The Captain's Vengeance

Also by Dewey Lambdin

The Captain's Vengeance

An Alan Lewrie   Naval Adventure

Dewey Lambdin

THOMAS DUNNE BOOKS

ST. MARTIN'S PRESS

NEW YORK

THOMAS DUNNE BOOKS.
An imprint of St. Martin's Press.

www.stmartins.com

Title page art by Wilhelm Melbye

ISBN 0-312-31547-3
EAN 978-0312-31547-4

First Edition: November 2004

10 9 8 7 6 5 4 3 2 1

To all my hard-working, common-sense East Tennessee kin-folk who went before, who lived in the shadows of McCloud Mountain and McLean's Rock in the Powell Valley time out of mind, just a "Hoot and Holler" from the Cumberland Gap. If they did try to pound some "down home" verities into me, I'm sorry that they didn't *all* take, and wish I'd paid more attention to the old tales, the centuries-old lore that was warp and woof of their "Bright, Sunny South," in those wondrous summer twilights when the kids and the dogs lay "plumb tuckered out" 'neath my Mamaw and Papaw Ellison's sheltering oak, and the "lightning bugs" swam above the lawn as thick as schools of minnows. It may be belated, but God bless you all for my "raisin'."

And, to my ex-wives . . . don't bother, I'm *still* too broke to pay attention.

Full-Rigged Ship: Starboard (right) side view

1. Mizen Topgallant
2. Mizen Topsail
3. Spanker
4. Main Royal
5. Main Topgallant
6. Mizen T'gallant Staysail
7. Main Topsail
8. Main Course
9. Main T'gallant Staysail
10. Middle Staysail
11. Main Topmast Staysail
12. Fore Royal
13. Fore Topgallant
14. Fore Topsail
15. Fore Course
16. Fore Topmast Staysail
17. Inner Jib
18. Outer Flying Jib
19. Spritsail

A. Taffrail & Lanterns
B. Stern & Quarter-galleries
C. Poop Deck/Great Cabins Under
D. Rudder & Transom Post
E. Quarterdeck
F. Mizen Chains & Stays
G. Main Chains & Stays
H. Boarding Battens/Entry Port
I. Cargo Loading Skids
J. Shrouds & Ratlines
K. Fore Chains & Stays
L. Waist
M. Gripe & Cutwater
N. Figurehead & Beakhead Rails
O. Bow Sprit
P. Jib Boom
Q. Foc's'le & Anchor Cat-heads
R. Cro'jack Yard (no sail fitted)
S. Top Platforms
T. Cross-Trees
U. Spanker Gaff

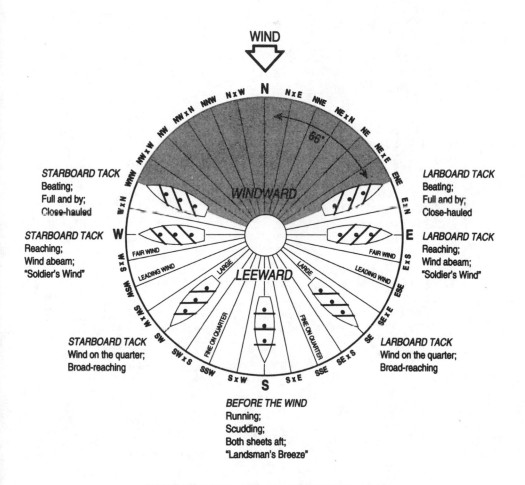

POINTS OF SAIL AND 32-POINT WIND-ROSE

The Captain's Vengeance

Praenda vago iussit geminare pericula ponto,
bellica cum dubiis rostra dedit retibus.
Praedator cupit immensos obsidere campos
ut multa innumera igera pascat ove.

Booty bade men double the perils of the surging
deep when it fitted the beaks of war
to the rocking ships.

'Tis the freebooter who longs to seize upon
the measureless plains that on many an acre
he may graze his countless sheep.

–*NEMESIS* III, 39-42
ALBIUS TIBULLUS

PROLOGUE

Gonzalo: Now would I give a thousand furlongs
Of sea for an acre of barren ground-long heath,
Brown furze, anything. The wills above be done
But I would fain die a dry death.

-*THE TEMPEST*, ACT I, SCENE 1
WILLIAM SHAKESPEARE

The Dry Tortugas 24°37' N, 82°45' W

*T*wo ships tossed, rocked, and heaved on a fretful sea, fetched-to and immobile, within easy rowing distance of the dry, low-lying, rocky islet—too small to be called an island, too large to be termed a cay. Bastard, barren places were these islets, neither Caribbean soft and beguiling nor American mainland coastal-marshily bleak. These islets did not belong to the Caribbean, but to the Gulf of Mexico, and lay far west of southernmost Spanish Florida, an afterthought of a distracted Creator, who had flung them like excess ochre droplets off a cosmic putty knife, once the last of the Florida Keys had been shaped.

Except for a small sand beach on the north side, off which the two ships lay, the islet's shore was rocky, gravelled and steep-to, with waves breaking vertically, strewn with broken shells, fragments of driftwood, bird skeletons, and russet humps of pine needles and palm furze.

The seas were lively and heaved four or five feet or more in a confused chop; deep-ocean blue-grey, changing to teal, aqua, or lapis near the shore—all under an achingly empty cerulean blue sky that was brushed by mares' tails, with only the rare stiff-winged albatross, frigate bird, or gull to show a single sign of life.

The two ships fetched-to off the northern beach were clattered, clanged, and slatted by those confused seas, rising and dropping, pitching at bows and sterns, and rocking in uneven, unpredictable fits and jerks. One of the fetched-to vessels was a typical bluff-bowed, three-masted merchantman, a tad high at poop and forecastle, wide and beamy and deeply laded. She gleamed with linseed oil 'twixt her black-tarred gunwale and her jaunty blue upper-works and bulwarks, with a hint of a wealthy trader's gilt round her bulging quarter-galleries, entry ports, and figurehead. Her motion, because of her greater tonnage and weight of cargo, was a bit easier and more predictable than the other ship's. A Tricolour flag of Republican France flew from the leach of her large spanker, which was still sheeted in to keep drive on her, and her bows pinched up to the winds, while her courses and topgallants were bag-reefed, her tops'ls flatted aback, and her jibs knife-edged full of wind. That linseeded gleaming wood was as pretty as a spanking-new, beeswaxed tabletop.

The second fetched-to vessel rode much more lively, for she was a schooner, much narrower in beam. Gaff-hung sails on her foremast and main fought a losing fight to drive her forward, whilst her two standing jibs, hauled taut on the opposing tack, kept her motionless—in respect to the islet, at least. Riding her decks, keeping one's feet as she slatted, was a feat worthy of gainful employment with a touring Gypsy circus. Her hired cap-tain, and her crewmembers, were managing it well. So were their employers.

The schooner showed the world a lovely face, too; black-hulled with a dockyard-fresh coat of the glossiest paint, not tar. That hull, so long, lean, and so sweetly sheer-lined, was boot-topped on the waterline and striped along the upperwork bulwarks with wide bands of a deep scarlet. Her masts, gaffs, and booms, jib boom and bowsprit, her coachtop 'tween foremast and mainmast, and her two small upper yards, were painted a hazy light blue–grey, and her sails . . . instead of new-from-the-chandlery *écru,* or well-worn and used parchment-like tan, had been dyed horizon-grey, as well.

La Réunion, she was called, as so she was named in the scroll-board on her stern and in her ship's papers that declared her a yacht, a nautical plaything for her idle-rich planter owners, and, registered as she was as homeported in a Spanish possession, she usually sported a gilt-tan flag with the two horizontal red stripes equidistant from top and bottom of a Spanish merchantman or pri-vate vessel.

For this occasion, though, in keeping with her secret name and her *other* papers, the purchased Letter of Marque and Reprisal declaring her to be a French privateer by name of *Le Revenant*—that is to say, "The Ghost"—that despised shit-brintle "rag" had been hanked on below a French Tricolour atop her mains'l's leach, a flag brighter and larger, as if *she* were the prize, not the three-master.

No matter how desolate or bleak the islet, *La Réunion*'s owners were in happy takings, eyes alight with the novelty of it all, sipping champagne and snickering as they watched the crew aboard the merchantman struggle to sway out and lower her largest launch. The sailors manning the check or snub lines were having a rough go of it as the prize ship juddered about.

"I thought you said *Capitaine* Balfa was a salty man," one young man demanded, "a bold, experienced freebooter! But he goes about that like a clumsy, drunken . . . Bayou Barataria coon-ass, ha ha!"

The hired captain of *La Réunion* (or *Le Revenant*), standing aloof of them, clamped his lips together to bite off what harsh response that petulant plaint merited, eyes slit in frustration. Jérôme Lanxade and Boudreaux Balfa went back a long time together, and a slur on Boudreaux might as well have been a slur on his own competence.

Dammit to hell, neither he nor Balfa owned this lithe schooner, only shares in the "enterprise"! It wasn't like the old days, back in the last war, when they'd commanded *five* ships at once, when the names Jérôme Lanxade—*Le Féroce*, for he had been called "The Ferocious"—and Boudreaux Balfa—*L'Affamé*, or "The Hungry"—had commanded respect and awe in every Caribbean or Gulf port. Then they could recruit an entire crew overnight at the snap of their fingers and fill every man's pockets with prize money or plunder. Under the old white-and-gold *fleur de lis* of Royal France, the heraldic red-gold of Spain . . . even the dreaded Jolly Roger or Black Flag, a time or two . . . their orders or slightest whims could have made *fish bait* of callow, capering lubbers like them!

Jérôme Lanxade turned to face his employers, hands clasped in the small of his back, a black-visaged glower of warning on his dark-tanned face. Just for a moment, he fantasised, again, of murdering every last one of them, of just *taking* this splendid little ship for his own and continuing the business for his own profit. Kill all the young men, not the girl, though. Oh no, not for a long time. . . .

He let his face soften and crease into a knowing smile.

"The seas are up, the prize ship's motion," Lanxade told them with what might have seemed to be infinite patience. "Nothing goes as quickly or smoothly as you wish aboard ship, *messieurs, mademoiselle.*"

Poseurs! he silently accused, though the girl was most fetching—even if she was the most bloody-minded of the entire bunch!

His employers dressed the part: jackboots and baggy sailors' slop trousers, colourful shirts under long-tailed and gaudy old-style waist-coats that they wore open; waist sashes crammed with pistols or daggers under the waist-coats; broad satin or velvet baldrics bearing costly short swords or swept-hilt rapiers; wide-brimmed hats adrip with egret plumes. . . . As if they'd tricked themselves out in fanciful garb and beauty spots and face powders for a pre-Revolution costume ball!

"One would wish, though, *M'sieur le Capitaine* Lanxade, that it goes competently, *n'est-ce pas?*" the young woman sweet-archly replied with an elegant lift of one brow, a leering smile at one corner of her sweetly kissable mouth, and a mocking salute with her wineglass.

Arrogant, wanton slut! Lanxade thought, unable to keep his eyes from caressing her curves, her slim legs on display for all the world to see in over-snug breeches and silk knee stockings, her *décolletage* made prominent by a tight and waist-hugging buttoned waist-coat, just long enough to flare over the tops of her hips like a corset. *Worst-named cunt in all Creation . . .* Charité . . . Angelette . . . de Guilleri!

Mlle Charité de Guilleri lowered her lashes and smirked over the rim of her crystal champagne glass, secretly delighted by their hired man's not-so-secret lust, *and* her heady power to deny.

"I still say we should just shoot them, make them to 'walk the plank,' or something," her cousin, Jean-Marie Rancour, spat.

"*Oui,* Jean . . . dead men tell no tales, after all," another of their party said. Unlike the rest, he was dark-haired and brown-eyed, was Don Rubio Monaster, while Charité, her brothers Hippolyte and Helio, and their cousin were the typical long-settled Creoles, with chestnut hair and blue eyes. "Just kill them and be done," Don Rubio asserted with what he was certain was an aggressive, decisive, and manly lift of his chin . . . for Charité's benefit and, hopefully, at some future time of bliss with her, his own.

"We've *done* that," the eldest brother, Helio de Guillieri, responded in a lazy drawl. "That Havana slaver's crew, remember, Rubio? We made *them* walk the plank, Jean."

"But we haven't done marooning yet," middle brother Hippolyte snickered. "Just about the only thing we *haven't* done."

"Kill or maroon?" Helio, as "leader," posed. "The old buccaneers practiced *égalité* and *fraternité*, they voted on things. Let's vote."

"Shoot!" Don Rubio Monaster quickly replied, but he was shouted down by those in favour of marooning their captives. Only Jean sided with him, and that not with a whole heart.

Mon Dieu, what a pack of . . . . Capt. Lanxade thought. "Marooned men tell no tales. No one ever comes here. They give these isles a wide berth for fear of shoals and reefs. Only piles of bleached bones will be found . . . if ever," he gruffly told them.

"I cannot shoot even *one?*" Don Rubio plaintively asked.

"Rubio, don't be greedy," Mlle Charité coaxed, sashaying to his side to drape an arm round his shoulders and lay her head next to his, as if cajoling her papa for a new gown. "We have seen how well you shoot. Those runaway slaves . . . *pim-pim-pim*, and all your doing, *n'est-ce pas?* If we run across another prize on the way home, we will leave things to you . . . won't we, Helio . . . Hippolyte?"

The other stalwart young fellows had no problem with that.

"If not, *quel dommage,*" Charité continued, "and you must quell your eagerness 'til the next voyage. Remember, Rubio, hastening the day of rejoining *La Belle* France, and throwing off the Spanish tyrany, comes first, last, and always. Before our petty amusements."

She blew teasingly at his ear, swept off his overly ornate hat, and tousled his romantically long, dark locks, then gave the embarrassed young fellow a quick and "sisterly" peck on the cheek . . . with a tiny flick of her tongue tip to tantalise before almost skipping away from him. "Ah, *regardeʒ* . . . the boat, at last!"

Don Rubio Monaster bashfully grinned, though following her every movement with downcast but lustful eyes; unsure, again, whether he'd been gulled by her . . . or slyly encouraged.

But for their mutual scheme, Don Rubio might have been shunned by her family. His father had been a grandee Spaniard sent to administrate the territory. Though a true Castilian of noble hidalgo blood never tainted by Moor or Marrano, whose sires had held titles since the Reconquista in the 1400s, his father had been so impoverished that a wilderness post's salary had been welcomed. Spanish overlord or not, his father *had* managed to wed a proud and exalted French Creole lady, heir to vast acreages upriver from the city, and had seen to it that the old French deeds of her family, the Bergrands, had become legitimate Spanish land grants.

Not so smart, though, to avoid taking the field against a Chickasaw uprising up near Natchez, where his noble father had been slain. Since then, the Bergrands had moulded him into more of a Creole than a Don, more a Jacobin than a Royalist after the French Revolution, too.

Spain was old, tired, and bankrupt, with nothing to offer but a corrupt and neglectful governance. The new United States encroaching on their borders were even worse, just *too* common, venal, grasping, and backwoods crude! Without a powerful protector, they would be swamped in buckskin, *awash* in the vile juices of "chaw-baccy"! *Non*, only a rising of their own— and a remonstrance of their *fait accompli* to the Republican Directory in

Paris could save them. *Everyone* was so sure of that, but so few really ever *did* anything about it, other than talk and talk in the *cabarets!* Only Hippolyte and Helio seemed capable of action, and he'd gladly become a part of their scheme. For the future, for . . . !

Bewitching Charité's costly Parisian scent lingered on Rubio's shirt collar, and he took a cautious sniff, even as he stood to watch the launch from the prize ship finally be rowed over to the schooner; feet wide-spread to balance, spring-kneed to ride the pitching of the deck as masterfully as he rode the most spirited stallion, with hands in the small of his back in unconscious imitation of their hired man, the daunting, dashing Capt. Lanxade. Chin up and alert, firm-jawed in spite of the swooping jerks and snubs, he would be dizzy and sick if he let himself. He would *not* be sick . . . he would be dashing.

Though *Maman* was delighted that her son had *entrée* with a family as distinguished and rich as the de Guilleris, one even richer and of longer habitation than her own, though he was coyly urged to lay suit to one of the older sisters, Iphegénie or Marguerite . . . though he was sure that either would be a pleasingly suitable and presentable match, and either would be amenable, yet . . . there was Charité, that coquette!

Oh, if only he could tell her what agony, and what ecstacy, her too-brief caress and kiss could cause him! How like the Golden Fleece he thought her long chestnut hair, how lambent he deemed her turquoise eyes, how generous her lips and mouth, how bountiful her breasts!

God above, not *lambent!* Don Rubio chid himself. He'd sound lame and prissy as a dancing master! No true gentleman wasted time on such limp tripe!. Like a born Creole grandee, he had no time for poetry or books, though girls *did* put a deal of stock in such—

A series of thuds alongside brought Rubio back from his fancies as the launch butted the schooner's hull below the entry-port and was hooked onto the chains. A moment later, *Capitaine* Boudreaux Balfa was clambering up the battens on his large and gnarly bare feet.

L'Affamé . . . more hungry for hog meat than booty! Rubio thought.

Boudreaux Balfa was typical of the shoddy, run-of-the-mill Louisiana Acadian, dressed in a homegrown rough cotton *écru* shirt, homemade and indigo-dyed knee breeches of the same *cotonnade* material. Shoes, or stockings, well . . . if nagged, rustics such as Balfa *might* don cowhide moccasins to attend church, knee-high moccasins to wade after his lost pigs in the swamps. Shoes and stockings Balfa *might* possess, for weddings or funerals . . . if at all! And, like most Acadians, the man was so abstemious that he wore his clothes until they were halfway between *mauvaises* and *usées;* meaning "tattered" or "threadbare." Atop his crown, Balfa wore a plaited palmetto-frond tricorne hat so old its wide brims sagged down nearly to horizontal . . . and looked as if rats had been at it.

"*Ohé*, Lanxade," Balfa gravelled in glum greeting to his old-time partner, sweeping off that shabby tricorne to bare a fierce and wiry thicket of unruly iron-grey hair, and studiously ignoring his employers. "See dat sky, dis choppy water? Feel dat wind? It'll be a good half a gale by sundown, by Gar. Let's get dis over wit', *cher*."

In his younger years, *Capitaine* Boudreaux Balfa had been a doughty figure of a buccaneer and privateersman, but time and shore living on a hard-scrabble plot of land had not been kind. He had thickened and grown a trencherman's gut, a shad belly, though not an ounce of him was yet soft. Balfa was as thick as a fierce boar hog.

"Ah *oui*, Boudreaux *mon cher*," Lanxade agreed. "We don't make a ceremony out of it, we can be fifteen *lieues* alee by sundown. In deep water, and scudding Large. Bosun, fetch them up!"

He took Balfa by the arm and together they walked back to the rails, away from the swaggering, tipsy revellers. Time had been somewhat kinder to Lanxade; he was still tall, lean, and flat-bellied, unbowed after the toils of peaceful employment on trading company *shalopes* upriver to Manchac, Natchez, St. Louis, and the old Illinois settlements, and back. But Boudreaux *did* imagine he heard a suspicious creak from somewhere near Lanxade's middle, which put him in mind of a well-hidden corset. And Balfa allowed himself a secret smile to note that his old compatriot's grey roots were showing, along with the telltale splotch of greenish walnut-husk oil on his ears that betrayed his use of hair dye to *remain* so dark and virile-looking!

Sure enough, a playful poke at Lanxade's *boudins* met well-stayed canvas and whalebone resistance. "Hawn hawn hawn!" He softly, nasally chortled at such vanity.

"Oh, shut up, you old *bougre*," Lanxade hissed back, stiffening to maintain his dignity. And his secrets.

"So, we kill dem, or we maroon dem?" Balfa asked off-handedly.

"Maroon," Lanxade told him, "for the *novelty* of it."

"Dem babies not tired o' killin' yet?" Balfa wondered aloud.

"Bored with it, more likely," Lanxade said in a harsh mutter. "I could say queasy of the consequences, but with this lot, I wouldn't count on it. Sated for now, but a few weeks ashore, and they'll wish to be back at it. Piracy's addictive . . . as we both know, *cher*. Pissing God *and* the Devil in the eye."

"By damn, dey wanna see *real* piracy, Jérôme, what say we jus' take dis damn' *goélette* for our own?" Balfa softly cackled. "Mak *dem* walk de plank, jus' like de ol' days, maroon *dem*, 'long wit' dem poor *salauds* down below, *hein?*"

"They're too rich and important to go missing, Boudreaux, and we'd swing for it," Lanxade countered, though not without a long pause to ponder it.

"But we won't for dat Dago *guarda costa* lugger? *Merde!*"

The Spanish government lugger, outbound from Havana, returning rebel slaves for execution at Mobile—along with a profitable load of other *nègres* and smuggled goods that her unscrupulous captain had meant to land on the sly—was their latest capture. The small crew of Spaniards had gone overside, as had the convicted rebels, though they'd kept the untainted *nègres* for sale to the *caboteurs*, the itinerant backcountry slave dealers. After the Pointe Coupee slave insurrection four years earlier, though, even a *blind* planter would have spurned such lash- or manacle-scarred slaves as cut-throat troublemakers, not with brigands such as St. John or St. Malo leading vengeful runaway slave bands in the swamps of Louisiana.

Those captives had held no value, except for sport. With their hands free, but with leg shackles linked and weighted with shot, their struggle to stay afloat had been *très drôle*, the strong futilely trying to buoy up the weaker after they'd been forced over the side, once the lugger had been stripped of everything useful, then sunk. The Spaniards had had it kinder; they'd walked the plank with only their arms roped, free to kick-swim to stay afloat, and alive, 'til the game had palled, and the youngsters had honed their marksmanship skills on them.

Now, there would be more fun.

Hoots and curses erupted from the schooner's crew, more wine was poured by their youthful employers, as the six remaining prisoners off the prize ship were fetched up the narrow and steep companionway ladder from the schooner's foetid orlop. Stumbling and sickly reeling, their eyes blindfolded and their arms bound, they were unable to help themselves.

"Time to die, bastards!" Helio de Guilleri taunted in English, though his intent was spoiled by tittering at his own wit and putting stress on the second syllable of "bastards."

"Go game, lads! Go game!" one of the older captives urged his mates. "They're nought but prinkin' Frogs an' Dons! Buck up, young sir!" he added as the youngest began to mewl and gasp in dread.

"Fack th' bloody lot o' ye!" another doughtier prisoner cried, head swivelling as if trying to see. "And th' Shee's undyin' *cess* be on yair black damn' souls."

"The Lord is my Shepherd, I shall not . . . *Britons* never never *never* shall be . . . !" others wavered.

"Shut the Devil . . . *up!*" *Capitaine* Lanxade bellowed, drawing a long-barrelled pistol from his waistband and firing into the air. "Christ, you damned noisy sons of dogs! Once we leave, you can scream all you wish. Stuff your faces with bird shit, drink your own piss . . . drink the sea and go even madder, for all we care. Loose their hands, men."

"But, *Capitaine,*" one of the de Guilleris objected.

"They cannot climb down into the boat, else," Lanxade snapped back. "Their blindfolds, *aussi* . . . take them off. Let them see what a fine estate we give them, ha ha!"

A mutual gasp of bleak realisation wheezed from the doomed men as they beheld the islet, providing even more amusement for the captors.

And with much eager poking, prodding, and shoving, the prisoners were forced to the entry-port, to lower themselves into the centre of the launch, where extra hands with pistols and daggers waited to receive them. Balfa and his oarsmen got down into the boat with them and steered towards the shore.

"Stroke, stroke," Balfa chearily directed, tapping the time on the tiller-bar. "A little song, *mes enfants!*" he urged.

> *"Ah! Suzette, Suzette, to veux pas chère?*
> *"Ah, Suzette, Chère amie, to pas l'aimin moin.*
> *M'alle dans montagne, zamie,*
> *M'alle coupé canne, chère amie,*
> *M'alle fait l'argent, mo trésor,*
> *Pour porter donné toi!"*

"Bastards!" the oldest prisoner spat back. "Kindest to kill us now and have done, ye gotch-gut shit!"

"Dat can be arranged, *cher,*" Balfa chuckled back.

"Don't!" the youngest pleaded, so agitated he looked as if he would fling himself over the side from fretting, with tears of relief in his eyes that their death was not to be *immediate.* "Like our vicar always said, Hope springs eternal, and—"

"Hope?" Balfa scoffed. "Dis de Dry Tortugas. *Comprendre* dry? Never know . . . *might* catch turtle. He blood you drink, he meat, and eggs you eat. Kill seabirds, *aussi* . . . same. Ah! Up oars! Bow men!"

The launch staggered through the last froth of surf and ground her bows into the raspy, pebbled grit of the beach. Bow men sprang to either side, thigh-deep in white-water spume, to steady the bows as a fresh wave lifted the boat a foot more ashore.

"Go over de bow, don't even get your feet wet, you. Out, *vite! Hope* . . . you like you' new home!" Balfa snickered as his oarsmen laid their blades in the bilges and waved their weapons at the captors to speed their departure. "You damn' *Anglais!* Dis pay you back for all I suffer. Prisoner, me. Kidnap, me, on your ships! Round us all up an' take us away from Acadia, an' don' let us take *nozzing* wit' us! *Gaol* us in England, firs'. We don' starve quick enough, us, don' get sick an' die, you damn *Anglais* ship us to Maryland! See how *you* like it dis time, by Gar! Damn' English!"

The prisoners were goaded at gun- or swordpoint at least twenty yards inland, past the overwash barrow full of wiregrass and deep, loose sand littered with feathers and shells.

"Oim Oirish!" one of the captives plaintively declared.

"All same, *aussi*," Balfa told him with almost a sympathetic air. "Dem *bébés* on de schooner, dey'd leave you nozzing, dem, 'cause dey all jus' crazy mean, but me, Boudreaux Balfa, I a sailor like you, I never let it be said I'm *heartless, comprendre?* So I give you a slim chance, me. Fetch it out de boat, men. You live, you remember, *hein?*"

Two crewmen trundled up a ten-gallon wooden barrico. Another slung a worn leather bag across the sand to land at their feet.

"*Bonne chance, chers!*" Balfa wished them all with a wide smile and a hearty laugh. "You stand where you are, now, 'til we get beyond de surf," he cautioned, wagging a finger in warning, "or we jus' have t'shoot, us. *Adieu. Allez, vite!*"

As the pirates scrambled to shove off and leap into their boat, one of the captives dared kneel by the leather sack and peer inside it. He wonderingly drew out a rusting old kitchen knife, paper, and . . .

"Crikey, 'tis a quizzin' glass, and a tinder-box, too. We can light a fire, does a ship ever pass!" he whispered in surprise.

"Sweet merciful Jaysus in Heaven!" the Irish captive cried in sudden glee as he swiped his fingers over a damp spot on the barrico and sniffed at it. "'Tis rum, by God! Ten bloody gallon o' *rum!*"

"What the Devil?" the oldest sailor puzzled, scratching at his grizzled scalp. He almost felt a twinge of hope, of gratitude to that . . .

The shot was inaudible over the loud swashing and raling of the surf, the wind that flapped their clothing, and the mewing cries of the seabirds that nested on the islet, flushed a'wing by their presence.

"Oh," the youngest lad said, as if he'd pricked his finger on a thorn, and clapped a hand to the inside of his right thigh. "Oh!" he reiterated, as if a wasp or bee had stung him, as he looked down at the blood on his white breeches. "Ah. Oh Lord!" as realisation came, as he fell to his knees and went as pale as the wave spume.

The other captives could see the tiniest wisp of spent powder smoke that blew westward from the schooner's small quarterdeck, ragging past the taffrails like the spirit of a hag that had ridden her mortal too long and must flee the coming of dawn.

"*Oh,* you bloody *bastards!* You goddamn' Frog sonsabitches!" the doughty older captive howled, shaking both fists at their tormentors. "We'll get ye, yet! We'll find ye, and cut yer damn' balls off, hear me? Ye'll all dance th' Tyburn Hornpipe 'fore we're done wi' ye!"

"Oh, poo," Don Rubio groaned, grimacing at his poor aim with a slim and expensive Jaeger rifle. "This boat's pitching, though." His compatriots cheered his expertise, even though he hadn't struck his mark in mid-chest.

"You said you wished to shoot just one, Rubio!" Hippolyte said in commiseration. "He'll die of that, right below his *organes!* What a bother he'll be for them, before he does. Ha ha!"

"Perhaps they'll *eat* him!" Helio quipped, eyes merrily alight.

> *Dé tit zozos-yé té assis,*
> *Dé tit zozos si la barrier,*
> *Dé tit zozos, qui zabotté,*
> *Qui ça yé di mo pas conné!*

They sang as well, hooting and capering, even assaying a nautical, buccaneer's hornpipe, though they hadn't heard a word that their captives had yelled from shore.

> *Monzeur-poulet vini simin,*
> *Croupé si yé et croqué yé,*
> *Personn pli tend yé zabotté,*
> *Dé tit zozos si la barrier!*

A Creole song, a slave song, one they'd all learned as children.

> Two little birds were sitting,
> Two little birds were sitting on the fence,
> Two little birds were chattering,
> What they were saying I do not know.
> A chicken hawk came along the road,
> Pounced on them and ate them up.
> No one hears the chattering anymore,
> The two little birds on the fence!

BOOK ONE

Gonzalo: I have great comfort from this fellow.
Methinks he hath no drowning mark upon him; his
Complexion is perfect gallows. Stand fast, good
Fate, to his hanging! Make the rope of his destiny
Our cable, for our own doth little advantage.

    If he be not born to be hanged, our case
Is miserable.

                    -*THE TEMPEST*, ACT I, SCENE 1
                    WILLIAM SHAKESPEARE

CHAPTER ONE

"*H*oy, the boat!" Mr. Midshipman Larkin cried his challenge to the approaching civilian cutter, though he had known who its passengers were as soon as they had stepped down into it on the distant quay ten minutes earlier; had been awaiting those passengers' return for at least the last two hours past.

"*Proteus!*" the Mulatto bow man shouted back, seated on the very tip of the cutter's bows, legs dangling to either side with a brass-fitted gaff staff across his lap with which to hook onto the chains. He shot one hand in the air for a moment, showing four fingers, proving that a captain was aboard.

"Come alongside, aye!" Mr. Larkin shouted back, then paced over to join the others of the side-party assembled to salute that officer's arrival back aboard. Larkin was a thatch-haired, ill-featured lout of a lad, all out at elbows and knees in his secondhand uniform, and that didn't even take into consideration the growing he'd done since signing ship's articles over a year before. Though it was a useless endeavour, he twitched and tugged his coat, waist-coat, and neck-stock into better order, shifted the hang of his shoddy dirk, and took a second to remove his battered, cocked hat and swipe his unruly hair with a "Welsh comb," that is to say, with his fingers.

Marine Lieutenant Devereux fiddled with his own immaculate neck-stock, harumphed to clear his throat, and cocked a brow as he regarded his short line of Marines under arms, in a last-instant inspection.

Though ships' officers did not usually stand harbour watches, the First

Officer, Mr. Anthony Langlie, was present, as was the Second Officer, the ever-cynical and recently wakened and yawning Lieutenant Catterall. The younger and cleverer Scot, Lt. Adair, also "toed the line" of a tar-paid seam in the starboard gangway planking, his sword loose and ready to present. Mr. Winwood, the Sailing Master, and Mr. Grace, the ship's other midshipman, also stood nearby, stiff-backed and chin-up with curiosity.

Thud! went the shabby cutter against the hull; a clatter of untidily "boated" oars. More, softer thuds as the cutter shouldered the proper captain's gig, and a grunt or two, some mumbles, as money changed hands for the short passage. Midshipman Larkin dared a peek outboard and downwards from his position at the opening of the entry-port, nodded to the neat-uniformed sailors in the side-party, and stiffened.

The Bosun, Mr. Pendarves, began his long, elaborate call as the dog's vane of the arriving officer's gilt-laced cocked hat peeked over the top step. At a whispered word, officers' swords were drawn, then presented before their faces; well-blacked Marine boots stamped on the creamy-pale, fresh-sanded planking; hands slapped glossy-oiled walnut musket buttstocks and fore-ends. At a word of command from Lt. Langlie, all hands present on deck stood erect and doffed their hats.

The arriving officer leaned back a little, gripping the tautly strung man-ropes for the last step of his ascent up the shelflike boarding battens that began level, and a bit aft, of the main chains. A visitor, unused to such ceremony, might have deemed the officer nonplussed to stillness by the elaborateness of his welcome. But it was simply his way . . . to seize the man-ropes just below their terminations set below the cap-rail of the entry-port's bulwarks, and jerk himself into the last step, instead of groping and fumbling the cap-rails like some stout "trullibubs" or senior dodderer more in need of hoisting aboard in a bosun's chair. He had barely turned his thirty-sixth year, this January of 1799, and was still almost boyishly spry.

That jerk was accompanied by a nearly playful hop or skip from the last batten to the snowy planks of the starboard gangway. When the officer doffed his hat, though, he did so with solemn gravity, so an uninitiated observer might have doubted his first, playful theory.

Said new-come "lubber" would have seen a slim man in his early thirties, who stood three inches shy of six feet tall, one who might weigh twelve or thirteen stone; still wider in the shoulders than the waist, a man whose snow-white breeches and waist-coat lay trimly flat, still.

He wore a good, hard-finished blue wool shoregoing coat, laced with butter-yellow gilt trim on the lapels, the stand-up blue collar, the side-pocket flaps, and cuffs, with nine real gilt buttons on each wide turn-back blue lapel. A fringed gilt-lace epaulet sat upon the officer's right shoulder, too, denoting him a Post-Captain, though one of less than three years' seniority.

Under that expensive coat lay a white leather baldric on which to hang his sword. A discerning observer would have appreciated that sword, a twenty-four-inch hanger, though he would have been puzzled by the scabbard, for it was of dark blue leather, not black, and both throat and drag were of plain brass, not gilded. The hilt, though, *was* gilded and most ornate; the typical lion's-head pommel that swallowed the back handguard, but the front guard that swelled to protect the user's fist was pierced-steel, like a scallop shell, with a smaller second shell at the hilt's forefront.

A discriminating man with a taste for blades would appreciate that the hanger was a Gill's and, when drawn, was nearly straight on the back edge, the first eight inches honed razor-sharp, while the lower edge was upswept to the point, so that it gave the *impression* of a curved-blade hanger.

A discriminating gentleman would have further "Ah-hummed" over the cut-steel square links of the officer's watch chain and fob, deeming him a man of good taste, too.

With the officer's beaver cocked hat doffed, an outsider would have seen a full head of hair atop his pate, still thick and all his own, of a middle, almost light brown, a tad wavy at his temples, over his ears, and loosely gathered into a trim nautical sprig of a queue atop his coat collar, bound with a bow-knotted black silk ribbon.

The officer was much too sun- or wind-burned for Fashion in the better sorts' *salons*, though. Not completely a gentleman, perhaps, the lofty observer would have sniffed; too much the "sea dog" after all!

The salute done, Lewrie clapped his hat back on his head and smiled at his First Officer, his darkly, romantically handsome Mr. Anthony Langlie. "Everything's in order, Mister Langlie?" he asked. "Nothing gone smash since I left the ship?" he gently teased.

"No, sir, praise God," Lt. Langlie reported. "The working sail set hung slack and allowed to dry, wood and watering done, and Mister Coote's requirements stowed below, sir. Did you, ah . . . find out . . ."

"I'll be below and aft, Mr. Langlie," Capt. Lewrie told him in a mystifying way. "Give me ten minutes, then do attend me, and I shall tell you all I have learned. Dismiss the hands back to their seeming drowsiness for now, sir."

"Aye, aye, sir," Lt. Langlie crisply replied, with a hand to his hat and a short sketch of a bow from the waist as Capt. Lewrie went down the starboard ladderway to the gun-deck, then aft past the bulkhead door and the Marine sentry, to his great-cabins.

"Cool tea, sir?" his cabin servant, Aspinall, enquired after he had helped him out of his coat, sword and baldric, and hat.

"That'd be handsome, Aspinall, aye," Lewrie replied, tearing at his neckstock and opening his shirt collar. "Why, hello, catlins . . . my littles! And what've you two imps been up to, hey?"

There were many glad trills and meows of welcome, much butting of heads on his Hessian boots; perhaps a tad too much standing on hind legs and whetting claws in *bienvenue* at his white canvas breeches. Those mischievous looks from both Toulon, the stout and well-muscled black-and-white ram-cat, and Chalky, the grey-smudged white yearling tom only half Toulon's heft, warned Lewrie that they'd be scaling up his thin shirt in their need to be newly adored.

"Miss me, did you?" Lewrie cooed to them, a hand for each, once he attained the chair behind his desk. "Damn my eyes, ye don't nip at *me*, Chalky! Hand that feeds, and all that? You'll get your 'wubbies,' no fear o' not."

"Yer tea, sir," Aspinall announced after several long minutes of discrete observation, as he sensed the cats' enthusiasms begin to flag. "Bridgetown didn't have no ice, though, sir. All used up for the season, I reckon. Cool from th' orlop, though, sir."

"Massachusetts Yankee ice *never* gets this far south" was Lewrie's surmise as he accepted the coin-silver commemorative tankard that the crew of his previous ship, the Sloop of War *Jester*, had given him just before they'd paid off at Portsmouth, and paced aft.

"Er . . . no luck, then, sir?" Aspinall dared to ask, when ship's officers would not. Lewrie flung himself onto the hard settee lashed to the starboard side, almost sprawled with one leg up.

"Not the answers I was looking for, Aspinall, no," Lewrie said, busying himself with taking another sip. The rob of lemons and sugar were dirt cheap in the Caribbean and the Sugar Isles, and tea was one of the most popular exports from England, so Aspinall brewed it by the gallon, every day or so, and kept it tepid, at least, in a pewter pitcher. Some days it was fresh, some days it was leftovers, clouded and so stout that it could rouse the deathly ill and make them prance hornpipes. Today it was fresh, and merely refreshing.

"No fear, though, sir . . . we'll find 'em, sooner'r later."

"I begin to wonder, Aspinall," Lewrie wearily said with a sigh, running his free hand over his hair and leaning his head back upon the oak of the hull's inner scantling and decorative panelling. " 'Pon my soul, I do."

Not only physically tired from his shore travels, from riding a hired horse far out into the countryside and back, Lewrie was starting to feel spiritually tired. No wonder, since he had done everything he could conceive of, had pursued every possibility no matter how tenuous, and it had all seemingly resulted in a titanic . . . nullity!

Toulon and Chalky, now that he'd alit, hopped up for a return bout of "pets" for the duration of the first mug of cold tea. By the refill, Toulon stalked off to claim his master's chair behind the desk, leaving Chalky to sling himself against Lewrie's thigh, wriggle and yawn, then stretch out half on his back with his paws in the air and "caulk" down, instantly don't-feel-a-thing asleep.

A forceful knock on the great-cabin door, the sharp thud of a brass musket butt on the deck, and the cry of "First Awf'cer, *sah*!" didn't even stir Chalky. "Come!" Lewrie responded.

"Sir," Langlie said, hat under his arm.

"You'll pardon me, Mister Langlie, do I not get up, hey?" Lewrie said, with a helpless shrug and a cock of his head in the direction of the fur-bag at his hip. "Take a pew, do. Aspinall, refreshments for Mister Langlie."

"Thankee, sir," Langlie answered, plunking down into a leather-and-wood chair that was *ensembled* with the settee, his hat in his lap, and fidgeting with expectation, not of the cool tea decoction, but of *news*, at last.

"Well, we found the mort known as Mistress Jugg," Lewrie told him, once he'd gotten his tea and had had a liberal draught of it. "Her, and the reputed girl-child that Jugg spoke of."

"Capital, sir!" Langlie enthused.

"No, no it ain't," Lewrie gloomed.

Two months before, Lewrie's frigate had taken an easy, and rich, French prize near the enemy-held island of Guadeloupe, in the midst of confounding and capturing Lewrie's old nemesis, the fearsome Guillaume Choundas. *Proteus* had sailed as an "independent ship" with Admiralty Orders fetched out by Foreign Office secret agents; the Honourable Mr. Grenville Pelham, an officious, over-vaunting twit, and his much abler aide, ex-Captain of Household Cavalry Mr. James Peel. Their mission, which everyone *but* Pelham could charitably call a "right cock-up" of a scheme, had been to discomfit Choundas and the French, first off; find a way to regain possession of the vast wealth of the French colony of Saint Domingue on Hispaniola from the victorious slave rebellion led by Toussaint L'Ouverture, second; *then* drag the Americans and their spanking-new Navy hooting and hollering into a *declared* war with the French. Or, run the Yankees out of the Caribbean if they didn't jump through the right hoops. The prize had been icing on the cake.

Lewrie had left their prize safely at anchor in Prince Rupert Bay, in the hands of the local Admiralty Court, with six crewmembers off *Proteus* for her Harbour Watch. Not two weeks later, though, their prize had vanished! The dimwits of the Dominica Prize Court had flung up their shoulders and mumbled, "Well, it's a myst'ry!" but the prize, her bonded cargo, and his five sailors and one midshipman were missing with her. Lost, absconded . . .

Had she been left at Antigua and auctioned off, she might have fetched them all over £15,000, and would still have safely *been* there!

The eternally sozzled incompetents of the Dominica Court admitted that a man *claiming* to be the prize's Quartermaster's Mate had come ashore at the sleepy port of Roseau, sculling a boat by himself, saying that, if a certain time period had elapsed without *Proteus*'s return to Dominica, his captain had left verbal orders to sail her to the court at Antiqua, to which Roseau's court was ancillary. They'd been so lax in their dealings, they couldn't even adequately *describe* him, but . . . they'd let him sail, anyway, the thoughtless clods!

Lewrie had left Midshipman Burns, his Bosun's Mate Mr. Towpenny, three other hands, and Quartermaster's Mate Toby Jugg aboard the prize.

And Toby Jugg was a man to be leery of.

After all, they'd pressed him off a Yankee brig engaged in smuggling arms to the French, and rebel slaves on Saint-Domingue, in the Danish Virgins the year before. American certificates of citizenship—either forged, false, or merely purchased from Yankee consuls—bedamned, Jugg had appeared as British as John Bull, and liable to the press, no matter where he was found. Jugg's plaint of an impoverished wife and daughter on Barbados had prompted Lewrie to suggest Jugg take the guinea Joining Bounty, to forward on to support his wife and child. He'd even *promoted* the man to Able Seaman, then Quartermaster's Mate, but . . . if Toby Jugg had found a way to overpower, or beguile, the rest of the hands, been glib enough to get them to desert with the prize to an enemy port, where they'd be safe from capture in the future for the crime . . . sell her off for *half* her potential value, and "go shares" so each would be rich and idle for life, well!

Had Jugg been aided by former "associates" who'd slunk into the bay to wood and water, or look for an easy capture; had he encountered criminal "jetsam" loafing ashore on Dominica, who'd put him up to it?

Dammit, Jugg had been the only Royal Navy Quartermaster's Mate in port, hadn't he? The court officers *said* the man had worn a Navy man's uniform, had an easy, gruff air of command about him as a Mate should, and sounded fluent in his English, so who else *could* it have been?

Waving his Admiralty Orders as an "independent ship" as a license to steal, Lewrie had taken *Proteus* in search of his missing men (and the value of the prize and her cargo!) with a vengeance. It had been a blow to his pride, to his offered trust, a slap in the face as bad as if his whole crew had mutinied! In point of fact, the missing Toby Jugg was becoming about as huge a *bête noire* to him as Guillaume Choundas had ever been!

Now, after weeks and weeks of searching, of quartering the sea, it appeared that the trail had gone completely cold, and any hope Lewrie had of rescuing his missing people was completely dashed. His last, best, hope had been here on Barbados, in the hills.

Lewrie, Padgett, and Cox'n Andrews had boated ashore, talked to officials, tradesmen, dock workers, and idlers. His clerk, Padgett, proved most useful in discovering that, for a while, a man named Tobias Hosier, formerly a *seaman* by trade, *had* farmed a small patch of land inland, in Saint Thomas parish, near a tiny place called Welsh Hell Gully, south of Mount Hillaby. Said Tobias Hosier had been *slightly* remiss in the tax collectors' books at Government House here in Bridgetown, *but* . . . his shortfall of 6s/8p had been made good about seven months before, which happily coincided with the time it would have taken for the note-of-hand on his Joining Bounty to have arrived by mail-packet from Jamaica, where it had been posted!

Any more information, especially a physical description of *this* Tobias (or Toby), as opposed to the two or three hundred other settlers anointed with that Christian name, any further information about him, would be the preserve of the parish authorities, Padgett was told.

That further search had involved runty hired horses, the roads being almost impossible for a more comfortable coach, and nearly six miserable miles upwards and inland, with nary a hope of even a mean dinner or potable refreshments along the way.

The local magistrate, your typical bluff squire, was not *available* (though his recumbent form could be espied, sprawled on a settee in his parlour, through the open double doors facing the front gallery of his imposing manor, and his snores were loud enough to unnerve the horses!). Both the vicar and his assisting curate were off "tending to good works"—though they *had* trotted off on their best hunters, clad in field clothing, bearing fowling guns, and animatedly conversing about "ring-necked *peasants*" or something such like, as the dour housekeeper of the vicar's manse told them, rather brusquely, between yawns. Evidently, folk did a *deal* of napping in Welsh Hell Gully.

Trust to Cox'n Andrews, though, to chat up the Cuffies who worked at the hamlet's tumbledown public house, where they dined, to learn that "Missah Tobias" matched the physical description of Toby Jugg to a tee, and where his acreage could be found. Off they'd gone, after an indifferent dinner, but two tankards of rather good ale to the good each, to seek out "Hosier Hall."

"Mistress Hosier, I presume?" Lewrie had said by way of enquiry. He stood with hat in hand, at the edge of the front gallery to a one-story house made of coral "tabby" blocks, ballast stones, and weathered scrap lumber. The gallery wasn't a foot off the ground, its planks uneven and sagging, though the long overhang of the roof, thatched from sugarcane stalks or bamboo or whatever fell to hand on Barbados, gave a more than welcome shade, and the raised gallery that spanned the entire house *did* provide at least ten degrees of relief from the noonday sun. "Or, should I say, Mistress Jugg?" Lewrie added, keeping a mild and unthreatening smile on his "phyz."

"Oh, saints presarve us!" the faded, fubsy woman cried, fanning herself with her stained housewife apron, turning pale and fretful under her tropical island colour. "Summat's happened t'Toby, are ye come t'tell me? Faith, I . . ." she said, gulping and collapsing in a rickety porch chair.

Past the open door of the vertical-board house, Lewrie could espy a girl-child in a simple shift, bare-legged and barefoot, coming out to the gallery from the inner gloom holding a squirming puppy. The taxes on windows that London enforced most-like also were imposed on Barbados, Lewrie thought. There was enough light, though, to note that a cradle took pride of place inside, one still rocking, one occupied by a baby in swaddles, and not above a year old.

"Allow me to name myself to you, Mistress," Lewrie said. "Captain Alan Lewrie, of the *Proteus* frigate. I've . . ."

"Toby's ship!" the woman cried, lips trembling now and both hands lifted to her mouth as if to press back grief or chew her nails. "Oh, God!" That sounded as if it was wrung from her by a mangle. "Th' poor man's daid, an't he? Oh, sway-et Jaysus!"

"Uh, *no*, Mistress Jugg . . . Hosier," Lewrie countered. "He . . ."

The wife was beginning to sob into her cupped hands; the little girl was beginning to blub, too, though for what reason she had yet to be told— Christ, even the babe in the cradle had wakened and added querulous, hiccoughy wail-ettes of its own!

"He's alive and well . . . we think," Lewrie was quick to inform.

"He's 'run,' d'ye mean?" Mistress . . . Whichever snapped, going squinty-eyed and flinty of a sudden, all grief quite flown her. "An' ye're here t'take him back, ye are? T'flog 'im? Court-martial 'im?"

"Find him, aye, Mistress . . . uh," Lewrie assured her, daring to put one booted foot on the gallery; thanking God that the Juggs/Hosiers could cut off their squawls so quickly. The girl-child still sniffled but hadn't worked up to a full-blown howl and was now almost content to clamber up into her mother's lap, still clasping the long-eared pup to her chest. And the cradled babe (trained to stealthiness, perhaps, by a visiting Muskogee or Seminolee Indian) had gurgled back to drowsiness. "Find our other missing people, too."

"*Missin'*, d'ye say, then? Missin'? Missin' *how*, sir?" Jugg's woman warily enquired. "Hesh up, now, Tess," she urged her girl.

Lewrie, daring to step up onto the gallery, even to drag up a second equally rickety chair and seat himself, fanning away the tropic heat and the many insects with his hat, explained about the missing prize ship and the hands he had left aboard to safeguard her.

"La, *arrah*," the woman said at last with a weary sigh. "Tess, cooshlin'. Jump down an' see t'yer brother. An' mind yer puppy don' make in th' house. Nor get in th' cradle an' smither 'im."

She waited 'til the little girl had slid down from her lap and had toddled off inside, dried her eyes for good and all with the hem of her apron, then heaved a long, bitter sigh and stared outwards, unfocussed, on her meagre acreage.

"Be mortal-cairtain yer sins'll find ye out," she whispered.

"Ma'am?" Lewrie gently asked, sure that the woman would confess Jugg's whereabouts, did he play his cards right a little longer.

"Pore Toby, *arrah*," she muttered with another long sigh. "All 'is work and sweat . . . all 'is good intentions. I *told* him, I did . . . I *pleaded* with 'im not t'go back t'sea. For sure, I knew in me bones, somethin' bad'd happen, and did it not right enough, Cap'm Lewrie? We *could* o' got by, we could o' made *some* sort o' crop, e'en did we hire out, th' both of us, but 'e wouldn't hear of it. Took all o' his savin's an' earnin's t'get this wee parcel, an' Toby'd not abide the idee o' losin' it, he didn't, so sure he traipsed down t'Bridgetown an' got hisself signed aboard a Yankee brig. Th' last night, 'e *tol'* me they was summat queer 'bout her, but they'd give him the two-crown advance he asked f'r, an' what they call a 'lay' o' th' profits that *sounded* handsome. Toby thought 'twas a slaver, I thought she might o' been a privateer," Mrs. Jugg or Hosier said with a half-amused shrug.

"The smuggling brig we took in the Danish Virgins, aye," Lewrie stuck in, in hopes to keep her reminiscing. "You received his Bounty guinea, I take it?"

"Aye, and sore welcome it was, for it cleared us o' taxes, an' went a fair way t'payin' th' vicar's tithe," the woman said brightly. "Covered th' storekeeper's ledger . . . crop t'crop, season t'season?"

Whatever surname she went by, Jugg's woman had at one time been a tolerably fetching wench, Lewrie judged. She was going stout, after two children, but had the sly eye and vixenish, sway-hipped carriage of a bouncy Irish sort; dark, frazzled red-auburn hair, snappy green eyes, high, merry cheekbones, and a wide and generous mouth. In the Caribbean, she was quite the catch for a man of Jugg's social position.

"What sins, ma'am?" Lewrie pressed. "The usual young tar's?"

"Privateersman's sins," Jugg's mate admitted, turning sadder. "Jumpin' ship sins, deserter's sins, Cap'm Lewrie. Navy ship or merchant. Hard masters an' such? Oh, he done a power in his younger days. But *nivver* mortal blood sins, I tell ye! Jugg, he said? Hmmf!"

"His real name's Hosier, then, I take it?" Lewrie slyly asked.

"Hah!" was her answer to that, and to Lewrie's mystification she went into the house, leaving him stewing on her porch. Not a minute later, though, she returned bearing a large painted mug much like a German beer stein, along with several tattered letters. She sat, then showed him the mug.

It was large enough for two pints, slightly tapering, with two stout handles and a china lid, like a teapot's. One side was crudely painted with a sailing ship, the other showed a tar-hatted sailor with a sea chest at his feet and a sea bag over his shoulder.

" 'Tis th' jug we keep on th' mantel," she coyly imparted. "Some o' th' time 'twas for flowers, summat small change, or sweets up where th' wee'uns couldn't reach. He called it 'Toby's Jug,' so that's where I 'spect he come up with a name for ye when ye pressed him. Hosier . . . 'twas a mate o' his wot 'slipped his cable' long afore, an' we took it when he lef' th' sea th' last time, and got this land. His real name is Paddy Warder, so 'tis. That's th' one he owned to, he tol' me jus' th' once, an' that I was t'forget it forever. An' so I did."

"So, he had a shifty past," Lewrie said cautiously.

"No more'n most wot end up out here!" Mrs. Jugg/Warder huffed.

"Mean t'say," Lewrie temporised, "might he have been tempted, then? Left aboard a rich prize, with so few other hands? Might he have kept in touch with mates from his rougher days?"

"Cairt'nly *not*, sir!" his woman angrily huffed. "Toby'd mended his ways, I seen t'that, an' 'twas only *need* that took 'im back t'sea! Look about ye, sir. What-all d'ye see?"

"Uhm, fields and crops . . . some creatures?" Lewrie flummoxed, sure that he'd blown the gaff to the wide.

"Five pigs an' a dozen chickens, an' them fair hard enough to feed up, Cap'm Lewrie!" his woman carped. "We *borry* use of a mule an' plough, then hoe, pull an' weed summat *back*-breakin', e'en do wee Tess when 'tis needful. Barbados an't like England, wi' nought but th' eldest son inheritin'. Faith, 'tis more like pore Ireland, with dividin' an' dividin' an' dividin', 'til we got but five acres o' mostly stony soil, an' half o' them in truck an' maize t'feed us an' keep body an' soul t'gither!"

"My condolences, Mistress, um . . . but I *must* enquire," Lewrie said, perched on the edge of the rickety caned chair, by then ready to duck or bolt did she feel like slinging something at him.

"Oh, faith, and 'tis th' rich'uns, th' titled squires own most o' th' land, an' *keep* it, hardhanded *English* fashion, sure!" she accused. "Foin gennulmen such's *your* like, Cap'm Lewrie, who'd press me man, then think ye'd shown 'im Christian favour do ye 'llow him *volunteer* t'be yer slave, 'stead o' whippin' 'im to't, sure an' no better'n them Cuffy sailors he said ye'd stolen on Jamaica!"

"He wrote you about that, did he?" Lewrie asked, after having a good, guilty squirm to imagine that the tale of his "accepting" runaway slaves from the despised Beauman family's plantations to take the King's Shilling (as it were) as Freedmen able to decide their own fate.

"Aye, an' he did," she huffily continued. "He wrote me letters in 'is own hand, mind. An't no scholard, is me Toby, but he can manage, sure. Writin', readin', an' ledgerin', good as any man, so's we won't be cheated like *some'd* try."

"And he said nothing to you of wishing to run, of any scheme to make off with the prize, or . . ." Lewrie doggedly pursued.

"Nought but four letters from 'im did I get, sir," she informed him, "th' last four month ago. Run? Aye, an' what sailor wouldn't?"

"Long before the prize disappeared, hmm," Lewrie muttered, his spirits sinking at the thought that he'd been on a wild goose chase all this time. "Might I be so bold, Mistress . . . Hosier . . . as to see the last couple of letters, to see if there's anything . . . *any* hint of . . ."

"Mummy, piddle!" little Tess urgently said from the cabin door.

"Swab it, then shoo that dog out, and—"

"No, mummy! *Baby* piddled," wee Tess amended. "See?"

Tess wriggled damp fingers, then the babe within began to carp and wail, so Mrs. Hosier (Whomever) leaped to her feet and scornfully flung her husband's letters at him before entering the house, there to make soothing but frazzled noises.

As Lewrie sorted the crinkly sheets, he could be forgiven (perhaps) for a slightly smug and amused "tetch" of relief that all of his three legitimate children, and both his by-blows, were long past swaddles, piddles, and "poops."

> *Thet damt Lt. Caterall hoo thinx himsef so Clevver but wat a Buffel-Hed!* . . . *Ferst Off.* Lt. Langlie [spelled correctly, for a wonder] *rites Capts. ward moon-caff in luv & Capts. pett & so is Lt. Adare* [phonetically, he supposed] *top lofty & too smart by haff a favryte. Capt. Loory* [a close approximation] *the idel basterd him & his catts all spoony over them tho thay Piss on hammok netts & we must sleep in them* . . . *Mr. Pendarves & Towpenny the Bos'n & Mate ar hard men never take calls from ther lipps & tis a hard life the Navy dear.*

Lewrie wished he could take the letters along or find paper and pen to make some notes, for Jugg had chuckled over the way some of the crew were getting their hands on smuggled rum or American corn whisky and where it was usually hidden; how the assistant and clerk to the Purser, Mr. Coote, the Jack-in-the-Breadroom, was working a fiddle in tobacco twists and sundries that he concealed in the fishroom; all about the breadroom and cable-tier rats being bred, where they were "pitted" in battle, how they were fed off wardroom flour and corn-meal, thanks to the "Pusser's" aide, too; how the Marine complement's Trinidad Hindoo mongoose was unfair competition . . .

What bloody mongoose? Lewrie silently gawped; *and how did they smuggle* that *aboard? We've never* been *t'bloody Trinidad!*

Oh, it was a rare and embarrassing glimpse into the lives of the people "before the mast," their complaints and sorrows so well hidden from officers under a mask of rote duty.

Jugg himself . . . sullen and truculent, embittered against those over him, those with Admiralty-ordained rank, or social position, with inherited money or soft hands. Indeed, he steered a quarter-point alee of mute insubordination, *boasted* of it to his wife, whether dealing with captain or officers as eagerly as he would with a main-mast or gun-captain with the power to order him about so brusquely.

Toby Jugg, or Hosier, or Warder—whatever he truly named himself— would never be a *glad* hand, no matter were he promoted to Bosun or Fleet Admiral! Yet Jugg, for all his simmering grievances, his ability to doff his hat, cry "Aye aye, sir!" and tug his forelock and smile while supping on his superior's *shite*, evinced no mutinous plots, schemed none, and reported none; nowhere in his letters did he *sound* like a man who would run. Begrudgingly, Jugg admitted that he had settled in *tolerably* well, that *Proteus* was a competently run frigate whose mates and officers knew their professions, and that she was mostly a *happy* ship.

> . . . *was rated Able rite off and struck for QwarterMasters Mate hah Me in a red wesket butt Sailing Master Winwood putt my name for'd & am now Rated & serving on the helm At lest Proteus is ever in the way of fyteing as all frigates & the Capt. betes the Kings Enemmys ever & Dear it looks fare to be prime for Prize Monie Capt. tho is madd for Qwim thay call him Ram Catt & not for his petts . . .*

Embarrassing, aye, to think how much of his personal, private life his sailors, and Jugg, knew! Jugg had learned about his American bastard son, Desmond McGilliveray, knew all about Theoni Connor back in London and his other by-blow, Alan Michael Connor; how his wife, Caroline, was chewing brass rags over his peccadilloes, and that there was a "dear friend" somewhere back in Europe (now *that* narrowed it down, didn't it?) who'd written anonymous your-husband's-a-swine letters, and how the hands—his trusted "ship's people"!—crammed fists into their mouths to keep from howling and chortling out loud over his doings!

> *thay reck her a lucky ship tho Dearun for her lawnching was rite Odd she wud not swimm & stuck on the ways as Proteus butt gott haffway when thay ferst name her Merlin butt change it & an Irish sawyer & hiz son whisper to her stemmpiece then she swamm & Capt. Loory is sayd to seen Selkies & sum say he has there favour sure.*

Jugg had also been struck that *Proteus* was a musical ship when the work allowed, and he'd quite enjoyed that.

> *Liam Desmond & his lap pipes ar capital we hev 3 gudd fiddlers &*
> *Mr. Rain (?) Saylmaker plays a Dago Gittar & even Capt. Loory*
> *plays tin whissle & lets us hev manie dear gay Irish tunes & plays*
> *them butt nott well poor man tho he dus not mind step & slip jigs nott*
> *like sum top-lofty English hoo'd shutt us up & call us mutinuss.*

He'd been coming round, Lewrie sadly thought, letting the note drop to his lap; *better the Devil you know, I s'pose . . .*

Jugg had had a snug berth, promotion and decent pay, shares in *Proteus*'s prize money, acceptable shipmates, and no obvious grievances. Most deserters took "leg bail" within the first few weeks, or months, aboard, 'til they established a personal investment. There were *some* who'd "run" after getting the Joining Bounty, before their kits were deducted, then enlist under a fresh name at another recruiting rendezvous, but Jugg hadn't had that chance. Perhaps wasn't even that sort, after all.

"Damn," Lewrie dejectedly muttered as Mrs. Hosier came back out to the porch and sat down again. A jutted hand silently demanded her precious letters, and he handed them over. She fondly straightened them and pressed them flat with a palm, as if ironing them, before she tucked them away in an apron pocket.

"Toby warn't th' one pirated yer ship, Cap'm Lewrie, not him," Jugg's wife said. "He'd never, else we'd lose ev'rything we've built up, did he haveta run an' change names, *again.*"

"I thought that he'd . . . if he had, that he'd come to Barbados to fetch you and the children," Lewrie confessed, a little chagrined. "You're sure you've not heard from him, he didn't . . ."

"Nary a word since that last letter," she firmly stated, chin up and sullen at his accusation. "Nor nary a sight o' him, at least twelve month or more, when the boy was quickened. Huh!" she snorted derisively, "*Had* he stole a rich prize, ye think I'd still be grubbin' at this farm, that we'd still be livin' in a pore *shebeen* like this? I'm cairtain ye already asked, down at th' harbour, an' know neither that prize ship, nor Toby, has come in here. An't it so?"

"Admitted," Lewried grudgingly allowed.

"So, when ye do find it, if e'er ye do, ye'll already know me Toby didn' steal her. An . . . an' whoever did, they'd not be th' sort t'let him live."

Mrs. Jugg teared up and began to blub again. "That sort'd want no witnesses, oh *arrah!*"

"Ma'am . . ." Lewrie said, springing to his feet at her upset.

"Damn 'is eyes, but I almost wish 'e *had* took her, sure, for he would still be livin', if he did!" She sniffled, blowing her nose on her fingers. "An' bad *cess* t'ye at findin' him, for you'd hang him, cairtain, do ye. Have to. La, la! What'll we do, wi' Toby gone?"

Lewrie blushed and dug into his breeches pocket for his coin-purse. He counted out about eight shillings and the odd pence in real coinage, and a wadded-up pound note. "Call it bringing his pay up to date, ma'am, and I'm sorry that I cannot do more. Navy paymasters . . ."

"I'd no take yer *charity*, Cap'm Lewrie," Mrs. Jugg huffed back, scraping up all her dignity. "But, aye, 'needs must,' sure. Call it hard-earned pay, but a beggar's price for me Toby's life, for all that.

"I'd fling yer paltry silver back, an' spit in yer eye, *arrah*," she said, rising, stiff-backed and arms crossed over her chest, "but th' pore can't *have* no scruples, not in this Life. Not like 'quality' folk like your foin self, sir. An' now I'll thankee t'be departin' me lands, Cap'm Lewrie."

"Of course, ma'am," Lewrie said, gathering up his hat. "Mind, *is* your husband innocent, and *if* I find him, I promise I'll fetch him back to you, safe and sound . . . unlashed and not dis-rated."

"Promises from yer like is 'fiddler's pay,' Cap'm Lewrie," she said, "for so 'tis been my experience, sure? How can ye promise such, when . . . oh, fash!" She swept her hair back from her brows in exasperation. "Don't go makin' promises ye don't *mean* t'keep. Or promises ye most-like can *never* keep, is my meanin'. I would admire, howiver it falls, that *somebody'd* write an' let me know."

"I shall, Mistress Jugg . . . Hosier . . . damme, which do you prefer? To which do I write, without confusing the post-boy?"

"Hosier'd do."

"Good-bye, Mistress Hosier," Lewrie said, bowing himself back off the porch and doffing his hat with a sociable bow. Despite what anger she felt, Mrs. Jugg (for so he thought her, anyway) dropped him a bobbing little housemaid's curtsy, then squinted her eyes in embarrassment the next second, to have such a servile habit so engrained in herself . . . *arrah!*

"So, the trail's gone cold as old, boiled mutton, sir," Langlie gathered, glumly sipping the last of his mug of cool tea.

"Phantom, spectral *false* trails are never hot enough to *cool*, Mister Langlie," Lewrie sourly rejoined. "We've wasted nigh onto two whole months, staggering from port to port, down the whole Windwards, and *no one's* seen them! Bloody fool's errand. The prize is most-like in Cartagena, Tampico, Havana, or Vera-bloody-Cruz by now, and has been all this time. Therefore, untouchable, 'thout a major military expedition! Damn!"

"And our people are most-like a long-time dead," Lt. Langlie further supposed. "Without Jugg as a culprit, I cannot imagine any of the others capable of the deed. Toffett, Ahern, and Luckaby were good men, and *certainly* not Mister Towpenny, or Mister Burns!"

"Unless that lack-wit Burns couldn't keep them in control, they found some liquor that we missed, and it got out of hand," Lewrie said to the overhead and the deck beams. "A fight, a knifing and a murder, and they ran off with the ship out of *fear*, not hope of gain. We both know how insensible poor tars can get. And how quickly. *And* so quick to quarrel on a bung-full of rum."

A goodly number of men who enlisted in the Army, a goodly share of sailors, willing volunteers or press-ganged failures, did it for a reliable daily issue of "grog." Where the term "groggy" came from!

"Well, we've searched everywhere we possibly could, except for Trinidad and Tobago, and the Dutch isles down South," Lewrie grumbled, cocking his head to a chart of the West Indies that had been pinned to the larboard side of his day-cabin for months on end. "We've prowled every cay and rock in the Grenadines and haven't found a sign of 'em. I'd say it's time, Mister Langlie, that we confess our failures, then sail back to Antigua and face the music. Then, on to Jamaica, where we belong. Damme, though . . . Captain Sir Edward bloody Charles . . ."

"Very well, sir," Langlie glumly agreed. "Shore liberty, sir?"

"Hmm? Oh, aye," Lewrie decided. "We've worked the people hard, and they've earned a run ashore. Bridgetown isn't a bad port for 'em. Lots to do . . . and the shore officials are reputed to be cooperative at huntin' down 'runners.' Larboard Watch first, at the end of the Morning Watch, and back aboard by Eight Bells, midnight."

"With the usual caution for troublemakers and deserters that if they run, or run wild, the starbowlines won't be allowed, sir?" First Officer Langlie said with a twinkle.

"Just so, sir," Lewrie tiredly snickered back. "And whilst the Larboard Watch is ashore, Mister Langlie, *you* are going to become some sort of legend."

"Sir?"

"There's trade in smuggled rum and spirits aboard," Lewrie said, reaching into a waist-coat pocket to withdraw a hastily scribbled list he'd made at a harbour tavern while waiting for a hired boat to convey him back aboard. "Here are the likely places to look. *This* time, at any rate. You will also have a word with Mister Coote in the privacy of your mess, and inform him that that jack-a-napes clerk of his sells smuggled tobacco at half the official price. Bits and pieces cut off Mister Coote's supply . . . God knows what all else he deals in, but he stashes it in a false-side keg in the fishroom, under the tiller flat."

"My word, sir, how did you . . . " Langlie all but gasped, sitting up straighter.

"Jugg's chatty letters to his wife," Lewrie chuckled. "The man is also skimming off your wardroom's flour and corn-meal to fatten the rats they fight in the cable-tiers and the forrud orlop."

"Rat fights, sir?"

"Rat on rat," Lewrie said, beaming, "for want of terriers. Wagers are laid on 'em, and I'll not have it."

"Well, now that you mention it, sir, I *had* noticed a diminution in the number of rats aboard, lately," Lt. Langlie said, making notes of his own with a pencil stub and his ever-present pocket notebook. "Though I did put it down to the midshipmen's appetites."

"They don't *have* that Brutus look, do they?" Lewrie mused. "No 'lean and hungry' air."

"Probably purchasing the dead losers from the fights." Langlie laughed. "Aye, sir, I will see to all of it."

"Damme, the people will think you have eyes in the back of yer head, Mister Langlie!" Lewrie crowed. "That you're a dark, devilish wizard who knows all and sees all. Most-like ask you to take augury on chicken guts, next. Hold one of those Gothick . . . seances. Speak to the dead . . . "

"Only for people who could pay, I would, sir," Langlie replied.

"*Speakin'* of chickens . . . "

"Sir?" Langlie enquired, pencil poised.

"Haven't some of the chickens gone missing, lately?"

"Well, aye sir, and so they have. Forgive me, but I did suspect that your *cats* had, um . . ." Langlie said, squirming and blushing.

"It's the mongoose, more like," Lewrie offhandedly told him.

"Beg pardon, sir . . . *mongoose*, did ye say?" Langlie gawped in perplexity. It wasn't often that his efficient First Lieutenant wore a bewildered, nigh cross-eyed expression, but he produced a passable facsimile.

"Mongoose. The Marines' mongoose," Lewrie assured him. "Blue riband, champion Hindoo rat-killin' emigrant mongoose. From Trinidad, or so I learned. It's been beatin' the sailors' best rats, and they don't much care for it, so it's creating bad blood. Find it, Mister Langlie, run it to earth. It's probably been keepin' its hand in by practicing on creatures in the manger up forrud. That's where all our chickens have gone, I'd wager."

"Find a mongoose and get rid of it, sir . . . aye," Langlie said as he scribbled into his little book.

"Well, if all else fails, definitely put a stop to the fights and *definitely* spare our fowl," Lewrie breezed on. "Do the Marines put so much stock in the beast, well . . . I don't much care whether it serves as a mascot with a red riband round its neck, 'long as no one thinks t'bring *snakes* aboard for it to fight."

"I s'pose I'll recognise a mongoose when I see one, sir?"

"Like an ermine or a ferret." Lewrie chuckled. "Like an smallish otter, with a talent for killin' cobras and such."

"Ah!" Langlie rejoined. "I see, sir. I think. Perhaps we may declare it the ship's official ratter . . . so long as no more wagers'r made on its prowess?"

"That's what I like about you, Mister Langlie." Lewrie smiled. "Your flexibility in the face of un-looked-for adversity. I believe that'll be all for now, Mister Langlie. That should be enough on yer plate, for the nonce."

"Oh, agreed, sir. Agreed!" Langlie said, rising and departing.

CHAPTER TWO

*H*MS *Proteus*'s return to English Harbour, Antigua, was actually not necessary, and mostly unproductive. The frigate's mail was still being held at Kingston, Jamaica, by the authorities of the West Indies Station, to which fleet she still putatively belonged, even after her long sojourn.

Thankfully, Lewrie's personal devils of late, Mr. Pelham and Mr. Peel, had long departed Antigua for other climes—all the way back to London, Lewrie fervently wished, so he could live his life free of their cynical machinations, ever more!

Antigua's Admiralty House atop Mt. Shirley held only one letter for him, and that from his new-found bastard son, Desmond McGilliveray, now a sixteen-year-old Midshipman aboard his uncle's (and the captain's) United States Navy Armed Ship, the *Thomas Sumter*. Desmond sounded as if he was thriving at his new profession, so eerily coincidental to Alan's own. *Sumter* had just embarked upon arduous and boresome escort duties to convoy a "trade" of Yankee merchantmen home and, most-like, would put back into her homeport of Charleston, South Carolina, for refitting and provisioning.

Young Desmond chirped right-merry over the prospects of how much prize money might result from *Sumter*'s—and her small squadron's—recent captures in the Caribbean: French merchant ships and several warships, too—ones that Lewrie had led them to, *twice*, using the reborn U.S. Navy as British cat's paws in Pelham's and Peel's scheme.

Desmond enthused how "half-seas-over" his hometown would be when they arrived with prizes in tow, how famous they might be once the news spread from Maine to Georgia, how eager he was to see his adoptive family once more. And, backhandedly, Desmond came close to boasting of a much better reception in Charleston society than he once had, strutting proudly in his uniform, a new-minted hero and promising gentleman seafarer. Which beat being shunned as a half-White, half-Muskogee Indian orphan all hollow, Lewrie sadly suspected.

Desmond happily enquired about Chalky, too; how large or playful the kitten had grown, etc. He'd been Desmond's gift, found shivering and cowering on the boat-tier beams of a French capture; rescued, then shyly presented to the father he'd never known, so heartbreakingly eager to please, to win Lewrie's affection, his claiming . . .

Lewrie looked over at the settee, where Chalky sprawled, teeth and little paws "killing" a cushion's tassel, and thought again, quite possibly for the thousandth time, that the lad had *meant* well, but . . .

His fears for Desmond's continued safety were allayed by news of Guillaume Choundas being detained on his parole aboard the USS *Hancock*, that monstrous frigate, which still cruised the Caribbean. Even so . . . did Choundas ever learn the boy's parentage, the seemingly indefatigable ogre *might* find a way to harm him, to get even with Lewrie. With a fond smile, Lewrie set Desmond's letter aside and pulled out the inkwell and one of his new-fangled, French-invented, steel-nib pens (one more parting gift from the lad off a defeated French *corvette*) to pen him a quick answer for mailing. After the British-American riots, when *Proteus* was last in English Harbour, he was pretty sure that the local authorities would wish them gone as soon as they'd wooded and watered. And not stand upon the order of their going, either! His working parties ashore were already limited to the docks area, and that under the wary guard of the local garrison! No, *Proteus* had already been absent long enough—it was time for a "fond" return to the bosom of Admiral Sir Hyde Parker's fleet on Jamaica, and the "warm" ministrations of the fleet's Staff Captain, Sir Edward "Bloody" Charles.

CHAPTER THREE

$\mathcal{K}$ingston—and Old Port Royal, or what was left of it, after the infamous earthquake many years before—was an ideal anchorage, protected from hurricane winds and winter gales by the Blue Mountains, but *Lord,* it could be a career-ender to approach if one were ignorant of its dangers! Lime Cay, Rackam's Cay and Gun Cay, Drunken Man's Cay, Christ, you could *see* those, could spot three miles of rocks and shoal-water reefs that stretched Sou'west to Nor'east, beginning four miles South of Fort Charles at the tip of the Palisades. The reefs, though, like Great and Little Portuguese and Salt Pond Reef on the Western approaches—it took an experienced master or a knacky harbour pilot who knew the sea bottom as well as he knew his wife's, and this time they had drawn the short straw and gotten a pilot with whom they had never worked, one so blithely casual and dismissive of impending danger, he had actually made that grave and sober Christian, Mr. Winwood, the Sailing Master, throw parallel rules and brass dividers and *curse!* He had come aboard with the dissembling *gravitas* of your practiced toper and had only started to slur, titter, and reveal himself as "three sheets to the wind" *after* they were committed, halfway into the maze inshore of the Great Portuguese!

And it hadn't helped the deck officers, the captain included, that mere seconds after they had made their number to Fort Charles and had begun the required gun-salute to the flag, that a signal had come in reply for her "Captain To Repair On Board"—which in this case meant for Lewrie to depart the ship (*instanter* if not earlier) and get his arse over to the fort, Giddy House, or Admiralty House, in haste.

"Well done, sir," Lewrie said, doffing his hat to Catterall and Langlie as he readied to disembark, "given the circumstances, and the pilot's state. Had I known, I'd have not asked it of you, yet . . . my congratulations for coping so well, Mister Catterall."

"Erm . . . thankee, sir!" Catterall responded, greatly pleased at the un-looked-for compliment, though still wheezing and swabbing perspiration.

"My permission to hoist a full bumper," Lewrie continued, with a sly wink. "You more than earned it, God knows. Gentlemen?"

With his reports, and bearing his log just in case it might be required, Lewrie took the salute of the crew and side-party, and went down into his gig, which had been towed astern in fear that his rapid reporting would be demanded.

The transition from sunlight to dim coolness almost made Lewrie sneeze as he stopped by the hall porter's station to ply a damp, cool towel on his face and neck before confronting Authority. The weather actually was quite mild, the daytime temperatures averaging in the low to mid-eighties, but no matter the season, the Caribbean sun was still a farrier's hammer. Combine that with Lewrie's trepidation of *rencontre* with "the Wine Keg," Capt. Sir Edward Charles, whose animus he'd roused through no fault of his own, after nearly half a year of swanning about as free of Navy control as so many larks, and it was no wonder that he could feel moisture under his clothes, in his nether regions.

Once dried, Lewrie put the best face on it and nearly marched down the long, gloomy hallway, the hard leather heels of his gilt-tasseled Hessian boots ringing off the plank floor and the hard plaster and shiny paint of the walls. He attained those fearsome double doors, so heavy and intricately panelled, so glossy with linseed oil or beeswax polish. Hell was *said* to be al-luring, Lewrie considered as he took a deep breath and heaved a sigh; from the outside, at least, before one got past its portals. He tugged his waist-coat, shirt cuffs, his sword baldric and neck-stock into pristine order, even gave the short ribbon-bound queue atop his collar a nervous tug before knocking.

The double doors resounded with a sound *not* unlike *Doom . . . Doom!*

"Go the bloody hell away!" someone inside shouted.

"Gladly," Lewrie replied without a thought, feeling as if he was back in public school (one of many he had attended at one time or another) and had come for a well-deserved caning, only to discover that the headmaster or proctor was sick! "May I take my frigate with me when I do?" he could not resist quipping.

There came a muttered something, mighty like a suppressed curse, then an aggrieved growl of "Enter!"

Lewrie pulled on the ornate brass handles and swung the doors back, revealing that dread office, that heaped desk awash under working papers, the bookshelves spilling over with loose stacks of it, and several wineglasses, all used since sunrise . . . Wait a bit!

"Mine arse on a band-box!" Lewrie expostulated.

The shelves were neatly stacked, all correspondence bound up in various coloured ribbons; the desktop could actually be *seen;* the books and ledgers were arranged in what Lewrie could only take for a proper order, and the only potables in sight was the coin-silver coffee set and tray on a sideboard 'neath the large North-facing windows, a set of porcelain cups, three candles burning under a more plebeian black-iron pot.

"So you finally turned up, have you?" scoffed the Post-Captain, standing behind the desk, minus his uniform coat.

"Captain Nicely?" Lewrie gawped in utter surprise.

"Unfortunately," that worthy said, waving a weary hand over the neat-but-daunting stacks of paperwork. "Come in, come in, Captain, and pray do pour yourself a cup, do you enjoy coffee. Take a pew, sir."

"Er, thankee, sir," Lewrie said, feeling much more at ease. He did pour a cup of coffee, stirred in some local sugar, and sniffed at the cream, then poured in a dollop of that, as well, taking an appreciative sip before seating himself, with his canvas-bound packet on the other chair. "Hmmm," he added, smacking his lips.

"Hope you don't mind goat's milk," Nicely said, "but it's fresher than cow's . . . just out back, d'ye see, drawn off the teat this dawn, so it has no time to go over. Does the sugar run low at sea, there's nothing like a dollop of sweet goat's milk."

"Up 'til now, I'd always thought it *too* sweet, sir, but . . ."

"Leave off the sugar, use a level teaspoon's worth, not a heaping," Nicely suggested, seating himself behind the desk and perking up brisker. "And what have you brought me, Lewrie . . . *more* paperwork to read, initial, pass on, and file? My, ain't *you* the fine gift-giver!"

In their brief acquaintance, Lewrie had quite liked Nicely; he was so aptly named! He was a squarely built older fellow, one of those gentlemen who simply oozed confidence, competence, and reliability. Nicely was a bluff older sea dog, but one with a wry and infectious sense of humour—or irony—to go with his merry blue eyes. Brisk, efficient, yet droll, he was a most congenial sort. Nicely had done Lewrie several kindnesses at Port-au-Prince before the evacuation of the Army from Saint-Domingue, when Nicely aboard HMS *Obdurate* had held temporary command of that harbour. And, after all, Lewrie had come in with complaints from Capt. George Blaylock of HMS *Halifax*. Nicely and Blaylock had been nigh mortal enemies since their midshipman days, and, since "the enemy of my enemy is my friend" applied to Royal Navy politics, Lewrie and Nicely had turned out to be "cater-cousinly."

"Sorry, sir, but I fear I must," Lewrie said, setting aside his coffee to hand over his bundled packet. "We've been under 'independent orders,' at the behest of some people from the Foreign Office, so . . ."

"Heard all about that," Nicely breezed off, "so I fear that you wasted a deal of ink and paper documenting your doings. *Sub rosa* they were, so they'll remain."

"I take it that Mister Pelham and Mister Peel returned to Jamaica before we did, then, sir," Lewrie surmised. "Well, damme!"

"It *sounded* like high adventures, Lewrie," Nicely said with a wry smirk. "Beats fruitless cruising, at any rate. Oh, some snippets of your activities *might* appear in the *Gazette* or the *Marine Chronicle* back home, but the bulk of it . . ." Nicely gave a shiver of denial. "A larger question'd be . . . where the Devil have you been *since?*"

"Well, that's a tad embarrassin', really," Lewrie replied and tugged at his neck-stock. He crossed his legs involuntarily.

"Oh, good!" Nicely chirped. "*Do*, Lewrie, tell me *all!*"

When the sorry tale was over, Nicely still beamed, as if he had known some of the affair beforehand or was sitting on a secret as smug as a broody-hen, with an I-know-something-*you*-don't-know smile.

"Why, damme, Captain Lewrie," Nicely chid him in mock displeasure as he rose and got himself a fresh cup of coffee, with milk only, and not a dab of sugar. "You've been . . . *yachting!* . . . you idle fop! Swanning from one liberty port to the next. Sightseeing every island in the Caribbean, and all at His Majesty's expense! Unlawful absconding with Admiralty property, too! Why, my predecessor would've hacked your balls off. Done 'em in sweet-meats, sauce and heavy cream."

"By the way, sir," Lewrie enquired, in hopes perhaps that what grief he was about to suffer might be delayed a moment more, like one of those head-master's canings. "Where *is* Sir Edward?"

"Dead as bloody mutton," Nicely told him with a grimace, spoon tinkling a little louder in his fine china cup. "Turned as yellow as quince and expired a week later. Physicians suspect 'twas his kidneys *and* liver, finally rebelled at all the cheap spirits he'd imbibed . . . since his mother's paps were taken from him, is my guess. 'Bugger all this, mate . . . it's mutiny,' I s'pose they said to each other, there below-decks as it were. He passed over three months ago, just after we brought the line-of-battle ships back from Halifax, once hurricane season was over."

"My condolences, sir," Lewrie soberly said.

"For 'the Wine Keg'?" Nicely scoffed.

"No, for you, sir," Lewrie amended, "I s'pose you had to give up *Obdurate* to take this, well . . . *call* it a promotion, at the least."

"Aye, I did, dammit," Nicely groused, seating himself once more. "Best two-decker on the West Indies Station, if I do say so myself . . . and I do! Staff drudgery, well . . . something I'd been fortunate enough to miss, 'til now. Sir Hyde gave me no choice in the matter, just said I was best for the post, how career-enhancing it'd be, and all of that flummery, then gave *Obdurate* to one of his favourite frigate Captains. *Then* gave said frigate to a *junior* Captain, shuffled another junior off a leaky sloop of war, promoted a brig-sloop Commander into *her,* made a Lieutenant into Commander for the brig-sloop . . . made a Midshipman into a Lieutenant in his flagship's wardroom as a replacement." Nicely had a bleak look out his windows at real ships at anchor, looking famished. "Interest and favour . . . or they all owe the Admiral money. Or he owes their *families.* But you know how the Navy works."

Lewrie refilled his coffee, stinting on the sugar this time.

What could be said? he wondered to himself; *Shouldn't have joined if ye can't take a joke? It's a cruel old world, and that's its way?*

"Didn't bury Captain Charles here, Lewrie," Nicely further griped. "Lumbered the old fellow into a beef barrel and filled it up with accidentally salted and condemned rum, then shipped him to his loving family in England. B'lieve it or not, sir, he actually *had* one!"

Lewrie could not keep his sniggering to himself at that news.

"Speaking ill of the dead?" Nicely chid him. "You heathen!"

"Springs to mind, sir . . . how *apt* it was to pickle him." Lewrie chortled, setting his cup down before he spilled or broke it as a wave of titters took him. "And, was there a *tinge* of saltwater in his keg, that's the closest he'd been to the genuine article in years!"

"If you can't say something good about the dead, say not a word, 'twas the old adage," Nicely replied, grinning himself, though.

"He's dead . . . good." Lewrie snickered.

"Aye, well . . . I doubt the rum was necessary. Sir Edward was a fair way towards pickling *himself* long before his 'casking,' damn his jingle-brained ways to hell. As much 'Miss Taylor,' 'Black Strap,' and rum went missing from stores, all with Sir Edward's signature affixed, 'tis a wonder he drew a *waking* breath, much less a sober one," Nicely confided. "One'd suspect malfeasance in office, selling it off by the odd hundred gallons to shore merchants, but no, I suspect he *drank* it. You cannot imagine what a bloody pot-mess this office was, and how much labour it's taken just to get it caught up!

"And the sorriest thing, Lewrie," Capt. Nicely continued, "is just how *little* work is necessary, now it's all tiddly and clackin' along like a hallway clock. I am *bored*, Lewrie, bored to *tears*. There are too *many* hours in the day. And damn you for havin' so much fun at sea . . . even if you *didn't* know where you were going or where you were when you *got* there!"

"My *sincerest* condolences, again, sir," Lewrie offered with his right hand over his heart and his eyes downcast, for a sober moment.

"Know what you're thinkin' . . . 'so long as it ain't me,' hey?"

"Something very like that, in truth, Captain Nicely," Lewrie had to admit.

"Yes, well . . ." Nicely gruffly said, shrugging. "Finish your coffee, Lewrie, and we'll coach down to the hospital. You've a little surprise in store."

"Sir?" Lewrie asked as Nicely flung on his sword belt, his ornate uniform coat, and got his hat down from a bookshelf. "The hospital, do you say?"

"Can't get your rich prize ship back for you, but we did recover your missing crewmen, picked 'em up from—"

"They're *alive*, sir?" Lewrie gawped, springing to his feet.

"Aye . . . most," Nicely said, with a brief *moue* of chagrin.

"And a Quartermaster's Mate name of Toby Jugg, too, sir?" Lewrie pressed. "He was recovered, as well?"

"*B'lieve* that was one of the names, Captain Lewrie. Why?"

" 'Cause he just *may* be the bastard who arranged her taking!"

"Well, let's go sort it out, then," Nicely said, leading the way towards the double doors. A stringy-pale and much harassed Lieutenant came barging in, shuffling a loose stack of papers and muttering under his breath.

"Fidditch!" Nicely barked, almost startling the poor young man out of a year's growth, making him go ashen, cutty-eyed, and fumble-fingered.

"Whistle up me coach, Mister Fidditch, there's a good 'Ink-Sniff' . . . you poor, put-upon 'catch-fart'!"

"Aye, aye, sir . . . directly!"

"Good lad, really," Nicely commented as they drum-echoed their boots down that long, cool hallway, "not a dab o' 'interest' with Admiralty in the world, though. And I need *someone* to abuse, damme!"

CHAPTER FOUR

*G*od bless ye, Cap'm Lewrie, sir!" Bosun's Mate Towpenny cried in delight as Lewrie entered their ward in the naval shore hospital on the Palisades peninsula. "Saw good ol' *Proteus* come in, we did, Cap'm, an' I told 'em t'wouldn't be long before we got reclaimed!"

Towpenny waved a hand at the large open windows that faced the harbour approaches, the louvred "Bahamian" storm shutters propped high to provide shade yet still allow fresh air to circulate. The windowpanes were small, though reasonably clear and clean; the lower halves of the sashes, quite tropically "homey"—but for the iron bars that kept "grateful recipients of His Majesty's care" from deserting as soon as they were ambulatory!

Lewrie took a quick census, his eyes darting about the room and plucking names from memory. Towpenny, Able Seaman Ahern, the teenaged topman, Willy Toffett, Able Seaman Luckaby . . . Midshipman Mr. Burns was not there, but most-like in a "gentleman's" ward, and . . . *Quartermaster Jugg?* His eyes blared and his lips parted in astonishment to see Toby Jugg sitting on a cot near one of the windows!

What the Devil's he doin' here? Why didn't he run if he . . .

"Ah . . . sorry it took a while, Mister Towpenny . . . lads," he managed to say, gulping down his shock after a moment. He strode about the room, clapping them all on the back, even the reluctant-looking Jugg, to congratulate them on their survival; squeamish, though, as he looked into Jugg's eyes and patted his shoulder with false *bonhomie*.

Squeamish, too, ready to clap a hand over his nose, as the reek of the hospital caught up with him; an age-old reek of blood, pus, and vomit, of fever-sweat and flesh rot. God, how many thousands had died here in the tropics of fevers, with battle wounds the *rare* cause!

It would be days, Lewrie had been told, before his hands could be released even on light duties after their ordeal. All were badly sunburned, some peeling in raw-beef sheets, their lips dryly cracked, exposed skin spotted with lanced and draining saltwater boils. Able Seaman Ahern was the worst off, still bedridden. He'd drunk seawater.

"Now, lads, just what the Devil happened to you?" Lewrie at last demanded, taking a seat on a cot and fanning away the heat.

" 'Twas two hours into th' Middle Watch, sir," Towpenny said, by way of a beginning. "Mister Burns, Toffett here, and Ahern over yonder, was the watchstanders, th' rest of us caulkin' below. 'Ccordin' to what they've told *me*, th' first thing they knowed, there come a *wee* thumpin' . . . of boats comin' alongside, sir, then nigh on two dozen pirates got on deck, and—"

"Blink of an eye, an' they was just there, sir!" Willy Toffett declared. "Knives an' cutlasses t'our throats, and 'twas nothin' that we could do, e'en t'cry out. Three or four t'each of us, Cap'm, sir."

"Not a sound did they make, sir," Towpenny started again, after bestowing a sour who's-tellin'-this? glare at young Toffett. "First I knowed, there were three on *me*, draggin' me out me cot. We'd took over th' wardroom cabins, d'ye see . . ."

A brief lark, a few days' luxury, that; to loll in private, in a small canvas-and-deal partition chamber normally reserved for officers or merchantmen's mates, in substantial bed-cots, not hammocks, with elbow room to yawn and stretch, not the fourteen to eighteen inches per man of swaying room on the gun-deck. *Convenient* to the weather decks, with fresh bedding and linens, real chairs and a glossy table at which to dine . . . as temporary civilian gentlemen of "the Quality."

"Black or dark grey boats and oars, dark clothin', and all done 'thout a sound above a whisper, sir," Towpenny related, still so impressed by their discipline that he shook his head in wonder, two months later. "Time they got us all bound, gagged and blindfolded, sir, and manacled down in the after hold, they'd got a way on her so quick they must've cut the anchor cables."

"Who *were* they, Mister Towpenny?" Lewrie pressed. "Privateers or pirates? . . . French or Spanish?" he asked, eying Jugg askance.

"Claimed t'be French privateers, sir," Towpenny related, "but we heard as much Spanish palaver as we did Frog, so we weren't sure, even at th' last. A day'r two outta Dominica, they fetched us up, we seen their schooner, the *Reunion*, they called her, but—"

"A *big* two-master she woz, sir!" Toffett stuck in, bouncing on his cot to add his share of their harrowing tale. "Masts, sails, and upperworks grey as dusk, Cap'm. Black-hulled, though. Black as them devils' hearts!" the young topman spat.

"Red gunn'ls an' boot-top stripe, too, don't forget, hey," Able Seaman Luckaby added through cracked and puffy lips.

"*Reviv*, or summat like that, woz wot *I* heard'm call her," Ahern croaked from a raw throat, propped up on one elbow. "*Two* names that bitch had. You heard it, right, Jugg? Wot woz it ye said?"

"The *Revenant*," Jugg gruffly supplied in a growl, seated apart on his cot by the windows, still. "Means 'The Ghost,' I think."

"Aye, sir," Ahern snarled. "A ghost she were, right enough."

"And it was reported that, ah . . . you went ashore by yourself to the Dominica Court's office, Jugg?" Lewrie asked, raising a hand to quell the indignantly excited babble. "I was told you were the one to ask permission to sail the prize over to Antigua?"

"Nossir, tweren't *me*," Jugg objected, his first sign of animation. He left off paring slices of anti-scorbutic apples that he ate off his knife blade to defend himself. " 'Twas one o' them pirates wot took Mister Towpenny's coat an' hat an' went ashore! Real tall, lean older man, wot spoke English right good . . ."

"Spanish an' French, just as easy" got tacked on.

" 'At's th' way o' h'it, sir!"

"Axed our names at th' point of a dagger, 'ey did!"

"I see," Lewrie said, after a long and leery pause to mull that over. It would seem that *all* his preconceptions about the taking of the prize had been as wrong as his guesses as to where she'd gone and might have been recaptured!

Damme, though, Lewrie thought; *Jugg's* still *lookin' as shifty-eyed as a pickpocket. I* still *think he knows more than he's telling! Old shipmates of his, did it? Did he* recognise *anyone or . . .*

Lewrie frowned, realising that, for now, he would have to take their collective word for it. Even Jugg's.

"What happened after that?" Lewrie asked, instead.

"Once we sailed, sir, they kep' us in irons down on th' orlop," Willy Toffett eagerly took up the tale. "Sometimes, they'd remember t'feed us an' give us water, sometimes not. Change out our shites or force us t'make in our clothes, the—!"

"Like we woz *nothin'*, 'ey did!" Ahern snarled from his bed-cot. "Like we'd be dead as th' rest, when 'ey got round to it!"

"Four, five days, 'twas rare quiet, sir," Mr. Towpenny related in a weary voice. "Felt like we were sailin' Large, the winds on the starboard quarter most th' time, bound mostly Westerly, Cap'm. Fifth or sixth day, we heard 'em clearin' for action, an' we were hopin' it was one o' *ours,* but . . . she turned out t'be a Spaniard, and she got took right quick. Wot'd they say 'bout her, Jugg? You savvied 'em."

"That she woz a Spanish cutter, mebbe a *guarda costa* or a *kind* o' gov'ment ship, anyways," Jugg warily supplied, arms crossed on his deep chest. "Made 'em right happy, by th' sounds of it."

"Smelled like a slaver, t'me," Mr. Towpenny abjected.

"Uush, 'at woz th' first'un," Ahern quibbled, "a slaver, sure! Can't mistake th' stink. 'Twoz th' *second* prize, woz th' *guarda costa.* Took . . . "

". . . a day'r two later, sir!" Toffett chirped up. "First, she woz a blackbirder, certain! Wot'd ye say, Toby? . . . She woz outta th' Spanish Main? Puerto Cabello?"

"Havana," Jugg gravelled. "Bought slaves at *Havana* t'sell down to Puerto Cabello, wot I could make out them sayin', Willy."

"Murderin' bastards," Ahern added, with a faint shudder of what he'd heard, even if he hadn't seen it. "Gawd, but there was a *power* o' murderin', both times, sor!"

"Murder?" Lewrie asked, appalled.

"Both times, 'ey'd start a'killin' folk, sir," Seaman Luckaby explained, black-visaged in anger.

"Ev'ry last Spaniard aboard both ships, sir," Mr. Towpenny said. "Some slaves, too, right, Jugg?"

"Old an' sick'uns, aye," Jugg grimly agreed.

"Lotta shootin', wailin', and screamin', sir," Mr. Towpenny said in a croak of horrible awe. "Down on th' orlop, we could hear 'em in th' water alongside, poundin' and scrabblin' at th' hull."

"*Keel-hauled* one, sir!" Luckaby shuddered. "Ropes rubbed right 'neath us, it sounded like."

"Shoved them *healthy* slaves down in th' holds atop us, round us an' ye never . . . !" Ahern griped.

"Chiefest delight seemed t'be killin' Spaniards, though, sir," Mr. Towpenny marvelled. "Like they were at war with *them* 'stead of us. Us, those slaves . . . we were more like icin' on th' cake. They'd get round to us when it pleased 'em.'"

"Moved us aboard th' schooner, th' last couple o' nights, h'it was so crowded 'board th' French prize, sir," Toffett said, "wot with a hundred'r more slaves t'see to. We knew we were next, though.'"

"So, how did you come to survive?" Lewrie queried, at a loss in the face of such capricious cruelty and bloodshed.

"Hauled us up, we heard 'em say they hadn't done a *maroonin'* yet," Towpenny said. "Wasn't that wot ye said they said, Toby?"

"Aye," Jugg was forced to admit. "Like 'twoz nought but a rare *game* they woz playin'. Whoopin' like Billy-O over it, and . . ."

"Oddest thing, that, sir," Towpenny mused, his grey-grizzled head laid over to one side. "When they fetched us up on deck the last time and set us ashore—the Dry Tortugas, it was, sir—we could look back from shore an' see 'em. Must've burnt their last two prizes, I s'pose, for t'were nought but *our* French merchantman and that black-heart schooner layin' off . . . Both were flyin' th' *Spanish* flag, along with the French, atop 'em. Yet, did they despise the Dons as bad as it seemed?"

"They weren't out of Guadeloupe?" Lewrie puzzled half to himself.

"Nossir," Towpenny countered, "and when they sailed away, arter maroonin' us, they woz bound Nor'west, straight as an arror, 'til they drapt below th' horizon, Cap'm."

"Spanish Florida, perhaps," Lewrie mused aloud, rising to pace with his hands in the small of his back, the engrained habit of a sea captain. "Mobile, Pensacola? Christ, other than New Orleans in Spanish Louisiana there's not a single settled port where they could sell off their prizes and slaves, 'til you get to Tampico or Veracruz, down in New Spain! Don't make sense. Jugg!" he exclaimed, stopping mid-stride and turning to peer at the man.

"Sir?" Jung warily replied.

"Did you ever hear them boast of their home port?"

"Could've been New Orleans, sir, mebbe," Jugg reluctantly said.

"Spaniards and Frogs, together, aye," Lewrie said, frowning and going to the windows to look out at the ocean, near Jugg's cot. "New Orleans and Louisiana were French, first, 'til '63. And New Orleans, so I've heard, draws seamen of every nation. The Frogs on Guadeloupe sell Letters of Marque to anyone with a *rowboat* and a full purse, no matter who it is. Other Frogs, Spaniards, British renegades, Yankee Doodles . . . *somewhat* honest privateersmen *or* outright pirates."

"*Acted* more like pirates, 'ey did, sir," Toffett grumbled.

"*Played* more like pirates," Seaman Luckaby sneered. "See, sir . . . there woz common sailors, like, then there woz some o' th' Quality sorts aboard 'at schooner, an' all o' us could hear th' diff'rence . . . 'twoz th' *way* they talked, d'ye see, sir . . . top-lofty an' lordly, not loud an' hard, like—".

"Though they were th' cruelest," Toffett stuck on.

"Mean t'say, sir," Luckaby forged on, "some of 'em *could* speak th' good ol' king's English, and—"

"Them lordley *fiends*," Toffett spat.

"Their Cap'm and him wot set us ashore on that island, sir . . . man called hisself Balfa," Towpenny agitatedly contributed. "On that last mornin', when they marooned us it woz, there were . . . *young'uns* who mocked an' jeered us, in English, sir. *Soft*-handed young'uns woz who I heard, couldn't bellow like full-grown tars, and—"

"An' 'ey *giggled,* for so 'ey did, sor," Ahern rasped from his bed, before pouring himself another mug of lemon-water. "Loik little misses at a dance, a'titt'rin' 'hind their fans."

"Hmmm . . . hear any other names, lads?" Lewrie asked them.

"*Think* the one played Toby in my clothes woz called Lanc'shire or somethin' like that, sir," Mr. Towpenny told him, "Lancs . . . Lang-thingummy?"

"Lotta first names, mostly, sir," Toffett offered. "Pierre an' Jacques, Pedro an' Pablo . . . nicknames? Mister Jugg said one o' their off'cers might o' been called 'Hungry,' an' t'other'un 'Fierce,' didn't ye say, Mister Jugg?"

"*Féroce,* meanin' 'Ferocious' in Frog," Jugg corrected gloomily, "and *L'Affamé.* Means 'Hungry,' aye. Never heard their real names, so which woz which, well . . ." the man trailed off with a confused shrug.

"No one's heard either nickname, I take it?" Lewrie probed them. "Nothing associated with a past, a repute, associated with either?"

"Nossir, sorry t'say," Mr. Towpenny said, after silently polling their ignorant expressions and helpless shrugs.

"Probably named themselves to better their odds at recruiting sailors," Lewrie said, sighing and shrugging himself. "That would be just *like* a gasconading Frenchman, t'claim he's successful. Well, let me say that I'm damned relieved to find you all relatively healthy and alive, men. We've spent the last two months runnin' down the Windwards searching for you. That prize bedamned, 'twas *you* we wanted to get back, and you can bet your last farthing, soon as you're able to come back aboard, your shipmates'll give you all a welcome worthy of the Prodigal Son. We'll have a 'Make or Mend' day *and* kill a fatted calf, the Purser's accounts no matter!"

That cheered them considerably, and they raised a hearty Three Cheers and a Tiger for Lewrie and their pending celebration.

"I'll just look in on Mister Burns, then go back aboard to let everyone know that you're alive," Lewrie said, basking in their cheers.

"Er, uh . . ." Mr. Towpenny gloomed up. "Ye can't, sir. Mister Burns is dead, sir."

"Them bastards *killed* him, sir!" Toffett barked.

"They bloody *what?*" Lewrie roared. "When? How? Did you see which of 'em did it?" His self-congratulatory mood had gone to ashes.

"Well, sir," Mr. Towpenny began, after another communal look and a sour swallow of bile that, as senior hand, it would be his forlorn duty to complete the sorry tale. "They set us ashore on the island . . . run us up th' beach at gun-point, an' this Balfa feller give us a few, um . . . things, 'coz even *he* said t'others woz 'crazy-mean,' and that *he'd* give us a sportin' chance, at least, almost like a Christian, he did, though I 'spect he woz a slave t'Popery. Ol' leather bag o' . . . stuff, an' he wished us good luck, an' they woz shovin' off, had oars in th' water an' was nigh onta a long musket-shot off, a'strokin' for their ship, when one o' them *buggerin'* high an' mighty sods aboard th' schooner just up an' *shot* him, sir! For the hellish *fun* of it, damn his blood! Pardon me French, sir."

"In his leg, sir," Toffett luridly described, grabbing his groin to show where the bullet had struck, "right close t'his weddin' tackle. Weren't nothin', we could do for Mister Burns, sir, with one ol' rusty knife that Balfa bugger'd left us. Ball was still in him, an' none of us with a lick o' doctorin', sir. Nought but seawater t'wash out th' wound with, so . . ."

"Lasted three days, he did, 'fore he passed over, sir, and wee Mister Burns, he went *hard*, sorry t'have t'tell ye, Cap'm," Towpenny gravelled, looking as if he'd tear up, as if it had happened just this morning, and not a week or more before. "No shelter, hardly any water t'drink, 'cept for rain squalls, an' that foul."

"Sucked outta our shirts an' such, sir," Toffett recalled with a grimace, as if in aftertaste. "Caught in 'at ol' wash-leather bag. Nought but a dram or two 'twixt th' six of us, was all it amounted to. Turtle blood . . . fish blood, and some gulls we knocked down with driftwood planks, sir? Ugh!"

They had dug with a grey-wood board in search of a fresh water seep but had hit porous limestone moist with saltwater. Amazingly to Lewrie, this Balfa creature had left them a cracked magnifying glass, a stained linen handkerchief and a flintlock tinder-box, that rusty knife, so a fire *could* be kindled once they'd found enough driftwood and sun-dry pine needles and palm furze. Most nights, though, they had shivered in the wind-swept chills in the dark, saving firewood for a beacon to any passing ship.

Raw turtle meat and blood, raw seabird flesh and gore doled out in meagre handfuls to last an entire day. The surf had been too heavy to "grabble," tickle, or spear fish . . . and the sharks too numerous and prowling almost into the glass windowpane of the waves that broke on their little beach. There'd been gulls' eggs for one afternoon, then the wonder of a hawksbill turtle that had crawled ashore to scoop out her nest in the sand. Craftily, they'd waited 'til she was crawling back to the water, totally spent, and had hammered, gouged, and pried her open with their bare hands and fist-sized rocks to kill her.

That night, they *had* lit a fire, to preserve so much meat; and had dug up her eggs like the Purser might dish out his rations, a bit at a time from the sandy "larder," a dozen apiece per day to assuage their raging hunger, and her massive, shield-like upper shell had made a catch-basin for the rare rain.

"Had t'bury th' poor lad there on th' island, sir," Mr. Towpenny said, almost piping his eyes. "Said wot words we had over him, put up a driftwood cross but we daren't risk th' knife t'carve his name on it. Poor little tyke. Warn't th' sort o' Midshipman like t'prosper in th' Navy, but he tried, I'll give him that. Weren't right, them bastards pottin' him like th' squire'd pot a rabbit, then leave him t'die. For th' fun o' it!"

"How long were you on that island, Mister Towpenny?" Lewrie asked, about as sorrowful as his sailors, after the dreary tale had been told of Midshipman Burns's sufferings before he'd died. "And how were you rescued?"

"Nigh on ten days, sir," Towpenny grumbled deep in his chest. "Got picked up 'bout two weeks ago. Fin'lly saw a sail o' *any* sort up to th' North'rd, and figgered even th' *Spaniards* couldn't do us worse in one o' their prisons, so we lit a fire, and she seen us and hauled her wind t'come about."

"Used our slop trousers t'make a big *smoky* fire, sir, just like Moses follered by day," Seaman Luckaby said with an ironic chuckling noise. "Stockings'd been burnt before, t'help cook that turtle."

"You were picked up naked from your shirts down?" Lewrie said, more than glad to conjure up a happier picture of their long ordeal.

"Burnt our tarred hats, too, sir, an' wearin' our wool jackets like shawls," Mr. Towpenny added, almost snickering, too, at the *outré* spectacle they had made of themselves.

"Thort 'at ship'd sail right past us, sor," Ahern said from his sick-bed, wheezing with happy remembrance of their deliverance. "But oncet 'at fire was blazin' good, wot with th' *vairy* last scrap o' wood on th' island, and God help us if she'd not come about!"

"Aye, and amen, i' faith!" his Proteuses chorused in cacophony.

"Sure, an' all 'at rum whooshed up like a fire-ship takin' light, sor, an' . . ." Ahern chortled, then blushed; silenced, he was taken by a fit of wheezing and coughing into his fist. And all of the other hands broke off from contributions and exultations, went red in the face, and found sudden interest in the floor or the odd strolling insect, their bare toes . . .

"The . . . *rum*," Lewrie posed, a skeptical brow lifted in query.

"Ahem, sir!" Mr. Towpenny finally spoke up. "D'ye see, sir, as I told ye, sir, that Balfa feller left us some . . . things, t'give us a sportin' chance, like he said, and, ah . . . one of 'em was a ten-gallon barrico o' rum, sir. Unwatered, d'ye see. Cruel! Oh, *cruel* it woz, that! Right, lads?"

"Oh, aye! Arr! Bastard!" came their enthusiastic remonstrance to that fiendish infliction. "Us t'do a 'Drunken Jack,' like 'at pore ol' pirate got found on th' coast o' th' Carolinas, nothin' but bones, an' an empty cask! Hellish temptation! But nary a drap o' *water?*"

"Die we must, sure an' we'd all go blissful," Ahern fondly speculated, "a'dreamin' 'twoz Fiddler's Green an' not a desert?"

"We rationed it out, we did, sir," Mr. Towpenny firmly stated, "just enough t'keep our spirits up, an' it *woz* wet, after all . . . savin' it for a *big* bonfire, did a ship come, d'ye see, Cap'm," he extemporised. "Eased Mister Burns, too, it did, thankee Jesus, *seemed* like it kept his wound from festerin' quick as it might've . . . give him at least a day or more o' life . . . t'make his peace with the Lord, so it could be counted a *blessin'*, do ye look at it *that* way, sir, and . . . "

"Any *left?*" Lewrie dryly asked.

"Well, er . . . nossir," Mr. Towpenny said, squirming on his rickety chair. "Th' bonfire took a power of it, sir, Flames nigh as tall as a cro'jack yard, an' *lots* o' smoke t'draw that ship down t'us."

"Um-humm," Lewrie commented; though picturing his sailors being rescued with their pricks swaying in the wind, short coats over their heads like be-shawled Dago widows . . . and every last man-jack as drunk as an emperor! 'Twas a wonder their rescuers hadn't backed oars, gone about, and rowed away and left them as a bad bargain!

"And you've lost your kits, I take it," Lewrie said further, as he paced back to the centre of the room. "Aye, we must do something on that score. The hospital charge you for these new slops you wear? By God, the skin-flints! I'll speak to Mister Coote, soon as I am back aboard, and suggest a whip-round . . . from forecastle, gun-deck, and the wardroom, all, to get you kitted out proper, again. So what pay you're owed won't vanish, and you won't have to sign away your prize money to shore jobbers for a quarter its future worth, either.

"As far as I'm concerned, you were on active duty all this time, so don't fear pay stoppage in your absence, as well," he further promised. "You did damed well, lads, to keep your discipline and your wits about you, simply to stay alive. Mister Towpenny, be sure that your keeping good charge will be noted, and rewarded."

"Thankee, sir . . . thankee kindly," Towpenny said, blushing anew.

"You'll all be back aboard in a few days," Lewrie told them as he picked up his hat and took a step towards the door. "In the meantime, I'd wish you to try to recall all you can about those so-called privateers who held you. Any *scrap* of information as to names, places, or gossip you heard . . . any clues as to where they were headed, as to who they really were. I'm sure Mister Jugg will prove helpful, since he can sort out French or Spanish words that might be confusing, right Jugg?" he prompted, giving that dubious rogue a damned chary glare.

"Aye, sir," the fellow answered.

"By the way, Jugg . . . we sailed as far as Barbados in search of you, of word of you," Lewrie slyly continued. "We rode up to call on your acres in Welsh Hell Gully. You've gotten your mail since coming ashore? No? Rest assured, your wife is well . . . There's a good crop coming up, and . . . both your daughter and infant son are in the best of health."

"Er . . . thankee, sir," Jugg all but gasped, sitting up straight in spite of his guarded caution, even as he went cutty-eyed to imagine what else Lewrie had learned about him from his fellow Barbadians.

"And your girl Tess has herself a reddish, flop-eared puppy," Lewrie added with a disarming grin. "*Almost* house-broke, but it looks t'be early days . . . I expect you'll hear all about it, in your wife's next letter. Well, I'll see you all later, lads. Keep your chins up, and take no more guff from the hospital staff than you must."

"Drunk as goats?" Lewrie asked Capt. Nicely, once they had met again in the hospital's cool, north-facing entrance hall.

"Staggering!" Nicely snorted with wry glee. "Falling-down, jig-dancing, gravel-swimming, talking-in-tongues, *raving* drunk, they were! Commander Mortimer of the sloop *Spritely*, which picked them up, was of half a mind to give them two dozen lashes for 'Drunk on Duty,' as soon as he learned they were Navy men! Thankfully, your Bosun's Mate, that Towpenny, had enough of his wits about him to claim the *pirates* were to blame, for leaving all that rum as a fiendish *torture*, with nary a drop of water about. Quite a fellow, to keep good order among them so long, given our tars' penchant for running riot and drinkin' themselves blind. Apparently, he found a length of hollow cane washed up on the beach . . . which was in his care at all times, mind, sir. They scuttled the barrico's top, and each man got two sips off it, as much as he could suck up, three times a day . . . morning, noon, and night."

"Aye, Mister Towpenny's a damned good man," Lewrie agreed.

"Though, once they saw 'twas a *Navy* ship their salvation," Capt. Nicely gaily went on, nigh chortling, "one of the survivors told Commander Mortimer they drank it up quick as they could, before somebody could take it *away* from them! 'Waste not, want not' is the old adage, ha ha, Captain Lewrie. 'Twas a drunken spree, the likes of which they will most-like remember all the rest of their lives!"

"And the 'heads' that required a stay in hospital!" Lewrie said, chuckling too. "I'd *like* to think they learned a lesson, but let sailors get a whiff of alcohol, and it's Bedlam."

"Speaking of, Captain Lewrie," Nicely cooed as they arrived at his waiting coach. "Once you've delivered your delightful tidings to your ship and crew about the fate of their mates, once the sun is well below the yardarm, it would be my pleasure to break out a bottle or two of capital 'cheer' . . . knowing that *officers* are as tempted by alcohol as the least foredeck hand. I'd admire did you dine with me ashore."

"And I would delighted to accept, sir," Lewrie gladly agreed.

"Shall we say . . . seven, sir?"

"So said, sir," Lewrie replied, laying his hat on his chest.

"My, um . . . grand though it is to get your sailors back, I do wish to extend my condolences upon the loss of your Midshipman Burns," Nicely sobered as they got seated facing each other, and a postillion boy raised the step and shut the door for them. "A lad of connexion to you, was he?" he asked, expecting the usual kinship or "interest."

Most Midshipmen, "gentlemen-in-training," came aboard as wards to captains, suggested to them by kin or neighbours, *direct* kin, such as Lewrie's bastard son Desmond was to his uncle, Capt. McGilliveray. But it was a *rare* lad, and usually a poor'un, sent aboard by Admiralty, especially those from the Naval Academy, as King's Letter Boys.

"No. No, he was not," Lewrie sombrely said, his sadness quickly returning. "In point of fact, 'twas Sir Edward Charles, your predecessor, who foisted him on me. Culled the West Indies fleet for the worst he could find.

Poor lad, he *meant* well, and he did *try*, but my *God*, what a witless goose! For those pirates, or privateers, or whatever they wish t'call themselves, to shoot him for sport, *deliberately* wing him so he'd take days to die, as if they'd rather stayed to *watch* his suffering! Like strangling kittens 'fore their poor eyes are even opened! By God, I'd give my right arm t'find the bastards who did that to him. I'd run 'em to earth, did it take a year and a day! And kill 'em slow . . . tooth for a tooth, eye for an eye, make *them* suffer! Swear to Christ, I—!

"Sorry, sir, to become so exercised, but . . ." Lewrie said as he came back to his senses, noting how speculatively Capt. Nicely eyed him; nose high and one quizzical brow raised. "Do forgive me, but it seems such a bloody, *murderous* injustice."

Nicely leaned forward, full of commiseration and true sympathy; of suppressed disgust for the crime, and what Lewrie took for a mutual desire to carve out Vengeance . . . or Justice. "What little I read from Commander Mortimer's report, Captain Lewrie, I am utterly convinced we . . . someone! . . . must pursue those devils. They may have Letters of Marque, but they're nothing more than cut-throats, and pirates, and a scurrilous stain on the honest seaman's trade, even 'pon the *dubious* good 'name' of privateer! We're knights-errant, d'ye know, sir."

"Knights-errant, sir?" Lewrie responded with a puzzled frown.

"There are *rules* for warfare, sir," Capt. Nicely insistently avowed. "There *must* be, else all is chaos and depravity. Someone must enforce those rules . . . We must! Standing armies came to be to replace barbarian gangs of land pirates, navies got formed to protect trade and poor seamen, innocent passengers, from the evil depredations of piracy. Oh, we also project power, fight our King's enemies, but mostly, we go about our lonely occasions, as nobly dedicated to the rule of Law, and the upkeep of Civilisation, as any of King Arthur's questing knights. To be the strong right arm for the helpless, the only enforcers of Justice that the seas know, Lewrie. Aye, we are just *like* the knights-errant of old, pure of heart!"

"Aye, sir?" Lewrie mildly rejoined, though stunned by the change in Nicely from being, well . . . "Nice!" . . . to what could be taken for a drool-at-the-mouth Turk in a holy, *hashish*-stoked hallucination!

Knew he was too good t'be true! Lewrie thought, wondering whether he should get out and walk back; *He's ravin' fit t'chew upholstery . . . like he's been got at by the Methodists or William Wilberforce!*

"I see, sir." Lewrie nodded, as if sagely enlightened instead.

"Tell me something, Lewrie," Nicely said, leaning forward with a crafty

look on his phyz, "could I give you a fair wind towards the pursuit and capture or destruction of these murderous scum, cobble up 'Independent Orders' to fetch 'em in before the bar of justice for all the world t'see . . . would
you be interested?"

"Oh well, I'd like nothing better, sir," Lewrie quickly vowed.

And of course he did, for such fervent avowal was pretty much what one
was *supposed* to say. It must here be noted, though, that he also fervently
speculated that wherever those pirates had run, there also might be his missing prize. There *was* the matter of how embarrassed he'd be, did the world
learn how he'd lost her, and had spent two whole months chasing a will-o'-
the-wisp.

Had those pirates sailed off to Pensacola, Mobile, or New Orleans, there
probably wasn't a hope in Hades of winkling them out without the use of an
entire naval squadron and an invasion force to capture or reduce any forts
guarding their lair, but . . . did he cruise off those harbours long enough,
surely they'd stand out to sea for another piratical cruise, where he could nail
them and punish the one, or all, who had perpetrated those cruelly useless
murders . . . poor Midshipman Burns's, the most especially.

"Aye," Lewrie said, with some heat and at least a scrap of hope that such
a feat could be accomplished.

"Good," Capt. Nicely crowed in gentle triumph, leaning back on his coat
seat with a satisfied grin. "Good! You're still of the mind that your man Jugg
might have had a hand in it?"

"Jugg, well . . ." Lewrie said, frowning. "No, sir. I no longer think he in-
stigated it. But I'm still convinced that he knows more about the people involved that he'd admit. Short of torture."

"We must 'smoak' him out, then, Captain Lewrie." Nicely beamed. "I
will put my mind to it, get in touch with a few people currently in port who
own knowledge of the Spanish Louisiana and Florida colonies, and might be
of avail to our quest. I do believe within a fortnight we could be on their
scent. Do you not object, sir, I know one well-connected fellow who could
dine with us tonight, so our campaign may begin at once. A tradesman."

"A tradesman, sir?" Lewrie asked, sharing an English gentleman's regard for people who actually *handled* finances, money, and goods.

"A merchant adventurer, so 'tis said, rather," Capt. Nicely added. "A
Mister Gideon Pollock, who works as the principal agent for the Panton,
Leslie & Company trading firm. Big in the Indian trade inland in the Americas. Pack trains and canoe expeditions. Pollock is head of Panton, Leslie's
affairs at New Orleans."

"A British firm that trades with the *Dons,* sir?" Lewrie gawped.

"His name arose, once your hands were fetched in, and aroused curiosity in, um . . . certain quarters," Capt. Nicely guardedly explained.

Mine arse on a band-box! Lewrie thought, with a sinking feeling in his nether innards; *But he don't mean somebody like Peel, or does he? What in Hell have I agreed to? Certain quarters, mine . . . !*

"Not made the man's acquaintance myself, yet," Nicely blathered on. "Though he comes well recommended, and his firm has, ah . . . proved *very* useful, in a most *quiet* way, to the Crown's interests in the Americas." Nicely tapped the side of his nose to assure Lewrie that it was covert and sometimes skullduggerish. "This Pollock fellow is reputed to be quite the neck-or-nothing sort when among the savages and brute settlers. Supper should prove int'resting, if nothing else, what?"

"Oh aye, sir . . . mirth, joy, and bloody glee, sounds like."

BOOK TWO

Trinculo: The folly of this island! They say
There's but five upon this isle. We are three
Of them. If th' other two be brained like us,
The state totters.

-*THE TEMPEST*, ACT III, SCENE 1
WILLIAM SHAKESPEARE

CHAPTER FIVE

*I*t was not often that Capt. Alan Lewrie, RN, actually sat down to dine with
tradesmen; nor, did he suspect, did Capt. Nicely, amiable though he was towards seemingly everyone with whom he came in contact. Tradesmen, even
those engaged in managing one's personal finances, like his solicitor back in
London, Mr. Matthew Mountjoy, the people at Coutts' Bank, his shore or prize
agent, well . . . they weren't *exactly* gentlemen, were they, even if they were
an hundred times wealthier than their customers.

Dining with tradesmen was not so much a downward social step as it
was running the risk of being dunned sometime 'twixt the fish course and
the cheese and port. Most "gentlemen" stayed in *debt* to tradesmen of their
acquaintance; a number fled like Hell at the sight of 'em.

Mr. Gideon Pollock, however, turned out to be a *most* congenial and in-
formative table companion, not that he had a chance to eat much.

And, so far as Lewrie knew, he didn't owe the man a farthing.

No, "nice" as Capt. Nicely was, as solicitous to Mr. Pollock as he behaved,
it was more a working supper than a social occasion, with Pollock "singing
for his supper" almost from the start. Pollock had no gossip, no books or
plays or ear for music to discuss; what he did discuss involved the fetching
of charts and maps, of sketching with his fork's handle or a well-honed
pencil stub, as he laid out the situation anent Spanish Florida and Spanish
Louisiana.

"Well, I rather doubt your prize ship went into port at Mobile or Pensacola,

Cap'm Lewrie," Pollock said with a chary expression once the reason for their supper had been explained to him. "Other than the small Spanish garrisons, a few priests and government officials, there aren't enough *customers* for the looted goods or the slaves. And not more than a handful of people with more than two silver *escudos* to rub together. No Prize Court to adjudge and condemn the ship, either," he said, rubbing the side of his nose, a nervous gesture that he evinced more than once that evening. "Nossir, I'd put my money on New Orleans. There, or Havana. What Spanish 'captain-general' of Florida there is, he's no more than 'governor of the mildew,' the mosquitoes, and palmetto bugs!"

Mr. Pollock also had a nervous habit of jerking his head up and to the right, now and again, with a wee throat-clearing whinny. It was quite unnerving. That, and watching his Adam's apple bob.

Pollock bore the complexion of a longtime sailor or huntsman, as creased about his eyes and lips as a Scots *ghillie*. He was slender and wiry, stood about two inches shorter than Lewrie but appeared to weigh no more than ten stone, and that with his suit and shoes on. He was high-cheeked and lean-faced, with rather remarkably vivd green eyes that seemed to droop at the outer corners, and a nose that put Lewrie in mind of a Welshman or Cornishman; it was long, prominent, and aquiline, with a hook-bump forming the bridge.

Not *exactly* English in his speech, either. Mr. Pollock sounded decently schooled, as if he might have been a second or third son from the squirearchy who had strayed from the expected church, law, military, or naval careers, or been "remittanced" overseas to hush up a scandal. He sounded *above* the station of tradesman but *below* the idle elegance of a gentleman. Less British, more . . . American somehow.

Capt. Nicely had introduced Pollock's firm as being thoroughly British, established in the Colonies long before the so-called French and Indian War, as the Colonials had referred to it. Lewrie imagined that he'd been among the Yankee Doodles, Dons, and French so long that their patterns of speech had corrupted those Pollock had been born with.

"We have offices in New Orleans, d'ye see," Pollock continued, "and I manage to get up there five or six times a year. Believe this, gentlemen, when I say that anything and *everything* is for sale in New Orleans. And the Cabildo, the Spanish Government House, could *float* on the bribes! A thoroughly corrupt people, are the Dons. Not that their ostensible subjects, the original French settlers, were a whit better. It'd be an easy thing to circumvent the Prize Court . . . Just sail your missing ship over to the south bank opposite the town, circulate some flyers—assuming your customers can read, that is!—and open her as an emporium. Once your goods are gone, you sell off the sails and fittings, then the ship herself. The slaves, well . . . there are itinerant dealers, the *caboteurs*, who'd meet you at the Head of the Passes and buy them off you, plunk them into their barges, and flog them off in the backcountry, 'thout hide nor hair of them ever appearing where the authorities'd have to take notice.

"Governor-General Carondelet banned the import of slaves born in the Caribbean in '96," Pollock said, with a rub at his nose and a jerk of his head, an "ahem-ish" whinny, and a tug at his costly neck-stock. "They're *s'posed* to be inspected and certified as genuine Africans, at Havana mostly, but . . . 'Black Ivory' is 'Black Ivory,' what with planters expanding their holdings. They're switching over to cotton, rice, and sugarcane, and for that the landowners need *thousands* of slaves."

"Er . . . how is it, Mister Pollock, that you, a British subject, come and go into the Spanish possessions so freely?. After all, we *are* at war with Spain," Lewrie asked, puzzled.

"Bless me, Cap'm Lewrie." Pollock chuckled over the rim of his wine-glass, not without another of those "ahem-twitch-whinnies." "Our firm damn' near keeps Spanish Florida and Louisiana a going business! Without us, they'd *have* no goods, no arms for their Indian allies, no comforts for themselves! Though merchants from Charleston or Savannah cut into us something frightful, we do manage to hold onto a profitable lion's share, so far. God's sake, sir . . . surely you don't think that Spanish merchants could do it! No, no, their goods have to come direct from Spain and are far too costly, and the bulk of American colonies neither make or export much of use to Louisiana or Florida.

"Dons rape, pillage, plunder, and *exploit* deuced well," Pollock sneered, "but they're utter failures at manufactury or trade. No high-nosed, haughty Spanish hidalgo'd be caught dead dirtying his hands with low-born doings. Ranch, run plantations, government work, but never in commerce. '*My* family rode weeth El Cid'," Pollock mock-declaimed in a Castilian lisp worthy of the royal court at Madrid, "'we drove ze Moor from *España* weeth our swords, *we* sail weeth Colombus, *we* conquered *Meh-hee-co* beside Cortes, sheenyor, how *dare* you shoog-yest . . .'!"

"So, their goods cost more than yours," Lewrie supposed, "and I expect they're overtaxed, too? So, you undercut, perhaps bribe?"

"But, of course," Pollock admitted, preening. "Frankly, were I king of Spain, I'd wash my hands of Louisiana and Florida, for they'll do no more with 'em than the Indians will. They're dead-broke—spiritually, morally, and financially—and haven't a hope of keeping them in the long run. No Spaniards emigrate there, but for government appointees and soldiers, and outside the port towns, there aren't two of 'em in every hundred square miles, but for priests or barefoot squatters. They simply *won't* change their climes to better themselves, as our good Anglo-Saxons will," Pollock declared. "So, sooner or later, they will lose 'em to the Americans. 'Til then, we at Panton, Leslie will stave off the inevitable. Therefore, the Dons *need* us," Pollock said with a sly wink . . . and another twitch-whinny.

Once peace had come after the American Revolution, the Yankees had *exploded* westward, over the mountains, up rivers, game-trails, or warpaths. Long-hunters, then settlers, then traders to service them; surveyors, speculators, and schemers hadn't been far behind. Each new "sovereign" state had veterans to reward with vast, vaguely bordered land tracts in lieu of pension monies, which soon became speculative stock-in-trade, some for as little as a farthing an acre!

Spain had one idea where her borders of Florida, and the edges of the Louisiana they had purchased from the French, lay; the Yankees had quite another—or simply didn't give a tinker's damn for them. Spain claimed the inland Indians were "allies and clients" whose territories expanded Spain's claims as far east as the Hiwassee River in the Tennessee Valley, and along the Tennessee (or Tanasi) River.

The industrious Jonathons, though, befuddled the tribes with a host of trade goods better than anything the Spanish could offer, with an ocean of rum and whiskey. They "rented" grants the size of Ireland for the "loan" of a musket, a stack of blankets, a cookpot, a good horse and saddle! And it was months, or years, before the rare, roaming Spanish soldier or official might stumble upon the unofficial invasion, then hie back to the coast to complain about the entire *towns* that had sprung up since their last visit.

Georgia, Virginia, and North and South Carolina had sent out a host of land agents to form development companies that issued speculative shares of dubious claim and value on these same tracts, when not arguing among each other as to who owned exactly what! The Yazoo Company, Muscle Shoals Company, Cumberland Company . . . Georgia alone had carved out a Bourbon "County" the size of France and had threatened war on the Spanish possessions, on Spain herself, if not certified.

North of Spanish claims, the new state of Kentucky had come into existence in 1792, then the closer and more-threatening state of Tennessee in 1796, which resulted in fresh hordes of hard-handed, cussedly independent-minded Americans coming to the eastern bank of the Great River, the Mississippi itself, down the Yazoo River to Natchez, down the Alabama into Florida almost in sight of Mobile, to Baton Rouge or Manchac *inside* Spanish Louisiana, down near New Orleans!

Pollock, thankfully, had the proper maps handy for his spiel.

Indeed, New Orleans was becoming the main *entrepôt* for Yankee frontier goods, rafted or barged down for shipment back East on American merchant ships, which was much quicker than over-mountain, upriver trade to the original Thirteen Colonies. Spanish and French companies either died or got co-opted; went broke or grew obscenely rich from the influx—which, unfortunately, filled New Orleans with "chaw-baccy" Yankee merchants, and Louisiana with unwanted land-grabbers.

Spitefully, the Spanish had banned American traffic on the river, in New Orleans, but that had been a failure, and the ban had been lifted the year before, in '98. *Nothing* seemed to avail.

"The Dons don't know what to do." Pollock let out a snicker, which, accompanied by a twitch-ahem-whinny, looked positively ghastly on him. "At least *with* American goods, a lot of money changes hands. And goods off Yankee ships that come upriver for cargoes are first-rate and cheap, so they can't really complain *too* much. My company thrives on wilderness goods, as well, I must avow."

"Your Indian trade, though . . . with the Spanish," Lewrie asked.

"Well, the old Indian trade is not as profitable as it was," Mr. Pollock replied with a wry smile, just as perfectly offputting. "The American trade makes up for it. They've no *money* in the backcountry, but both they and the Indians have hides, furs, whisky, and tobacco to barter with. And, so far from East Coast manufactures, and so hard it is to get finished goods westward in carts, small waggons, or mule-back . . . the small, poled flatboats, well . . . here Panton, Leslie is, with *British* goods at decent prices, heh heh heh!"

Gawd, he sets me teeth on edge when he laughs like that! Lewrie thought with a cringe; *Was I a Yankee or Indian, he did that just once, I'd run like hell . . . or scalp him!*

"So, sooner or later the Americans overwhelm Louisiana and the Floridas, you expect, sir?" Lewrie asked.

"Indeed, Captain Lewrie," Pollock gravely agreed. "There's a good chance all this trade, ours and the Americans through New Orleans, is drawing even *more* settlers than do the empty lands! I'd give them no more than

five or six years before the Yankee Doodles just up and *take* the place, and
have done. Either the United States acting as an organised polity, or the frontier states acting on their own."

"Indeed!" Capt. Nicely harrumphed in surprise.

"Kentucky and Tennessee, their settlers below the boundaries, are so
isolated from the rest of the States, they might as well still answer to London, sirs." Pollock chuckled. "Physically and politically too, d'ye see . . .
ahem. The backwoods have little in common with those 'civilised' sorts
'cross the mountains. The settlers are rankled by the games played by speculators and diverse state governments, the broken promises of pensions . . ."

"Like the Whisky Rebellion?" Lewrie asked with a knowing smirk.

"Very much like it, aye." Pollock laughed. "Americans are the most stubborn, anarchy-minded, personally independent folk, ever I did see! *Some*
over-mountain people aspire to personal fiefdoms, like the rebellious state of
Franklin that sprang up in East Tennessee just a few years ago. The Indians
are no real challenge, not really, and the Spanish aren't much better at pro-
tecting their holdings, so . . ."

"Might be a good idea to encourage that sort of thing," Captain Nicely
posed, "since it should be in our interests to rein in the Americans, before
they get *too* big and powerful to deal with, hmmm?"

"Well, I dare say . . . heh heh," Pollock responded, sounding as if Capt.
Nicely had broached a topic best left alone.

To Lewrie's puzzled look, Captain Nicely softly imparted, "There are
plans afoot, Captain Lewrie, I may tell you in all confidence, o' course, for
some, ah . . . lands lately in rebellion against the Crown that *might* be recovered, Admiral Sir Hyde Parker has corresponded with our British North
American forces to, ah . . . effect the taking of the Mississippi. If necessary.
To that happy conclusion, we would need free entry to a strong military and
commercial base. Mobile or New Orleans, control of the west bank of the
Mississippi, if nothing else, hence, to control its entire length, and hold the
Yankees snug in their kennels."

"Enticing the breakaway backwoods Americans in the new western states
to, ah . . ." Lewrie gawped. *What* have *I got into?* he wondered.

"Depend on us for their economic well-being, aye," Nicely said.

"I thought we were to speak of finding pirates, my missing—"

"I only give you the background, sir," Capt. Nicely cautioned. "Sir Hyde
instructed me to reveal this much to you, before you sally forth to haunt the
coasts. Sir Hyde told *me* that Mister Pollock, in his capacity as a trader allowed
into Spanish possessions, could aid your search . . . provide information anent

New Orleans, the identities of notorious brigands who might've been involved in taking your prize and committing their . . . atrocities, then send you coded letters by way of his smaller vessels."

"I assure you, Captain Lewrie, that I know where all the bodies are buried," Pollock intoned, with another of his ghastly grins. "And who is most likely to be your perpetrators. I cannot give you *active* assistance without, *ahem* . . . revealing my, and my firm's, ties to the Crown, 'thout being garotted as a spy by the Dons, but . . . "

"In the meantime, whilst I haunt the coasts, you'll really be . . . spying, anyway? To aid any future, ah . . . descent on New Orleans or Louisiana?" Lewrie sourly realised, aloud.

"One observes, one notes. Quite innocently . . . *ahem!*" Pollock rejoined, looking quite happily "sly-boots."

"And here comes dessert!" Nicely suddenly exclaimed as supper plates were whisked away by his house-servants, and an intricate cut-crystal serving bowl was trotted out. A jumble or trifle, most-like?

A shit cobbler? Lewrie dubiously thought as he took note of the dish's *brown* colour, all streaked with what looked like crust, and some whitish creamy layers. There were some suspicious yellow lumps, too.

"You're reputed to be a man possessed of a fine palate, Captain Lewrie," Nicely enthused, hands a'rub in gleeful expectation. "But I dare say you've not tasted the like o' this in all your travels!"

"I dare say *not*, sir," Lewrie squeamishly confessed, his eyes fixed upon the dollops being spooned out in smaller bowls. "What—"

"Caribbean and New World, sir!" Nicely boasted. "All regional ingredients. Rum and sugar, molasses for thickening. Bananas, fresh off the bush. And sweetened chocolate beans, pulverised and boiled to a milk paste. I call it a chocolate pudding pie. Taste, sir!"

"Good God in Heaven!" Lewrie had to splutter in amazement once he'd had a tentative, tiny spoonful. "It's Ambrosia! Why, I never . . . bloody marvellous!"

"Once we've eat our fill, we'll retire to my parlour," Captain Nicely simpered 'twixt avid bites of his unique concoction, "where we may have our brandy or port, and consult the charts, so Mister Pollock may further enlighten us regarding our mission, Lewrie."

Our mission, is it? Lewrie thought with a brief check. *I know he's bored shitless, but . . . oh, well. At least the pudding's good!*

CHAPTER SIX

*S*o, Mister Pollock, what's the best way to get at 'em, in your estimation?"
Capt. Nicely eagerly enquired, once a parlour table had been cleared of dec-
orations, and the maps and sea charts assembled. He took a slurp from a
snifter of brandy, then used it to anchor a corner of a chart. "Should it be
necessary, of course."

"Well, sir, *ahem*," Mr. Pollock carefully began, "you will note that New
Orleans is situated a fair piece or better up the Mississippi River, an hundred
miles or more. The river is somewhat unique in that its silt deposits form this
massive delta on either bank that extends so far out into the Gulf of Mexico.
The rules of Nature do not obtain in Louisiana . . . The streams don't flow
into the river, they seep *out* in sloughs and bayous, and those meander and di-
vide into a trackless maze. The land south of Baton Rouge is flat as a tabletop, and but a few feet above sea level, *ahem*.

"No cellars or basements in Louisiana, sirs! Nor will you find the dead
buried in the ground, hah hah! And what appears to be solid ground is so saturated, you may sink into spongy, saturated 'quaking' prairies . . . if not an
outright marsh. *Rich* soil, yes, refreshed by the annual floods, where it's
arable. But it also makes for swamps you must see to believe."

"Grand place for Frogs, then . . . swamps," Lewrie japed.

"As to getting upriver to New Orleans . . ." Pollock continued.

What the Devil's that t'do with capturing my pirates? he asked himself,
cocking his head to one side as Pollock "prosed."

"There are several nevigable entrances to the Mississippi delta . . . the Southwest Pass, South Pass, and the Southeast Pass. I prefer the Southeast, myself, as closest to Jamaica, so . . ."

They want me t'take Proteus *into the Mississippi?* Lewrie gawped.

Lewrie took note that the chart was British, reading the description: *The Entrance of the River Missisipi* (misspelled) *at Fort Balise, Taken in the King's Ship Nautilus in the Year 1764* (Oh Christ, rather a *long* time ago!) with fathoms indicated in Roman numerals, and soundings in feet shown in Arabic . . . rather a *lot* of Arabic numbers, hmmm.

There was a mud bank, there was a large white expanse he took as a featureless alluvial island, and a hellish-shallow swath of soundings in feet betwixt; a narrower channel to the West of the featureless island where Fort Balise was situated, and a note above the fort, indicating that ships anchored there to lighten themselves before attempting to cross the river bar. East of the blank might-be-an-island was illustrated what Lewrie first took for the faithfully reproduced tracks of several drunken chickens, or wee little "fishies." More on the eastern mud bank, hmmm . . . A closer perusal with a quizzing glass revealed that they were supposed to be an enormous maze of trees that had washed downriver; heaps that had drifted to the mud bank and had aided its formation. Hmmm . . . *"Printed for R. Sayer & J. Bennett, No. 53 Fleet St. as the Act directs, July 1779."* Rather a long time ago, too! More trees littered the north bank of the tri-furcated channel.

Well, just thankee Jesus! he exultantly thought.

"A formidable fort, is this Balise, sir?" Nicely asked.

"Not really, Captain Nicely," Pollock said, shrugging. "Simple stone water bastion, faced with earth and its guns old and rusty."

Lewrie turned his concentration to his glass of brandy, let his eyes roam the parlour's furnishings, and stifled a yawn, giving Mr. Pollock's explanation but half an ear, and ready to stroll to a large bookcase and pull down a novel he'd heard of but hadn't yet read.

Pass a L'Outre was a shortcut to the Head of the Passes, where all the forking channels came together; bloody grand for someone. Up halfway at a Northwest bend was a better bastion, Fort Saint Phillip; ho-hum. Halfway to New Orleans was Pointe a La Hache, but no fort, so who cared? Ninety miles up past the Head of the Passes was the great Nor'east bend called the English Turn, and Fort Saint Leon, a substantial obstacle, though.

"Know why they call it the English Turn, sirs?" Pollock japed.

Now that's unattractive on him, too! Lewrie thought, grimacing.

"When the French still owned Louisiana, we actually put a fleet this far upriver," Pollock said with a lopsided smile, "but the old governor, Bienville I think it was, made such a belligerent display, *daring* us to come get slaughtered, that we fell for his bluff and put about . . . right there," he said, tapping the map with a forefinger.

"What's the current?" Nicely enquired, frowning.

"Five to six knots, sir," Pollock supplied. "It takes nearly a week to ascend the river. Boresomely slow passage. In small vessels, and with the help of hired locals, one *could* approach the city up the various minor rivers and bayous. Bayou Teche, Bayou La Fourche, from Atchafalaya Bay, or from Barataria Bay further west, where there is a lake and a major bayou of the same name. Very few people live on the coasts, but they make wondrous hidey-holes, and privateers and pirates have been reputed to use them, now and again."

Lewrie abandoned the idea of borrowing the novel and returned his interest to the chart at the mention of "pirates" and the coastal lairs they might be using.

"Do you envisage an overland expedition?" Pollock grimaced in distaste for such an endeavour.

"Through the swamps?" Nicely said, shying from the idea, too.

"Wouldn't have a corporal's guard left by the time you got to New Orleans," Lewrie said, chuckling, half his mind on *that* topic, too, still intent on the passes into the aforementioned bays. "Snakes and hornets, alligators . . . biting, bloodsucking insects? God help the poor, tasty British soldier subjected to *that!*"

"Captain Lewrie, when a Lieutenant in the last war, sir, did a stint ashore in the Spanish Floridas," Capt. Nicely explained. "With the Creek Indians up the Apalachicola, was it not, Lewrie?"

"Aye, sir. Once was enough for me," Lewrie said, mock-shivering. "Does Sir Hyde intend a descent upon Spanish Louisiana, I could think of no *worse* way to go about it."

"Um, then," Nicely grunted, sounding hellish disappointed. "If it must be a *coup de main,* and nothing stealthy, then, Mister Pollock, what about coming in from the East? These tempting bodies of water, this Lake Pontchartrain or Lake Borgne, for instance. Looks to me as if our pirates could hide in there, too, hey, Lewrie?"

"How large a vessel was it?" Pollock asked.

"A *large* two-masted, tops'l schooner," Nicely quickly answered. "Might have six to eight feet of draught, if laden with booty?"

"Well, one *could* enter the Mississippi Sounds and get to Lake Borgne below, ah . . . here. Below Cat Island, there is Pass Maria, and a vessel could find sufficient depth to *enter*. As for any ships they *captured*, though, hmm . . . *ahem*. They'd be much larger, with deeper draught, and there'd be no place to strip them of goods and fittings, 'less they did it in plain sight."

"And getting to New Orleans itself from there?" Nicely added.

"From the West shore of Lake Borgne it's fifteen or so miles to the city, *or*, one *could* enter Lake Pontchartrain from Lake Borgne by the Rigolets Narrows," Pollock hazily surmised. "But, *that* pass is guarded by Fort Coquilles, and once into Pontchartrain—a *very* shallow body of water, I must tell you—there is still Fort Saint John on the city's northern outskirts, to guard that approach, and the fast water route down Bayou Saint John."

"If we *did* invade New Orleans from there, Lewrie," Capt. Nicely prompted, "sometime in the *future*, ah . . . how does it look to you? If our pirates could use it to get their goods into the town, couldn't a military expedition use the same route, perhaps?"

"Well, sir . . ." Lewrie stated, then took time to read the depth notations and slowly shook his head. "Mister Pollock is right. The ships of the line and the troop transports would have to lay off this Cat Island, outside the Sounds, and you'd need hundreds of cutters and barges to pull it off, lots of gunboats and bomb ketches to reduce this Fort Coquilles, too, I s'pose. I could sail *Proteus* up there and take fresh soundings for you, if Mister Pollock thinks the pirates *might've* used this short approach to the main market for their loot."

"Yes, hmm," Nicely grumbled, sounding guarded.

"If our presence, scouting and sounding their water approaches didn't give the game away, of course, sir," Lewrie added. "For later."

"Perhaps a covert approach," Nicely posed, "in a civilian ship flying, oh . . . an American flag might suit. Sound and scout this way to the city . . . perhaps even sail up the Mississippi right up to the town! Take a look at their garrisons, their river forts, ah . . . just in case we are forced to use blunt force, and risk the English Turn once more, hmm?"

"Whilst I'm looking for pirates, sir?" Lewrie asked, grinning widely at how eager (yet cagy) Capt. Nicely looked to have an active part in whatever it was that Admiral Sir Hyde Parker, the general in charge of their Canadian possessions, and far-off London might have in mind. "Of course. My frigate could back you up should you get into trouble. Just so long as you're near the coast, not actually upriver beyond that . . . what did you call it? . . . the Head of the Passes?"

Poor fellow, bored to tears! Lewrie thought sympathetically.

"Do you personally wish to scout the city, though, sir, posing as an Ameri-can," Lewrie japed the so pleasant and good-humoured Captain Nicely, "I'd strongly advise you to learn how to chew a quid of tobacco and how to spit. 'Tis hardly a skill one quickly learns. And, I'm told that neatness counts, sir, hah hah!"

"Ah ha!" Nicely rejoined, though not looking quite so amused by his joshing as Lewrie would have imagined. "Lewrie's first command was a cap-tured French *corvette*, I'm told, Mister Pollock," he added as he turned to face that worthy. "Admiral Hood renamed her HMS *Jester*. Given Captain Lewrie's wit, one does *not* wonder why, hmm? He's such a *droll* young wag." Nicely's smile was feral, an I'll-get-you-for-that.

Why ain't he laughin'? Lewrie had to wonder; *Did I put him in a pet? Fact is, he couldn't pass for American in India!*

"Excuse me, sir," Nicely's longtime Cox'n, now the *majordomo* of his un-welcome shore establishment, interrupted as he slid back the pocket doors to the parlour. "Your other visitor, a Mister Peel, is arrived, sir."

Peel! Lewrie gasped to himself, feeling his supper and two bowls of "chocolate pudding pie" turn to liquid in his bowels; *Shit, and God help me! Is* he *a part o' this, whatever it is?*

And whatever it was that Capt. Nicely was so sphinx-faced about Lewrie feared that it would not be a duty *quite* so straightforward as hunting down pirates.

CHAPTER SEVEN

*A*pleasure to see you once again, Captain Lewrie," Peel said, once the introductions were done.

"I just wish I could say the same, Jemmy," Lewrie rejoined with a tart grimace. "Not when you wear your 'official' spy phyz, though."

"Who says that I wear it *now*, Lewrie?" the darkly handsome and well-knit Foreign Office agent said with a smirk.

"You're here, damn my eyes," Lewrie spat back. "That's proof enough for me."

"Oh, ye of little faith," Mr. Peel—James Peel—mocked with a mournful "tsk-tsk" and a shake of his head.

"Oh, I of scars aplenty," Lewrie said right back, scowling.

"You know each other, sirs?" Pollock dared ask.

"Yes," "No!" Peel and Lewrie said in the same instant.

" 'Tis good to see you again, Mister Pollock," Peel said. "Your business thrives?"

"Indeed it does, Mister Peel," Pollock allowed. "Well-met, sir."

"Oh, Christ," Lewrie whispered, passing a hand over his brow as he realised that Pollock and Peel might have worked together before, and what *that* signified!

"Thank you for coming, Mister Peel," Capt. Nicely bade him. "I s'pose you've already eat, but . . . "

"Aye, I did, sir, but thankee," Peel pooh-poohed.

"Perhaps coffee and a dessert would not go amiss, hey?"

"Your chocolate concoction, Captain Nicely?" Peel brightened. "That would be capital, indeed!"

"We were just discussing where Captain Lewrie could best search for our murderous pirates, Mister Peel," Nicely said, inviting all of them to sit. "And some details of that, ah, other matter," Nicely concluded with a wink towards Peel. "Have you learned anything as to the identity of who some of the bastards might be, sir?"

"I did, sir," Peel rejoined, turning to Lewrie. "Pardon me for taking the liberty, Lewrie, but I spoke with your surviving crewmen at the hospital . . ."

"Was Toby Jugg, or whatever his real name is, involved?" Lewrie demanded.

"No, I don't think he was," Peel stated. "Not that he isn't a shifty fellow, at bottom. But he's innocent of your prize's taking. Wrong place, wrong time, that sort of thing. I'm convinced of it."

Mr. Peel steepled his fingers under his nose, an unconscious imitation of his old mentor, that master spy of Lewrie's past acqaintance, the now-retired Mr. Zachariah Twigg.

"However," Peel alluringly added, "that's not to say that Jugg didn't *know* at least one or two of the leaders. The one who declared himself when he marooned them, who called himself Boudreaux Balfa for one. Mister Pollock," Peel said, swivelling about, "you're much more familiar with Louisiana and New Orleans. That name ring a bell?"

"I've heard him mentioned, yes, Mister Peel," Pollock intoned. "*Ahem* . . . (twitch-whinny) he made a name for himself during the Revolution as a privateer. An exiled Acadian, from old French Canada, he is. I think he lives somewhere down Bayou Barataria now. Used his profits to buy land and retired from seafaring, so I've been told. A widower, I think I also heard? Went by the sobriquet of *L'Affamé*, 'the Hungry,' at sea."

"Your Toby Jugg sailed with him years ago, Lewrie," Peel said, with a sly delight to impart that fact. "Your Jugg admitted to me he didn't *want* to be recognised. Something about cheating this Balfa of a share of old booty. And, in the years since, he's thickened, aged, and wears that thick beard, so, thankfully, Balfa didn't tumble to his presence. Else he might've lost his ears, Jugg told me."

"Put him to the Question like the Spanish Inquisition, did you?" Lewrie cynically supposed.

"Hardly *that* extreme!" Peel laughed heartily. "Though I did get him in quite a sweat when I interrogated him alone."

"Good!" was Lewrie's sour comment to that news.

"The long, lanky one who impersonated him in your Bosun's Mate's clothes," Peel prosed on, "your Jugg might have known, as well. Got it garbled, o' course, the other sailors. Another name to conjure with, Mister Pollock," Peel said, turning about, again. "Lanxade?"

"Oh, him!" Pollock exclaimed in instant recognition. "He has a fair amount of fame in New Orleans, too, *ahem* (twitch-whinny). He and Balfa must have ended up with four or five privateers at sea, towards the end of the last war! Jérôme Lanxade. Made umpteen *thousands* from privateering . . . some say from *piracy*, too, 'fore the war, and perhaps for a time after. Spent it like water, though, gambled deep, and lost most of it. Or, spent it on the, ah . . . *ahem!* . . . the faster ladies."

Pollock actually looked as if he would blush!

"What is he doing now, and where could he be found?" Peel asked.

"In any b-b-*bordello* in New Orleans, actually," Pollock admitted. "He's infamous for it. High-born French Creole lady or tavern drabs, no matter, and 'tis said no husband, father, or beau sleeps sound if Jérôme Lanxade's on the town."

"We have a good physical description of Balfa from Lewrie's men. What does Lanxade look like? You've seen him yourself, Mister Pollock?" Peel casually pressed, his eyes alight as the game took foot.

"Each time I return to New Orleans, yes," Pollock supplied them. "Hmm . . . very tall and lean. Very long and spiky waxed mustachios in the Spanish style . . . uncommon vain, he is. Still tries to twinkle in style, but, oh . . . he'd be in his fifties, by now, I think, so his appeal of old is fading. Dresses in the highest fashion . . . garish, loud colours, but very fine material," Pollock told them, head cocked most parrot-like in forced recollection. "I'm *told* that he employs dye to keep his hair and mustachios dark, and . . . rapier-thin though he still is, good living put a gotch-gut on his middle, so there's some say he wears a canvas and whale-bone corset to maintain his manly figure!"

"And his activities, of late?" Peel asked.

"Oh, I do believe he only sails the Mississippi, now," Pollock responded, snickering a little at any man who'd held such a fortune and squandered it, now reduced to the Prodigal Son's beggary. "Works for some trading company, captaining *shalopes* up to Natchez, Manchac, Baton Rouge, and the west bank settlements like Saint Louis. Jérôme Lanxade . . ." Pollock pondered with a long sigh, ruminating. "Him, I can see returning to a life of piracy and looting. From what little I know of Balfa, though, I'd have thought he'd have more sense."

"And Lanxade was known, in his privateering days, as 'the Ferocious' . . . Le Féroce?" Peel almost happily concluded.

"That was the name connected to his repute, yes, Mister Peel." Pollock assured him. "Once gained, how hard it must be to dim . . . "

"There's your principals, Captain Nicely, Captain Lewrie," Mr. Peel told them, beaming, turning away from Pollock as if he had wrung him dry of all that was necessary.

"A description of their schooner, and the names and descriptions of the leaders," Lewrie said, pleased as well. "So I'll know who to whack when I cross hawses with 'em. Excellent work, Mister Peel!"

"Well, there is the matter of where a penniless Jérôme Lanxade got the wherewithal to outfit a ship and hire on a crew," Peel said in caution. "What he promised this Boudreaux Balfa to come out of retirement. Your sailors also spoke of some others aboard the schooner, the morning they were put ashore on the Dry Tortugas . . . "

"The young 'uns, d'ye mean," Lewrie said, recalling what he had heard in the hospital ward. "The titterin' cruelest ones?"

"It is also quite intriguing to me," Peel continued, "that our pirates, but for the seizure of your prize ship, Lewrie, seem to take great pleasure in only attacking *Spanish* vessels."

"Hmmm . . ." Capt. Nicely sagely stuck in as Peel's coffee and pie at last appeared, silencing them until they'd been set by Peel's chair on a round wine-table, and the servant had withdrawn.

"Who backed them, and why, you wonder," Nicely supposed, once they were alone again. "Where the seed money came from?"

"Most-like, they both fell on hard times, as Mister Pollock suggests," Lewrie dismissed, "they're bored, and piracy's the only trade they know that pays. Reliving their wild and misspent youth! Began with a cutting-out raid in a brace o' rowboats and moved up from that. The schooner might be their best, and latest, capture, is all."

"Mister Pollock," Peel said, turning to that worthy again, after a pitiable grin at Lewrie's supposition. "What's the mood among the old French Creoles with whom you deal? Have you heard any expression of dis-satisfaction with Spanish rule, of late?"

"Of course, Mister Peel!" Pollock quickly assured him. "They barely tolerate 'em in the best of times. They'd despise *anyone* other than their fellow Frenchmen ruling them. No one else in the world is, *ahem!* . . . cultured enough to even rub shoulders with 'em. There's a long-simmering revulsion, ever since old King Louis sold Louisiana to the Spanish."

"Anything *beyond* a grudge, of late, though, Mister Pollock?" Peel further enquired. "The talk in parlours and streets, your store, any more fervid? Any rumours of revolt?"

"My dear sir, there has always been, *ahem!*" Pollock told him with an amused chuckle and a twitch-whinny. "Creoles, though, are an excitable lot. As are most folk from Catholic lands, who speak their Romance languages. *Talk* is all they're *capable* of. To hear the rants in the *cabarets*, one'd think they were on the edge of armed rebellion, but . . . perhaps it's something in the climate that enervates them, or something, but they are quite *incapable* of ever really *doing* anything, in the end. The food and wine's too good, heh heh!"

"But what if it was different this time?" Peel posed. "What if a small group of malcontents . . . young, excitable, and endowed with the will to take whatever act is needful . . . very like the cruel ones your sailors experienced, Lewrie . . . *was* of a mind to rise up against the Spanish. Do recall what your men told me of their schooner: she had two names, *Le Revenant*, or the Ghost, and *La Réunion*. Reunion with whom? With the new, Republican France? Hmm?"

"And you want to go sound 'em out?" Lewrie scoffed. "Feed 'em money for their little revolution, then spring a British invasion on 'em? Well, good luck to you."

"Exciting as that sounds," Peel seemed to demur, "as valuable to Crown interests as that may turn out to be . . . assuming that such a cabal exists, and would be more amenable to British possession than Spanish . . . or American, eventually! . . . I fear I have more pressing items to pursue. Mister Pollock is our eyes and ears in New Orleans. He can smoak out any hint of actual rebellion . . . which His Majesty's Government would be more than happy to abet and encourage, and, exploit.

"*If* this suspected cabal indeed *is* violently anti-Spanish, with the wherewithal to succeed," Peel grimly added. "Unless it turns out to be a forlorn and pointless *geste*, only a *piratical* cabal arranged merely for profit . . . In that case, naturally, it must be Scotched."

"You're saying I can't whack 'em 'til Mister Pollock tells me I can?" Lewrie snickered between sips of brandy. "You have an uncanny way of making simple things hellish complicated, James."

"Mister Peel is correct, though, Captain Lewrie," Nicely praised with his eyes alight with what Lewrie deemed a Crusader's fire. "This *must* be explored. Should orders come to proceed against the Spanish, we must scout out New Orleans's defences, determine the best route for invasion for Admiral Parker's part of the expedition, *and,* put paid to these pirates, all in one. You spoke to Sir Hyde, Mister Peel? Lord Balcarres, the royal governor, as well?"

"Dined with them, sir," Peel smugly told him, "soon as I ended my interviews with Lewrie's sailors."

"It would appear your mission has grown, Lewrie," Nicely stated.

"Sir?" Lewrie nigh squeaked in dread, secretly crossing fingers in his lap.

"Here's what we'll do," Nicely declared, up and pacing energetically, all but swinging his arms at full stretch to clap hands. "Sir Hyde has allowed me to, ah . . . coordinate things, so! Mister Pollock, your ship will sail soon for New Orleans? Good. Your role will be to discover whatever intelligences that Mister Peel requests. Lewrie!"

"Sir?" Lewrie reiterated, even more concerned, of a sudden.

"You are to go to New Orleans with Mister Pollock."

"*Me,* sir?" Lewrie managed to splutter, taking a brief moment to glare hatefully in Peel's direction.

"Take your Quartermaster's Mate—Jugg's his name?—with you so he can identify as many people from that schooner as he may," Nicely forcefully ordained. "They didn't recognise their old shipmate the first time, there's good odds they won't, the second. Take some hands along . . . your real brawlers and scrappers. Pass yourself off as an American, or . . . "

"Hindu'd be easier, sir," Lewrie spluttered some more, tittery with disbelief. Self-amused, too; sarcastically so, to imagine that he could be taken for anything other than British for longer than ten seconds. Hindee or Chinee *might* be easier!

"What . . . ever!" Nicely snapped, pausing in his pacing to bestow a glare at him. "If, as Mister Peel suspects, someone funded the . . . Lank-diddle and Belfry, whatever their names are, we must learn if they're in it for the money, or for France. If for France, discover as much as you can. If for the money, make sure you stop their business. Blood in the streets, bodies floating in the river, the ships burning at dawn! If you can't get at 'em at sea, carry the fight to their parlours, and let 'em see the reach of the Royal Navy, and His Majesty's Government, when we're aroused!"

"That's not . . . *ahem!* . . . the sort of aid to the Crown my firm usually *supplies,* Captain Nicely," Pollock objected, leaping afoot in consternation.

"Subtlety, d'ye see. To the Dons, I'm a mere trader. A useful trader. If I take Lewrie and a pack of bully-bucks to New Orleans, all my years of, ah . . . covert good works will end. I, and Panton, Leslie, could be banned, at the best. We could all be arrested . . . exposed, and publicly strangled, at the worst.

"Besides," Pollock continued, turning to point accusatorily at Lewrie. "What does *he* know of covert doings? How obvious may *he* be, I conjure you, sir? Why—!"

"He's damned good, really," Peel interrupted, idly spooning up chocolate pudding pie, trifle, jumble, whatever, as if Pollock's thin shrieks of alarm, and Lewrie's red-faced surprise, were a street raree of only fair amusement.

"I *am?*" Lewrie roared. "Last time, you thought me an idiot!"

"My dear Lewrie, it ain't like you haven't done this, before," Peel pointed out. "Apalachicola, in '82. The Far East in '84 or so. Genoa and Leghorn in '94? Actually, Captain Nicely, I rather doubt if you really wish blood in the streets. A thorough sounding-out'd suit our purposes, anent the pirates' financing and organisation. A viable invasion route, well . . . Lewrie is a most knacky Sea Officer who knows the practicality of transporting troops and guns to the best place for a successful, and *quick*, victory. And what's needful to support it so it is successful. Really, Alan . . . that's your main task."

"*Sea* Officer, Jemmy!" Lewrie fumed. "Wouldn't an Army officer be better for . . ."

"Gawd, who'd put trust in a *soldier!*" Nicely guffawed. "Nought but idle fools who bought their rank and haven't worked a day since! Peel's right, Lewrie. You're better suited. Though it would be nice could you eliminate the known leaders of our pirates. Without their expertise, men of less repute might find it hard to keep their crews together. Put an end to 'em."

"Far be it from me to cry 'croakum,' sir," Lewrie tried to say as calmly and reasonably as he could, though he was nigh *shuddering* with anger to have been . . . "bamboozled" . . . again! "But I thought I was to hunt 'em down at sea. Just how did I—how did this—turn into . . . spying?"

"Your record precedes you, Lewrie," Nicely told him, obviously trying to praise, but failing badly. "Sir Hyde, the Governor-General, the Admiralty . . . Mister Peel's Foreign Office," he said, waving one hand in Peel's direction, prompting a brief bow from the seated Peel, "all think you can do it. Sir Hyde said you're the very man for the job, no error."

"It won't work, won't work at all," Pollock mournfully groaned.

"I can't see how it possibly could." Lewrie heavily sighed.

"Fine, we're agreed!" Nicely declared.

It went downhill from there, o' course.

BOOK THREE

Gonzalo: All torment, trouble, wonder, and amazement
Inhabits here. Some heavenly power guide us
Out of this fearful country!

–*THE TEMPEST*, ACT V, SCENE 1
WILLIAM SHAKESPEARE

CHAPTER EIGHT

Crack!

"Shitten, goddamned son of a whore!"

Quickly followed mere seconds later by another faint *crack!*

"Take that, you son of a bitch!"

Crack!

"And that . . ." *Crack!* "And here's one for you, too, you!"

Phfft!

"Well, shit."

"Damn me eyes, sor . . . sorry," Ordinary Seaman Liam Desmond, in the stern of the ship's gig, congratulated in his own fashion. "That's five outta twelve, this time, an' on th' wing, too, sor!"

"Should've been six, but for this . . . thing," Capt. Alan Lewrie griped, holding the rifled musket out from him as if it were a stunned-rigid viper. "Well, let's round them up," he said with a sigh.

"Needs spaniels, we do," Landsman Furfy, Desmond's inseparable friend, commented in a throaty aside. "Warter spaniels, wot kin swim for 'em, right Liam?"

"Out oars . . . give way all," Toby Jugg ordered from the stern-sheets, waggling the tiller-bar a few times as if to scull the gig to faster motion, so the rudder would bite against the river current. It had been a wrench to Lewrie, but taking his longtime Cox'n, Andrews, to New Orleans would be a bad idea, Pollock had sternly advised. Cox'n Andrews was Black, a former house slave from Jamaica who'd run away to sea and freedom. Disguised as a civilian, though, his "protection" of being in the Royal Navy, and therefore untouchable by slavers, couldn't be of help to him if taken up by the Spanish authorities. Even a forged certificate of manumission would be of no avail, since it was issued by *British* authorities. So, volunteer to go despite the circumstances as Andrews had, as had several of the Black sailors who had "stolen themselves" from the late Ledyard Beauman's plantation on Portland Bight on Jamaica to sign aboard *Proteus*, Lewrie had reluctantly left Andrews and the others behind.

Lewrie, in the eyes of the bow with his rifled musket, levelled a chary gaze on Toby Jugg once again as he steered the gig towards the nearest slain duck, wondering still if the man was truly trustworthy, and dearly missing Cox'n Andrews, who'd been a strong right arm several times over. Now, though, he must place faith in the enigmatic Jugg, who had let his beard grow even longer, making him look even more piratical and *outré?*

"Ware oars, larboard," Jugg grunted, hauling off to starboard as a drifting log approached on their left, from upstream.

The Mississippi looked sluggish at first glance, its surface as smooth as a marble slab under a nearly cloudless sky, reflecting blueness and the sun like a lying masquerade. But beneath that mirror, it was an onrushing, hungry beast, roiled by deadly undercurrents and eddies; and it kept its secrets, evils, and perils in its silty, brown-red depths, mere inches below its opaque surface, where no eyes but those of the dead and river-drowned could ever probe.

Now and then would come a visible danger—trees or giant snags, some entangled into rafts as big as a house foundation ripped from the banks an hundred, a thousand miles upriver, surging along deceptively slowly, and it was the wise boatman who steered very wide of them. The banks were littered with tree limbs, whole forests of them, so convoluted that geese, ducks, snakes, turtles, and other local creatures made homes in them, next to the carcasses of unwary deer, elk, and cattle.

It took two of the gig's six oarsmen, by turns, to keep the boat abreast the current, and even with all six straining to put their backs into it, upriver progress was slow. Thankfully, the Mississippi wafted most of his kills down within reaching distance. Lewrie could even reach out from the tiny bow platform on his stomach to pluck one himself and drop the duck lolling-limp and dead into the boat, leaking blood and river water.

He could not swim, had never learned. And it was a rare sailor of any nation who could, excepting the Dutch, of course. Swimming, so the old salts said, just prolonged the inevitable and attracted some finned horror to come eat you alive. Deliberately drowning might be preferable!

With brisk oarswork and much "short-tacking" about, they recovered three of Lewrie's latest kills. The Mississippi took the other two, last seen bound downriver for the Southeast Pass and the sea at a rate of knots. To chase after them would have required a half-mile descent of the river and an hour of hard rowing to get back to where they'd started!

Fetching the last fat grey-and-white goose caused their gig to stray close to the southern bank, where the tangled, dead-grey trees and snags had piled up deepest and abounded with wildlife; this set his boat crew to goggling, oohing, and aahing over the creatures new to them. Since the crack of gun-fire had died away, the beasts had reemerged and acted as if they'd never seen humans this close before.

"Ooh, 'ey's another possum!" Ordinary Seaman Mannix exclaimed in wonder, "carryin' 'er babbies hangin' off 'er tail, kin ye 'magine?"

"Snowy egrets!" said burly Seaman Dempsey. "Dere's plenty o' profit dere, lads. Quality's mad f'r egret plumes, d'we shoot some."

"Cottonmouth snake," Toby Jugg laconically commented, spitting over the side. "Get ye 'fore ye get th' plumes, ya daft bastard."

"Baby raccoons, yonder!" a teenaged Irish topman named Clancey breathed in amusement. "Wee li'l highwaymen, masks an' all? Loik wee bears! Wonder do they make good pets? They do, Oi'd wish me one!"

"No, ya wouldn't," Jugg spoke up again. "They get t'be grown, they turn mean an' snappish, no matter how ya treats 'em. Ol' cap'm had one . . . 'til it bit 'im, that is." Jugg grinned in sweet reverie.

"Warshin' their food, ain't that a wonder, though?" Clancey insisted.

He, Furfy, the plume hunter, even Desmond, looked forward, each with a silent plea in his eyes, like children at a parish fair, as if begging their captain to shoot, trap, or fetch them something, to order the boat put in so they could scrounge about among the "rarees" . . . to pet or adopt some adorable but be-fanged "something."

A splash and a crackling racket among the dead branches whipped their attention shoreward once more. The cottonmouth snake had nabbed one of the baby raccoons, and the rest were scurrying for their lives.

"Eyes in th' boat, then, an' mind yer stroke," Jugg commanded, as if bored with the ancient struggle of survival.

"This thing's had it," Lewrie said of his improvised "fowling" piece. "Back to the ship, if you please, Jugg. And three of our fat ducks'll be your supper tonight, lads."

That promise perked them up considerably, and, turning athwart the stream, they made the gig fairly fly across the river towards the northern bank, where Mr. Pollock's broad-beamed and shallow-draughted trading brig, the *Azucena del Oeste*, was anchored. Jugg kept the gig aimed a bit wide of her jib-boom, so they fetched up close-aboard and just a bit to the right of the starboard entry-port and the main-mast chain platform.

It wasn't an officer's place to do such, but Lewrie reached out with the boat-hook to play the role of bow man, snagged the fore-most dead-eyes and stays, then passed the gaff to the larboard bow oarsman as he swept the gig's painter round the after-most and tied it off; a perfect arrival, all in all.

He should have been cheered by their prowess at small-boat work, by his recall of rusty skills; there were a round dozen ducks or geese heaped on the mid-ships sole of the gig, confirming his reputation as a keen shot, yet . . . it went without saying that cheered he was not. The *how* of being here, the fact of being halfway up the lower Mississippi and not on his own quarterdeck, still rankled. He was, in fact, still irked—pissed!—might even attain to "mad as the very Devil!" if he stewed on his situation for a bit.

It did not help his sullen mood that no courtesy due a captain could be shown by the trading brig's crew, either. The Second Mate on her quarter-deck leaned out and peered over the bulwarks for a second, then disappeared, leaving Lewrie and his hands to scramble up the man-ropes and battens with only casual notice taken. As a Post-Captain, he was of course first out of the boat and aboard, yet . . . without all the usual twittering naval ado he'd come to take for granted.

After years of traditional welcomes-aboard, Lewrie was reduced to the status of "live lumber," a mere . . . passenger!

Jugg, as senior hand, and Liam Desmond were allowed to paw over his string of kills to select two ducks and one of the wild geese for the hands' mess, whilst the brig's typical one-eyed and peg-leg ship's cook and his helper came to take the others for gutting, stanching in boiling water, plucking, and roasting.

It appeared that tonight would be a game-feast, for, whilst he and his Navy sailors had been birding, others from the brig's wardroom had been hunting ashore in the forbiddingly dark woods on the northern bank. Two daintily lean yearling doe deer hung over wooden buckets on the larboard gangway stanchions. They had already been gutted, washed out with river water, hooves and scent glands axed off so their meat wasn't tainted, and their throats cut to drain into the buckets so the cook could try his hand at making blood sausages. Mr. Caldecott, the brig's hearty First Mate, was just beginning to skin and butcher them, surrounded by a clutch of hecklers and bemused "advisors."

The *Azucena del Oeste* had become becalmed the afternoon before and had been forced to come to anchor for the night. Dawn had brought a contrary light wind, with fitful zephyrs from out of the East-Northeast, which in this stretch of river just below the English Turn, made for a "dead muzzler" right down her throat, against which the brig had no chance to make a foot of headway, unless back-breakingly rowed with long galley sweeps. Not being Navy, and in no particular hurry to get hernias, Pollock and his ship's Master, a Mr. Coffin, had decided that they'd take a "Make and Mend" day of ease, secured with both her best and second bower anchors, with the river chuckling about her hull and frothing from her anchor cables, as if she still was making three or four knots.

Once secured about two long musket shots from the north shore, they had tried their hand at fishing. Last night's supper had been a "mess" of catfish; big ones, Lewrie had been enthusiastically informed. The catfish had resembled be-whiskered, shiny-hided sharks, scaleless, and as big-about and long as a stout man's thigh, and just about that meaty. Pollock had said they were reckoned a fine treat, after being breaded with crumbled ship's biscuit and powdered day-old toast, fried in deep iron skillets and lard. "Just be wary of the bones!" Pollock had warned.

'Least I'm eatin' well, Lewrie could conjure to himself in consolation. He had also thought that, for a rare once aboard a ship, he could sleep in as late as his idle nature desired. But one night out to sea and the sounds of the brig making a goodly way, the sounds from the watchstanders changing at four in the morning, had roused him, and that had been the *last* night he'd enjoyed a lubberly "All-Night-In." A half of his life spent at sea had engrained wary and wakeful habits in him, and it was a rare morning when he could roll back over and "caulk" even for a slothful extra hour! Even if the brig belonged to Mr. Pollock and his company, even if she had a most competent Master in Mr. Coffin, with a full complement of tarry-handed Mates, he still haunted her deck in fretful and enforced impotence, like a coachman who was forced to ride inside for once, far from his familiar reins.

"Well, how was the air-rifle, sir?" Pollock enquired, coming up as cordial as anything in hopes perhaps that Lewrie's approval (as if *that* held sway with Admiralty!) might result in a profitable contract.

"Fine, does it work, sir," Lewrie replied as he unslung the gun from his shoulder. "When it doesn't, it might serve as an oar, a club, or a punt pole."

"Yet you bagged a dozen, I see . . . *ahem*." Pollock twitch-whinnied and beamed like a horse dealer trying to palm off a half-dead sway-back for a thoroughbred, did he wink and smile often enough.

"Ah, but the ones lost to misfires," Lewrie told him as he held the air-rifle 'twixt thumb and two fingers, as if the firearm *was* that aforementioned dangerous asp.

"About what the Austrians said, too," Pollock said with a disappointed sigh. "Still, there's hopes the Yankee long-hunters, the local swamp-runners and Indians find them knacky. So quiet-like, fast-firing? Tell you what, sir. I'll make you a present of it, e'en so."

Lewrie was tempted to tell Pollock where he could shove such a handsome offer, that he wouldn't take it on a penny wager, but suspected that Mr. Pollock might think repacking it more trouble than it was worth. After all, he still had eight dozen of the Girandoni air-rifles crated up, a dozen to the crate, and stowed below.

Back in England, the Girandoni might have a curiosity value to someone, did Lewrie hold onto it long enough. Surely there would be a collector so eager he'd trample small children to lay hands on one, to say he had it, if nothing else.

There were other air-powered sporting arms made in Europe, but usually only to single custom orders, whereas the Girandoni rifle was the only one mass-produced for military service.

In 1780 the Austrians had ordered nearly two thousand of them from Bartolomeo Girandoni for sharpshooting skirmishers from several regiments' light companies. It fired a lighter .51 calibre ball, one even lighter than Lewrie's prized Ferguson breech-loading musket that he'd picked up during the Revolution, or the fusil-musket he'd gotten as a grim souvenir after his disastrous Florida expedition in 1783.

The Girandoni *looked* more like a sporting arm; the fore-stock was half the length of a typical three-banded musket, ending about one foot ahead of the trigger guard. The fire-lock mechanism looked much the same as a flint-lock, but it lacked the dog's-jaws, the flint, and the raspy frizzen to strike the flint, as well as the powder pan that ignited a powder charge. Its buttstock was detachable, made of iron, and formed the pressurised air flask—it came with three.

What was most promising about the Girandoni air-rifle was that a skilled user could get off twelve shots in about thirty seconds and never have to ram a ball down the muzzle! Twelve lead balls could be loaded down a tube in the fore-stock, all at once.

Pull back the brass lever along the bottom of the fore-stock and a ball would pop into the opened breech from below; return the lever to its slot and the breech was sealed; cock the lock, take aim, and squeeze the trigger, and a complicated clock-work spring valve opened from the buttstock, and there would come a faint, barely perceptible, *crack!* as the ball was propelled at 700–800 feet per second!

It was said (by Pollock, who was hot to flog them off on *some*body!) that it was accurate on man-sized targets beyond one hundred yards, not the fifty or so of a smoothbore musket. Nowhere near as good as the two hundred yards of a European Jaeger or Pennsylvania rifle, but *they* were very slow to load and needed a greased patch to grip the rifling. Perhaps this time, quantity could make up for quality and incredible accuracy.

The main drawback was that the user might as well hire a clock-maker to go along and keep the Girandoni working properly, and the oil-soaked leather seals on the air flasks leaked like an entire litter of puppies, as Lewrie's last shot at ducks could attest. There had been a serpentine hiss, then a *phfft!* of low-pressure air and sealing oils, which put Lewrie in mind of a sailor betrayed by his bean soup. And to pump the flasks back to full pressure, propping the detachable rod against a tree or wall (in his case, the ship's main-mast) for the last, hardest strokes looked like slow, strenuous buggery.

"Well," Lewrie responded, shamming real gratitude, "it does have its curiosity value. Thankee, sir. Most kind of you."

Even if his round-dozen waterfowl had used up all three flasks and four dozen lead balls, and he was a better wing-shot than that!

"We'll be under way by dawn," Pollock informed him, turning his face northward, going gloomy again. "The wind will come Westerly or Sou'westerly, in my experience. Enough for us to weather the English Turn and Fort Saint Leon. Another stretch of river, one more big bend, and after that 'tis an arrow-shot, the last twenty-odd miles, to New Orleans." He sounded loath to arrive.

"Then we'll be about our business . . . whatever it is," Lewrie rejoined. It had not been a joyful "yachting" voyage; Pollock was in a permanent fret of exposure, of letting his firm down, ruing the day he'd made Peel's acquaintance, and had begun to nibble round the edges of *espionage,* as the Frogs called it. He had never before been asked to do anything quite so *overt* and was definitely "off his feed" with qualms. Ruing the night he'd dined with the forceful, brook-me-no-arguments Capt. Nicely, too, Lewrie shouldn't wonder. On Peel and Nicely at least, he and Pollock saw eye to eye, if on little else.

"God help us," Pollock said, all but chewing on a thumbnail.

"*Might* get lucky," Lewrie japed. "Murder those two whose names we know straightaway, and put the wind up the others, hey?"

Pollock shuddered, glared at him, then toddled off without one more word to share, *muttering* a fair slew of imprecations, though.

Lewrie leaned on the bulwarks and plucked at his "costume" cotton shirt, most slack and lubberly fashion. Pollock had advised that he and his small band of Navy men dress as anything but sailors. They had been forced to don thigh-long hunting shirts over rough trousers, older, battered tricornes or low-crowned farmers' hats. Ruing costs like the meanest skinflint, Pollock had issued them all powder horns and deerskin cartridge pouches, long hunting knives to hang on their hips to make them appear more like huntsmen or a pack of bully-bucks he'd hired on to escort his goods into the hinterlands . . . or protect his new-landed assets in his New Orleans warehouses and store. All of which—the clothing, arms and accoutrements, "surplus to requirements" infantry hangers and such—had been produced from Pollock's warehouses in Kingston and sold at a so-called discounted price to Capt. Nicely. Lewrie could sourly suspect that he and his handful of disciplined sailors had been charged passengers' fare just to come along, as well!

Lewrie heaved a befuddled sigh and contemplated once again just how he had been finagled into this dubious adventure. Capt. Nicely had proved to be *much* cleverer than Lewrie would have credited him. And not half so nice as he appeared.

Not a day after their shore supper, Capt. Nicely and Mr. Peel had been rowed out to *Proteus* at her anchorage and had come aboard in stately manner, with a strange young Lieutenant and Midshipman in tow.

With Nicely wearing a gruff but-me-no-buts expression on his face, and Jemmy Peel cocked-browed with a sardonic you-poor-dense-bastard look, Nicely had introduced the young Lieutenant as one Thaddeus Darling, the Midshipman as one Mr. the Honourable Darcy Gamble.

Since *Proteus* had lost the unfortunate (and regrettable) young Mr. Burns, Admiral Sir Hyde Parker had decided to appoint the much tarrier and more promising Mr. Gamble into the frigate. He came off the flagship, and such an appointment usually was a signal honour for the recipient captain. The lad was upwards of his majority, eighteen or so, and while attired in a well-to-do lad's best uniform and kit of the finest quality, right down to his ivory-and-gilt trimmed dirk, he was touted as a bright lad who'd been properly seasoned at sea duties since his eleventh birthday; a welcome prize, indeed!

"You're short a Midshipman, Captain Lewrie," Nicely had almost gushed in seeming sincerity, "and I prevailed upon Sir Hyde to assign you his very best . . . and one close to his heart," Nicely had added in a confidential whisper, with an encouraging wink, "in reward for your previous good service to the Crown."

"Honoured, indeed, to welcome him aboard, Captain Nicely, sir," Lewrie had bowed back, temporarily disarmed, though still a *dab* leery.

"If you do not mind, then, sir, I will read myself in, and put up my broad pendant, according to Sir Hyde's orders?" Nicely had said further, whipping an official document from his coat's breast pocket.

"Beg pardon?" Lewrie had gawped, all aback. "Say uh?"

Lieutenant Darling produced a paper-wrapped packet containing a red pendant, much shorter and wider than the coach-whip commissioning pendant that forever flew from *Proteus*'s main-mast. He handed it off to Midshipman Grace and bade him hoist it aloft. And to Lewrie's chagrin, the red broad pendant bore a white ball, indicating that Capt. Nicely would have no flag-captain below him!

There was much too much blood thundering in Lewrie's ears for a clear hearing of Capt. Nicely's bellowing recital of Navy officialese, but the sense of it was that Sir Hyde had temporarily appointed him as a *petit* Commodore without the actual rank, privileges, or emoluments of a permanent promotion.

". . . and take upon yourself accordingly the duties of regulating the details of your *squadron,* in making the necessary distribution of *men,* stores, provisions, and in such other *duties* as you shall think fit to direct!" Nicely had thundered, casting a baleful eye at his "flagship's" goggling captain. Lewrie had whirled to seek confirmation or aid from Peel, but Peel could do nothing but offer him a side-cocked head and a helpless shrug. That "distribution . . . as you shall think fit to direct" sounded hellish-ominous!

To make matters even worse, *Proteus*'s crew thought they had been done a great honour in recognition of their prowess, and they had actually cheered Nicely's pronouncement. And his decision to "splice the main-brace" and trot out the rum keg for a drink free of personal debts, the "sippers" or "gulpers" owed among them, had raised an even heartier second!

Fickle bloody ingrates! Lewrie had fumed.

"Ah, sir, um . . ." Lewrie attempted once Nicely had turned to face him.

"You speak highly of your First Officer, Mister Langlie," Nicely had said sweetly, "nearly ready for a command of his own, as I recall you praising, so . . . perhaps a spell of actual command, with me as his advisor, as it were, will properly season him for better things in the near future, hey? No fear, Captain, your Order Book shall not be supplanted or amended while I'm aboard as, ah . . . 'super-cargo' or acting Commodore. I shall not interfere in your officers' habitual direction of your ship. Though I did bring along Lieutenant Darling to stand as a temporary Third Lieutenant, I assure you that he shall strictly adhere to your way of doing things and will be subordinate to Lieutenant Langlie, not me."

"*What* squadron?" Lewrie had baldly asked, after jerking his chin upwards to indicate the broad pendant.

"We, ah . . . stand upon it," Nicely had had the gall to confess, with what seemed a dab of chagrin to "press-gang" him out of his command, so he'd be *available* to fulfill the rest of his scheme.

"Christ on a . . ." Lewrie had spluttered, close to babbling.

"We may add two cutters later on, once you've reported . . . "

"Mine arse on a . . ." Lewrie had fumed, nigh to mutiny.

"So, you're free, d'ye see, Captain Lewrie. Needs must—"

"*Bluck!*" Lewrie had squawked, shaking his head in ashen awe at how deftly he'd been made "available"; he hadn't seen *this* coming!

"Sir Hyde and Lord Balcarres insisted, d'ye see," Nicely hurriedly added, "once I'd laid our enterprise's sketch before 'em, so you must adopt the old Navy adage, 'growl ye may, but go ye must.' "

"Mine . . . Arr!" Lewrie tongue-tangled. "Gahh!"

"So glad you understand," Nicely had cajoled. "Well, I'm dry as dust, and I fetched off a half-dozen of my best claret. Shall we go aft and toast the success of our venture, sirs?"

And, damned if, after the wine had been opened and Lewrie had sloshed down two impatient glasses, his cats hadn't come out of hiding and had made an instant head-rubbing, twining fuss over Captain Nicely, as if they'd been just waiting for his arrival their whole little lives!

Damned traitors! Lewrie could but accuse in rebellious silence.

And Nicely had been so maddeningly, bloody *nice* that he'd cooed, "mewed," and conversed with Toulon and Chalky, to their evident delight, even suffering Chalky to clamber up his breeches, roll about in his lap to bare his belly for "wubbies," and scale Nicely's heavily gilt-trimmed lapels to play with his epaulet tassels, touch noses with him, shiver his tail to mark him, and grope behind his neck with a paw at his ribbon-bound queue.

Christ, what a . . . He sighed to himself, sagging weary on the bulwarks, on his elbows and crossed forearms. *What an eerie place this is!*

He'd been up the Hooghly to Calcutta and had thought that lush and exotic; he'd been to Canton in trading season 'tween the wars and had goggled at the many sights of the inaptly named Pearl River below Jack-Ass Point. Both had been Asian, crowded, teeming with noise, and anthill busy with seeming millions of strange people intent on their labours. Louisiana, though . . .

First had come the barren shoals, bars, and mud flats of the Mississippi River delta, so far out at sea, the silted-up banks on either hand of the pass and the lower-most channels' desolate ribbons of barrier islands, with the Gulf of Mexico stretching to horizons when seen from the main-top platform, just a few miles beyond them. Skeins made from dead trees, silent and uninhabited, only heightened the sense of utter desolation.

Once past the Head of the Passes, the land spread out east and west to gobble up the seas, the salt marshes and "quaking prairies" impossibly green and glittering, framed by far-distant hints of woods; yet still devoid of humankind, and abandoned.

Now, here almost within two hours' sail of the English Turn and Fort Saint Leon, the river was darkly, gloomily shadowed by too many trees, all wind-sculpted into eldritch shapes, adrape with the Spanish moss that could look like the last rotting shreds of ancient winding sheets or burial shrouds after the ghosts of the dead had clawed their way from their lost-forgotten graves to the sunlight once again. The cypresses standing in green-scummed, death-still ponds, the hammocks of higher land furry with scrub pines, bearing fringes of saw-grasses like bayonets planted to slice foolish intruders . . .

Oh, here and there were tall levees heaped up to protect fields and pastureland, rough entrenchments of earth that put him in uneasy mind of Yorktown during the Franco-American siege, raised as if to hide whatever lurked behind them from an interloper's view. There might be a gap in the levees where someone had a seasonal sluice-gate to flood and replenish his secret acres. There might be the tiniest peek of a farmhouse's roof and chimneys, faint wisps of cook-fire smoke at times; the larger pall of bittersweet white smoke as a field was burned off for a fresh seeding with sugarcane or cotton.

But, all in all, it seemed such a thinly settled place, a spookily off-putting land so daunting that only the desperate, the forlorn, would dare attempt to tame it or wrest from it a farthing's profit, or sustenance.

There came a promising little zephyr of wind from the West at last, a welcome bit of coolness after the sullen, damp-washcloth heat of even a winter's day in Louisiana. Lewrie's flesh beneath the stifling closeness of his clothing goose-pimpled to that zephyr. As if to a forewarning, but of what?

CHAPTER NINE

L ewrie wasn't sure exactly what he was expecting once *Azucena del Oeste* weathered the last bend of the Mississippi, abeam a Westerly wind, and began a long "reach" up the centre of the river's widening channel. To hear Mr. Pollock, Capt. Coffin, and his mates gush about New Orleans, it was a blend of Old Port Royal, Jamaica, the old pirate haven, London's East End docks for commerce, Lisbon for quaintness, and Macao in China for sin.

Lazing on the starboard foremast stays and ratlines just above the gangway bulwarks, using his telescope on things that caught his interest, he watched New Orleans loom up at last. Like most realities, though, the city proved a letdown, compared to the myth.

Near the city, the levees were higher and better-kept, on the east bank at least, with a road atop them bearing waggon traffic and light carts. The road sometimes crossed wooden bridges above sluice-gates and canal cuts that led to planters' fields. Even here, though, Spanish Louisiana still looked thinly populated. One would *expect* a modicum of commercial bustle so close to a seaport of New Orleans's repute, but . . .

The river widened and ran arrow-straight, finally, and Lewrie could espy buildings and wharves, another vast, sloping levee in front of low but wide warehouses. Dead, bare "trees" turned out to be masts of a whole squadron of merchant ships tied up along the quays, along with a confusing tangle that looked like a gigantic log-jam. Nearer up, the log-jam turned out to be a fleet; hundreds of large log rafts or square-ended flatboats that had been floated, poled, or sailed to the docks from the settlements far upriver. Those would be sold off and broken up for their lumber once their voyages were done, Mr. Pollock had told him.

But for church spires and a few public buildings, nothing was taller than two stories, though. Within the last mile, Lewrie could estimate the city as only ten or twelve city blocks wide, and might straggle north towards Lake Pontchartrain another half-dozen blocks. Within throwing distance of the town, swamps, marshes, and forests took over, again; brooding, foetid, and primeval.

"That's it?" Lewrie grumbled in disbelief. "That's all there is to it? What a bloody gyp!"

The river wind brought the tang of "civilisation" from toilets and garbage middens, from horse, mule, donkey, oxen, and human "shite," from hen coops and pig sties; and the Mississippi wafted even more evidence— drowned rats, cats, and dogs; wilted vegetables and husks of fruit; butchers' offal; and turds. Evidently, not only was no one interred belowground in marshy Louisiana, but no drains or sewers could be dug, either! The river that close to town had gone from leaf-mould and silt tobacco-brown to a piss-yellow, shit-brindle colour.

"It ain't that bad, sir," Mr. Pollock said from below him on the gangway, having heard his disappointed muttering. "'Tis a very wealthy town, for all that. A most pleasant and delightful one, too."

"Wealth? There in that . . . village?" Lewrie scoffed.

"Consider it a London, Bristol, or Liverpool in their youngest days," Pollock replied with faint amusement. "So recently settled a port city, much like a new-found Ostia serving an equally unimpressive Rome a generation or two after its founding. An Athens or Piraeus in the days of Demosthenes, a Genoa or Marseilles when the Gauls had 'em? Even in their heydays, the fabled ports of antiquity were nowhere near as impressive as present-day London or, say, Lisbon, Lewrie. Ancient Alexandria, Jerusalem in the times of the temple, fabled Babylon, or the hellish-rich Troy of Homer's myth weren't all that big, either. Nothing like Paris or London. Though I doubt the modern world has, or the ancient world had, New Orleans's match when it comes to wealth and vital location."

"It looks no bigger than Kingston, English Harbour, or Sheerness," Lewrie said with a grunt as he jumped down to the deck.

"Think of Baltimore on the Chesapeake, sir," Pollock countered with a wry grin, "Philadelphia or Charleston. Neither are particularly impressive to look at, but rich? Oh, my my, *ahem!*" Pollock gushed, making another of his throat-clearing twitch-whinnies. "Port-au-Prince or that shabby hole, Cape François, on the north shore of Saint-Domingue. You've been to both, I'm told. Nothing to write home about, but consider the vast wealth that passes through those ports each year."

"Sodom and Gomorrah?" Lewrie queried with a smirk.

"Neither known for trading wealth," Mr. Pollock primly replied, " 'less you consider that their, ah . . . reputations drew hordes of rich visitors. As does New Orleans. The most, um . . . entertaining town within five hundred miles in any direction, *ahem*."

"Well, hmmm," Lewrie speculated. Though even at less than one mile's distance now, New Orleans still appeared small and sleepy, with no sign of anything wondrous, amusing, or sinful about it.

" 'Tis a mortal pity it's so hard to get at," Pollock said on, half wistful and half wolfish, "for its sacking by a British expedition would go a long way towards erasing the Crown's war debts."

"*That* rich?" Lewrie gawped, turning to regard the approaching town more closely, seeing it in a much better light, of a sudden.

At least I see what makes him happy, Lewrie thought, comparing Pollock's relaxed stance and evident appreciation of New Orleans to his earlier sullenness on the voyage.

"All the wealth of the West pours down here to New Orleans," Mr. Pollock nigh dreamily praised, eyes alight with Pound Sterling symbols, "from the joining of the Ohio and Missouri Rivers. Spanish Louisiana extends to the Great Lakes, and our Hudson's Bay Company's territory, then far west across the great unknown to Spanish California."

"There for the taking," Lewrie speculated, idly fantasising if anyone would miss a wee chunk of it, the size of Scotland or Ireland, say . . . and dare he call it "Lewriana"?

"For the settling, eventually," Pollock mused on most happily, for once. "There's very little there now, but for Indians and game. A few wretched settlements like Saint Louis . . . crossroad or river hamlets. But someday . . . as the Americans spread out, as we spread west from Canada, the wealth flowing down to New Orleans is certain to be tremendous."

"Of course, Panton, Leslie & Company already trades with the isolated rustics and tribes up yonder?" Lewrie asked smirkily.

"We, ah . . . and the Hudson's Bay Company, *ahem!* . . . are laying the foundations for a *British* presence, should the Crown desire such, sir," Pollock assured him with a soft voice.

"Hemming the Americans in," Lewrie decided. "Even if they get to the east bank of the Mississippi, and south from Tennessee to the Gulf, in Spanish Florida. Hmmph!. Take 'em a century t'eat that!"

"*More* than enough room for them. Let us reclaim a bit of Spanish West Florida, as far east as Mobile, say, and we will have an unassailable buffer against any American expedition against the meat of the matter . . . New Orleans," Pollock speculated, fiddling at his open shirt collars and throat.

Capt. Coffin ordered the brig's hands aloft to reduce sail now that New Orleans had finally been fetched. Her helm, though, was put up, not down, to steer away from the quays, levee, and other shipping, pointing the brig towards the opposite bank.

"We never go to the town docks first," Pollock told Lewrie in answer to his puzzled look. "We go alongside our hulk, yonder, to unload the lighter goods, the, ah . . . most desirable luxury items."

"Why not use the piers, sir?" Lewrie wondered aloud.

"Land cargo direct to the warehouses, Captain Lewrie, and the Spanish customs officials must levy their duties," Pollock said with a wry smirk, "and not get tuppence in bribes. A portion of our goods are *always* part-owned by 'em, on the sly! *Bulk* cargo is charged duty, which keeps their superiors in Havana and Madrid happy, and what sells on this side of the river is pure profit to the Dons in the Cabildo."

"So, you sell directly from these decks, I take it?" Lewrie asked.

"Oh, no! We transfer the goods aboard our *store* ship, heh heh . . . *ahem*. That hulk I spoke of, yonder," Pollock told him, pointing towards the south shore. "Damn my eyes, those bloody Yankees . . . they've a *new* store ship ahead of ours, the conniving . . . "

In actuality, there were four hulks opposite the city, all half sunk or permanently mired in the mud and silt of the south bank; all cut down to a gantline, with masts above their top platforms removed, and cargo-handling booms rigged below their main-tops in lieu of course sail yards, just above their waists and main cargo hatches.

The one that Pollock had indicated, the second-most downriver, had once been a three-masted ship of about four or five hundred tons, he judged. She was very old, with a steeply steeved jib boom and bowsprit still jutting upwards from her wide, bluff bows. She had, like an aged whore, though, been tarted up to the point of gaudiness.

Her wide and deep gunwale was painted a bright but chalking and peeling red, her upperworks and bulwarks canary yellow. Remarkably, a permanent shed had been built over her long quarterdeck, making an open and airy peaked-roof awning. A second construction had been erected over her forecastle, from figurehead to the stump of her foremast, with the once-open "heads" and roundhouse toilets fully enclosed, all scaly with shingle siding and roof.

She now sported two entry-ports leading to her starboard upperdeck gangway, each with two pair of stairs and landings of sturdy wood planking and timbers permanently attached; each beginning at the waterline atop a pair of floating platforms to accommodate patrons' sailing or rowing boats, where even now a clutch of boats and some extremely long, lean, and narrow, and *very* low-sided strange craft were tied up.

Even more oddly, a wide entryway had been cut into her side, as wide as double doors, down level with her lower deck where a 3rd Rate warship's heaviest guns would be housed. Instead of stairs, though, a wide, long ramp led up to that entryway from another timber-and-log landing stage; and all were so arranged that the stairs and the ramp would float up or down with the tide.

Bold white lettering on the red gunwale stated that she was the Panton, Leslie & Co. Store, with further information in smaller letters announcing her days and hours of operation and touting the significant range of goods readily available. Along the gunwale, near the tops of the stairs and ramp, were giltwork frames tacked on about white bare spaces, which were daubed and littered with both new and old printed broadsheets regarding newly arrived goods for sale.

The hulk flew a company commissioning pendant, and the red-gold-red crowned merchant flag of Spain, as did their trading brig. Lewrie thought that it would hardly be possible to fly a British flag in *this* port, not without instant seizure by the Dons ... or boarding and burning by the sullen French Creoles, yet, it was another *outré* wrench to his already-wary sense of vulnerability. So far from British aid!

"Told you she's a *store* ship, not a stores-ship, *ahem*." Mr. Pollock hooted. "Below-decks, we've goods counters, storage shelvings, and glass display cases, good as any emporium in London. Aisles wide enough for the most fashionable ladies' skirts, too."

"You need to repaint," Lewrie said with a droll grin, pointing at the new-come American hulk that sported red-white-blue on gunwales, lower hull, and bulwarks, and huge white stars on the blue; giant American "grid-iron" flags flew from every mast stump. Astern of Pollock's hulk was a small, dowdy store ship flying a French flag; the American was just upriver of Pollock's, and a fourth that flew a Spanish flag lay beyond.

"Damn those interlopers to Hell and gone, Lewrie, damn 'em all!" Pollock fumed. "Do I show half the usual profit this time, I will be flat amazed. You, sir! They won't know you, you could go aboard her and see how fine their goods, how low their prices, browse about!"

Spy? Lewrie drolly thought; *Me?* He was just about to say it when Jugg ambled up, wringing his wide-brim farmer's hat in his hands, as if loath to intrude, and clearing his throat for attention.

"Beg pardon, sir, but . . . 'at th' head o' th' line?" Jugg said. "Can't rightly say from here, sir, but damned if she don't look *peculiar* like our missing prize. D'ye not think so, Cap'm?"

Lewrie looked nonplussed for a second, wondering if the task of finding her could *possibly* be this easy, then spun as quickly as decorum allowed to eye her with his telescope.

The *Azucena del Oeste* was edging in nearly alongside her store ship's landing stage, making the viewing angle acute, so he couldn't make out all her details . . . perhaps half her stern gallery and transom, but a slice of her starboard side, yet . . . she seemed at least a *tad* familiar, a ship he'd seen before.

"Know her, Mister Pollock?" Lewrie asked, his gaze intent upon the strange ship.

"Never clapped eyes on her before, sir," Pollock glumly stated.

Lewrie could make out royal blue upperworks and bulwarks; *that* tweaked his memory. She bore ornate carvings about her stern gallery and sash windows, her arched taff-rail and lanthorn posts, and quarter-galleries; mermaids, cherubs, seahorses, and dolphins, all the work of decent carpenters, and painted in white, pink, and pale blue, decorated with gilt filigrees, and *they* twanged his chords of memory, too, that last sight he'd seen of her in daylight after her midnight taking as she sailed off for Dominica.

Her name-boards did not match, though; nothing decorative, but merely rectangular planks that didn't equal the size or shape of those that might have once adorned her, leaving faint bands of pale timbers not darkened by sea, sun, linseed oil, or tar. At his acute angle, he could barely make out a crudely *painted-on* name, not carved intaglio: *Fleur de Sud*. That name most definitely did *not* match his dimmed recollection!

Her lower hull, her quickwork! His last sight of her, she'd been heeled over heavily, exposing a badly maintained hull below the waterline, and before he'd turned away to deal with *Proteus*'s demands, he could recall thinking that she might not fetch the *highest* price at auction, for she hadn't been completely coppered against barnacles and ship-killing teredo worms. Along her waterline and for about two or three feet below it, she'd been coated with linseed-soaked felt, tar-paper, and stark white-lead paint, before the proper bronze-greened chequerboard of copper sheets began.

Penny-pinching ship's husbands, a miserly master, or a dearth of sheet-copper in the French Antilles, where she'd departed after her last slap-dash beaching to burn off seaweed and chip away barnacles . . . forced to make do with all the copper that could be had outside a European port, tacked on down where it mattered most, on the hope that if she got weeded, it might be where it could be gotten at by her sailors when still under way, heeled well over to leeward as her people hung in bosun's chairs on her windward side?

"Damn my eyes," Lewrie exclaimed at last, taking his telescope from his eye. "I do b'lieve you're right, Mister Jugg. That's her, to the life. Damme, we found her, right off? Why, this all could turn out simpler than we first thought!"

Uh-oh! Lewrie thought a second later; *Fate, forget I said it!* Saying such hopeful things, he had learned from hard experience, was about as bad as whistling on deck, a dare to Dame Fortune to come boot him up the arse . . . as she usually did . . . again!

CHAPTER TEN

Silks, satins, cambrics, and lace; cards of steel sewing needles and pins from Sheffield; bolts of cloth, from sheerest cotton or linen to winter-weight, hard-finished broadcloth and kerseymere wools. Dolls so lifelike one expected them to move or speak, dressed in miniature to exhibit the latest styles from Paris, for one of which Lewrie greedily spoke up, as a gift for his daughter, Charlotte. There were stacks of gentlemen's hats in every style, gloves for gentlemen and ladies, from canvas duck or deerskin work gloves to the thinnest, snuggest kidskin.

There were cases of elegant shoes and boots, ready-made, ready-to-wear, that went swaying up on a yardarm from *Azucena del Oeste* to the stout landing stage, thence by ramp or yardarm into the emporium hulk. Wooden casks and straw-packed crates bearing gin, sherry, fine clarets, ports, Madeiras, and aged brandies emerged, followed by bales of ready-made shirts, boxes of neck-stocks, boxes of spooled ribbons and flouncings. Ornate penknives, workaday jackknives, needle-thin smallswords and scabbards, slim hunting hangers, old-style swept hilt rapiers and matching daggers . . . pocket watches, fobs, and chains; ormulu clocks, mantel clocks, and hallway clocks. Duelling pistols cased, dragoon pistols by the dozen to the box, pocket pistols, rifled German Jaegers and Pennsylvania hunters, fowling pieces, blunderbusses, coach-guns . . . flints, powder flasks, bullet moulds and lead nippers and vent picks. Spices, sealing waxes, tallow and beeswax candles for entertaining, thick votives, and short, stubby prayer candles!

And coffee beans, sugar cones, and licorice whips, cinnamon sticks, bitter blocks of chocolate, teas and tea caddies, mote spoons; everyday tableware, sterling silver compotes and candelabras, coffee and tea services, complete sets of silverware . . . and the trading brig was only half unloaded!

"The rest will be landed on the quays, the rougher goods," Mr. Pollock announced as they took a break for supper aboard. "Ready-made slop clothing, cruder shoes and such for the planters' slaves, rough muskets and Indian trade goods. The sort of junk our agents will fob off among the Yankee settlers, too. Another day, and we'll empty her of the quality goods, then slant over to the docks to unload the rest."

"Then what do I do?" Lewrie asked as they shared a succulent supper aboard ship. "Do I just loaf about, go ashore and prowl, or . . . "

"Don the guise that your Mister Peel chose for you, Mister . . . Willoughby," Pollock said, winking craftily as he reached for a bottle of hock. Being back on his home turf had cheered up the little fellow most disgustingly wondrous, Lewrie thought. "Stand with a tally as the cargo is broken from the hold. You are ostensibly in charge of my new-hired protective force, *ahem*. Temporarily employed in support of our dowdy commercial doings. Such a dangerous-lookin' chap, really . . . "

Pollock stroked a finger down his left cheek to sketch Lewrie's teen-years duelling scar on his own face. Lewrie knew he was being twitted, paid back for all the bloodthirsty teasing he'd used upon the unsettled Pollock on the voyage.

"I still don't know as I care much for—" Lewrie objected.

"Willoughby's a common name, after all," Pollock breezily said with a dismissive wave of his hand. "You might even claim to be American, it's so common on both sides of the Atlantic. And your accent isn't so Oxonion or top-lofty that you could not play the part of a *new-come* American, to the Spanish and Creoles at least. An emigré from old England to the New World, as are so many. And it is your sire's name, so . . . "

"Well," Lewrie replied, sulkily accepting a glass. "For a bit, I thought Peel was having too much fun building me a *persona*, without a thought as to whether it'd be plausible."

"In a private moment, *ahem!* . . . Mister Peel might have said to me that Willoughby was a name you'd not *forget*, were you ever flustered," Pollock twinkled, barely concealing a grin. Aye, Pollock *was* enjoying himself at last, and that, right maliciously, too!

"In my cups? A 'melting' moment?" Lewrie gravelled. "Were I stuck for an answer to 'hello'? *Damn* that smarmy bastard!"

"You can't pose as anything *but* a former serving officer." Mr. Pollock pretended to commiserate, losing his grin. "You're much too weathered and roguish-looking to play a clerk, after all, sir. Even the way you walk will cry 'Sailor,' soon as you step ashore. To be a cashiered Royal Navy officer, fled to the United States in search of a seafaring post to remake your fortune, is frankly perfect. *Ahem*."

"And so easy for my dim wits to remember?" Lewrie groused. "I see the sense of it. Aye, I think I know how to play it."

"Assure me, pray do," Pollock entreated.

"I'm an overaged Lieutenant," Lewrie almost sing-songed what Peel had had the gall to *write down* for him to study on the voyage. "Was, rather. Little patronage or 'interest,' lived mostly on my pay and never had a speck of luck with prize-money . . . one command, early on. A despatch cutter. Glorious fun, but then I was advanced aboard a Third Rate seventy-four, and that was boresome blockading, with no chance to advance. And no adventure or fun, either."

"Mmm-hmm," Pollock encouraged 'tween sips of pepper-pot soup.

"Competent, but no one's pet," Lewrie impatiently recited his false biography, one slightly borrowed from his own past aboard the 64-gun HMS *Ariadne* as a Midshipman, the despatch schooner HMS *Parrot*. "Started in the American Revolution, second or third son of a freehold family, but nothing grand. I'm thirty-six, so I spent a lot of time 'tween the wars on half-pay, knocking about in the merchant service, so I can bore people to death with tales about the Far East, Canton in China, Calcutta . . . and know what I'm saying. Mate aboard a 'country' ship, not with the East India Company . . . that'd be too grand for me."

"Quite," Pollock primly simpered over the bowl of his spoon.

"Back in the Navy in '93, when the war broke out," Lewrie went on, by then bored with repeated recitations. "Impress Service, not sea duty, though. Deptford, 'cause my old Captain Lilycrop held that district . . . ."

"As were you, for a time," Pollock pointed out.

"Aye, I did, damn yer eyes. Then," Lewrie muttered, taking time to sample his soup and take a drink of wine. "Um . . . I learned one could make a 'shower o' tin' crimping merchant sailors even with legitimate protections, farm lads. Fiddled the books, too, over the costs of recruiting, claimed more than I brought in . . . took bribes from merchant captains t'look the other way, and—"

"And you ended out here, in my employ," Pollock concluded for him, as if laying a permanent claim upon him. "The very sort of tar-handed fellow we need, who knows his way with artillery, good with an assortment of weapons . . . knows how to lead men. Useful but ruthless, none too squeamish if heads need knocking together? Hmm, though . . . " Pollock stopped of a sudden and gave Lewrie a skeptical appraising, up and down like a disbelieving London tailor presented with a crude, "Country-Put" ape to garb. "What you now wear will do aboard ship, but . . . " he speculated for a long moment. "Before I turn you loose on the city to do whatever it is you'll do to seek your pirates, I fancy you should adopt better togs. Now employed, you might be accepted all the more as a flash dandy, now you have the 'chink.' New Orleans is hip-deep in dandies. Think of it as a way of, ah . . . blending in. Do you own shore-going attire, Mister Willoughby . . . *ahem?*"

"Never had need of 'em," Lewrie gruffly replied, wondering what new horror might be foisted upon him. "Ev'ry stitch o' 'long clothes' I own are back in England."

"Then we must come up with something suitable, mustn't we?" Mr. Pollock decided with a lazy, feral smile and a chuckle worthy of a Covent Garden pimp. "Can't have you looking *too* elegant, but . . . I think that a bit of the gentleman, with a bit of the 'Captain Sharp' will suit your needs right down to your toes, heh heh."

"Oh, bloody joy," Lewrie warily groaned, sure he'd despise Mr. Pollock's choices, even if he did know his home ground and its tastes to a tee; and half worried that the wretched little man would *charge* him for new clothing!

"Couldn't I lurk about in what I'm wearing?" Lewrie asked him.

"You'd look like a costumed spy right off," Pollock warned him. "Best to appear as close to the locals' style as you may and be taken for what the town expects to see from a man of your new station. As for *lurking* . . . "

"How else do we find the pirates who—"

"Time enough for that," Pollock assured him. "All in good time."

CHAPTER ELEVEN

Christ, I'm a Covent Garden pimp! Lewrie sourly thought, taking in his new "suitings" in a wavy, speckled old *cheval* mirror aboard the emporium hulk. *One o' the canting crew, a pickpocket . . . an Amuser!*

Mr. Pollock had suggested a touch of "Captain Sharp" and by God he'd delivered: a tawdry ensemble usually sported by "buttock brokers" and confidence men, professional gamblers and ne'er-do-wells, or those who blew snuff in a cully's eyes in a dark street, then robbed him of all he had—the Amusers of ill repute.

He'd been given a tightly woven and wide-brimmed planter's hat made of the slimmest straw or cane fibres from Cuba, nigh as big about as a washtub, what local settlers called a "wide-awake," since it was nearly impossible to see whether the wearer was asleep or awake underneath its cooling shade if one had one's head down. Below that, he now was clad in an exaggerated tailcoat, assured that it was "all the go" in Paris, London, or Madrid. The lapels were extremely wide, the square cut-aways didn't come down to his waist, there was no *way* it could button together over his chest, and its long scissor-tails fell to the backs of his knees. The sleeves were almost excruciatingly snug, and puffed up where they joined the shoulders, putting Lewrie in mind of a gown his wife, Caroline, was partial to. The tailcoat was bottle green, but made from an extremely glittery fabric.

Under that, he wore a shiny, nubby-silk waist-coat weaved in vertical stripes—salmon, burgundy, white, and tan, with lapels of its own, best displayed overlaid upon the coat lapels, so very snug, short-waisted and double-breasted that he found it hard to breathe.

Sensible neck-stocks were no longer the *ton;* no, one had to wear a florid paisley Frog invention, the *cravat,* which even tied could do double duty as a child's bib or a diner's napkin, and tickled his chin every time he moved, it was so big, wide, and puffy.

Pollock let him keep his own watch, fob, and chain, but tricked him out in *trousers,* much snugger and more stylish than his accustomed slop trousers at sea; they were white, and fitted so close to his calves that he had no trouble donning a horseman's top-boots.

A small pistol fit into his coat's breast pocket, its twin in the small of his back. He could wear his own Gills' hanger, but on a flashier snake-clasp waist belt. Finally, with a cherry-ebony walking stick to fend off riffraff and mendicants—it hid a slim eighteen-inch sword as well—he was simply "the crack," and "all the go"!

Before Pollock trusted him to survive on his own versus suspected pirates, though, that worthy sent Lewrie and Jugg, still dressed as an idle bully-buck, aboard the Yankee emporium hulk to check out their wares and prices. "Think of it as a dress rehearsal!" Mr. Pollock had chirped. Jugg also went well armed; *his* clothes were so loose he could carry a whole armory, so much so that Lewrie feared he'd give himself away by the clanking!

Damn Pollock, and Commerce! Lewrie thought after only a few minutes aboard, in the main display area on the lower deck. The prices were chalked on slate or penned on brown paper scraps atop the baskets or bins, altogether a mind-boggling array of international currencies and exchange rates. Louisiana should ask payment in *centavos, escudos,* or silver dollars, even old pieces-of-eight, but, like the rest of the Caribbean and the New World, local currency amounted to whatever was at hand, including Austrian Maria Theresas (*all* dated 1780!) as well as Dutch, Danish, French, or Portuguese coinage. Try as he might to make the calculations in his head, to recall prices and what sold the quickest, Lewrie couldn't keep things straight without a surreptitious jotting with a pencil stub and a folded-over sheet of foolscap. With his nervousness over being caught out, and without any decent ventilation belowdecks, and a winter's day in New Orleans sullenly hot and muggily humid, he was quickly reduced to a muddle-headed puddle.

People always said *I was too dense t'make change, but Lord!* he fretted. And whenever sales clerks looked his way, he broke out in a fresh sweat, reducing his original sour opinion of his appearance from "pimp" to a "whore in church" or a guilty-looking, potential shoplifter! And Pollock's list of prime items to be compared in price, which he *thought* he'd mostly memorised, had quite flown his head. What he'd do when spying-out pirates, he couldn't imagine!

The American emporium seemed to be doing a thriving business at that somewhat early hour, in spite of the closeness. Elegantly gowned Creole ladies and their ever-present slave maids swished about slowly, more sashaying or parading than shopping, as if borrowing the Spanish custom of strolling the city squares each evening, eligible young ladies circulating clockwise and the young men strutting in the opposite direction. They tittered behind their fans, and they softly giggled and peered over the lace fan-tops.

Hang Pollock and his junk, Lewrie thought; *There's women afoot!*

And some of them were quite pretty and fetching; some of mixed race but *almost* White, some raven-haired but blue-eyed, the majority with sandy or light brown hair, and green, blue, or amber eyes, which put him in mind of Caroline. This gave him a check for an instant but did not deter him from circumspect ogling . . . fantasising, undressing them with his imagination. He looked down for a moment into a discreet bin back at the rear of a glass display case of medicaments and saw a pile of paper-wrapped cundums, priced at . . .

Um, pesos to pounds, that's one pound, seven shillings to the do<u></u>en, or two shillings thruppence each, and that's highway robbery! he rapidly figured, then felt his mouth almost drop open in astonishment. *Amazin' what you can do, do you put yer mind to it!* he told himself.

Pepper, salt, and thimble prices might be Chinee chicken tracks to Lewrie, but something *prurient* ever would spark his interests!

"Help you, sir?" another roving clerk suggested from behind the counter.

"No, no, just looking about," Lewrie tried to reply glibly, languidly, though the interruption almost made him leap from his own skin with an *Eep*! Fresh sweat awoke, he blinked rapidly.

"But of course ya are, sir," the clerk sarcastically accused.

"Ye kin help me, then," Jugg said at his elbow. "I'd admire a half-dozen *cigaros,* them slim'uns, no bigger'n yer little finger, an' a wee flask o' whisky. Yer payin', are ye not, Mister Willoughby, as ye promised?" Jugg hinted, all but digging him in the ribs with an elbow, all chummy-like.

"Um . . ." Lewrie stammered, turning to peer bug-eyed at Jugg, who was smiling fit to bust. "Well, this once I s'pose," he said, though feeling the urge to clout the impudent bastard silly, clap him in irons in the cable-tiers, then have him flogged bloody for his egalitarian "sauce"! Sailors and officers, English and Irish, were akin to oil and water—they *never* mixed.

"Need a deal more of 'em for th' rest o' th' lads, so we will, sor, 'fore we saddle up an' head for th' backcountry," Jugg continued.

"Prospectin' for land, are ya?" the clerk asked in a friendly manner, no longer considering Lewrie a sneak-thief.

"Hopin' t'do some tradin' in the east bank country, ain't we," Jugg confided, as if inspired. "Got th' lads t'gether, got the Cap'm here t'lead, an' only lackin' trade goods t'make a payin' proposition, right, Mister Willoughby?" Why, the bastard had the nerve to wink!

Huh! What? Lewrie silently flummoxed, peering at the bearded rogue as if he'd never clapped eyes on him before.

"Perhaps find some land to claim, as well," Lewrie said at last, as if that was a secret wrung from him; his reply certainly was wrung! "Store or trading post, eventually. Um . . . might as well let me have a flask of whisky, too."

The clerk fetched out their purchases, then produced a flintlock tinderbox with which to light Jugg's *cigaro*, making him lean over the counter to do so. With a fiendish little grin, Jugg handed Lewrie one, and he had no choice but to get his lit, too, and puff it into life. The clerk named a figure, Lewrie dug into his coin-purse to show British coins, paid the translated rate, and then, at the clerk's request, went up the civilian-style stairs of the awning weather deck to smoke them.

"Thankee, sor, I owes ya," Jugg gleefully muttered round his lit and glowing *cigaro*.

"Bloody hell, Jugg! Now see hear, my man . . ."

"Ain't on th' ship, sor," Jugg idly pointed out, rocking on the balls of his feet and exhaling a jet of smoke before pulling the cork of his quarter-pint flask of whisky with his teeth and spitting it out overside. "An' this ain't play-actin', not 'gainst th' sort o' people wot took th' prize ship an' marooned us, kindly beggin' yer pardon, an' all, Cap'm, sor. You're t'be a cashiered awf'cer, I'm t'play an Irish ne'er-do-well, mebbe spent some time among th' Yankees an' caught 'at Democracy fever? Man like me'd never tug 'is forelock, nor scrape an' bow t'him wot just *hired* me on, d'ye see, sor?"

"I s'pose . . ." Lewrie muttered, heaving a bitter sigh and still highly irked for the vast gulf to be spanned 'twixt a Commission Sea Officer of the King and a common seaman. Even in a sham!

"Just till we're back aboard good ol' *Proteus*, Cap'm, sor, then I'm back in yer harness, like," Jugg vowed, turning earnest. "We step outta character, d'ye see my meanin', an' them pirates'll scrag us in a dark alley 'fore we kin say 'nay,' sor. Just playin' parts, we are."

"Damme though, why do I think you *enjoy* it so bloody much?"

"Went t'plays in Dublin an' London, I did, sor," Jugg happily told him with a droll grin. "*Some* parts them actors played looked to be more fun than others, Cap'm, sor!"

"Christ! Just . . . don't develop bad habits you can't break later, Jugg," Lewrie cautioned, unable to do much more to the man, not in public at least, not as long as they were stranded so far from the Navy's discipline.

"Oh, aye, and I won't, on me honour swear it, yer honour, sor!" Jugg vowed quite theatrically, dropping into a deeper "Oirish" brogue. "On me poor mither's eyes, i' 'tis. Faith . . . and *arrah!*" Jugg japed. "An' an't these th' *foinest* sway-et *cigaros*, Mister Willoughby, and Oi thankee kindly fer 'em, and at'all and at'all."

"Oh, stop yer gob," Lewrie said, slumping in surrender, though ready to turn away, run to the nearest rail, and laugh in spite of all.

He took a puff on his *cigaro*, but it had almost gone out after being amateurishly neglected. Lewrie hadn't even been tempted to partake of tobacco since he'd hocked up half his lungs among the Muskogee Indians in '83, the last time he'd been involved in a similarly covert expedition. Jugg blew ash off the glowing tip of his own and offered it to relight Lewrie's.

He was bent over and sucking to reignite his when a boisterous pack of shoppers came tramping up the sets of stairs leading from the landing stage, and Lewrie turned his eyes to look at them.

"What the Devil?" he whispered, half coughing, for the pall of fresh smoke had been trapped beneath the wide, drooping front brim of his "wide-awake" hat, making his eyes water.

"Yankees, sor," Jugg muttered from the side of his mouth, "an' a rare lot they are, sure."

Outré might have been a better choice of words for the Yankees, rather than "rare." They were frontiersmen, of a certainty, clad in long-fringed hunting shirts of homespun cloth or supple, but stained, deerskin. They wore home-spun trousers stuffed into the tops of knee-high boots, deerskin trousers laced inside calf-length moccasins, or loose and flapping over ankle-high beaded moccasins. At every hip was a fighting knife that looked as if it had started life as a double-edged broadsword or Scottish claymore. Some wore nearly civilised coats and shirts, though none of those wore neck-stocks or cravats, and their headgear ran the gamut from tricornes to flat-brim farm hats, shapeless, spreading cone-topped slouch hats, cast-off Army cocked hats, Jacobin-type stocking caps, an assortment of ratty straw . . . "things," and several masked and tailed fur caps that *departed* life as honest and upstanding foxes, raccoons, and possums. One man, a particularly blank-looking and pimply malevolence whose eyes almost crossed, had on a black-and-white fur cap that fixed Lewrie's gawping (teary, blinking) attention.

"Whut?" the fur cap wearer truculently said, noticing that he was being ogled like a whirling Persian Dervish in Hyde Park. "Air ye lookin' at *me*, mister?" Which growl brought the others to a halt.

"I, uh . . ." Lewrie spluttered back. "I don't believe I've ever seen your species of hat, sir. It isn't . . . *cat*, is it?"

"*Polecat!*" the wearer of that hat snapped back, "Ye wanna *make* somethin' o' h'it?"

"Now, Georgie," the much better-dressed apparent leader of the gang cautioned as "Cross-Eyes" thumped closer to Lewrie and the rest sidled behind him to watch the confrontation. He heaved a little sigh as if to say, "here we-go again," as he stayed by Georgie's side, as if to intervene . . . or referee should it come to blows.

"Polecat is what they call a . . . skunk?" Lewrie asked, determined to stand his ground and glad for all the weaponry that he bore, of a sudden.

"H'it is," Georgie said, "an' what *of* h'it?"

With "Georgie" only six feet away from him, Lewrie could note that the skunk's mask had been left on, as well as its long, bushy and luxuriant black tail with two white stripes. Tiny yellow glass beads had been sewn into the eye sockets, and the lips of its long, sharp muzzle had shrunk back from two rows of wee teeth, as if it still grinned.

"Don't they, ah . . . smell rather bad?" Lewrie enquired, taking what he hoped was a casual but expert puff on his *cigaro*.

"Yeah, 'ey do. So?" Georgie rumbled from deep in his throat.

"Well, I'd expect it took a deal o' work to skin and tan it," Lewrie replied with studied nonchalance. "Upwind all the time, I'd wager." This close to him, the unforgettable odour of skunk, merely a slight tang of it, reawoke Lewrie's memory of the genuine, undiluted article, and he strove not to wrinkle his nose.

"Huh! Soaked h'it near two weeks in a cold, fast crick a'fore I could touch h'it," Georgie boasted, partially disarmed from his anger.

"Wisht *Georgie'd* spent 'at long soakin' in wawter," another of his buckskinned companions hooted.

"Whyever did you kill it, if it took so long and smelt so bad?" Lewrie further enquired.

"H'it piss me awf!" Georgie said with an affronted snort. "Got inna m'chicken coop, a'stealin' ay'ggs, an' 'en hayud th' gall t'spray at me. Huh! 'At's th' *las'* thayng he ever done."

Lewrie couldn't tell which reek was worse, the skunk-fur cap or Georgie in general. Both shared a sour-corpse musk, mixed with wood smoke, crudely brain-tanned leather, old sweat and wet tobacco, sour-wet wool and felt, mud-soiled feet and toes, and scrofulous crotch and armpits. Taken altogether, the frontiersman was a positive mélange of aromas and could have kept his cats, Toulon and Chalky, sniffing in sheer ecstacy for *hours,* their little jaws as agape as miniature lions to savour the subtlest effluvia!

"Stout fellow!" Lewrie exclaimed to further disarm him, holding out his unopened flask of whisky. "Capital work!"

Georgie stared at him, glareful, as if wondering if he was being twitted, then at the offered flask, eyes aswim as if having trouble in focussing on anything that close. Georgie finally took the flask, bit down on the cork, pulled it with his brown teeth (those remaining, that is) and spat it to the deck. He shifted a quid of "chaw-baccy" to the other side of his mouth, tipped the flask up, and drained it in two or three long gulps.

"I don't s'pose there's a market for skunk-fur caps," Lewrie wondered aloud to the better-dresed fellow who seemed to be their leader. "During the Revolution, Benjamin Franklin's coonskins were all the rage in Paris. The Frogs were mad for 'em."

"No, I doubt they is." The man chuckled as the tension evaporated. Georgie ripped off a stentorian belch, then beamed at Lewrie with a dank, quid-dribbly smile. "You're a tradin' fellah, are you, Mister ah . . ."

"Alan Willoughby," Lewrie said, extending his hand; and pleased that despite Peel's cynical sneer, he had no trouble recalling it.

"Jim Hawk Ellison," the other said, shaking hands. "We're down from Tennessee. Say 'thankee' for the whisky, Georgie."

"Thankee, mister," Georgie said, almost bobbing now.

"So, what line o' goods ya handle, then, Mister Willoughby?"

"Oh, this and that, what sells best upriver or on the eastern bank." Lewrie shrugged off. "We're asking about first, before we buy any goods, Jugg and I . . . This is Toby Jugg, one of my men. Say hello to Mister Ellison, Jugg," he smirkily suggested, getting a bit of his own back after Jugg had twigged him.

"Mister Jugg," Ellison offered. "How do?"

"Mister Ellison, sor?" Jugg said, knuckling the wide brim of his hat first, then hesitantly taking Ellison's hand, as if that congenial social convention was only for gentlemen, outside his experience.

"British, and Irish, ya sound, sirs," Ellison decided, his face tweaked up into a wry expression. "A long way from home, are you?"

"Well, weren't *you* British before the Revolution, as well, sir?" Lewrie posed, about ready to hock up another lung in dread that they'd been found out not an hour after setting off on their own. "In a manner of speaking, that is?"

"Hah!" Mr. Jim Hawk Ellison hooted with mirth, flinging his head back for a second. "I s'pose we were, at that. And some of our rich folk from the coasts . . . the first states . . . sometime act as if they still were, at times."

"From Tennessee," Lewrie speculated, "that makes you a long way from home, yourself, Mister Ellison. What, uh . . . line do you follow?"

"Land speculatin'," Ellison replied, as if it was of no matter. "On the eastern banks," he added, as if to mystify, with a shrug and a wink.

"Oh, you're with the Yazoo Company, then?" Lewrie asked.

"No, they're too big a fish for me." Ellison chuckled. "Call it a private venture. Some friends and associates of mine in Nashborough . . . that's our new state capital, ya know . . . thought to put a company of their own t'gether. The Robertsons, Donelsons, and Overtons got the real power, but they're lookin' west to the Mississippi, t'other side o' the Tennessee River, now they got the middle of the state sewed up. I come from North Carolina first off, right after the war ended. I read for the law in Salisbury, but sorta followed our militia over-mountain t'East Tennessee, liked it better, an' never left. Had a hand in startin' the state o' Franklin, with John Sevier and them, 'til Virginia an' both Carolinas run it under. Drifted on over t'Nashborough just before Tennessee got statehood, an' ya know what, Mister Willougby? Not a bit o' credit, nor profit, ever come from any of it."

"Oh, what a pity," Lewrie commiserated, though it was disconcerting to be the recipient of such a tale of woe right off. *English* gentlemen would never blurt out the details of their lives so early in a *passing* acquaintance-ship, nor nigh-brag upon their failures in life to anyone, English or not, close kin or not. Though he *could* recall a unique Colonial American trait in the Loyalists he'd met when serving with them during the Revolution; ask what day it was, and he'd get a full hour's discourse. He put it down to Yankees springing from a much smaller circle of society, their rusticity and isolation resulting in a belief that everyone they met was almost kin. Besides, he could sneer, when you came down to it, Americans *had* no other diverting amuse-ments!

"So, you've come south in Hopes of better?" Lewrie asked.

"And ya know what they say . . . 'hope springs eternal,'" Ellison almost gaily admitted. "Oh, I had a land grant, from servin' with the Army for a spell. Sixty-four hundred acres, the Continental Congress and the state o' North Carolina said I was t'have. But by the time they got through squabblin' over who could *issue* my grant—Congress an' three states!—and all of it in Franklin, I hadta sell up for ten cent an acre. Not much t'show for four years o' fightin', the Cow Pens and King's Mountain, Camden and—"

"You whipped Banastre Tarleton?" Lewrie exclaimed. "And King's Mountain . . . I still own one of Major Patrick Ferguson's breech-loader rifles, that—" He clapped his mouth shut, but a sorrowful second too late. Trying to be congenial and sociable, he was betrayed by his dislike for Tarleton and his enthusiasm for fine firearms.

"Do tell," Ellison cagily said, almost peeking from beneath the brim of his hat. "Thought we'd captured 'em all at King's Mountain."

"Well, some few'd been bought before . . ." Lewrie flummoxed. He could almost *feel* Jugg's eyes rolling behind his back, perhaps hear a *sotto voce* "Christ, you're hopeless!" movement of his lips!

"So you were a Loyalist, then?" Ellison enquired. "A Tory?"

"Royal Navy," Lewrie confessed with a grunting sound. "Got it from some Cape Fear Loyalists before they went north with Cornwallis to Yorktown. They put it up on a bad wager when we put into Wilmington. And thankee for whipping Tarleton, too. Met him there briefly . . . when he was stabling his cavalry mounts in the pew boxes of Saint James's Church, the haughty bastard. And I ran into him in England, too. At Bath, it was, in the Long Rooms one night," Lewrie continued, and *most* of it true, whilst he'd been at sixes and sevens on half-pay, after paying off his first temporary command, the *Shrike* brig. "He and Benedict Arnold both, the same night, in point of fact. Still wearin' their uniforms, as if they'd *ever* be employed again!"

Lewrie felt that some un-English loquaciousness was called for, so he prosed on. "Tarleton was the same top-lofty, arrogant shit, but Arnold, well . . . I s'pose it was because his wife, Peggy, was with him at the time, but he was almost pleasant. Skint and miserly with his poor stack o' coin, but pleasant. When he wasn't frettin' over what he had lost at the tables, and doin' sums in his head t'see could they afford another bottle o' wine, that is."

"And how'd a British Navy officer and his man get into Spanish New Orleans? Don't ya know they'd throw ya *under* the *calabozo* if they learn you're here?" Ellison asked with a cynical snort.

"Ah, but I'm not British any longer, d'ye see!" Lewrie rejoined with a sudden burst of inspiration. "And Jugg, well . . . what Irishman would claim *that*, if America's open to one and all looking for a fresh start, I ask you?"

"Amen t'that, sor," Jugg seconded with enthusiasm. "An' after wot Admiralty did to ya, an' all, *arrah*."

"Jugg, for God's sake," Lewrie spat, spinning to blow Jugg's ears off, but stopping a rant at the sight of the man's sly look. "It is *not* a subject I bandy about to just . . ." he spluttered. Admittedly, he didn't know *where* Jugg was going with it, nor did he have a single clue what *else* he should say to re-establish his manufactured identity.

Knew I'd muck this up! he scathed himself, the very details of his false background a sweat-soaked, confusing muddle in his own head.

"Just got here, did ya, Mister Willoughby?" Ellison probed.

"Ah . . . two days ago, aye," Lewrie told him. Dare he say that they'd come on the Panton, Leslie ship *Azucena del Oeste?* Would its Spanish registry save him from exposing the whole enterprise? Or was it widely known as a spy ship, the company that owned it deep in the Crown's pocket? "On the *Azucena del Oeste*," he cautiously added.

"Yeah, I saw her come in," Ellison casually said, with no *more* suspicion than previous to his tone. "Panton, Leslie carries good wares. Have some arms aboard, do they? You'd be amazed how the easterners from the wrong side of the mountains think t'settle without decent arms, nor enough flint, shot, and powder. Like all the Indians just up an' flew away soon as we became a state."

"I believe they do," Lewrie informed him. "Most especially, a quantity of Austrian air-rifles, quiet as anything, but very accurate. Better than a musket, but not as good as a Pennsylvania rifle. Decent price they're asking, too, I think. You ought to at least take a look at 'em, if for no other reason that they're a rarity, sir."

"Hmmm . . . maybe I will, at that," Ellison mused aloud, rubbing his chin. "Well, I haveta go catch up with my wild men before they wreck the place," he added with a wry grin. "They get a snootful, and they're like the old bull in the china shop, don't ya know. Maybe we will run into each other again, long as we're both in New Orleans? I favour the Pigeonnier cabaret, if you're lookin' for entertainment on the town. Got hired rooms nearby."

"Thankee for the suggestion, Mister Ellison," Lewrie said with a relieved grin, shaking hands with the fellow once more, though he hadn't the first clue as to what a cabaret was or what sort of amusement might be found in one, especially one called the "Pigeon Coop."

"Mister Willoughby . . . Mister Jugg," Ellison gallantly said as he doffed his hat and sketched a brief, jerking bow in *congé,* forcing them to lift their own lids and show a "leg."

Ellison had not taken two steps when he turned about, though.

"By the by, Mister Willoughby, that was quick thinkin', the way ya handled Georgie," Ellison told him, greatly amused.

"Er, ah, thankee, Mister Ellison."

"For a minute there, I thought you'd riled him beyond all temperance. When that happens, he's a *very* short fuse. The most warning ya have is him sayin', 'Ah'll kee' ye,' then it's 'Katie, bar the door.' "

"Ah *kee'* ye?" Lewrie parroted, head cocked in query.

"That's country for 'kill you,' sir," Ellison warned, not half as jovially as he'd been just a moment before, then knuckled the brim of his hat, spun about, and went below to the emporium proper.

"Think I blew it, do you, Jugg?" Lewrie felt need to ask, once they were alone at the starboard rails. "By God, I do!"

"Permission t'git ragin' drunk, sor," Jugg replied.

"*That* bad?"

"F'r when 'e comes sniffin' about an' askin' me 'bout ya, sor. An' gits me three sheets t'th' wind t'do it, sure," Jugg added with a wide grin of expectation. "I'll set him straight, no fear, sor."

"By God, somebody should," Lewrie bemoaned, back turned so he could not hear Jugg's scathing, mouthed "Amen!"

CHAPTER TWELVE

*T*he de Guilleris—Helio, Hippolyte, and Charité—with Don Rubio Monaster, and their cousin Jean-Marie, were "at home" to receive guests. To the casual passerby who took note of their guests' arrival nothing could seem more innocent. First came *Monsieur* Henri Maurepas, the prim and eminently respectable banker, a man known in New Orleans as the de Guilleris' parents' factotum and financial advisor who stood *in loco parentis* to keep the youngsters reined in whilst their elders, the dashingly handsome Hilaire and the beauteous Marie pursued rounds of country pleasures on their upcountry plantations.

Their other two guests—*Capitaines* Lanxade and Balfa—might have drawn more attention as they arrived; more envy than anthing else for those two old rogues and their tales of derring-do were always welcome in French Creole parlours.

Nothing could seem more innocent—*café au lait*, sweets, and fresh-baked biscuits, bright laughter and vicarious thrills. Though, inside the grand upper-storey *appartement* on the Rue Dauphine, everyone sat stiffly upright in expectation, or slumped in boredom as Henri Maurepas droned on through his dry financial summary.

". . . results in a profit to the Reunion Enterprise of four hundred fifty thousand Spanish dollars," Maurepas fussily related. Monsieur Maurepas was one of those gotch-gutted minikins, what crude Americans would call "shad-bellied," though a fine satin waist-coat and a gold watch chain tautly

spanned that "appliance." The balding Maurepas patted his shiny pate and
fiddled with his little oval spectacles, awarding them a wee smile as he
summed up his report. "The bank has deducted its tenth part, as your agent.
A twentieth part goes to Monsieur Bistineau to cover those bribes he paid the
Spanish authorities at the Cabildo to land untaxed goods. Another forty-five
thousand dollars, I shifted into the Revolutionary Fund, for purchase of
weapons, shot, and powder to arm new recruits. Less a further ten percent
each due *Capitaines* Lanxade and Balfa, and shares to reward their sailors,
ah . . . that leaves ten percent to be divided equally between you young people, as the principals, that is to say . . . nine thousand silver dollars each." He
ended with a short, seated bow to every person present. "Which shares are
now deposited in your accounts, to draw upon as you wish."

If he thought he'd made them happy, then he was wrong. Rubio Monaster
went poutily red-faced; penniless Jean-Marie Rancour, whose family had
fled bloody Saint-Domingue with nothing, went pale and gaping in disappointment. As for the doughty pirate *capitaines* . . .

"You cheese-paring *bougre!*" Boudreaux Balfa erupted, leaping to his
feet. "You an' dat Bistineau *salaud,* too, him! He gets dem goods for *nothin',*
den sells 'em dear, an' bribin' de Spanish he done did *all* de time, by damn!
Normal bid 'ness wit' Bistineau. *Eh, merde!*"

"We can't go back to our crew with promises or bank slips. We need to
take them their shares, in *coin* . . . now!" Capt. Jérôme Lanxade demanded,
rising with his left hand on the hilt of his smallsword and with a wee creak
from his own "appliance," that bone-stayed corset that kept his own *boudins*
from resembling the banker's. "They will not wait for their money. They
signed on for a quick payout, with nothing up front but wine, rum, and rations, and had to provide their own hammocks and sea kits! They're waiting
aboard *Le Revenant* where we hid her for their money . . . and I tell you,
banker, they will not wait *long!* They have no trust in lubberly *accounts,* they
want silver and gold!"

"But, *Capitaine* . . . that much specie in one batch will weigh so much, my
bank does not hold reserves *that*—!" Maurepas tried to demur.

"Your bank, *m'sieur,* and you yourself, entered into our scheme with as-
surances to us that you did so from pure patriotic fervour. Do you now wish
to see everything fall apart because you refused to take risks?" Helio de
Guilleri accusingly spat, still slumped upon a table edge by one arm. "This is
for Louisiana's freedom. For France!"

"After what the gallant French people did to throw off the despotism of
King Louis and the *ancien régime,*" Charité de Guilleri chid him from her

seat at the other side of the table. She sat erect and prim, hands clasped together in her lap as she would at Mass with her family. "After the example even the bumpkinish Americans showed us when they wrote their Declaration of Independence, *m'sieur* Maurepas . . . that they 'pledged their property, their lives, and their sacred honour' to oust the perfidious *Anglais?* Freeing Louisiana from Spanish tyranny and declaring ourselves part of Republican France is just as noble a cause. Shame, *m'sieur* Maurepas, for shame!"

"*Mademoiselle,* I would do anything for our coming revolution, but a *successful* revolution must have a sound financial footing, and I cannot assure you that foundation without being somewhat circumspect," M. Maurepas insisted, dabbing at his face with a handkerchief, ready to polish the lenses of his spectacles of the irritation-fog that his skin had generated. "Money is power, young people . . . as powerful as massed artillery, for it *buys* the guns, the shot and powder, it clothes and feeds the brave—"

"Pays their damned *wages,*" *Capitaine* Lanxade nastily growled.

"Keep de ship dat *make* money afloat, an' ready to fight, money." Balfa gruffly added. He had sat back down and was now squashed into a hairy hog-pile of muscles, his arms crossed over his chest. "An' not enough money, by Gar! Forty percent for de men, dat's only . . . uh, one hundred eighty t'ousand dollar, only four t'ousand dollar apiece, and dey can drink dat up in a week! Mebbe the *bank* only take five percent, and dat revolution fund go short dis time, mebbe so, *hein?*"

"But we agreed upon a—" Maurepas said in a scandalised gasp.

"Two hundred and forty thousand silver dollars to be shared by our hands," Lanxade proposed, stroking his mustachios and twirling a tip as if the matter was settled. "That's fairer. That will be over five thousand dollars per sailor," he loosely guessed.

"Perhaps *m'sieur* Maurepas, in the pure revolutionary spirit," Charité sweetly and calmly suggested, "might reduce his bank's share to seven and a half percent . . . just this once? And perhaps our wise advisor will also speak to *m'sieur* Bistineau about reducing his firm's upfront cut as well, since he will make such an outsized profit from our goods, which cost him nothing but his complicity? If you take pains to point that out to him, *m'sieur,* I am sure he will act in the patriotic spirit."

"But . . ." Maurepas spluttered.

"And we still have the prize ship to sell," Charité continued in her sweetest parlour manner, the epitome of a soft-spoken and well-bred Creole lady, "which might reap another fifty thousand dollars or so? If not here, then at

Havana, Veracruz, Tampico, or Cartagena. I think our *capitaines* are right, *m'sieur* Maurepas. If our crew is not well rewarded, they will melt away, and we'll lose the means to earn future profits. No more money for the Revolutionary Fund . . . and no hope of freeing ourselves of Spanish rule . . . until those despicable Anglo-Saxon *Américains* take all the Southwest from them."

"*Then* where would we be?" Don Rubio grimly added, always eager to second anything Charité proposed. "They'd make *us* American, please God save us from that fate. Brr!" He mock-shivered in disgust.

"No more than five percent to the fund," brother Helio proposed to the banker. "When the ship is sold, a second deposit, of course . . ."

"Five thousand dollars per sailor," Maurepas haggled, "making a total of, um . . . two hundred twenty-five thousand. Else, you would have to wait until I purchase coins from Veracruz or Havana."

"Pah!" Balfa hooted, scrubbing his grey locks in frustration. "*Six* t'ousand be better. Dat be two hundred seventy t'ousand, and I better be on my way wit' it down Bayou Barataria *tonight*. Sixty percent for de crew, like de ol' days, dat."

"Then perhaps you and *Capitaine* Lanxade, for the good of the revolution," Monsieur Maurepas slyly countered, "might agree to reducing your share from twenty percent to fifteen, to be split between you. Merely for a short time . . . 'til the ship *is* sold, of course. For my part, I will agree to seven and one half percent, temporarily. After all, the sailors' requirements come before the officers', *n'est-ce-pas?*"

"You thieving *bougre!*" Capt. Balfa roared in protest. "Take de food out de mouths of *ma famille*, you? *Nom d'un chien!*"

"Only 'til the ship is sold off, *messieurs?*" Charité quickly seconded, batting her eyelashes at Balfa, who was immune, and then at Capt. Lanxade, who most assuredly was not, despite his deeply held reservations about her ruthlessness. Still and all, Lanxade considered, she'd be a delightful temporary lay. Lanxade preened his mustachios a bit more and struck a noble pose intended to impress the mort.

"*Naturellement, m'sieur* Maurepas," Lanxade declaimed, "the wise leader sees to the needs of his men first. *Bon!* Seven and one half percent to me, and to Boudreaux as well . . . just this once, *hein?* It *is* necessary, though, that Balfa and I take the crew's share to them as soon as possible. *Tonight* would be best."

Banker Maurepas quickly scribbled on the back of his prepared notes, heaved a wee sigh, then removed his glasses. "With a pittance of two and one half percent in the Revolutionary Fund, the crew will split fifty-five percent, or fifty-five hundred dollars, per man and that, I regret to say, is the best I can manage. Until the ship is sold off."

The de Guilleris, sister and brothers, their cousin Jean-Marie, and their hired buccaneers shared equally glum expressions with each other, then reluctantly gave their consent to such a division.

"*Bon,*" Maurepas said, gently slapping his expensive calfskin book shut and rising. "I will make the adjustments once I get back to the bank and will have the specie ready . . . no later than tomorrow evening. Tonight is out of the question, *Capitaine* Lanxade, but tomorrow, for certain. Will you bold gentlemen require your shares in coin at the same time?" he asked, forcing himself to be genial, fingers crossed.

"I will gladly let you carry me as a depositor in your strongboxes, *m'sieur* Maurepas, but for a mere thousand in silver dollars or *pesos*," Capt. Lanxade grandly announced, with an elegant bow and "leg."

"You gimme five thousand," Balfa tetchily demanded. "My *famille* need t'ings from town, dem."

"It shall be done. Well!" Maurepas said, brightening. "I think that concludes our first, successful work towards the freedom of Louisiana, don't you? *Adieu, mademoiselle, messieurs,*" the banker said as he made a graceful bow and leg in *congé,* clapping his narrow-brimmed, high-crowned townsman's "thimble" hat over his heart and departing the cool and airy apartment on the second storey of the elegant *pension.* Despite M. Maurepas's apparent gaiety, he once more felt the pangs of serious misgivings that he'd ever been damn-fool enough to become part of their bloody scheme! His reputation! His neck, did the Spaniards discover his complicity! Those brainless . . . *brats* who were *sure* to over-reach themselves or boast immoderate to the wrong people! Dear as reunion with France was to him, sweet as it would be to oust every last arrogant sham-hidalgo Spaniard, surely it *could not* rest on such a slender bundle of reeds! Where were the wise *adult* patriots?

"Need a drink, me," Balfa huskily decided. "Wash de foul taste of *bankers* away. Let's go, Jérôme. Now we so damn rich, I'll buy."

"Don't you have shopping for your *famille* to do first?" Capt. Lanxade reminded him, "if we head down the bayou tomorrow night. I'll meet you at the cabaret, later." Lanxade only slowly gathered up his hat and cane, his elegant new kidskin gloves, bought by the dozen on credit from M. Bistineau's store. Mlle Charité had crooked a finger and glanced to the empty chair by her side when Balfa's attention was distracted, and Lanxade was curious to see if his sham "nobility" and selflessness had improved his chances at putting the leg over.

"*Oui*, later, *cher*," Balfa glumly said, gathering up his things as well. "Mademoiselle Charité, Helio . . . Hippolyte, Jean-Marie . . . *adieu*." He bobbed them each a sketchy bow, then clopped out through the hall door, his feet, shod for once in silver-buckled shoes and not the wooden *sabots* he kept for mucky weather or town visits, drumming on the parquet.

"And I thought there was *money* in piracy," Cousin Jean-Marie moaned, absently chewing on a thumbnail.

"There is, Jean," Helio said, going to the side board for wine. "There would be, if you didn't spend all your time at the Pigeonnire, playing *Bouré*."

"Next trip, there'll be more," Hippolyte prophecied, joining his brother for a glass, as well. "There's sure to be. We could sail off to the west and take a rich ship full of Mexican silver and gold."

"That would require a better ship than *Le Revenant*, young sir," Lanxade idly responded, carefully seating himself beside the desirable Charité, who today was forced by societal conventions to wear her hair up and a gauzy but *somewhat* chastely lined high-waisted, puff-sleeved gown with dainty flat shoes on her silk-sheathed feet instead of knee boots. Her light, citrony scent was maddening to Lanxade's senses!

"But did we take another fast schooner as fine as *Le Revenant*," Charité eagerly said, turning to face Capt. Lanxade and batting away like Billy-O with her long lashes, her blue eyes glittering, "may not two small ships equal a bigger, *Capitaine*? I *know*, you are our most experienced . . . mentor, in these matters, but could not two schooners, crewed by, oh . . . perhaps no more than *sixty* men, double our chances?"

"Well, *mademoiselle*," Lanxade replied with one "experienced" eyebrow cocked, "I dare say two schooners would suit me better for the taking of a much bigger and well-armed treasure ship, *oui*, but . . ."

"And with two ships, we could place dear old *Capitaine* Balfa on his own quarterdeck again, as he most desires," Charité suggested. "Once we *have* the two schooners, of course. With two, we could seize a single ship full of coin and reap three or four times the profits of a string of poor captures, could we not, *m'sieur?*"

"Assuredly, Mademoiselle Charité," Lanxade all but simpered.

"Then we could afford the arms and pay with which to raise our rebel army," Charite almost giddily fantasised, fanning herself with a laced silk and ivory folding fan, "and approach even more *capitaines* to join us. Then there would be no shortage of sailors. *Quel dommage,* that, for now, we seem to have so many men for our one little schooner. Two *capitaines?* Why, at this rate, it will take us years to build our secret fund with *m'sieur* Maurepas's bank!"

"It would be a grave mistake to pay off crewmen just to save a few *sous,*" Lanxade frostily said as he twigged to what she was driving at. *All for her foolish rebellion, but nothing for those who make it come about?* he sarcastically thought; *She's mad . . . the rest are just greedy!* "After all, who will form the backbone of our liberation, if we disenchant the ones we first recruited?

"We carry a large crew so we can sail and fight the prizes that we take, *and* defend *Le Revenant,* you see?" Lanxade explained, striving for patience with them. Did he make them angry, he'd lose his berth, and the loot that went with it, more than he'd made in three years of the river trade. Lanxade knew in his bones that nothing would come of their scheming, but at least it was profitable while it lasted. "This is so aboard any privateer in wartime, the cost of doing business, *non?* If we do not lavish profit on our hands, they'll jump ship, even strike out on their own in competition with us, *n'est-ce pas?*" he instructed, with the simpery, bemused air of tutor to pupil. "Capable and *ruthless* sailors cost dearly. But they are worth their weight in silver."

"Ah, *mais oui,* I understand," Mlle Charité said with a heave of her chest, most wondrous to Lanxade's lascivious covert oglings. "You are right as usual, dear *Capitaine* Lanxade. Forgive us our ignorance and lack of experience with such things, but . . . it is so frustrating for the coffers to fill so slowly, to *glean* but not to *reap* the funds to reunite us with beloved France! We all know that but for you and *Capitaine* Balfa and your sailors, we find so little support, so thin the contributions from other patriot Creoles. Our poor people," she bemoaned as she drew a delicately embroidered handkerchief from her tight sleeve and dabbed at her eyes. "We Creoles . . . so proud and prone to florid speeches. We can be so enthusiastic, but . . . so lacking when it comes to conclusions, or acting on them. So many swear they wholeheartedly support what we propose, but will they join us, fund us, or take up arms? Act? Really *do* anything?" she sneered. "Like those snails, Maurepas and Bistineau! All is profit, profit, profit and gain, and freedom is someday, someday, someday . . . if it isn't *too* much trouble!"

She heaved another heavy, fetching sigh, nigh a hiccough.

"Forgive me, *Capitaine* Lanxade, but my lack is patience."

"I quite understand, *Mademoiselle* Charité," Lanxade cooed with a comforting, avuncular warmth to his voice. Had they been alone, without her brothers or calf-headed cousin or that prinking "dago" Don Rubio with his sheep's eyes, he would have put a supportive male arm about her, offered a broad shoulder on which she could incline her weak head! "We all share your impatience, my dear."

Lanxade *did* lean closer, like a parish priest taking confession in the open countryside on his rustic circuit.

Charité de Guilleri bestowed upon him a grateful, wide-eyed grin for his support. Then slithered to her feet in a rustle of satins and crossed to the sideboard for the glass of wine that Helio offered.

Bitch! Lanxade thought, seething; *She did it to me again! The minx, the mort, the . . .* Lanxade *knew* he was being played like a flute, but there'd come a time, someday, when he'd *take* what he wanted if—

"There is another matter, *Capitaine*," Charité said, once she had taken a sip or two of an excellent and effervescent white wine. "That odious British trade ship from Panton, Leslie & Company has docked, and has more people aboard than usual. Helio has heard rumours that Panton, Leslie has close ties to the British government. Do you think they might be trouble, *Capitaine* Lanxade?"

"Oh, in the American War, they might have had a contract to the British Army in Florida," Lanxade airily dismissed with a soft chuckle. "They still profit off the Indian trade, with the Cabildo's connivance . . . the American trade up the Great River, too. But I myself have met many of them, sailed upriver or down, and camped with them many times, and there is nothing mysterious about them. If they have extra people aboard, perhaps it is to guard the mule trains or learn the trade."

"Half a dozen hard, *well-armed* men," Helio contributed, frowning in concern, "led by a man with fighting experience. I sent a slave to look the ship over, and he heard this man respectfully called *capitaine*. He has a scar on his left cheek, so he's certain to have been a soldier, but he walks like a *sailor* . . . They *all* do. What need has Panton, Leslie of sailors to guard their trade by land?"

"Might the *Anglais* send a pack of cut-throats or spies to look for their missing ship and the ones who took her?" Jean-Marie cried, leaping nervously to his feet.

"A lone prize, taken so far from here?" Lanxade scoffed. "Not even the British are that vengeful! They're fighting a war with both France and Spain. Their hands are already full."

"Nonetheless, it is . . . disturbing," Don Rubio said, slinking near Charité as if to offer needful male comfort to allay any fears. Which offer almost made Capt. Lanxade curl his upper lip, twirl at his mustachios, and sneer at the hapless, lusting fool. Or turn gruff at the importunings of a possible rival!

"Shouldn't we look into it?" Hippolyte suggested fearfully, as if Jean-Marie's dread was catching.

"Well, if you must," Lanxade replied with a shrug. "This fellow and his bully boys will be easy enough to locate in a town as small as New Orleans, and if they *are* British sailors . . . sailors of any nation . . . they *must* come off their ship to get drunk and pleasured, must they not, *hein?* Watchers to track them, even talk to them once they're in their cups? You can manage that, I expect."

All five of them stared at him, as if silently demanding more.

"I can ask around as well," Lanxade allowed them, shrugging as if it was a bootless chore, but one he'd do despite how futile such a task would surely turn out to be. He got to his feet at last, since it didn't look as if his employers and fellow conspirators would offer *him* a glass of that white wine. "You should worry more about a crowd of Americans who just sailed down from Tennessee. Backwoods rustics in stinking skins, but *they* are led by a man who *also* has the bearing of a soldier. *And* he was asking about the procurement of *large* quantities of arms, powder, and shot. Another pack of would-be *filibustero* freebooters, by the look of them."

"*Let* them have a slice of the east bank," Helio sneered. "The damned Spaniards have all but given it away already! The Lower Muskogees, Choctaws, and Chickasaws will make short work of them."

"They might be useful, though," Lanxade tossed off as he gathered up his hat and cane from the commode table by the apartment's door.

"Americans?" Helio and Hippolyte scoffed. "Hah!"

"Many of them war veterans promised land instead of pensions, but have neither," Lanxade drolly pointed out. "Shuffling from one hard patch of ground to the next, when the land plays out . . . or the rich and powerful snap it up, *messieurs, mademoiselle?* Such motherless ne'er-do-wells will do anything merely for the *promise* of better. And if part of Lousiana was promised to them . . . far north of here, of course . . . what sort of army would they make to oust the Spanish?"

"They're heathen Protestants!" Don Rubio exclaimed with all the disgust that both his hidalgo-Catholic-Spanish father and the French Creole Catholic Bergrands had drummed into him with his mother's milk. "They're Anglo-Saxons, and they have no *Spanish*, much less knowledge of our beautiful French."

"We Creoles would be drowned in a *flood* of heretics," Helio de Guilleri quickly added.

"Our glorious language, our genteel way of life, our *people!*" Jean-Marie Rancour piped up, turning even paler. "They'd sweep us from the face of the world! They're hideous, they're—"

"Ambitious, and powerful in their numbers," Lanxade interjected. "Draw a border far to the north, along the Arkansas River, let us say. The Yankees are not at war with France, not a real war, and are mostly of two minds about the French, or Creoles. Without us, they would not be free of the British, and for that they are thankful still. Their priests direct their anger at Spain and its Inquisition. *Mon Dieu*, Americans are so English, they still despise the Spanish for the *Armada!* The United States *may* end up with every last stick of Florida east of Pensacola, but with American settler-veterans fighting to carve out their own little empire in our service, in the *northern* half of Louisiana, all the way to Lake Michigan . . . hmm?"

"But, we're so few, and those bumpkins breed like rabbits. They would swarm us under in a generation, Lanxade!" Don Rubio objected.

"Ah, but what if an entirely *new* country . . . Louisiana . . . came to be. For that, do you not think that the Directory in Paris might not suspend their wasteful war against the British . . . to recover just as much 'empire' as we lost in '63? Steal it from the haughty *Anglais* and the grasping United States?

"The chance of such a coup would *assure* our reunion with France . . . that we all hold dear," Lanxade dangled before them, almost playfully. "Hmm? Oh well, it's just a thought . . . *adieu, messieurs* and *mademoiselle.* I will do what I can to sniff out those newly arrived and mysterious *anglais* for you, before Balfa and I take the silver down to pay our impatient sailors. I will send you a report before we go. Once more, *adieu.*"

"What an *odious* idea!" middle brother Hippolyte declared with a grimace once Lanxade was gone. "Even temporarily associated with those . . . brutish animals, pah!"

"The Americans press us so closely, even now, though, Hippolyte. The time may be shorter than we think before they march into Florida. The time we have in which to raise a rebellion," Charité glumly considered, pacing the parlour with a silent, graceful gliding motion that her town clothes enforced upon her, the artful attainments drilled into her by her parents, tutors, and dancing-masters.

"If that happens, Louisiana, and our city, are doomed," cousin Jean-Marie brokenly muttered, as if contemplating being driven from a second refuge. "And we think it's bad enough under the Spanish!"

"Good for business, though," said Helio, the most levelheaded among them, the eldest de Guilleri who would inherit the bulk of their lands and the resulting responsibilities. "New Orleans is already the most thriving port on the Gulf. With Yankee industriousness . . ."

"Shame on you!" Charité stormed, so outraged that she stamped a dainty foot on the floor. "Does the struggle to become French again mean so little to you, after all we've *done?* After all our hopes and plans? Saint Domingue, Martinique, and Guadeloupe are *bursting* with thousands of good Frenchmen who would flee here and join us. Swedish and Danish ships come here to trade as thick as mosquitoes. How many stout Republican soldiers and settlers could be smuggled here in those neutral ships, once Paris is aware of our movement? We must send another letter, many of them. Each of us writes two, claiming to be, ah . . . Maurepas, Bistineau! Bergrands and Boisblancs . . . LeMoynes and D'Ablemonts, the leading citizens! Urging them to come to our aid, on the *sly!*"

"Sister, *chérie,*" Helio had to point out. "The Spanish are the only allies the Directory has in the world. Even if they meant to betray the Spaniards, how would they sneak an army here, with the *Anglais* stopping and inspecting every ship they come across?"

"If they could, though," Don Rubio objected, "the Spanish can't spare troops or ships to fight them. And with our schooner, and soon even more vessels, the decrepit Spanish Navy could not move soldiers from Mexico or Cuba as long as that British Navy blockades *them! Oui,* more letters to Paris, and . . . what if we *did* hire on a few bands of Americans?"

"What? But I thought you—" Jean-Marie blanched.

"As backwoods troublemakers," Rubio Monaster expounded with an evil snicker. "To raid Spanish posts, massacre the soldiers, and loot them. We'd let them keep all they take, so we would not have to *pay* them. We begin a campaign of torching Spanish properties around the city . . . dressed in buckskins, so American visitors get the blame. I think Yankee patriots dressed as Indians when they dumped the teas in Boston harbour, ha ha!"

"I'd rather try to make a pet of an alligator," Helio objected. "You cannot trust them, no matter how destitute and dog-eyed they look at the moment. Give a Yankee a cubit, and he'll take an *arpent!* They *have* no lasting gratitude in their souls. Look how thankful they were after Yorktown, and how they turned on the France that saved them not twenty years later, and now make war on our commerce, did not declare war on the British to help *our* Revolution in '93, did not *give* grain to keep the suffering French people from starvation, but *sold* it!"

"Enough, *cher* Helio," Charité demanded, pressing fingers to her forehead as if suffering a *mal de tête*. "*Capitaine* Lanxade is a fool. Useful in his way, but still a fool. Helio is right. We can never rely on the Americans. They would betray us eventually. But until we can urge the Directory to come to our aid, and quickly, we must do *something* to rouse our sleeping fellow Creoles. Rubio, your idea has some merit. We must look into that."

Don Rubio Monaster almost wagged his nonexistent tail at such rare praise from her.

"And let's not forget that we must look into both the American backwoodsmen's arrival, *and* those suspicious strangers off the Panton, Leslie trader," Charité announced. "They're men, after all, and men *always* find themselves a cabaret, a grog shop, or a *bordel* after the hard journey is done. Who knows, they might even come right to us in our favourite *boîtes?*" She chuckled. "If either party looks to be a danger to us, then . . . what better could we do than go to sea to take even more prizes, while they search for us here, *n'est-ce pas?*"

"*Chère* Charité, I swear if you are not the heart and soul of all we do, of all we dream," her brother Helio exclaimed with heartfelt admiration for her quick and clever thinking.

Yes, and sometimes it seems I am the only one with any sense at all! Charité Angelette de Guilleri smugly thought as she gave her elder brother a hug for his praise.

"A young woman who would make any fortunate man a most formidable and sensible wife," Don Rubio Monaster dared to say, colouring at once to blurt out his dearest desire.

"Why, thank you, Rubio, aren't you so *sweet?*" Charité brightly, "sugarly," replied, batting her lashes and acting the guileless Creole coquette for a moment.

A nice boy! she deemed him, though; *Good puppy . . . sit up, beg! But so slavish, mon Dieu! Oh, quel dommage . . . he has his uses, too.*

CHAPTER THIRTEEN

$\mathcal{A}$h, well," Mr. Gideon Pollock said with a heavy sigh of disappointment, once Lewrie had related the results of his hours spent "shopping" and comparing prices. "I suppose I must delve into things myself."

"Sorry, Mister Pollock," Lewrie replied with a whimsical shrug. "But I fear my forte ain't in Commerce. Without making notes, which'd have got me thrown out on my ear, I couldn't keep track of it. Whereas you know to the farthing what's a fair price. No scribblin' necessary with you, d'ye see. It's all up here," he said as he tapped his forehead.

"Um, yayss . . . *ahem,*" Pollock said with a somewhat dubious expression, and another of his cough-twitch-whinnies; questioning, perhaps, whether Lewrie possessed *anything* inside his skull.

"At least Jugg and I *did* meet with that Ellison fellow, him and his reeky gang," Lewrie pointed out. "Seemed quite the 'Captain Sharp' to me. He admitted he was tied up in that state of Franklin affair."

"Well, that would depend on who are his employers," Mr. Pollock grudgingly allowed, fretting round the super-cargo's spacious cabin on the *Azucena del Oeste,* transferring possessions from his sea chests to a leather valise, "tut-tutting" and "ha-humming" to himself as he sorted out clean shirts, stockings, neck-stocks, underdrawers, and his slim wardrobe of waist-coats and trousers. "I would expect that Ellison most likely is an agent for richer men, as he baldly stated to you. In what *capacity,* however . . . *ahem.* After he left your ken, though, Mister James Hawk Ellison came aboard our emporium hulk."

"As I suggested," Lewrie reminded the man, hoping that his day's work had borne *some* fruit, "that he look at the air-rifles and—"

"Which he and his fellows did," Pollock said with a crafty grin, interrupting his packing long enough to turn and smile at Lewrie. "And they were all *most* desirous of arms and ammuniton. Not merely muskets or pistols, but heavier ordnance, as well, hmm! Mister Ellison asked of the availability of brass four-pounders, or old regimental guns . . . brass six-pounders, or 'grasshopper' guns, Coehorn mortars and such."

"Aha! I knew the man wasn't straight!" Lewrie boasted, since it looked like he might be the *only* one to do so over his covert delvings. "So, he's the vanguard of a Yankee invasion?"

"His service during the Revolution, which Ellison revealed to me as quickly as he did to you," Pollock smugly said as he carefully folded a pair of white silk stockings, "does worry me a bit. Oh, that he's involved with some sort of filibustering expedition, I have no doubt. I fear, though, that is our Mister Ellison *still* a serving officer in the American Army, he just *might* have been sent to New Orleans by an incredibly aspiring man by name of General James Wilkinson, Lewrie. An aspiring man, indeed, *ahem*."

And damn all spies, Foreign Office, amateur, or otherwise! Lewrie sourly thought; *Twigg, Pelham, Peel, this clod, they're all the same . . . smug when they know something you don't, and damn' near pissin' themselves for you t'beg 'em t'tell it to you!*

"And who is James Wilkinson when he's up and dressed?" he asked finally, in almost a rote monotone, which lack of enthusiasm stopped Pollock dead in his tracks and made him turn, twitch-whinny, and glare.

"Wilkinson is the senior officer in charge of the American Army, which garrisons the states of Tennessee and Kentucky, Lewrie," Pollock archly cooed, "which is rather ironic, since before Kentucky became an established state in the Union in 1792, Wilkinson was scheming to seize the whole damned thing and make it a personal fief! He might have done the same for Tennessee, had he not been opposed by a set of politicians, lawyers, and planters even richer and more influential than he could ever hope to be. General Wilkinson came down to New Orleans himself in 1787, when the former Captain-General of Louisiana recruited him as a secret agent. He's known to the Dons as Agent Thirteen . . . bad luck for someone, hey? Wilkinson's well thought of by many in the Congress and just *may* end up the Commanding General of the United States Army in a new administration! He's rumoured to be close to Mister Thomas Jefferson and his faction, and Jefferson's rumoured to be planning to oppose their current president, John Adams.

"Horrid idea, that," Pollock quibbled, looking disgusted with Democracy's machinations. "Set terms for public office keep bad men in place too long, and depose good'uns . . . when *our* way lets us call a by-election if one of ours proves himself a criminal or a fool."

"They're an odd people, our Yankee Doodles." Lewrie snickered. "The way that fellow Ellison just blurted out his whole life story to me in the first ten minutes . . . prosed on worse than a jobless Irish poet! You think Ellison and his crew were sent here to spy out things for Wilkinson? If he can't have Kentucky or Tennessee, he still hopes to strike out on his own and take Louisiana . . . for the United States, or *himself?*"

"A very good possibility, given his past proclivities, Lewrie." Mr. Pollock sagaciously leered before returning to his packing. "If Ellison reports on how weak the Spanish garrisons are, Wilkinson *may* invade the Muscle Shoals, Yazoo, or Alabama River country right off. The Spanish have very little control there. Acting on Jefferson's behest, he would raise his political prospects to the top of the heap with such a land-grab . . . and eclipse any of his potential opponents."

"If the Americans start a war with Spain, it wouldn't be much of one," Lewrie surmised. "Not with re-enforcements so distant. Not as long as we're at war with 'em, and the Royal Navy in the way. And the American Navy to guard the approaches to the Gulf . . ."

"Unless we side with Spain against the Yankees, Lewrie. So we gain concessions in Louisiana *and* Florida to buttress the Dons. Then we also tear them away from France's embrace," Mr. Pollock dreamily speculated, head cocked to one side. "Didn't think o' that'un, did ye, hey? *Ahem.*"

"My word, I—"

"Cheaper than mounting an expedition from Jamaica, and another all the way downriver from Canada," Pollock wheezed with merriment at the possibility. "My firm with an exclusive franchise from the Crown in these lands for good service . . . Ah!" Pollock took a long moment to savour that outcome, then suddenly sobered. "Unless," he grumped, "Ellison's been sicced on me to catch me selling arms, acting on suspicions inside the Cabildo . . . or General Wilkinson's way of eliminating a British firm *he* suspects. Or, is in competition with commerical cronies backing *his* secret plans. Either way, avoid Ellison and his men like the plague, Lewrie. You've bigger fish to fry, heh heh! You've our mysterious pirates to smoak out . . . Lanxade and Balfa need running to earth. For now, those Yankees are an idle distraction. For my part, I shan't sell them more than a few trade muskets . . . profitable though such a transaction would be. There's too much risk from exposure, and a very public trial for spying. Quickly followed a public garotting," Pollock warned, involuntarily massaging his own neck.

Executions in Spanish lands didn't required a gallows—going for "the high jump," doing the "Tyburn hornpipe." The Dons preferred sitting one down in a stout chair, then slowly strangling the convicted with a garotte . . . one agonising twist of the ropes at a time.

Such qualms on Pollock's odd features quite made Lewrie feel at his own throat and swallow a few times.

"No sense in arming the competition, sir?" Lewrie asked instead.

"Quite so, Lew— Pardon, Mister Willoughby." Pollock beamed. "I might even aspire to report Ellison to the Dons, do they importune me for a large consignment of arms. Or try to bribe me. And all of it well witnessed by my clerks, heh heh! Commerce, Mister Willoughby, is not quite so dull an enterprise as you'd imagine, *ahem*. When spryer and younger, and moving pack-trains among the Cherokee and Upper Creek Indians in the Revolution . . . fiercely in competition with Americans such as McGilliveray & Sons out of Charleston, well . . . it was a war to the knife, and no quarter!" Pollock modestly preened over his past derring-do and skullduggery. "Panton, Leslie gave as good as it got!"

Sure as Hell I won't mention Desmond to him! Lewrie considered.

"Well, I think we're ready to go ashore," Pollock announced. "Whyever are ye not packed, Mister Willoughby?"

"Ashore?" Lewrie gawped back. "First I've heard of it."

"Oh, so sorry," Pollock gaily said, not sounding sorry at all. "Best for your *persona*, do you take shore lodgings in a modest *pension* or boardinghouse. The cost is middlin', and the local cuisine's most delectable, bein' French, d'ye see? Best get cracking, Willoughby, or it will be completely dark before we get you settled."

"I don't have a shore-going bag," Lewrie complained, springing to his feet. "No one told me I needed one, and—"

"No matter," Pollock objected, "for I'm sure we have a suitable valise aboard . . . for which I may gladly offer you a handsome discount, seeing as how it will go towards furthering the Crown's interests."

"What if I just lease or rent?" Lewrie dubiously wondered.

"Oh no, that'd never do, Lewrie," Pollock quibbled. "For once we come back aboard, it'll have been *used*, and I could not in good conscience flog it off on someone else as good as new."

Damn him, I knew *he'd find a way t'pry me loose from a guinea or two!* Lewrie thought; *Tradesmen! Bah!*

"We'll allow your Navy lads shore liberty, along with the brig's crew as well." Pollock further blandly announced.

"But I haven't warned 'em yet," Lewrie quickly rejoined, fearing what-all they might blab when in their cups ashore without a stern lecture. Would some of them "run" was another instant worry.

"Then you'd best be at it, shouldn't you," Pollock said, tapping a foot in growing impatience, and eagerness to savour the city's joys. "If you do not mind, I will take part in that, *ahem*. Your man, Jugg, should be given a roving brief and a freer hand, since he most likely, in my cautious estimation, has been to New Orleans before and knows his way about . . . and knows the names and faces of those we seek, from his past, ah . . . employments? I propose that Jugg temporarily report to me, not you. Now 'til next morning, say, 'til Eight Bells and the start of the Forenoon Watch, for your hands' return, so they may carouse ashore?"

"That'd do, I expect," Lewrie begrudgingly said, "Uh, what'll I need ashore, how much should I pack, then?"

"Oh, no more than a change or two of clothing," Pollock guessed. "Your current 'sporting' togs and a fresh shirt and stockings will do. Take those shipboard things you wore on the way upriver, the hunting shirt and such . . . as if that's all you own at present. A full purse, it goes without saying . . . and all your, um . . . weapons. One cannot tell what sort of footpads one may come across."

"You're so reassuring," Lewrie said with a faint sneer as he opened the cabin door to go forward to his own small accommodations.

Not one hour later he was ashore and cozily ensconced in one of Pollock's "open and airy" *appartements* (as the Frogs termed them) in a *pension* at the corner of Bourbon Street and Rue Ste. Anne. His rooms were two storeys above the ground floor, up narrow, rickety stairs, and any felons who wished to scrag him couldn't *help* making the most hellish racket on their way up to get at him, he cautiously reasoned. It actually was a promisingly pleasant place, a tad spare when it came to elegant furnishings, but it was clean and (relatively) bug-free, with bed linens, towels, and drapes still redolent of boiling water and soap, fresh washed. The "airy" part came from three complete sets of glazed doors that served for gigantic windows, all of which led out to a wraparound upper balcony fronted with intricate wrought-iron railings, and even the stench from the bricked streets with too-narrow sidewalks and no drains or gutters by the kerbs wasn't *that* bad, for all the detritus seemed to end up in the sunken centres of the cobbled streets, where, Lewrie suspected, it stayed till the next rainstorm flushed it asea . . . or down the street, where another neighbourhood could enjoy it!

Not a true set of rooms, really; he'd gotten one large, open, high-ceilinged chamber as a parlour, fitted out with a mismatched set of chairs and a settee, corner tables, end tables, a faded carpet, and some cast-off horrors for framed paintings and such, aligned along Rue Bourbon. A wide, stub-walled archway at the Ste. Anne end delineated the bedchamber, further separated from the parlour by a pair of sham Chinee folding screens.

He'd packed in a hurry, though taking time enough to place his pair of twin-barreled Manton pistols deep in his new valise, a pair of pocket pistols in his clothes, his hanger on his hip, new sword-cane in his hand, and a wavy-bladed and razor-keen Mindanao *krees* knife up his left sleeve, a "remembrance" he'd picked up off a piratical Lanun Rover in the Far East.

Lewrie had had time, too, to warn his men about the parts they were to play—adventurers signed on as Mr. Pollock's muscles—and that they should not get so drunk that their time in the Royal Navy got blabbed as *present-day* status. Poor Furfy had the hardest time understanding.

"Desmond, a private word," Lewrie had bade the happy-go-lucky Irish rogue. "You've a sensible head on your shoulders, though I fear your mate Furfy's not the quickest wit was ever dropped."

"An' that he is, sorry t'say, sor," Desmond commiserated. "A grand feller Furfy is, a fast friend, but . . . nary th' sort o' man t'even *sham* clever."

"You'll look out for him special, Desmond," Lewrie charged him. "Furfy is a good sailor, aye, and I'd hate to lose him or let him get in trouble if liquor frees his tongue, or ties it."

"Oi'll see to it, sor, swear it," Desmond soberly vowed, though how "sober" he'd be himself within the hour was doubtful. Let sailors get at drink, and they'd be senseless, roaring drunk in a turn-about of your head! Faster than you could say "Luff"!

"I knew I could count on you, Desmond," Lewrie had replied, not quite relieved, but close. "You might keep the lads together, keep an eye and ear cocked to their doin's, too, and not a word about *Proteus* or our mission. "Just enjoy the first day, and we'll probe, later."

"Ye kin count on me, sor," Desmond had assured him, though all but dancing in place from one foot to t'other to be away and ashore in search of pleasures and deviltry.

⚓

Now, Lewrie was on his own. Pollock had quickly steered him to this *pension*, a place he'd obviously stayed before, for he was on good terms with the proprietor and his wife, then had nearly jog-trotted to his own lodgings—a much nicer place, Pollock smugly and thoughtlessly informed him, located in the middle of Rue Royale, 'twixt Ste. Anne and Rue Dumaine. Pollock said that they should breakfast together next morning at eight, that Lewrie (Willoughby, rather!) should not spread himself *too* widely on his own spree among the Creoles, and should keep a clear head. A caution (more than one!) to not go off half-cocked should he encounter Lanxade or Balfa straightaway; merely on their descriptions, he just might end up accosting the wrong man, do one of them in too publicly, even should he slit the throat of the *right'un,* and end up arrested; at which juncture, there'd be nothing Pollock or Panton, Leslie & Company could do for him but deny they'd ever *heard* of him, and wasn't it such a shame for a new-minted *American* who'd come aboard their ship to go Lunatick and kill somebody, the damned rank stranger!

"Rest assured, Mister Willoughby," Mr. Pollock confided, close to him and "chummy" enough for the passersby to witness, smiling wide as anything. But his cautions were muttered from the side of his mouth (and an unattractive sight that was for "Mr. Willoughby," in truth!) so no passersby could actually eavesdrop. "I shall begin my own probes in the morning. Subtle, casual . . . nought that draws attention," he said, as if despairing that Lewrie/Willoughby could do the same.

"New Orleans can be a delightful port of call," Pollock said, practically dancing, like Liam Desmond, to be on his way. "There's a cabaret not too far off, the Pigeon Coop? Many locals are regulars there. You may casually pick up an earful. Just don't gamble with 'em! The games are all 'crook.' See you in the morning, ta!"

And with that, Lewrie was abandoned on his own. He re-entered his *pension* and clumped up the stairs to unpack. Once there, utterly alone, he wandered about the confines of his set of rooms, intently studied the wallpaper for a few minutes, and took a refreshing sundown, river-wind turn on his wrought-iron upper balcony. Oil or candle lanthorns were being lit in front of the many residences, even as those outside shops were being extinguished. Folk were strolling below him, softly speaking and chuckling at their ease in a rather pure Parisian French or in a mangled local patois that he suspected was Acadian. There now and then was even a snatch of lispy, high-born Castilian Spanish, along with another garbled version spoken by the poorer-dressed. Pollock had told him that the bulk of the Spanish in New Orleans were humbler peasant-raised Catalans. Some Portuguese, some German small-hold farmers from above New Orleans on the Côte des Allemands, even some Spanish Canary Islanders had settled in Louisiana, undoubtedly *very* desperate for land or a new beginning; or perhaps the Spanish authorities were desperate for settlers of any kind!

Dammit, I'm stuck in this dump! Lewrie groused to himself as he leaned on the railings, which gave out an ominous creaking. *I'm famished, I'm badly in need o' wine, and Pollock just up and leaves me t'rot, the hideous "ahemmin" bastard! What self-respectin' spy'd leave* me *free t'blunder about without a minder or something? A bear-leader?*

Looking back on his previous fumbling attempts at masquerading civilian and innocent, Lewrie ruefully realised that he'd been the sort who *needed* minding. Why, one could almost imagine that Pollock *trusted* him to acquit himself well on his own! Aye, did one have an optimistic bent and a *very* creative imagination! Perhaps it wasn't neglect at all, but grudging respect that he'd survived those previous missions and had implicit faith that Lewrie could be circumspect enough to survive 'til morning! Had Mr. James Peel had a private word with Mr. Pollock and "buffed up" Lewrie's dubious credentials to convince him to take him along?

Or, Lewrie glumly suspected, Pollock was simply too eager for a *rencontre* with his "shore wife"! The Captain and First Mate, on their passage to New Orleans, had discretely hinted that, no matter how prim and upright Mr. Pollock publicly presented himself, he was a mere mortal after all and had found himself a *luscious* "Bright" Free Black to warm his bed when in New Orleans; kept her in some style year-round at his permanent lodgings. Mr. Caldecott had even winked and alluded that Pollock might've succumbed to blind lust for an Octoroon female *slave* and had bought her for *thousands*, his usual parsimony bedamned!

Damme, am I scared *t'go out on my own?* Lewrie asked the new-lit stars above the streets; *Mine arse on a band-box if I am! After all, I'm better armed than most Press gangs!*

A succulent meal, even a Froggish "kickshaw," a "made" dish in savoury, but suspect, foreign sauces, a bottle of wine or three, even an idle hour or two at the cabaret both Pollock *and* Ellison had named . . . then, as Benjamin Franklin had advised, "Early to bed, early to rise." Hah!

How much trouble could I get into in that *short o'time?* Lewrie asked himself as he went back inside for his hat, coat, and cane.

CHAPTER FOURTEEN

*L*e Pigeonnier held another whole new set of scents that would've entranced Toulon and Chalky for a day or *more*. The acrid smell of hot tobacco leaf and the head-high pall of smoke from it; the wet reek of chewing tobacco and ejecta in the metal spit-kids along the long bar and spaced conveniently round the club's stygian interior. More hot smells from candles with badly trimmed wicks, beeswax, cheap tallow, or frontier rush dips. There was the faint aroma of bad breath and wine-breath combined, of elegant clothing too long unwashed, bodies that suffered from the same benign neglect, the slightest tinge from a hastily rejected supper spewed up somewhere in the cabaret and slovenly swabbed at; the reek that arose from the back of the club and wafted through the opened rear doors from the outdoor toilets. Hungary Water and cologne, mostly sweet and flowery, tried to mask human stink, but they could only do so much.

And there was the enticing odour of drink: the musk-sweetness of wine, the sweet tang of rum, the even more noticeable but mellower scent of aged brandy, or corn whisky down from the hinterlands. The ice-pinchy smell of juniper berry gin, the yeasty sourness of a variety of beers or ales . . . though it was a long way from English porters, stouts, and malts, and Lewrie had never heard a good word said for Spanish or French brews.

Here and there, in pools of somewhat honest light, dice rattled in leather cups and clattered on tabletops. In others, men, even a few bawdily gowned women, hunched over cards. "Van John" to the English, or *Vingt-et-Un* to the Frogs, was being played. Some jostled and perspired round a Pharoah table or a numbered wheel Lewrie supposed was a roulette game. He caught a few words here and there, enough to inform him that most cardplayers played Piquet, a popular local game called *Bouré,* or an American game of incomprehensible nature; it *sounded* like it was called Poke Her.

"M'sieur?" a bartender asked from the other side of a long oak counter.

"Ah . . . let me have a whisky," Lewrie decided, having grown more than fond of the American decoction. "The *aged* corn whisky, not that watery-lookin' poison." He'd been warned off *that* last year!

"L'Américain, " the servitor said with a faint sneer as he got up a stone gallon crock, removed the stopper, and poured a small glass half full, stating its price as twenty *pesetas,* in a tone that accused Lewrie of having no palate, no class, and no business in a real Creole establishment. Even tossing the man a silver British crown made no impression on the publican's *hauteur.*

The custom of the house was to elbow up along the counter, rest a foot on a wood rail, and drink standing up. Were one sitting, then one was mostly gambling; Lewrie only saw a few seated patrons risking the house cuisine. At some tables, mostly far in back, Lewrie could espy people hunched over their glasses and muttering conspiratorily with each other. To his mind it *looked* as if they were conspiring . . . greasy leers, rubbed "money" fingers, Gallic shrugs, and stony glares.

Christ, they all *look like well-paid pirates!* Lewrie goggled.

At some tables, though, it was men *and women* draped upon each other in the dim candlelight. Now that his eyes had adjusted to the gloom, Lewrie took note of scantily clad young women in morning gowns and sheer dressing robes traipsing up the stairs to the upper storey on the arms of jaunty, eager men, whilst others clumped downwards almost alone, trailed by jaded and spent patrons who barely held hands with them, the women's hard eyes already prowling for the next client.

It took Lewrie a long minute or so to unmoor his gaze from the whores; it had been rather a long while since he'd had a free moment for "doing the needful," and some of them were more than handsome. He all but shook himself from the idea; there was *work* to do! He scanned the vast, dim room's expanse, recalling his crewmen's—and Mr. Pollock's—descriptions of Lanxade or Balfa. But after ten minutes he had to admit to himself that those cut-throats weren't present. He looked the room over again to see if there was a single soul he *knew.* But none of his hands were in the Pigeon Coop, nor could he spot sailors off Pollock's ship; obviously, this cabaret was too high-toned for the common tars.

He *did* think he saw one of the *Azucena del Oeste*'s mates trotting up the stairs past the music gallery on a whore's arm, but he wasn't so sure he'd wager on it.

A fetchin' whore, he has, Lewrie decided to himself, noting that his glass was empty, of a sudden, and turning belly-first to the bar to whistle up the serving man for a refill. In the private screen of his coat-tails, he felt a tightening in his groin, a pinching from the fork of his tight trousers' crutch as his lubricious nature awakened.

Glass topped up, Lewrie turned back to face the room just as a nigh nakedly "dressed" Mulatto *demimonde* came slithering by, her arm brushing men's fundaments or thighs, "all quite by accident." He gawped, gulped, looking at the size and springy rounded shape of her "poonts," exchanged a brief, red-faced smile . . . before a patron down the counter looped an arm round her waist, drew her to him, and gnawed at her bare neck like a long-lost lover. Off they went up the stairs.

"Lubricious Nature" began to whisper, which awoke his old companion, "Amatory Fever," who began to gibber, leer, and cajole . . .

Damme, *I'm tryin'* t'spy *here!* Lewrie pointed out to his groin.

It was a forlorn hope, though, any continued "spying." On both sides of him, it was all elbows and shoulders, *troops* of foreigners in full cry in alien tongues, and the local French patois was so nasally "hawn-hawn" and rapid he could barely make out one word in four, those mostly harmless and plebeian. He was being jostled at the bar, just a whisker short of intentional insult for an English gentleman, who held a larger personal space than most. Even the music played by a string trio from the old-style gallery irritated him, a jiggery-pokery of gay but jangly airs . . . when not some mournful dirges, half-Spanish, half-Moorishly minor keyed.

He thought of crying off and heading home to bed, but surely! His first night ashore in untold months, out of uniform and anonymous, in a port town as sinful as Old Port Royal on Jamaica. How *dull* it'd be to wash out his stockings and underdrawers alone, yet . . .

The press at the counter got to him. He scooped up his change, wafer-thin foreign "tin," felt to see if he still had his coin-purse, then began to wander the main room.

"Mon Dieu, Jean!" Hippolyte whispered maliciously. "Where did he get such a tawdry ensemble? That fellow there in the wide hat?"

"Why is he walking so oddly . . . all hunched over?" Helio asked.

"An *Américain* clown," Jean-Marie Rancour dismissed. "Back to what we are discussing . . . We *know M'sieur* Bistineau cheats us. Why *does* he get five percent off the top, when I've heard that criminals who deal in stolen goods pay the thieves *first* to get them. Lanxade *said* it's his normal cost of doing business," Jean insisted in a hot mutter, both elbows on the table round a wineglass, "And how do we know we can trust Henri Maurepas, either, if he misreports on—"

"Papa trusts him implicitly, Jean," Helio declared. "Not once has he ever doubted *him*. He manages all our affairs. Papa knows . . . "

"Papa knows how to spend, *cher* brother," Charité impatiently countered. "He has no real head for the intricacies of business. It is beneath true gentlemen. Of course, M'sieur Bistineau is cheating us, and there is little we, or old Henri Maurepas, can do about it . . . so long as Bistineau is the only trader who'll accept our goods, dare to have them in his store. Later on, well . . . "

"Later on, perhaps we'll confront Monsieur Bistineau with steel," Helio, as the eldest, announced. "His son Claude will inherit. Isn't Claude one of us, the one who presented the scheme to his father, out of patriotism? Perhaps we should talk to Claude . . . "

"He is the only outlet," Hippolyte grumbled, turning his glass round and round. "If not the Bistineaus, I can't think of another of *French* blood who'd be bold enough. All the rest who could handle our goods are Americans these days, anyway," he glumly stated.

"*Mon Dieu,* business, business, business!" Charité exasperatedly complained. "We are here to celebrate, *n'est-ce pas?* Our cause gains cash, it advances . . . We have hurt and frightened our Spanish masters. And . . . we have money to spend . . . like sailors." She twinkled to buck them up. "Like buccaneers of the grand old days. *A votre santé!*" she gaily proposed, raising her champagne glass.

Charité de Guilleri had enjoyed the freedom of movement that a buccaneering costume had given her on their first raiding cruise, and even before that she'd found it extremely droll to go out at night in the company of her brothers, or other sporting young males of her set, disguised as a man who could witness the games, pleasures, and amusing places that men could enjoy, whilst "proper" young ladies were forced to sit at home . . . to hear the curses and uproariously funny and lewd stories and jests that a staid husband would *never* bring home to a genteelly sheltered wife after a night out with his contemporaries.

Tonight, Charité wore a silk shirt with a stylish broad cravat, a snugly tailored waist-coat over that, and a man's wide-lapeled, nip-waisted coat, unbuttoned and loose enough to disguise her breasts. A pair of fawn-coloured trousers, snug as a second skin, and riding boots, covered her legs. Her long chestnut hair was pinned up high and concealed beneath a tapered-crown tall hat that was forced to ride far back on her forehead, as if cocked in a saucy, devil-may-care manner. And, like her brothers, or any New Orleans "gentleman," Charité bore a small pocket pistol in her coat, a pencil-thin dagger in a hidden sheath up her left sleeve, and a gilt-handled sword-cane behind her chair.

To help her disguise along, she had fashioned a narrow mustachio from gauze and her own hair clippings, attached to her upper lip by paste. Admittedly, it required a lot of fiddling to assure her that it wasn't coming loose, and it didn't take well to wine or brandy, but the surprise she elicited with it had been amusing.

Should Papa or Maman, any of her respectable family, ever learn that she went out without a female chaperone or body slave . . . that she went out after *dark,* and to such low dives as the Pigeon Coop, dressed as a man especially, well! Charité would end up on one of their isolated, dreary swamp plantations, and it could be a year or longer *être dans la merde*—"Up Shit's Creek"—before they relented!

Nor would it help for them to learn that Charité long ago had become "tarnished treasure"; that she had surrendered the particular commodity that fetched a high bride price. Charité wasn't sure which would shame her family more: to be caught in her disguise as a "false, de-sexed" carouser, to have squandered her precious virginity, or to be tried and executed by the Spaniards as a dangerous revolutionary pirate!

Each, though, all of it together, made Life so piquantly exciting. "Down with your tired old conventions and morals!" was, in her mind, as revolutionary a slogan as "Down with Tyrants and Aristos" in the Place de Bastille.

It was thrilling to be, to act, so Modern!

"Look!" Helio said of a sudden as the tawdrily garbed stranger wandered over to a nearby gaming table. "Your gaudy fellow, Hippolyte . . . See that scar on his cheek? Our slave Aristotle said the man who leads the bruisers off the Panton, Leslie ship, the one he heard them calling '*Capitaine,*' has such a scar. He is fairer-haired than that *Américain,* that El . . . El-isson. I think it's the same man!"

"Why is he *walking* that way?" Charité wondered, snickering.

"Too-tight trousers," Helio sneered. "Cheap, ready-made."

"A stiff-leg sailor." Hippolyte tittered.

"Ah, but which leg, *mes amis?*" Cousin Jean-Marie giggled. "Is he a sailor, he's one *en rut*, hee hee!"

"*Zut, Jean!*" Helio chid him. "Our sister is present!"

"Your sister is not here, tonight, *mes frères,*" Charité pointed out. "I am *Armand, comprende?*" She leaned back in her chair, one arm slung over its back in studiedly "male" fashion, appraising their potentially worrisome stranger over the rim of her champagne glass with her eyes half-lidded. "Mmmm . . . the scar makes him look . . . dashing. Very intriguing. Almost handsome," she cooed, half to herself. Then she abandoned her male pose to whirl and chirp girlishly at her tablemates. "We must talk to him, one of us! Get him to drink with us . . . tell him some jokes or something. Get him drunk and sound him out to see who, and what, he is . . . see if he *is* trouble."

"El-isson, or that *Capitaine* fellow?" Hippolyte quickly objected, blanching. "It's best if neither of them know us."

"We *must* beard him," Charité insisted. "In drink, he may blab or even wish to befriend *us* to help him with whatever it is he's come for. If *Capitaine* Lanxade is wrong, and he's seeking pirates . . . we could pretend to help discover them!

"*Oui!*" Charité exclaimed, to their appalled expressions. "We send him on a goose chase down the bayous, looking for truly *desperate* cut-throats. La Fourche, or Bayou Terre aux Boeufs, not Barataria, you see? And, if he's not a spy, we learn it. Come *on*, one of you! Have you no spirit? Must *I* do it?"

Oh là, how delicious! Charite thought suddenly.

Which would be sweeter: to sham the idle, elegant Creole *gentilhomme* and befuddle the man's wits, or reveal herself, beguile him with her novelty, her modernity! Perhaps even to *seduce* him, then get him to talk unguardedly, half-sodden and nigh spent? True Jacobin patriot girls, heroines of the glorious Revolution in France, had applied their wiles in such a fashion to ferret out Aristos and sympathisers. Could she do no less for *their* coming liberation?

She looked back over at him. *No, it wouldn't be such a* horrid *chore*, Charité decided, her lips parting in an expectant smile, with a *frisson* of pleasure-to-come swelling inside her. *He is certainly not . . . unattractive!*

Charité felt her nipples harden at the thought, felt them swell and pucker against the caressing silk of her shirt, the tautness of her waist-coat. That made her squirm a bit more on her chair, blaming the snugness of her trousers' crutch-fork for the restless, warm feeling that ghost-tickled up her innards, and clasp her knees together, clutch her buttock muscles as if . . .

"The Devil take you all," she said with a bold laugh, draining her champagne glass and tossing her head in frustration, in a mad-cap finality. "*I'll* be the one to beard him! Just you watch this, you . . . timid *garçonnets!*"

With what appeared to others as a dashing stroke of her mustachios, but was really reassurance that that "appliance" was still firmly stuck on, Charité de Guilleri sprang to her feet and began stalking her prey.

CHAPTER FIFTEEN

*B*onjour, m'sieur . . . you are new to Le Pigeonnier?"

Alan Lewrie had been trying to make sense of the dealing, discarding, and redealing of the "Poke Her" game, yet not get so close that the players might object, when that "sweet" voice stole his attention.

"Hey?" was his bright rejoinder.

"I ask if you are new, here, *m'sieur*. You are not a familiar face" came the reply, from a slim, short, over-elegant fop, who put him in mind of cheap dolls sold at fairs, a "Bartholomew Baby."

Lewrie beheld a saucy, possibly half drunk cock-a-whoop so pale-complexioned he couldn't have seen sunlight since his christening; so lean-faced and pert-chinned, so young he had no need to shave, yet, but with an oddly lush mustachio; three or four inches shorter than Lewrie, even with the help of riding-boot heels. The idle jack-a-napes lazily twiddled an empty champagne glass 'twixt the lean fingers of his right hand, with the other challengingly poised akimbo on his hip.

For a second, another whippet-thin fellow came to mind: Horatio Nelson, his old squadron commander. Lewrie's second recollection was sorrier: his Sodomite half brother, Gerald, or others of that "Molly's" idle and depraved "Windward Passage" crew.

"You buy me champagne, *m'sieur?*" the wee fellow asked, his blue eyes twinkling, his cheeks as dimpled as a randy chambermaid's.

"Sorry, lad," Lewrie gruffly responded. "Not t'give offence but . . . I don't think we're in the same regiment."

"You are new to New Orleans, I take it?" the mininkin persisted, smiling even wider. "British . . . or American? *Vous parlez pauvre Français, peut-être?* The poor French, perhaps? *Un peu,* but a little? You will need the translator, and I am he, *m'sieur!* Vairy *bon marché . . . pas cher,*" he gaily beguiled. "That is to say, 'inexpensive.' The 'cheap'?" he added with an amused titter.

"Nothing personal, young fellow, but . . . I don't need help with the language, and I *won't* buy you a drink, and you ain't my sort, so *do* toddle off, won't you?" Lewrie rejoined, beginning to get irked. "If you aren't a pimp . . . *un entremetteur* . . . I've no need of you, or your services, thankee. *Comprendre* 'no thanks'? Try someone else."

"Ah, yes! I can introduce you to a girl, *m'sieur.*" The elfin imp brightened, attempting to step closer, which set Lewrie to backing up a matching step or two. "None of *these* drabs, *non!* You would be interested, *m'sieur* . . . your name escapes me, sorry?"

"Didn't set it loose," Lewrie huffed. "Willoughby. Now do—"

"Willoughby," the cheeky little bastard slowly struggled to say, nodding somberly for a moment as if the name was a talismanic spell to be forgotten at one's peril. "*Very* solid. *Very* Anglo-Saxon. You are new to New Orleans, and you wish a girl. You are *un Américain,* come down the Great River on a long, lonely, and pleasureless travail. Or you came *up*river on a ship, a long, lonely, and pleasure-denying time, *aussi, n'est-ce pas?* You have heard of the Creole ladies, and come to the Pigeonnier to seek one, but alas . . . they *never* come out to such a place. They sit lonely and sad in their rooms, *m'sieur* Willoughby . . . you have a Christian name? They wait for you, bold traveller, I—"

"Oh, bugger this!" Lewrie growled, "and bugger you, too! Scat! Shoo! I don't *like* boys, *comprenez?*"

"But I am *not* a boy, *m'sieur!*" the fellow whispered so alluringly and girlishly, long lashes batting, that Lewrie was stalled in his tracks, despite whatever revulsion for the "back-gammoners' brigade" he felt. *Damme, is he or isn't he?* he wondered; *he . . . she . . . a specialty of the house? Oh, the Devil with it . . . him, she, it!*

"*Adieu, m'sieur* . . . or whatever," Lewrie all but snarled back, exasperated enough to risk open insult and a knife fight. "*Bonsoir. Hasta la vista . . . vaya con Dios . . . auf* bloody *wiedersehen,* 'bye!"

"*Such* a pity," the wee chap said with a disconcertingly fetching pout, raising hands to hat and lip. "*Adieu,* and *bonsoir* to you as well, m'sieur Willoughby."

"Same t'you, as . . . Jesus!" Lewrie gawped in astonishment as the hat was lifted high enough to reveal a bounteous beehive of silky chestnut hair, as half a broadly grinning upper lip was mockingly "exfoliated." The . . . she/he/it/whatever dimpled prettily and laughed aloud, sticking out a taunting tongue as the hat was quickly clapped back on, and the false mustachio got restuck.

She—Lewrie wasn't *exactly* certain that she *wasn't* truly a girl at that moment!—sashayed away, swaying slim hips that *swayed* the female way, leaving him red-faced to be so twitted, the butt of a gargantuan joke! He shrugged and shook his head to cast off his puzzlement, then toddled back to the bar for a very needed refill of drink, leaving the publican an extra *peseta* or three this time. Once there, he tossed off the "heel-taps" of his last one, then craned his vision about the large cabaret to see if someone he knew had deliberately set him up for a wry jape and was now chortling in a dark corner, but no . . . not a single familiar face, form, or distinguising article of clothing could he spot, not a single guffaw, grin, or smile directed at *him*. *Was she or wasn't he, dammit?* he speculated, nursing his insulted feelings on smoky-sweet and mellow aged "corn squeezings." *Was she bait t'get me somewhere dark, where some hostile bully-bucks could knife me all quiet-like? Or just rob me down t'me skin?*

He leaned both elbows on the bar, hunched over his whisky like the Creole dandies, Catalan peasants, and few raw-boned Yankees did it.

Lewrie would have hauled out his pocket watch to find how late it was, would that act not perk up potential pickpockets, much like a red flag waved at a bull. The Pigeon Coop's clientele certainly *seemed* to boast more than its fair share of cutty-eyed sharpers!

One more glass, he gloomily determined, still stewing over his mocking, and he'd be off to his hired set of rooms, no matter how dour a prospect that was, call it an early night, and—

A sharpish *clack!* sounded from his left as a gilt-handled cane came down flat on the bar counter to claim space for its owner, and to summon the publican.

"I am *so* sorry, m'sieur Willoughby." The smooth-cheeked "fellow" chuckled as he insinuated himself—herself?—alongside him. "But it was *very* amuse . . . amusing? . . . to see your face when I accosted you. To see your *étonnement* . . . astonishment . . . over my little jest."

"And which bastard put you up to it?" Lewrie snapped.

"Why, *no* one, *m'sieur*" came the reply, with a soft, intimate laugh. "I do this to many people. To pretend to be a man is the only way a girl could enjoy a cabaret. They are *such* fun, but as you see, *ladies* are *barred*. Only the *putains*, the whores, come here, and I do not wish to be taken for one, *n'est-ce pas?* I sincerely apologise for causing you any uh . . . embarrassment, *m'sieur* Willoughby . . . and I do earnestly beg your forgive . . . forgiveness."

"Well, hmmm," Lewrie growled, turning to face . . . whatever, though he still had his doubts, dreading an even crueller twitting did he relent. *Hmmm, though!* he thought, looking down.

In the short time since their parting, the . . . whatever . . . had untied the broad cravat and let it dangle like a short scarf, undone the upper buttons of that lace-ruffled silk shirt, and had freed the top buttons of the satin waistcoat, revealing, hinting at . . .

There were damn' few boys, in Lewrie's broad experience, could sport such a flawless décolletage; nor spring free such neatly bounteous breasts. Not even rolled-up stockings could sham those!

"If you buy me champagne, *m'sieur* Willoughby," she (*definitely* a she, Lewrie was now *almost* completely certain!) inveigled with her eyes and mouth lazily grinning, for knowing exactly where he had been gazing, "and I will teach you how to play *Bouré,* a most amusing, and very Creole, card game. I am Charité . . . Charité Bonsecours, though I disguise myself as Armand," she told him, their gazes now directly bold and all but inseparable. She borrowed the surname of another proud and respectable Creole family of long standing on the spur of the moment. "For when I wish to go out and . . . play."

That sweet expression on her face, that tone of voice, and her play on words, those female long lashes being batted at him, and her angel-whore's coyness, all but made Lewrie go *"Eep!"* and snatch at his suddenly reawakened crutch.

"What else do you play?" he barely had the wit to ask, "Other than *Bouré* . . . and jests on 'Johnny Newcomes'?"

"Oh, there are many other delightful games that I enjoy," she sultrily intimated, shifting from one foot to the other, which slyly shifted a hip to brush against his. "I promise you will not be disappointed, *m'sieur,* ah . . . I must know your Christian name. If we are to be . . . intimates?" she cooed.

"'Tis Alan . . . Alan . . . Willoughby," he replied, coming nigh a cropper over his own masquerade, grinning it off with an appraising leer. "I'll allow you the champagne, and the cards. For now. Just so long as you don't play *me,* again . . . Charité." In a gruffer, warning tone he added, "Fool me once, shame on me. Fool me twice, then look to your life."

"I stand warned, *cher* Alain." Charité throatily chuckled back, not daunted in the least. "Let us get a private table in the back, a deck of cards, and a bottle of champagne. And I assure you, *cher*, I shall have no reason to fear for my life."

Her false mustachio had sagged completely off one side of her mouth, and her eyes and voice were so sweetly, soberly candid that he could not help but assent and whistle up the publican for glasses and a bottle. She leaned close enough to gently touch her rather cutely formed nose on his near shoulder for a flirtatious second, as if sealing a bargain, before breaking away to waft towards a dark rear corner of the cabaret to claim a table for two.

Damme, this is daft! he chid himself as he flung coins on the counter; *Is she a sham, I'll* never *live it down! If not, well . . . it might be the sort of tale ye dine out on for bloody* years!

CHAPTER SIXTEEN

*L*aw, Jim Hawk, ye won't b'lieve h'it!" Georgie insistently whispered, reeking of "time-killing" whisky, fried chicken from a street vendor, and "chaw-baccy." "H'it's th' oddest thang ever I did see, an' had I not, I'da never thunk hit real," Georgie said as he and Ellison "lurked" beneath the stranger's wrought-iron balcony.

"Simmer down an' tell it, Georgie," Jim Hawk Ellison coaxed as he leaned away from the aromatic scents, "an' kindly keep your skunk-skin cap downwind, how 'bout. It's still pert ripe."

"We kep' an eye on 'at Willoughby feller, like ya asked us to," Georgie began to explain, though all but wringing his hands confusedly. Confusion with Georgie was a given, though, Ellison had found. Bright help was hard to find lately. "He left 'at tavern place, I follered him, like ye tol' me. But he come back hyar with another *fella*, Jim Hawk," Georgie nigh moaned, waving a hand at the balcony, and the dim single candle still aglow in one of the windows. Ellison was sure he was blushing as red as ripe vine peppers. "Come nigh t'chokin' on ma chaw . . . way they wuz a'pawin' an' a'gropin' at each other, an' . . ."

"With another *man?*" Jim Hawk gawped. "Well, he is *English*, but . . . that's a surprise. A big'un." Ellison scrubbed his chin thoughtfully, speculating on how Willoughby's secret proclivity could be used, if he turned out to be a British spy; he hadn't bought the man's "new-come American" pose for a second! He'd come off that Panton, Leslie ship, hadn't he? And that company and the British government might as well be tight as ticks together.

"Sure it wasn't a way t'sneak a fellow spy up there, so's they could have 'em a parley, on the sly? Just with their heads close . . ."

"Nossiree, Jim Hawk!" Georgie adamantly objected, wringing his skunk cap in his hands. " 'Twuz a lantern burnin' o'er th' door when they got hyar, an' I seed wot they wuz a'doin', plain! They wuz all arm in *arm,* had their clothes un-sheveled an' their hands a'roamin' round *inside. Kissin',* a time'r two, too, right out in front o' God an' *ever'body,* hotter'n foxes in heat! An' 'at little feller with 'im a'cooin' an' a'titt'rin' like one o' them rum-hot whores we had on th' Natchez Trace!"

"Hmmph!" Ellison commented. "What'd this other fella look like, then? Ye git a good look, so we can find out what *he's* up to?"

"Real short an' slimmish, Jim Hawk," Georgie related, screwing up his face, "an' cleed all dandy-like, in rich clothes. Struttin' as proud as a banty-rooster! Had a right mystifyin' mustachio, too. One minute, h'it wuz thar, next h'it warn't, an' he'd git all giggly-shrieky. They git to th' door, thar, wot with all th' kissin', his hat come off an' he had s'much hair piled up on his haid, hit looked like a wasp's nest, an' I coulda *swore* I thought I saw a *titty,* but . . ."

Ellison lowered his chin to his chest and slowly counted to ten, as his mentor had told him to, back when he'd thought to read for the law in Salisbury, North Carolina, before blurting out foolishness when in court. He pinched the bridge of his nose and heaved a *heavy* sigh.

"Mightn't it o' come to ye, Georgie," Ellison asked in a slow drawl of seemingly infinite patience, "that your little fella might've been a girl dressed up in men's clothin'?"

"Wull . . ." Georgie began, then subsided, abashed. "Oh."

Comes th' dawn! Jim Hawk Ellison sourly thought; *Oh, indeed!*

"Wull . . . 'at's unnat'ral, too, ain't h'it, Jim Hawk?" Georgie spluttered, giving his hat another wringing, freshly aggrieved.

"How long they been at it?" Ellison asked, glancing upwards.

" 'Bout near a hour, I reckon," Georgie muttered. "I *thought* to shinny up thar an' see wot-all they wuz a'doin' . . ."

"You didn't, did you, Georgie?" Ellison asked, alarmed.

"Naw." Georgie chuckled. " 'Em iron poles is slick, an' 'at balcony ain't as stout as you'd a'reckon, so . . ."

"Good!" Ellison nigh barked with relief, much louder than he'd meant to on the dark, silent street. "I'll take over, Georgie. Here. Go git yerself somethin' t'drink, maybe have yerself a Creole gal. A real 'un," he said, digging into a pocket for some silver Spanish dollars. "Don't go blabbin', mind, do ya git a snoot-full. This business is nobody's but ours, right?"

"Damn' right, Jim Hawk, an' thankee right kindly," Georgie said with a wide grin of delight. "But . . . yew figger this out, ye'll tell me wot h'it means, won't ye, Jim Hawk?"

"Be th' first t'know, Georgie," Ellison promised.

Ellison slunk into a dark shop doorway and wrapped his coat snug against the past-midnight river and swamp mists, thinking that if the sky started raining whisky, Georgie Prater would be the sort to hold a fork . . . and he'd most-like drop that!

The game was getting even more complicated than he'd imagined when he'd been appointed to scout New Orleans by Congress—and without General Wilkinson finding out about it! Ellison had been limited in his choice of skilled and smart backwoodsmen and volunteer soldiers to go along with him, men unknown to the Tennessee or Kentucky garrisons, who were likely already enmeshed in Wilkinson's schemes. So, beyond a few men of past acquaintance and a surveyor or two borrowed from civilian pursuits, he was pretty much stuck with dregs—well-muscled, well-armed dregs who'd be good in a fight, but . . .

Jim Hawk Ellison now strongly suspected that this Englishman, this "Captain" Willoughby, was on a mission very much like his own to New Orleans, and Louisiana. A new American citizen as he claimed, or not—Willoughby couldn't disguise his educated accent for very long, no matter how "aw shuckin's" he tried. He was a man used to command, his sobriquet of "Captain" either naval or military, with a volunteer pack of muscle accompanying him who toed the line when he spoke. But who was he working for?

General Wilkinson was out of the question; he'd never trust the British, even someone *formerly* British, to be his eyes and ears before he put his own invasion scheme in play. There were secret, but widely known whispers of a British move against the hapless Spanish. Though Ellison doubted an expedition could make it all the way down the Mississippi quietly, past American settlements on the eastern bank.

It made more sense to launch it from Jamaica, overwhelm the few defenders in a few brisk, brutal days' combat, and take New Orleans as the main prize. Without the city, Louisiana was useless anyway, Jim Hawk had long before realised.

Or Willoughby *could've* been hired by Virginia, South Carolina, or Georgia, and was here as part of a sectional land-grab. There were already secret agents aplenty in the town from those governments, he had been warned. Yet he'd come on a Spanish-flagged, British-owned ship, in the guise of a bootless adventurer?

Ellison had spent half the night dashing from one oddity to the next, from watcher to watcher to hear their reports, and was, in the backcountry vernacular, " 'bout plumb tuckered out." Even more *outré* was what happened in the alley behind the Maurepas bank, as sack after sack of money had been spirited out the door into a couple of farm waggons, surrounded by a gang of heavily armed men, as piratical a crew of cut-throats as ever he did see! And what was *that* about, Ellison wondered, a bold midnight robbery?

He'd been tempted to whistle up his own lads and try to rob the robbers! A sudden flood of money could, when delivered to Congress, be the funds to pay for America's fore-ordained growth. The United States Government *was* mighty "skint," still paying for the Revolution years after their independence had been won. With enough money, they would not have to wait for a more assertive President in office, but . . .

At least Ellison had sicced one of his better men on the trail of those waggons, to see where they'd gone. That had been the best he could do, since most of his others had been let go for the rest of the night and were mostly "drunk as Cootie Brown" by then.

And there went a shot at a little *personal* profit, too; profit beyond the promised reward for his covert service, which he doubted if Congress could actually *pay*. There was land he craved, in the Powell's Valley of East Tennessee, among good people he'd come to know, like the McLeans and Bowmans . . . good neighbours, with a few pretty daughters to choose from, did he ever have a chance to put down roots and marry.

Jim Hawk Ellison drew a quid of tobacco from a pocket and cut a chew off. He'd prefer his pipe, but that was impossible if he didn't wish to betray his vigil.

"Damn you, Willoughby," he whispered, eying the candle's glow enviously. "Whatever you're up to, you're costin' me sleep. Even if ye *are* a Godcursed Sodomite, you can lay down on th' job!"

"Mmm . . . *mon amour formidable*," Charité coo-muttered, draped delightfully light, incredibly smooth and baby-soft half atop him as Lewrie billowed the sheet high above them to float downwards, creating a cooling zephyr. "Alain, *mon coeur*," she added with a sleepily sated smile as she shifted her lazy embrace.

"Charité, *ma petite biche*," Lewrie answered in kind, chuckling deep in his throat, recalling endearments he hadn't used since Phoebe Aretino, his Mediterranean mistress. He was *pretty* sure he had just called her a "little doe." And Charité was certainly that.

Only four inches above five feet without her boots, with slim hips and the wee-est little bottom, the faintest wisps of pale blond fluff below her knees, above her quim, and beneath her arms, a narrow waist that gently tapered inward above the talc-smooth swell of her hips; narrow shoulders and slim arms, but with the most heavenly, *perfect* breasts ever he did see, or kiss, or suckle, or lick, with darker tan areolae and cunningly puckering square nipples to worship as well.

With her hair unpinned in the privacy of his rooms, a positive flood of chestnut hair spilled down her back to her waist and now lay like a light blanket over both of them.

They had shared two bottles of champagne whilst she'd taught him *Bouré*, which had surprisingly resembled *Ecarte*, with antes tossed out first. Five cards each, dealer announcing trumps, but before any play, one could discard or fold completely, build one's hand with the replacement cards, then follow the leader's play in the proper suit or trump with a higher card, or over-trump with a higher card of another suit, thereby taking tricks. The second dealing and the discards, she told him, were similar to that rube-ish Yankee Doodle derivative that they called Poker or Poquet, not "Poke Her" as Lewrie had imagined he had heard it. Two other young Creole gentlemen had joined them, once Lewrie had picked up the game, introduced as the Darbone brothers, the older one as Claude, the younger as Baltasar.

"Pardon, *messieurs*," Lewrie had taken note, "but you and, ah . . . Armand bear a striking resemblance."

"Most Creoles do," the elder brother Claude had replied with a smirk. "Light-coloured eyes and chestnut hair . . . many from Normandy arrived first in Louisiana, before the Acadians or the Spanish. And we do marry back and forth, *n'est-ce pas?* Armand, your mustachio's slipping again. *Fais attention!*" he'd sing-songed, as if they and she were long familiar with each other's company in the Pigeon Coop; this had set Lewrie's sudden possessive "teeth" all ataunt-to, jealous even before having her.

He'd lost fourty Spanish silver dollars at *Bouré,* and that was at small-to-middling stakes, the lion's share to Charité, or "Armand." At five British shillings to the dollar, that was only ten pounds, at least—nowhere near "gambling deep," and a cheap lesson at the price. And the Darbone brothers *had* bought two other bottles.

And once the last "bubbly" had been poured and drunk, Charité had bid them a firm, no-more-gambling goodnight and had requested a gentleman to see her safely home. And though the Darbones seemed to grumble over that more than a bit, they had stood aside as Lewrie had seen her out to the street and round the corner towards Bourbon Street and his *pension.* Once in the relative anonymity of the dark streets, she had flung herself into his arms.

Admittedly, Lewrie had taken a callous, *common* moment or two to grope her like a sack of grain, to discover if he'd been gulled again, intensely relieved to reach inside her open shirt and determine that she definitely *was* a girl, and not a lying set of laundry items, that there was no "wedding tackle" artfully tucked away somewhere. It was only then that he committed himself to a kiss, then they were off to the races, barely able to stay clad as they jog-trotted breathlessly to his *appartement* and dashed upstairs past the scandalised *concierge.*

"*Vous comprenez, cher* Alain," Charité had seriously insisted, even as she was slinging coat, waist-coat, and cravat to the wide, and hop-tugging to get a boot off, "this does not mean a commitment of any sort between us."

"Completely!" Lewrie had most happily barked back, shedding his garments in fervent flurry. "None offered on my part, and *damn'* thoughtful of ye t'mention it! I say, *ma chérie* . . . take a pew on the settee, and I'll have those boots off quick as a wink!"

Giggling, guffawing, tugging first from the front, then turned away from her with her boot 'twixt his legs, her other foot shoving in the middle of his back, or the cleft of his buttocks; and then Lewrie attended to her trousers, her ankles on his shoulders, and she laughing and squirming as delighted as an infant tickled mid-bath, a bold, hearty laugh not usually heard from genteel young ladies.

All but one candle snuffed, the amber shadows and flickers of light gilding them, Charité stood and slowly lifted the long hem of her lace-ruffled shirt, performing for him as he sat to wrestle out of his boots, and he was struck dumb, completely entranced, for the girl looked him right in the eyes as she did so, her coltish young thighs almost chastely crossed at the same time, and her laughter turned much softer and huskier, as if it was a dare.

"Oh . . . that," Charité said with a sheepish expression when she unstrapped the sheath of her poignard from her left forearm and tossed it into a far dark corner of the sitting area.

"And, oh . . . this 'un," Lewrie echoed, unbuttoning his cuffs and pushing up his left sleeve to expose his own sheathed *krees*, removing it and tossing it to join hers in the corner.

Completely nude, as perfect as a young Venus on the half-shell, she knelt to help him take off his boots, only pretending to struggle with the right one so she could turn about and present her delightful wee *derrière*, then chuckle deep in her chest as Lewrie "helped out," bracing a bare left foot on her mounds and enticing Venus Dimples and wriggling his toes.

Finally barefooted, he stood to peel his shirt upwards and off, but she knelt again and unpinned her hair to let it fall like a glossy silk avalanche, spilling down her back and over her breasts. She shook her mane to free it all, then swept it forward like a stage curtain as she scooted forward on her knees to press her face into his groin, and Lewrie gave out a groan of instant pleasure as soft, sweet lips were put to his straining member, as dainty little fingers gently took his measure and tickled feathery-soft down the shaft.

He tossed his shirt away and lowered his hands to her shoulders as Charité made yummy-good appreciative moaning sounds and whispered, "Oh, *la grosse verge, cher* Alain! *Si grande et dure. Si ardente pour moi?*"

Big . . . hard . . . eager for her? "Bloody right!" he exclaimed as he flung back his head and shut his eyes, lost to her tantalising ministrations. He felt like he sported a marlingspike, a belaying pin, and if he didn't top her that very instant, his heads would explode—both of them! And where did a girl that fine learn *that?* Lewrie wondered in a brief moment of concern, one that quickly passed. Was she *so* experienced, so *widely* ploughed, that he'd need to dig into his valise for a sheepskin cundum?

Before he *did* burst like a 12-pounder, he drew her up and away from his groin, got her to her feet, swept that concealing hair behind her shoulders and embraced her, savouring how smooth, soft, and wee she was as she eagerly pressed against him, lifting her arms about his neck and silently urging him to lift her off her straining toes.

She was not quite as light as the elfin Phoebe Aretino that he remembered, but he had no trouble hefting her up, her face level with his, to support her bottom with his hands, and slowly walk towards the bedstead as she rained kisses on him, now making faint, kitteny whimpering sounds. He sat her on the high edge of the bedstead, her legs scissored about his waist, and began to reward her, kiss for hot, wet kiss, slowly roaming to her eyes, her ears, down each side of her neck, then to her breasts.

Charité leaned back on the palms of her hands, luring him to a matching lean forward, her head thrown back and her mane beginning to whip and toss with each pleasured roll of her head, her hips starting a slow, metronomic sweep from left to right and back again, supporting herself on her hands and the strength of her legs, beginning to thrust and recede, even squirming impatiently to snare his prick and lure it in, and Lewrie squirmed as well to lower his member, now stoutly upjutting as a jib boom, to meet her. Quim and cock met at last, darker wrinkly nether lips gently parted as the head slid so *easily* into her, one heavenly inch, as if dipped into a brazier-warmed pot of honey . . .

"Oooh . . . Alain!" she whimpered, freezing in place. "*Mon Dieu, le préservatif, 'l'anglais,'* please? The . . . protection?"

"Arrr!" he good-naturedly groaned, a single second of madness away from spearing her to the root. But he turned away and went to his valise. Spare shirt and hunting shirt went flying, as did rolled stockings, a clean, pressed neck-stock, and spare underdrawers, flung upwards without a care to where they landed, as if he was a highwayman rifling a coach passenger's bags for hidden jewels.

He heard her softly tinkling laughter and turned. She'd rolled over on her stomach and was peeking between the bedstead curtains in full amusement, chin resting on her forearms crossed atop the massive mahogany footboard. Lewrie shrugged and grinned back at her, at last found his cundum packet and unbound the tied ribbons to lift the flap and pull out a whole handful, showing them to her before returning to the side of the bed.

By then, Charité had rolled back to the bedside, quickly, eagerly posing herself. Her hands grasped the upper canopy railing and, half standing on the short assisting ladder with one dainty foot, and with her other slim leg resting on the mattress, thighs far apart, she pretended to swing slightly, almost childlike, as she watched in wide-eyed wonder to see him sheath himself and bind a cundum on. Once done, her welcoming, warming, growing smile was all the invitation he needed.

He embraced her about her thighs, pressing his face against the soft-fleshed and fragrant warmth of her firm, flat stomach, kissing up to her breasts again to restore his slightly cooled ardour, squeezing gently at her bottom; kissing slowly downwards over her belly that was almost shuddering, quivering under his lips and the tip of his tongue.

Sliding over and sitting down where she'd been when he left her, Charité leaned back on her hands again, parted her sweet thighs, lifted her knees, and resumed the left-right squirming of her hips, and the upward, forward hungry thrusting of her groin, as steady and gentle as waves breaking at a slack tide.

"*Mon Dieu,* please! *Maintenant* . . . now, *cher!* I can't take any more!" Charité huskily begged, clawing him upwards, sliding her body to the very edge of the high bedside, then embracing him in a death grip as frantic as someone about to drown. Lewrie rose, stepped up, dragged her to him with one hand at the base of her spine, and guided himself back to the pleasure seat. Succulently hot nether lips, slick and engorged . . . that first inch into Paradise swiftly, even more easily regained . . . both of his hands seizing her hips and another, short half step to the bedside, gliding in, gliding up ward . . . half his manhood all at one steady, gentle thrust . . . an inch more, then one more . . . drawing back and hearing her sob in shuddering want . . . then *all* of him, *ramming* himself home, eliciting a startled shout as he felt his cap bumping against the sea-bed of her depths, sunk to the root, and she clung to him desperately, legs clasped high around him, ankles crossed on the back of his hips and demanding, quickening his pace. Head and long, glossy hair tossing and turning, she whined and groaned, whimpered, and laid her head on his shoulder for a little time, softly bawling like a newborn calf, a trickle of saliva from her gasping, panting mouth on his skin . . .

"*Je vais jouir!*" Charité cried at last, "I am going . . . aahhh." A baby shriek, a broken, quivering-whimpering sudden sinking away, arms and thighs turning flaccid and limp, though her quim pulsed, squeezed and suctioned like a Chinee finger-puzzle, as if to draw all of him in and keep him secreted forever, and for a few, floating moments of absolute ecstacy, nothing else in the universe existed for him but their groins, his shaft, her gulf. Even the sounds she made, the endearments she grunted, receded, and all he could hear, cared to hear, was the hot, sweet liquid sound of sex before his own moment arrived. A long, inarticulate deep-voiced lion's roar, and he burst so *deep* into her, losing *all* cognizance, a siege-mortar's shell exploding, trails of violent smoke spreading outward, outward behind the red-glowing jutting embers of his passion. And his arriving restored her strength for a few minutes, to clamp damply sweet thighs and arms about him, force-squeeze her belly muscles to match the last upward jerkings he used to tease her, fiercely clinging, kissing, and stroking in pleased reward.

She fell back onto the soft, yielding feather mattress finally, one arm over her eyes to get her breath back, legs wide apart as if to wish him gone from her, but Charité needily moaned in limp protest when he finally shrank away and withdrew. He stripped off his used cundum and clambered up into bed with her, scooped her to him, and pressed his length along hers, gently nestling her close, and both of them all but purring in delight.

"Fantastic," he whispered into her ear, drawing forth her happy chuckles and fondly closer pressing, her head on his chest. "Charité, darlin', you are simply marvelous. So sweet, so handsome . . ."

"I please you?" she asked, almost hesitantly, her head averted, as if fearing he hadn't been.

"Two steps past Saint Peter's gate into Heaven itself," Lewrie truthfully avowed. "You're a little peek of Paradise, *chérie*."

"You do not ask if you . . ." Charité said, sounding small and meek as she turned her head from one cheek to the other to peer up at him.

"Sort of got the, ah . . . impression that I did," Lewrie teasingly muttered back, giving her a warm squeeze, a cozy jounce. She slow-blinked her eyes and nodded her recumbent head, then the most beatific smile slowly blossomed on her face, a longtime, committed lover's expression that told him all. She slid up his body 'til they were face to face, draping herself on him, one sticky-damp thigh slyly insinuated between his as she said, "*Oui, très bon, aussi* . . . you did. You will, *encore*. Or should I go now, and let you sleep?"

"Sweet little dear'un!" Lewrie protested, holding her tighter. "Cundums in London came by the dozen! One down, eleven to go . . . ?"

"Hah!" she cried in bawdy delight, laughing with joy. "You are *that* formidable? Then as our backcountry 'Cadiens say, '*laisser les bons temps rouler*'!"

CHAPTER SEVENTEEN

*A*nd the *"bons temps"* did, far into the night.

Charité entranced him, amazed him with her eagerness, even stunned him a few times with her expertise. One moment she was as sweet, loving, and fond as a blushing new bride, purring like a cat with half-slit sleepy eyes. The next moment she could be as fierce in her ardour at kissing and foreplay as a milkmaid, a Jill, tearing at her Jack with only five minutes to spare in the dairy barn's loft.

And she was *so* skilled at other times, almost suspiciously so; she chuckled, so pleased with herself, like the costliest courtesans who had experienced it all, yet still beguiled with believable eagerness.

She'd start half the fun, shyly "bride-like" one time, then as demanding as a boa constrictor the next. She could slink across the room to fetch something, wine or a washcloth, and taunt him with her nudity, certain of her comeliness and its effect on him.

She'd hike a leg over a chair-back, twine about a bedpost and bare everything, as bawdy as the cheapest jade ready to take six pence for a "knee-trembler" in a dockyard alley. And she must have seen a good collection of "risible artworks" somewhere, good as any his father, Sir Hugo, ever had squirrelled away, for some of the "poses" she struck looked damnably familiar to him! Lewrie reacted, of course, just as he had in his wide-eyed, pubescent days . . . to the detriment of their upstairs maids and serving wenches!

Then there were good old-fashioned Christian fucks with him on top, plunging away like Billy-O, followed by turn-about, with Charité riding St. George atop *him* like a jockey whipping into the last corner at the Newmarket race course. Followed by a return to the side of the bed, ankles crossed behind his *neck*, and squealing like a shoat . . . followed, perhaps finished off, by another turn-about, bent over face-down and her legs thrashing and dangling before him, and her nails clawing at his hips, her teeth gnashing on the bed linens.

"Oh la, Alain, *mon cher amour*," Charité said with a sleepy sigh, spooned with him in the light of a fresh candle, watching his face in the conveniently placed *cheval* mirror. "I am *so* glad you come to New Orleans! To Le Pigeonnier, tonight of all nights . . . What *does* bring you to my city?"

"A dowdy brig with a weedy bottom," he lazily quipped. "Nothin' at all like yours, sweetlin'. Uhmmm . . ." he purred, taking some more fondling strokes of the temptingly yielding aforesaid.

"No, do not tease!" She prettily pouted, making a *moue* at him. "You are British, I think. So many things you say that I do not hear Americans say . . . Is it not dangerous for you, with Britain and Spain at war?"

"Used t' be British, love," Lewrie told her, dredging up his new biography, just in case he was too sated, drink-muzzled, and jaded to make a mistake, even with an intriguing girl with nothing to do with piracy. "Used t' be. But . . . they sort of got tired of *me,* so off I went and turned American. New start."

"You were a . . . criminal, fleeing British law?" Charité posed with a fearful, fretful sound of sudden concern, tossing herself over to face him abruptly.

"No, I'm not outlaw, dear'un," Lewrie assured her with a grin. "I've already faced my court and been sent away. A court-martial, in London. I was in the Royal Navy . . . once. Lieutenant Willoughby, if you can feature it, Commission Sea Officer. God, Crown, and Country . . ."

"Oh la, what happened?" she all but wailed in commiseration.

He fed her the whole fiction, chapter and verse, that Peel had penned for him, that he'd rehearsed with Pollock before coming ashore. Drink made it come out slurred, slow, and believable; weariness after all their sporting made it sound plausible even to his own ears, with just the right touch of tiredness with his *own* life, even bitterness.

Damme, I could've become a Drury Lane actor! he cynically cajoled himself as she seemed to eat it up like plum duff. Especially the part about India and the Far East, the Great South Seas . . .

"How grand!" Charité marvelled. "What fun, to see elephants or tigers, rajahs or even . . . real *pirates!*" She was as excited as a tot on Christmas Day, pounding pillows so she could sit up on the headboard and listen raptly. "You must tell me *everything* of your adventures . . . the next evening we are together. That is," she shied, going miss-ish, and meek, "uh . . . if you *wish* to . . ."

"Oh, aye!" Lewrie swore, "no doubt o' *that*, sweet'un," suddenly engorged with desire to have her again, night after night of heavenly, bawdy bliss. "Truthfully . . . I cannot get enough of you!"

She rewarded that ardour with a soul-kiss, snuggling him down alongside her. After a long, purring moment, she asked, "You had to come back when the war began . . . from the Far East?"

"Aye, but late. Too late for a shipboard commission," Lewrie said, spinning his lie again. He departed from the script, creating a chapter on the fly from his own experiences. "I finally got aboard a perfect *scow* of a Third Rate ship of the line as Fourth Lieutenant . . . fourth out of five, d' ye see? Went to the Mediterranean, worked out of Gibraltar. That's a place t' see, too, *ma chérie!* We took part in the Toulon expedition, in the time of the First Coalition, when the damned Spanish were our allies. I rose to Third Officer, but we sailed home for repairs, and she ended up dropping her bottom in Portsmouth harbour. Too long laid up in ordinary, weeded, wormed, and dry-rotted, so they had to scrap her. That was . . . '95, it was. I thought I'd board another ship, but . . . things didn't work out the way I wished."

He sketched a miserly three months ashore on half-pay between assignments, before being forced to *beg* for employment, the best, and soonest, opening being in the Impress Service! Ashore!

Midshipmen making Lieutenant, if they turned up two hundred "recruits" by Christmas; intercepting merchantmen in Soundings and pressing most of the crew, leaving just enough to work her into port; splitting the seamen's pay with the ships' masters, to boot! Brothel, tavern raids in connivance with publicans and "Mother Abbesses," of inflating *per diem* pay and the rum and ale bought to gull volunteers, lodging costs, and pocketing the difference . . . The bribes from weeping parents, wives, and employers to spring a swept-up man . . .

"And you . . . profited from all that?" Charité asked him, hesitantly, though his tale had lit her merry blue eyes with delight.

"Had to," Lewrie gruffly seemed to admit, " 'cause I needed the money so *perishin'* bad!" he cynically barked, for that was his father's excuse for disowning him and shipping *him* off to sea. "Life ashore costs more than sea duty, and every officer but the titled wealthy are forever in debt, and even a goodly share o' *them!* Everyone else was working a 'fiddle' on the King's money, but *me*, they caught! I never seem t' be able to prosper or hold my luck for long, d' ye see, love."

"How *terrible* for you . . . for your family, *quel dommage!*" she actually sounded *affected* by his fraud. The candle's glint revealed a hint of *moisture* in her eyes, to Lewrie's chagrin.

"No family to shame, really," Lewrie lied. "I was a third son, and we were never that close."

"Poor Alain!" she groaned, hugging him close to her. "And was there ever . . . a young lady whose heart was broken to see you shamed? Were you ever affianced, or . . ." she meekly asked in a wee voice, her head nigh buried in the crook of his shoulder.

"What the money was *for*," Lewrie told her, forcing a credible hitch into his voice. "I *was* wed. Daft thing for a mere Lieutenant t' do. Our Navy thinks married Lieutenants are useless . . . lost to the Service, with their minds half-ashore. But . . . she died."

He blushed tomato-red, covered his chagrin by busying himself at his wineglass; that was a lie most *damnable* to say, as if a word was parent to the *wish;* as if he'd called fickle Fate to heed him and harm Caroline!

"*Mon Dieu*, no! *Pauvre, pauvre* . . . poor, dear man!" she said in a shuddery tone, quivering against him.

"Sweetest, kindest . . . not a rich match, no, but . . . Caroline was my landlord's daughter, when I lodged in Portsmouth," he grunted.

Damn, damn, damn! he chid himself; *Why'd I give her real name? This won't do, it's gettin' too personal! Should've said, "No, never wed," should've said Cheapside, 'stead o' Portsmouth, where I really was with the 'Press! Christ, let's hope she wasn't listenin' all that close . . . or geography's not her strong suit! Else, I'll never put a leg over again. And God help me, I want to!*

"How did it . . ." Charité asked, and he could feel moisture on his shoulder; she was really *weeping* for him! He felt like such a cad, but . . . in for the penny, in for the pound. It was too late to recant.

"She got sick soon after we wed," Lewrie continued, his voice most believably husky, with many a pause to marshall fresh stages in a tale of woe. "All the coal smoke . . . she began to suffer a wracking cough, sometimes spotted her handkerchief . . . We tried an apothecary at first. Then a naval surgeon I knew. He sent us to a proper physician, who sent us to a *London* physician, and it all cost so bloody, bloody much, and . . . nigh onto an hundred pounds, yet she *still* went weaker and paler, wasting away. And carrying our first child as—"

Charité flung herself on him, trembling fingers pressed on his mouth. She kissed him with a fierce, life-giving hunger for almost a whole minute, then sank her head into the small of his neck, *sobbing!*

You mis'rable, fraud bastard! Lewrie scathed himself, glad that she could not see his face. He *wanted* her yet wasn't sure he could look her in the eyes, not after this. His wife, Caroline, *had* sickened once, when he'd been so far away in the Mediterranean, and it had been a near-run thing that she'd lived and, recalling *that,* and his being so estranged from her sweetness now, his own eyes grew moist, but . . . the shudders that took him, that *could* have been mistaken for response to his old grief for a dead wife, were the result of sour *amusement!* At himself, mostly, for being such a charlatan, for being such a *good* liar!

"You stole to save her. Oh, Alain. That is so . . . noble," she said at last, rising on one elbow and swiping her tears. "You were almost . . . ad-mirable!"

"Didn't help, though," Lewrie said, flinging an arm over his eyes as a mask. "I was court-martialed and flung out. Signed aboard a Yankee ship in Falmouth as a mate and got by. But the captain, an idiot, wrecked her off the Cape Fear. Ran her on a shoal they call the Lump, 'twixt Old and New Inlets into Wilmington. I decided to *be* an American . . . New world, new life? . . . and damned if aboard my next ship, as Second Mate, a British frigate didn't stop us and nearly press me 'cause they said my certificate was fraudu-lent? Hah!"

"So, you come on a Yankee ship to New Orleans?" she asked, and he fret-fully caught what sounded hellish-like . . . connivance, gentle, beguiling *probing* in her tone; this made him forget his false tales and perk up and take notice.

"No," he answered, wondering why she sounded so curious about his means of transport. "I came on the *Azucena del Oeste.* She's the Panton, Leslie & Company brig. British-owned, but Spanish-flagged, if you can fea-ture it. They hired me on at Charleston, after I cooled my heels there a few weeks, looking for another ship. Where I washed up when Wilmington had nothing to offer," he quickly stuck in, about to confuse *himself.* "As a new American, I can go inland, up the Mississippi to the Yankee settlements. They talked up the opportunity . . . and this part of the world, like it was the Promised Land. 'Get in on the beginning,' they swore. A little outside my normal line o' work, but for command of river boats now and then, but . . . it *sounded* damn' promising. And . . ." he paused, allowed himself some bashfulness, as if coaxing a shy miss to bed; back on his stride once more. "*Indians* to see . . . hundreds of miles of unspoiled wilderness! I s'pose I like the idea of a . . . a fresh, new *adventure*, and nothing the same, twice! A share of the profits, for my share of the risk, and . . . do I find a parcel of land that suits, well . . . start my own freehold."

"That is what you do for Panton, Leslie, Alain?"

"Filled in as a ship's mate, on the way here. Head up guards for their pack-trains," Lewrie speculated, as if he meant it. "Hoist my own 'broad pendant' someday . . . commodore of the canoes or barges, if their river trade from New Orleans gets that big."

"So . . . you would come back often to New Orleans, *mon cher?*" Charité teasingly asked, her blue eyes merry and beguiling once more. She leaned against him, stroking him with a sleek, soft thigh, breasts pressed against the side of his chest. And Lewrie was delighted that her near-side nipple was beginning to stiffen.

"Now, would you find that so extremely . . . pleasurable?" he teased right back, immensely relieved that they seemed done with his bogus *curriculum vitae* and were back to intimate trifles. He stroked her bare hip, purring to her, his voice deep and inveigling.

"Alain . . ." Charité posed, frowning in thought and coyly biting on her delectable lower lip for a second or two, "New Orleans is going to be a *très* important seaport, no matter how far from the ocean. The American trade up the Great River, what our planters grow . . . not only the cane for sugar, molasses, and rum, but now the rice and cotton, and both so much closer to get than from India or China, *n'est-ce pas?* If our businessmen need to send goods out where they can make profit, other than in *Spanish* ports," she sneered, "we will need ships of our *own*, else the Yankees or Spaniards rob us blind. The, uh . . ."

"The carrying charges, aye," Lewrie said with a nod and a sip of his wine, "the freight. So?"

"Upriver, up and down all the bayous, there are so *many* rich men," Charité slyly enthused, cuddling up to him so she could look him directly in the eyes, "men who would *pay* to have ships of their own to carry their goods, to bring in the fine things they desire, even *from* China or India! They would form the, ah . . . syndicates, *oui?* to create a *fleet* of their own ships. And, those rich men would pay a *capitaine* extremely *well* to manage the nautical details that they do not know . . . *n'est-ce pas, mon amour ami?*"

"What? D' ye mean they'd hire *me* on?" Lewrie laughed, picturing that fantasy. "So I could be an underpaid mate again?"

"*Non*, Alain . . . a *capitaine* of your own ship," Charité cajoled, "The sort of ship our rich men would *pay* you to design and have built, then command! With a share in the profits, perhaps? And later, after the profits grow *very* huge, you command *all* the ships, one of the syndicate *directeurs*. A seat on the board of a firm as important and rich as your old British East India Company, *peut-être?* A seat on the board of a bank . . . a planter with hundreds of *arpents* of land, with the town house and the country mansion, *aussi!* Hundreds of slaves to work your lands and make you even richer, to serve at your every beck and call . . ."

And I'm t'mount you every time you feel an itch, hey? he thought in amusement; *Though, damme . . . it* does *sound tempting!*

Lewrie shammed a far-off, speculating expression, one eyebrow cocked. Was Charité posing a legitimate proposition? Or was it merely a girlish daydream? She could not be much older than nineteen or twenty in his estimation, not that long away from dry tutors and even drier chaperoning nuns, raised as bleakly as most Catholic girls were. Though, she *had* galloped a good distance from whatever tutors and nuns had driven into her, Lewrie cynically thought. And dammit . . .

She was absolutely lovely. From her speech and manners—minus her odd penchants for drinking, card-playing, men's clothing, and fucking notwithstanding—Charité obviously came from good family and ran in rich (though sporting) circles. So . . .

Why ain't she married off and cloistered already? he worried; *That's the way they do it in Popery, ain't it? Get 'em engaged soon as they're fourteen, wed 'em off at seventeen? Damme, why hasn't some beau-nasty put in a bid . . . or does she scare most of 'em off? Black sheep? Blotted her copy book, has she?*

"Now, that'd be, ah . . . that'd show the bloody Royal Navy!" Alan decided to tell her, just to see where it would lead. For *if* someone in New Orleans wanted his own ship, they came much cheaper if *pirated*, and even an innocent interest in a ship of his own might smoak out a seller who'd been involved in stealing ships, and Charité would be the one who might steer him to that seller, that supposed "syndicate" that backed the piracy; and her all unwitting! And in the meantime . . . she'd be his temporary "ride," even if nothing came from it!

Oh, what fun! Lewrie lewdly chortled to himself.

"Captain Alan Willoughby, of the Willoughby Navigation Company! I rather like the sound of that," he exclaimed.

Charité broke out in giggles, gave him a congratulatory embrace, then sat back and took away his wineglass to set on the nightstand on her side of the bed. Lewrie snuggled down in bed, expecting a hug . . .

She spun about and leaped atop him, pinning him to the mattress and his hands to the pillows, shifting demandingly astride of him.

"You have the six *préservatifs* remaining, *mon coeur?*" Charité coo-asked, writhing against his groin, her face and eyes alight with greed. "Ooh, *très bien!*"

"*Laisser les bons temps rouler!*" Lewrie hooted in return.

CHAPTER EIGHTEEN

*M*r. Pollock appeared to be in fine fettle when Lewrie trundled into the eatery he had specified for breakfast. Bright-eyed and bushy-tailed, as some might put it, in point of fact, and bubbling over with *bonhomie* as he untucked his napkin from under his chin and courteously rose to greet him.

"Ah, good morning to you, Mister Willoughby. I trust you slept well? The set of rooms I suggested proved pleasing?" Pollock gushed.

"Barely a wink," Lewrie replied as he dragged back a chair and sat down at the table, smirking, despite his seeming complaint.

"Oh, so sorry," Mr. Pollock said, frowning in concern as he sat down himself. " 'Twas a quiet place when I lodged there. Nothing too disturbing or dangerous, I trust?"

"The company I kept, actually," Lewrie said with a worldly leer.

"*Ahem!*" Pollock shied, primly nigh-appalled. "This will not . . . descend to *common* talk, will it, Mister Willoughby? A gentleman never tells, after all, ah . . . *ahem!* What?"

What a fine *hymn-singer he is!* Lewrie wolfishly thought; *After what my lady concierge told me about him and his "shore wife." Kept her* there, *beforehand! A lovely near-White Octoroon she said! Put* me *to spyin', my man, you'll never know* what *I'll discover!*

"I didn't intend to give you chapter and verse, no," Lewrie said to soothe Pollock. "Most p'culiar, though . . . I wandered into the Pigeon Coop cabaret you mentioned, and there was this most adorable wee fellow . . ."

"Hey, *what?*" Pollock nearly screeched, blanching. *"Ahem?"*

"She was a *girl,* Mister Pollock . . . play-acting in men's togs," Lewrie quickly assured him. "Made sure o' *that!* A full inspection . . . keel to truck. She *said* she was from a proper Creole family here in town . . . out for a stolen night of gambling and fun whilst her folks are in the country. Well-spoken and mannered, obviously educ—"

"Well, I rather doubt *that,* Mister Willoughby," Pollock drawled back, once he'd gotten over his utter shock and no longer looked like he'd dive out the window shutters in disgust; now he was condescending and simpering with superior local lore. "*Proper* young Creole ladies never indulge in such, in such low haunts. *Sons,* however, are expected to, are even encouraged to sloth, indolence, and vice. Daughters, good'uns, might as well be raised to be nuns. No no, sir! I suspect you were spun a merry tale by a cunning bawd who earns a high 'socket fee,' *ahem!* . . . for her ah, novelty," Pollock tut-tutted, blushing.

"Didn't ask for tuppence," Lewrie rejoined quickly, boasting a bit. "Well, a brace of champagnes, and she *did* take me for ten pounds at *Bouré* before we left the cabaret. Intriguin' game, that, but never a word about being for hire. Oddest, most intriguing girl, too . . ."

Pollock winced, as if Lewrie *would* descend to Billingsgate smut to describe his evening, but was saved by the waiter's arrival. A cup and saucer was placed before Lewrie without asking, and a stout coffee was poured. "The omelettes are quite good here," Pollock said instead.

"French style . . . piss-runny and underdone?" Lewrie scoffed.

"A Catalan Spaniard owns the place, so they're properly done," Pollock advised. "Quite succulent with their ham or bacon." To which suggestion Lewrie took heed and placed a hearty four-egg order.

His coffee was stout and strong, the best ever passed his lips, but with an odd, bitter aftertaste, a tang that put Lewrie in mind of the ink-black council brew the Muskogee Indians inaptly termed "White Drink" that caused copious perspiring, pissing, and purifying puking.

"South American or Mexican coffee beans, hereabouts," Pollock explained, "though I do prefer the Turk or Arabica. The climate and soil in Louisiana is much too damp for coffee, and sometimes subject to frost. With the war on, the locals eke out their imports with the local equivalent, chicory. Tasty, once you develop a palate to it. With sugar and cream. Lots of cream, I'd advise, which makes what the French call a *café au lait.*"

"Hmmm . . . better," Lewrie agreed, after a liberal admixture and a second taste. A smallish platter of little crescent-shaped sugared rolls sat between them, on which Pollock had been snacking before his own breakfast arrived, and Lewrie tasted one . . . or two or three. A French breakfast, he'd found in his Mediterranean travels, always did lean towards a lot of breads.

"Towards the end, the girl seemed quite taken with me," Lewrie continued his tale, in a confidential voice.

"Indeed," Mr. Pollock frostily commented. *"Ahem?"*

"She mentioned the possibility that ex-Lieutenant Willoughby, RN, might make his fortune as captain of a New Orleans–owned merchant ship, maybe even end up master of an entire fleet of merchantmen, did I play my cards right. All sorts of hints that their new crops of rice and cotton are the coming thing, and that she was on good terms of *some* sort with a fair number of the rich and powerful who'd fund the ships I'd design, or go survey and buy for 'em. Damme, but these . . . whatevers are good!"

"She did, did she?" Pollock mused aloud, perking up and giving at least one ear to Lewrie's tale. "Well, well . . . oh, but that might have been but wee-hours 'pillow talk,'" he piffled a moment later as he tore one of those little rolls in two, stared at both bites, as if unable to decide which to swallow first, and mulled all that over.

"Not the sort of offer one hears from a common trull, don't ye know," Lewrie pointed out. "Usually, the well-pleased strumpets hint at 'going under the protection' of the lout, is he a gentleman of any means . . . or making him her bully-buck and pimp for a cut of the profits t' keep her safe on the streets. Lurk near her rooms . . ."

"Indeed." Pollock icily glared at him.

"Well . . . or so I've heard," Lewrie replied, shifty-eyed, making a throat-clearing "Ahem" of his own before furthering his point. "The way she suggested it, her understanding of syndicates and such, and her air of . . . actual *gentility* was what convinced me that it might be—"

"Dressed in men's attire, I b'lieve you said she was?" Pollock interrupted.

"Aye, and with a false mustachio pasted on her upper lip, too," Lewrie sulkily insisted.

"Well, surely . . . *ahem!*" Pollock brightened, bestowing upon his breakfast partner an almost pitiable look, "a girl out on the town who dresses so . . . perhaps well-raised *once*, as you described, I grant you . . . might delight in spinning phantasms about herself, about what she could *do* for you. Telling you everything or anything she thought you wished to hear once she'd sounded you out. Either for your monetary support and, uh . . . protection later on, or . . . scalping you for ten pounds, or fourty Spanish dollars, was her night's earnings. Anything she dreamt up afterward was moonbeams, and you her, ah . . . pleasurable, but unwitting, baa-lamb, Lew . . . Willoughby."

"Well, now really!" Lewrie objected, though not too strongly. There *was* a sordid possibility that he'd been gulled. God knows, it wouldn't have been the first time! He crossed his arms and grumped.

"And was this after you fed her your, ah . . . alias?"

"Aye," Lewrie replied, tight-lipped.

"And did she supply one of her own?" Pollock asked, nigh leering.

"Charité Bonsecours, she said she was," Lewrie told him. "And in the course of our card game, she introduced me to a pair of brothers by name of Darbone, who sat in with us."

"Oh, sir," Pollock commiserated with a world-weary shake of his head. "She was their handmaiden most-like! An attractive lure to get you bedazzled, off your guard, and skinned by a pair of sharps!"

"They barely won five silver dollars each off me, ten at most," Lewrie countered, "and they *each* bought a fresh bottle of champagne to keep the game going, 'cause . . . well, I got the impression as we were intent on leaving for my rooms that . . . they seemed more jealous than disappointed. *And,* sir! If she was their man-trap, why wasn't she in a revealing, gauzy gown, with her poonts hangin' out? Why suited, booted, and damn-near spurred?"

"I know of the Darbones, though I cannot recall . . ." Mr. Pollock deeply frowned, almost chewed on a thumbnail. "I know most of the established Creole families, if just in passing. What were their names?"

"One was Baltasar, t'other, ah . . . Claude," Lewrie dredged up at last. "They were all fair-haired, chestnut-ey, I'd say, and blue eyed. In fact, they all three bore a striking resemblance to each other."

"Oh, half the Creoles in Louisiana fit that description," Mr. Pollock pooh-poohed. "They all marry their distinguished cousins."

"So one of the Darbone brothers said, about the resemblance . . . nothing about the cross-eyed cousins part," Lewrie replied. "She was a very fetching girl, most . . ."

"Hmmm . . . pity you were not intrigued enough to follow her home and get to the bottom of the matter," Pollock grumpily commented.

"By cock-crow, 'twas all I could do to hand her down the stairs to the door!" Lewrie countered with a smug look. "Had an old captain, said whenever he made a grand night of it ashore, by the time he'd come back aboard, he hadn't had a wink, and one more passionate kiss, or a cold breakfast, would've killed him!"

"And one had hopes you *wouldn't* boast, *ahem,*" Pollock despaired with a heavy sigh. "Still . . . Charité Bonsecours, didje say? Hmmm, how old? Under twenty, or about twenty, ah-ha. I can't say that I am able to place her, though French Creole families don't trot their females out, in the main. Not *quite* as bad as Hindoo purdah, but . . ."

"Well, perhaps your wife, being a local lady, might know 'em," Lewrie offhandedly suggested, slyly watching Pollock's reaction.

"My *wife!*" Pollock instantly bristled. "How did you—"

"My *concierge,* your former landlady, told me she took the young lady you boarded with as your *épouse,*" Lewrie said, intrigued, and wondering what it was he'd said to nettle the man.

"Yes, well . . . *ahem,*" Pollock said, strangling, purpling, and tugging at his neck-stock. "My wife, of course."

"Once we've eat, shouldn't we call on her to ask what she knows about the Bonsecours and the Darbones?" Lewrie coyly hinted, his mien as seemingly guileless as the densest, most uninterested cully.

"I doubt there's need of that, Mister Willoughby," he snipped back, as if scandalised by the suggestion. "Colette is, ah . . . *ahem!* indisposed."

She that *ugly?* Lewrie maliciously thought; *Is he ashamed about her, 'cause she's not lily-white or he's proper-married somewhere? I just have t'clap eyes on her 'fore we leave New Orleans!*

"Wouldn't it be worth it to run this Charité Bonsecours to her lodgings, then?" Lewrie suggested, "to see if she knows what she was boasting about? If I posed ready to bolt your employment and enter theirs, it might lead to the ones who back our pirates. I might even get hired to be a pirate captain myself!"

"I s'pose we could . . ." Pollock somberly mused. "It might not cause *too* much harm. Could you dissemble well enough. Ah, breakfast!" he cried, instead, glad for the interruption.

Middling large platters were slid before them, holding omelettes as big as roof shingles, oozing cheese and done to a perfect firm turn, laced with bits of red onion and bell pepper. Each platter bore slabs of ham as large-about as ox hooves, half an inch thick. A woven straw basket of piping-hot *croissants* arrived, too, a fist-sized ball of soft and sweating fresh, salted butter, and an array of local preserves.

"Tasty," Pollock enthused over each ravishing bite, "and all for a song, don't ye know. You'll not find *this* in an English four-penny ordinary . . . which is the equivalent cost, here. I've come to love New Orleans . . . though not its summer climate. Or its current owners," he muttered from the side of his mouth.

"I expect it'd be much cleaner, were someone other than the Dons in charge," Lewrie said, snickering. "Put in gutters or something . . . shovel up the horse dung, hire indigents to sweep the garbage into the river, at least. Town drains . . . gurgle, gurgle, gurgle!"

"We'll not talk of *that*," Pollock warned in a faint whisper.

"Dung and garbage?" Lewrie twinklingly quipped. "Why not?"

"The, ah . . . change of ownership, *ahem*," Pollock hissed, leaning closer in the act of reaching for the salt cellar.

"Oh," an only slightly chastened Lewrie replied.

"As for our *other* matter, sir," Pollock continued to mutter. "Both Lanxade and Balfa have been seen in New Orleans within the past two days. Done up in new finery . . . Balfa in shoes and stockings, for a rare once, and shopping like an unexpected heir. You ride well, do you, Mister Willoughby?" Pollock suddenly queried, putting Lewrie off his stride with the question.

"Hmm? Aye, main-well, in point of fact," Lewrie answered, at a loss. "We plan to gallop out to their secret 'rondy' and scrag 'em in broad daylight?"

"Their present whereabouts are unknown to me, their *exact* location," Pollock said, shying back again by Lewrie's aggressive air. "I merely suggest that we go for a long ride today. You're new here . . . I, as your putative employer, must show you the sights, orient you to the city," Pollock explained, buttering a roll. "It may be that whilst gadding about, we either spot them and their lair, or make discrete enquiries *of* them. *I'll* do that part, I'm known, and, ah . . . harmless, ha! In the course of things, we could also survey Lake Pontchartrain, what the lay of the land looks like to you."

Well, I wasn't going to draw sword, yell 'Yoicks, Tally Ho,' and charge at the first sight *of 'em!* Lewrie told himself; *I ain't a total* fool. *A passin'-fair fool at times, but . . .*

"Are we not successful today, we could ride tomorrow as well, does the weather turn off fair," Pollock suggested, louder this time, as if nattering with a new employee for real, playing the genial host to a brand-new city. "Out east, there's still land going begging, if you can believe it. We'll take a good look at it, shall we?"

We find Lanxade and Balfa, though, we whistle up my sailors for a 'boarding action' and leave 'em bleedin' on the cobbles like steers in a Wapping slaughterhouse, Lewrie grimly decided to himself, steeling himself to action; *Aye, let's be at it. And that other nonsense.*

CHAPTER NINETEEN

*S*hameless!" Helio de Guilleri spat, still seething after what she'd done; *had* been seething since she and that lout, a common sailor, a despicable Englishman, had left the Pigeon Coop hours before.

"Do quit stomping about, *cher*," Charité lazily scolded, covering another weary yawn, "or Madame D'Ablemont below us will be angry and send the *concierge* after you. I told both of you that someone had to sound him out, to see if he was dangerous to us. And I did," she concluded, with a well-hidden, secretly pleased grin.

"Oh, *please!*" Helio snapped, angry enough to want to seize her and deliver a good shaking. "You debased yourself!"

Charité paused over her light breakfast of melon, strawberries, and rolls, fixing him with an imperious glare, one elegant brow cocked in vexation. "If my good name, and our family's, worries you so much, *mon frère*, why is it only *now* that you deplore my nighttime prowlings, when you were more than aware of my nature before?"

"*Nom d'un chien*, Charité!" Helio barked. "The man is a lowly, a common . . . Anglo-Saxon. An *Anglais*! A *Protestant Anglais!*"

"Ah!" Charité responded, as if her brother had announced a revelation. "So . . . I am only to 'play' with dashing and proper Creoles of good family, *cher*? Is that what you demand? I am *always* the soul of caution and discretion, and so I was with him. Besides, he believes I am a Bonsecour, so no gossip will touch the de Guilleris."

She switched from a frostily arch coo of annoyance to a twinkly merriment the next moment. "I had the courage and skill, and the allure of my sex, to beard him when *you* never could, and I think him harmless to us. Alain Weelooby," she said, butchering the name, "*was* a British Navy officer, but he was court-martialed and found guilty of theft, in their Impress Service, now a mere hired hand with Panton, Leslie. He is a widower, an embittered life-long failure, just scraping by, though he dreams of making a fortune at last in the Americas," she told them, outlining all she had learned from him in the wee hours. It was almost hilarious to her to see the stricken looks on her brothers' faces as she laid out his bleak biography.

"He will go north on the river, leading his company's *shalopes,* or help guard their pack-trains," Charité blithely informed them. "He has *read* all about the 'Noble Savages,' the Indians, and is panting to *see* them! The usual printed lies, and *Monsieur* Rousseau's idiocy," she sneered between sips of *café au lait.*

"So he *says,*" younger brother Hippolyte objected, a skeptical frown on his face. "But, what is an *Anglais* Navy officer doing here, just months after we took one of their prize ships? It doesn't sound like coincidence to me! Panton, Leslie is said to have ties to the British government, even if the Spanish let them come and go as they please. Everyone knows that. They *might* have sent a clever *spy.*"

"*Cher* Hippolyte," Charité replied with barely patient scorn in her voice. "What sort of man steals from his own Navy? Is that their idea of a trustworthy spy . . . a thief stupid enough to be caught out? Would they even trust such a man with expense money for his espionage, lest he drink it up or abscond with it? If the British *do* send a spy to New Orleans, I think they would choose someone more . . . upstanding. I believe him," she stated, dismissing their qualms. "His arrival *is* coincidence . . . and he is harmless. And malleable." She chuckled.

Charité nibbled on a melon slice whilst her male relations sulkily dithered. Men, she had found, were hopelessly easy to manipulate. Her new Alain might be even easier than *most* . . . though he was a sweet, gentle, but hungry *amour;* rather endearing and impressive in his own fashion, she happily recalled. But a man, one too easily distracted by his sensual side, his greed, to ever be a real success at anything; so easily led by his *verge* wherever she wished.

Yet he did possess nautical knowledge and skills, she thought. Alain was an experienced fighting officer, hard-handed . . . Oh, but how those hard hands delighted! Could she lead him, one cautious step at a time, into their service, Charité found herself fantasising? He *could* be just venal *enough*. With piles of loot, gold, and . . . *her* as his reward, which way would he jump?

Charité had planned to go right to bed after a cool bath and a restorative light breakfast, yet here it was well past eight o'clock in the morning, and Helio and Hippolyte were still intent on belabouring her daring, her long, shameful absence.

She'd always thought it so unfair that *they* were allowed to rut like yowling tomcats, to strut, preen, and stagger, but *she* had to be cloistered with sewing, music, lessons in grace and wit, and those few books her house would claim? When younger, she'd been the apple of her father's eye and had been allowed to learn riding, fishing, and sword-play . . . as Papa's condescending *jape*, his amusing girl toy, with never a thought that she might *enjoy* such things. She was crushed when, on her thirteenth birthday, Maman had demanded she be corseted, straitened, and reined in, and Papa had so easily agreed that "playtime" was over, and she must become just another limp, pretty, *useless* . . . young lady!

As for her brothers' worry about her *amours!* Despite the pious claims of Society, the bishop and priests, the severe Ursuline nuns, and city fathers, Charité could count the real virgins among her contemporaries on one hand. As for those already showing when led to the altar, *pah!*

Once inside their family's city *maison*, Charité had deftly deflected their sullen anger with a concocted tale of fearing she'd been followed home by some determined skulker, even if she'd had the foggy street to herself. She'd hooted with glee to see them clatter off in high dudgeon, swords and pistols at the ready.

By the time they'd clomped back upstairs, having discovered not one whit of her skulker, she'd just been emerging from her bath, which kept them redfaced and at bay 'til she'd taken her own sweet dawdling time getting patted dry, have her hair dried and combed by her maid. She took even more time in choosing a gauzy morning ensemble sure to scandalise them by its sheerness.

Charité knew that she was being unspeakably cruel to them . . . but damned if they didn't deserve it for being so hypocritically censorous and scolding!

"It might have been that *Anglais* you spent . . ." Helio grumbled, censoring himself to *name* what she'd been doing so bluntly. "Or one of his men."

"It was not my Alain," Charité sweetly whey-face lied.

"We saw that American, El-isson, walking towards his lodgings," Hippolyte pointed out. "He might have been coming from our street."

"I know what he looks like, and it was not him," Charité said, daintily nibbling on a buttered and jammed *croissant*. "Besides, what would the Americans care of my doings . . . *our* doings? Are they not in competition with Panton, Leslie? If the new-come Americans are spies, I would think they were only keeping an eye on *Alain*."

"Well . . ."

"Think, *mes frères*," Charité insisted, abandoning her breakfast for a moment to look them in the eyes. "The Americans scheme to seize Louisiana, and our dear city. If they suspect that Panton, Leslie is helping the British do the same—you *said* everyone knows that, but for our dim Spanish masters, it seems!—then the Americans keep an eye on *them*. My Alain is a strange, new face, leading a band of hard men. To expand their trade advantage, or to scout for an invasion?"

"But *someone* followed you!" Hippolyte insisted.

"Mere curiosity," Charité dismissed, covering her guilt over her lie by busying herself pouring a fresh cup of coffee. "Would *you* not be curious to see Alain with an elegant young *man* who becomes a *girl* at dawn? Was I Armand the *raconteur* or Charité, *n'est-ce pas?*"

"Stop calling him Alain . . . *your* Alain!" Helio shouted.

"Why not, Helio?" she asked with a half-lidded leer, "when we are on such intimate—"

"Gahh! You're immoral, brazen!"

"It runs in our blood," Charité shot back, shutting Helio down, for she'd touched a sore spot on their family's escutcheon. Papa was a devilishly handsome, distinguished-looking *roué* who enjoyed *amours* in every quarter, reputedly even comely house slaves. Their elegant Maman, perhaps in spite, spent *protracted* visits on nearby plantings, ostensibly on a round of "good works" with the poor, but . . . And Helio and Hippolyte, cousin Jean-Marie, even that hopeful grandee Don Rubio, they were all of a piece!

"Let us be honest about our forebears," Charité soberly intoned. "Our men were never bold Christian adventurer *chevaliers* obeying King Louis to conquer these lands. Our womenfolk weren't virtuous, virginal bourgeois *filles à la cassette*, come straight from a convent in France to the Ursulines convent here."

"Charité!" Hippolyte exclaimed, all but covering his ears.

"No sweet little 'casket girls,' with their dowry trunk direct from the King for their goodness," Charité scoffed. "Oh là, never the street whores swept up to be auctioned off as wives. *Never* dregs from prisons . . . excess *peasant* girls turfed off the estates of the great, heavens no!"

"You are so scandalous, so . . ." Helio spluttered.

"We may be richer, but no better," Charité remorselessly continued. "Louisiana then, as now, is still *sans religion, sans justice . . . sans discipline, sans ordre, et sans police. Sans moralité,* too, the lot of us. And nothing the hated Spanish, the Americans if they take us over, or the *British* will ever be able to change our Creole soul. No matter how long they hold us in bondage."

"If that's so, Charité," Hippolyte gently asked, near a broken heart, "then what is the point of our hoped-for rebellion, if we free ourselves from Spain, yet remain so . . . if we reunited with beloved France, but—"

"Oh, Hippolyte!" Charité laughed, worldly-wise for her tender years, and rising to go to him and take his hands in hers. "We will be *free* to be French again. Free to take *joy* in being *sans moralité* . . . of being ourselves . . . Creoles. Then, *laisser les bons temps rouler,* and to *hell* with rest of the world!"

"Even so," Helio, the far more practical brother, said. "You must not see . . . your Alain again," he somberly decreed, playing the role of *pater familias* in their papa's absence. "Even if he doesn't spy on us, he's drawn the *Americans'* attention, and sooner or later he'll draw the Spaniards'. Our cause, our movement must grow in secret 'til we're strong, well armed, and ready to strike. We can't afford the risk of exposure."

"I told you, Helio, he thinks I'm a Bonsecour," Charité calmly explained, though chafing at being *told* what to do. "He only knows you two as the Darbone brothers. He has no way to find me, or either of you."

"He could spot you, one of us in the markets, and follow one of us here," Helio fretted. "Anyone he asked could steer him right!"

"Then I will cut him off as a *passing* amusement," Charité was quick to rebuff. "Alain aspired once to be a British officer, one of the gentlemanly class. And we know how mannerly and reticent *les Anglais* are, *n'est-ce pas?*" she said, chuckling. "They do not press themselves where they are not wanted. I snub him in public, deliver a 'cut-sublime,' it would tell him that I am . . . unattainable. Does he find our address, I do *not* have to answer his notes. One from me to him at his lodgings, saying that I am affianced and never to be his, well . . . he *had* his one glorious night, like a footman with a great lady," Charité affected to sneer, though her heart was not in it, "and he'll know he is much too lowly to ever aspire to—"

"Then do it," Helio demanded.

"Only if he becomes tedious," Charité snapped, whirling back to her breakfast table to sit down and spoon sugar into her coffee, pour fresh cream, and stir. She saw that that seemed to satisfy them.

"Though lowly footmen have their uses," she could not help suggesting, twiddling one foot under the table in anxiety.

"What?"

"He is a trained naval officer, or was once. Alain might come cheaper than *Capitaine* Lanxade, or that buffoon Balfa," she schemed aloud, making it up as she went along. Unwilling to be ordered about, certainly; to give up a pleasureable relationship just because Helio *said* to. Averse, too, because Alain Weelooby (however one *said* that!) had amused her, gratified her . . . touched her heart, and she doubted if she *wished* to give him up, unless her brothers' fears were proven.

"*Non non, mon Dieu, non!*" Helio erupted, squawking like a jay. "What are you *thinking?* If the British didn't trust him, why should we?"

"He has no love for Creole freedom, for us, Charité!" younger brother Hippolyte chimed in, in similar screechy takings. "He'd sell us out in a heartbeat. He might *be* a spy. What a horrid idea!"

"We're in more danger of being sold out by faint-heart *Creoles*, Hippolyte," Charité pointed out. "Both of you are illogical. Alain is a spy, or he is not. He is trustworthy, or he is not. He may be useful, or he is not. The only way to discover if he's a danger to us is for me to continue seeing him, sounding him out. You cannot argue both ways," she said, as if the subject was resettled.

"Whether this . . . Weelooby creature is a British agent or not," Helio gravelled, disgruntled at his sister's refusal to obey his dictates, "perhaps it would be best if we *all* avoided any involvement with him, before he discovers we're not the Darbone brothers, or that you, sister, aren't Charité Bonsecours, and he becomes suspicious . . . "

"Even if Alain is really harmless?" Charité asked, smirking over the rim of her coffee cup.

"*Capitaine* Lanxade has paid our crew from our last cruise, but he *said* they could spend it in a week and drift away from us without a good chance for more," Helio reminded them. "If we left town, went back to sea on another raiding cruise, made another pile of money . . . "

"Yes, we could!" Hippolyte enthused, suddenly in better fettle. "If agents look for us here, we could fool them and be where they cannot find us. The Gulf of Mexico is a very big place."

"Before poor Jean loses all his booty money at *Bouré*," brother Helio snickered. "Even if the cruise is fruitless, by the time we get back, *M'sieur* Bistineau and old Maurepas will have the prize ship sold and there'll be *something* to show for it!"

"And we can set Aristotle and the other boys to keep an eye on Alain and his party," Charité chimed in. "If he goes upriver or inland with trade goods, doesn't linger in New Orleans and ask after us, then he's harmless. Will *that* satisfy your worries, Helio . . . Hippolyte?"

"Mmm," her brothers grudgingly allowed.

"*Bon!*" Charité chirped. "Then I can continue seeing him after we return. And if we're to leave town, I must give him a reason why. After all, a mysterious, sudden disappearance might spur him to ask too many questions. No, think of it!" she insisted, to their sudden querulous expressions. "If I must go upcountry to the family plantations to . . . comfort my sick *grand-mère,* and you two 'Darbones' must tend to farm business or take a hunting trip, a *harmless* Alain will accept the tale and make no enquiries, you see?"

They may not have liked it, but they could see the sense of it. Charité, both sated and pleased with their surrender, dabbed her lips with her napkin and rose from the table, secretly thrilled to have one more meeting with her entrancing, yet possibly dangerous, Englishman.

"Oh là, dear brothers, but I am going to bed," she said, rising. "If you wish to scheme or plot . . . or continue to complain about me . . . then do it quietly. In one of your thoroughly masculine coffeehouses, *peut-être. Bonsoir, chers . . . bonjour,* rather.

"And don't clatter going down the stairs," she added, swirling at her bedchamber door to face them for a moment. "Your chase after my pursuer has already upset poor Madame D'Ablemont once this morning."

"Better safe than sorry," Helio said in a harsh whisper as they gathered up their stylish hats, canes, and gloves to go out for coffee and their own breakfasts. "What did the old buccaneers say . . . 'Dead men tell no tales'? Not a word to Charité about it, but . . . before we sail, I think we should eliminate this pesky *Anglais.* That American, El-isson, too. He was too winded and too hurried, like he *had* followed her, when we saw him. What do *you* think, Hippolyte?"

"Both at once," his brother casually, happily agreed. "We get Rubio and Jean to help. They're both excellent shots. And Rubio will love it. *Oui. Bon.* Let's kill them!"

CHAPTER TWENTY

Another day, another guided tour, Lewrie thought.

They'd not found Lanxade or Balfa; indeed, they'd been rumoured to have departed New Orleans for parts unknown. Even with Toby Jugg, the only witness they'd dared bring along on the expedition, wandering the port on his own for days on end, they'd not turned up one familiar face from the pirate ship's crew—or recognised a single one of the elegant young sprogs on the buccaneer schooner's deck the morning that Lewrie's prize-ship crew had been marooned.

So this morning involved "that other nonsense" that Lewrie and Pollock were charged to perform, and frankly, though Lewrie thought it a bootless endeavour, he had to admit that it was *pleasureable* work.

The morning was slightly overcast, but balmy. There was a faint breeze that felt refreshing, and it was not mosquito season, though a goodly tribe of flies were present round their horses.

He'd been shown the Cabildo and the cathedral their first days on foot, strolled the streets and pretended to shop . . . round the fort guarding the town centre and the levees, out Rue de l'Arsenal to the garrison barracks and the storehouses to count Spanish noses one day; rode to Lake Pontchartrain's shore through the reclaimed marshes that were now greengrocer produce plots to sniff round decrepit Fort Saint John, and the reeky Bayou St. John that threaded right into the city.

This morning Pollock suggested a brisk canter out to the east, along the

Chef Menteur road towards Lake Borgne, across the Plain of Gentilly, near Bayou Bienvenu, with a promised *alfresco* dinner at the end of it. Lewrie was a good horseman, but it had been a while since he'd spent *that* much time astride. In point of fact, his thighs were chafing, and his bottom was stiff and sore!

"Damme, Mister Pollock, I didn't think you meant to emulate Alexander's march into Persia!" he griped at last, trying to rub his ass.

"Almost there, no worries," Pollock gaily replied.

"Almost where, the middle of another swamp?" Lewrie carped, as Pollock checked his horse to a slow walk from a canter in the shade of a tall cypress grove.

"What do you make of the country hereabouts, sir?" Pollock asked.

"Well, it's green, frankly," Lewrie said with a scowl as he cast his gaze about. "Hellish lot o' trees, and such. All these fields . . . the usual marshy sponges, I s'pose, 'neath the prairie grass?"

"Quaking prairie, such as we've seen before? No. Not quite," his guide told him, sounding a tad pleased with himself. "Take note of the *variety* of the grasses, the sandier nature of the soil. Oh, rainy season will turn the sand and clay into a perfect quagmire, but in the winter, or a warm and dry springtime, it's . . . passable. Grazeable."

Lewrie took note that their horses' hooves left fairly shallow prints and didn't throw up *much* mud, except for the lower places . . . but they'd crossed a *fair* number of rivulets and seeps.

"Not much quicksand out here, either, sir," Pollock mused.

"Nor much market for it, either, I'd expect," Lewrie quipped. "Bad for egg timers and watch-glasses, hey?"

"The bulk of the grasses here, Mister Willoughby," Mr. Pollock irritatedly explained, "are not *marsh* grasses, like those round rills and along the bayou channel. They're *dry-land* grasses. If the soil along Lake Pontchartrain won't support troops, artillery, or waggons, do you not think that this terrain might be more practicable? Please leave off your japing and take a good look, I conjure you!"

"Well, aye, I s'pose the land here is higher and dryer," Lewrie allowed, dismounting and squatting to dig up a handful to crumble in his hands, wondering again why anyone in his right mind would send a *sailor* on a chore like this, instead of a soldier . . . or a farmer! He was, at best, a "gentleman-farmer" on his rented acres in Surrey, one who might "raise his hat" but little else. That was his wife's bailiwick, what her experience and knowledge from an agricultural childhood in North Carolina had taught her; what their

hired estate manager and day labourers tended to without Lewrie having to
do much beyond shout encouragement, heartily agree like the Vicar of Bray,
then toddle down to the Olde Ploughman tavern for an ale.

"Firm enough to support . . . things, perhaps?" Pollock hinted.

"Aye, I think it *might* be," Lewrie dumbly agreed.

"Mount up, then, and we'll ride on to the end of the road and have our
meal," Pollock suggested, pleased with Lewrie's opinion.

"Bring any liniment?" Lewrie asked with a grin, taking time to massage
his buttocks, with the reins in his hands.

"Sorry, no . . . Said you were a horseman." Pollock snickered.

They dismounted and spread a groundcloth at the end of the Chef Menteur
road, on a sandy, beach-dune hillock on the western shore of Lake Borgne.
A vast expanse of open water—seawater—stretched out before them to the
south and southeast, the lake's horizon mostly limitless, except for due east,
where, cross a fairly narrow channel or river, the swamps began again and
made a vast, reedy, and marshy island that blocked the view; here and speckled with a few straggling groves of scrub trees.

Once the horses had been hobbled and let to graze, once they'd been led
to fresh water to drink, Pollock did provide a decent spread, Lewrie had to
allow. There were crusty, fresh *baguettes,* mustard and butter in small stone
jars, and pickles in another. A choice of roast beef or ham was wrapped in
one cloth, and several pieces of crispily breaded and fried chicken were
wrapped in another. A glass apothecary jar contained cold, cooked beans in
oil and vinegar, and there were two bottles of imported hock. Pewter plates
and utensils, spare chequered napkins, and proper wineglasses . . . Pollock
had seen to everything.

Another thing Lewrie had to admit to himself as he concocted a thick,
meaty sandwich (or was it, as his cabin-servant, Aspinall, had cheekily
termed it, a "Shrewsbury," for the *real* lord who'd first built one at an all-
night gaming table?) and took a bite: risky though this expedition might be,
he was actually beginning to enjoy it!

A night or two in a comfy shore bed, with fine coffee or hot chocolate delivered to his bedside by one of his *pension*'s servants; of sleeping lubberly,
civilian "All-Night-Ins" with no emergencies to summon him on deck; and
a myriad of coffeehouses, cabarets, wine bars, or eating places from which
to choose had seduced him utterly. And the victuals, the viands, the delicious
variety, all but a few low dives preparing piquant, unforgettable dishes, ah!

And Charité Bonsecours and her enthusiastic *amour* to savour . . . to contemplate another bout after the first and *second*, well! He was, but for a troop of nubile and nude nymphs feeding him ambrosia . . . or grapes . . . in the fabled Lotus Eater's Paradise!

"Out to the Nor'east, yonder, is Cat Island," Mr. Pollock intruded, rattling out the folds of his inevitable chart to lay between them as they dined. "Between Cat Island and the mainland is the inlet they call Pass Maria, ah . . . here, *ahem.*" Pollock indicated with a forefinger, which left a dab of mustard on Lake Borgne. "There is deep water on the seaward side, you see. Near to Ship Island, as well. This swampy island before us, t'other side of this channel, has a fort at the north end, Fort Coquilles, to control the pass into Lake Pontchartrain, but . . . there's nothing to guard against ships entering Lake Borgne . . . coming right to the shore on which we sit, Willoughby! In your valued opinion, could Fort Coquilles prevent a landing here?"

"What calibre are their guns?" Lewrie asked, measuring distance 'twixt thumb and forefinger, and laying them on the chart's scale. It was a full five miles from the fort to the channel mouth.

"I've heard boasts that they're twenty-four-pounders," Pollock supplied. "Ships' guns, on naval carriages."

"They'd not have a hope in Hell," Lewrie told him, sure enough of artillery, one of his chiefest delights since his first experience of a broadside on the old *Ariadne*. "No mortars? No big'uns?"

"Only light Coehorn mortars on the landward walls, I have discovered, over the years," Pollock guardedly declared. "Our Spaniards are a boastful lot when shopping. Do you use my telescope, you can almost make out the fort to the north and east of us. It's placed on firm ground, so I'm told, at this island's tip. The Pass, the lakes, are too shallow for deep-draught ships, so I suppose the fort was set in place to counter *small* vessels and gunboats from getting past it."

"Could I get some bomb-ketches in here, within three miles of the place . . . shallow, improvised bombs up this channel a little way, with ten-inch sea mortars, I could pound it into ruin," Lewrie stated, standing and peering through the borrowed telescope. "Buoyed up with 'camels' to either beam, to get 'em up this slough. Wood-based light Coehorn mortars in launches and pinnaces to sail right up the island's west side, *that'd* keep their heads down and their buttocks clenched!" he hooted in anticipatory mirth. "Two . . . three combined companies of Marines from off a few ships of the line could go with the small boats and assault it from the rear. Landward walls of a *sea* fort aren't designed against a strong assault." He lowered the glass and looked down at the channel.

"Though I don't much care for the current. Looks fast to me," he said, frowning at the eddies, swirls, and bent-over reeds. "Take a slack tide, and how long *that'd* last . . . else the mortar boats could not breast the tides under sail, and rowing'd be sheer buggery. Make less than a mile an hour, slower than a man could walk it."

"Or Fort Coquilles could be ignored, if it can't reach to this shore with its guns," Mr. Pollock mused as Lewrie sat back down, handing him the glass to stow away. "Then . . . in your professional opinion, could a large force be landed here? Where we now sit? It's not over thirteen miles from here to New Orleans, over a fairly good road, too. Mister Peel, being a cavalryman at one time, suggested that this might prove the best route, when we talked before leaving Kingston."

"Beats sailing an hundred miles up the Mississippi River from the Gulf," Lewrie cautiously allowed, "or God knows *how* far down from from Canada, aye. How *large* a force could be landed here, though . . . " Lewrie mused, shrugging. He fixed Pollock with a sharp, leery eye and grinned. "And did Mister Peel drop a few hints, hey, Mister Pollock, as to what he thought the size of the force required could be?"

"Well, *ahem!* . . . he did mention a squadron of horse, merely in passing, d'ye see," Pollock responded.

"Oh, I'm sure he did!" Lewrie said, laughing. "Old habits die hard. *Tarra-tarra* . . . 'draw sabres and charge'! Peel, no matter his influence in London or Kingston, no matter his knowledge of any secret plans already drawn, Mister Pollock, ain't a sailor. He and his Army contacts see the problem from this hillock inland, with nary a worry 'bout how they're t'be *gotten* here. He really should've chosen an infantry officer in disguise for this part of our mission, not me."

"Mister Peel, ah . . ." Pollock hesitantly explained, "said that the crux of the matter *was* the getting ashore, and that you, sir, had the wits to solve it, or, *ahem!* . . . Scotch it, should it not prove to be practical."

"Mine arse on a band-box! Peel said *that*?" Lewrie gawped. "It is news t'me that . . . hmm. Well, well!"

And all this time Peel's good as told me I'm an idiot! Lewrie thought; *A useful idiot, now an' again, but . . . hmm, well, well!*

"Horse transports are even rarer than hens' teeth, sir," Lewrie laid out to his guide, suddenly in much better takings, even finding professional delight in sketching out a plan on the chart. "I expect only one or two might be available on short notice, so . . . let's say no more than two or three troops of cavalry, not an entire squadron. A couple of batteries of horse artillery, nothing heavier than four- or six-pounders, too. *Troop* transports aren't that common, either, so . . . no more than three or four regiments of foot, with *their* four-gun batteries of equally light artillery pieces."

He'd anchor the invasion fleet off Cat and Ship Islands in deep water; sail or row barges, launches, pinnaces, and Coehorn mortar boats from there into Lake Borgne . . . dead of night, all that! . . . even *tow* some astern of the extemporised bombs, which could fire far inland to suppress any opposition as the troops were going ashore. Light infantry, fusiliers and such, ashore first to scout and skirmish their way west to protect the fairly small landing ground, which was not quite as big as a cricket pitch, really. Some light regimental guns next, their limbers stuffed with cannister and grape, not solid shot. *Then* cavalry and horse artillery, followed by the rest of the regiments . . . the line companies and grenadier companies, the Marines for the Bayou Bienvenu, near where they sat.

Aye, the bayou, by God! A Heaven-sent highway in its own right, that (so Mr. Pollock assured him) meandered right into the northern suburbs of New Orleans itself, fed the Marigny Canal, hard by the many farm plots and cart paths behind Fort St. John and the shore of Pontchartrain!

"Takes most of the supply waggons or pack-mules off the single road," Lewrie said, chuckling. "Supply boats, gigs, launches, cutters . . . shallow-draught stuff off every vessel can get up Bayou Bienvenu. Pole 'em if they can't be rowed! Cuts down on the number of draught animals to transport or feed, too! Less hay and oats, more shot and powder, more troops. Who are fed *worse* than horses, really. Hmmm, swivels and two-pounder boat-guns on the bayou boats, to keep the Dons well back, and up to *their* necks in muck."

Seven miles from New Orleans, the chart showed a large tongue of higher, dryer ground to the north of the Chef Menteur road, framed by great groves of cypresses. The surprised, scurrying Spanish garrison would, in his limited military judgement, think that the perfect place to rally, to form a defence line and fight. Firm ground on which to emplace heavier guns than the landing force could boast, and Lewrie couldn't see a way round it without a thrust into Lake Pontchartrain in boats to land infantry *behind* that solid ground, to take the Spanish in flank or rear before they could get sorted out and unlimber their artillery pieces . . . or just *after,* and sweep them up, thereby shattering the frantic resistance even further? Or could cavalry do it on their own, unsupported? Lewrie grimaced as he imagined that it might take a whole squadron of horse to be landed, after all!

"It's . . . feasible," Lewrie said at last, grimacing with doubt, despite his tentative statement of approval, "with a brigade of foot, a battalion of Marines, *and* Peel's damned squadron of cavalry. One day to land, sort out, and march past here. Fight a battle here, on this firm ground, if cavalry can't seize it right off, then . . . whistle up the bandsmen for the march into New Orleans. Land a second brigade?"

"Once New Orleans falls, a second or third brigade could sweep up the forts down the Mississippi, one at a time," Pollock contributed.

"Whilst a squadron of frigates sails *up* to help reduce them by direct fire," Lewrie supposed.

"Then what small, wretched garrisons there are at Mobile and Pensacola could be overwhelmed?" Pollock asked. "Nor more than fifty or an hundred men to each, really. Mounting guard over the mosquitoes and the mildew, heh heh!" Pollock scoffed.

"A touchy endeavour, even so, Mister Pollock," Lewrie counselled. "Where do we get *that* many tropic-seasoned troops, and transports in sufficient number? If they come from England, it would depend on whether it's hurricane season or not, or how long they have to languish aboard their ships and still be healthy, whether they go ashore on Jamaica for long during Fever Season before the Army has things done all 'tiddly,' and Yellow Jack kills two-thirds of them. You have pen and paper?"

Lewrie sat cross-legged and jotted. *Four* brigades, say, and 12,000 infantry; average transport 300 to 350 tons with two men per ton of displacement; 600 to 700 men each—say, no more than 500 to 600 for health reasons in the tropics . . . It would take twenty-four transports, with another dozen for supplies. Nearly 500 cavalry mounts plus artillery nags (assume a quarter died or broke legs on-passage) so plan on seven or eight rare, specialised horse transports, and an equal number just for fodder and oats, and the light artillery could have eight animals per gun, not the usual six, in case the soil was soggy . . .

He broke off and gazed out at Lake Borgne and the open sea, in disgust. "Hundreds of barges and cutters, all coming t'this wee patch o' mud. And *our* Army in charge of it? Hmmm, I don't know . . . "

"Something wrong?" Pollock asked, taking fret from his tone.

"Anchored so far off, bloody miles of choppy, shallow sea they must cross," Lewrie gloomed. "Unless it's flat calm, it'd take *days* to land them, and the Spanish would have time to react. Our wonderful Army just doesn't have 'quick' in its vocabulary, Mister Pollock. A large force would hamper itself, a small, quick'un could be knackered. Saw at at Toulon in '93 and '94, and that was a *proper* harbour, with wharves, cranes, and all. This sand spit ain't! It'd be treacly chaos to get 'em landed and sorted out quickly, then march them west . . . up a single sandy *track*, one weeded bayou. Did we get a *regiment* ashore per *day*, I'd be very much surprised. I'd be surprised all the more did the general in charge dare lurch into motion before a *week'd* passed!"

"Our soldiers can't be *that* slow, can they?" Pollock asked with a crushed look on his ill-formed phyz. "Wolfe . . . Montreal. . . ."

"A fluke," Lewrie spat. "Hah! You know, Mister Pollock . . . it might be better did we just slip the Dons a note and ask 'em what they'd *take* for Louisiana. Cheaper in the long run, especially when it comes to the lives of our soldiers, ha ha! Trade 'em Gibraltar or something?"

"Oh, for God's sake, Lewrie!" Pollock grumped, so nettled that he quite forgot the agreed-upon alias.

"I'll write Admiral Parker, and Mister Peel, an appreciation," Lewrie promised, digging into their food basket to build a roast beef sandwich. "This *is* the quickest, easiest route to the city's conquest, though I will have to include its warts . . . and my reservations."

"That is, after all, one of the reasons Captain Nicely, Mister Peel, as well, insisted on your presence," Pollock told him. "Sooner or later, we *must* have New Orleans. Louisiana and Spanish Florida, too. To keep the Americans hemmed in and humble, on *their* side of the Mississippi. To pay the Spanish back for switching sides and taking hand with the French in '96, to boot!"

"Well, that'd be sweet, I grant you." Lewrie chuckled. "Damme, is that a twist of ground pepper by your leg? *That's* what's missing on this beef!"

Pollock handed the paper twist over, then picked up the sheet on which Lewrie had marked his figures. He carefully tore it to bits, as fine as confetti, then let the soft breeze scatter it.

"Put nothing more on paper," Pollock warned him. "Trust all to your head, or let me, ah . . . translate the numbers into innocent debits and such in a ledger book. Things to be *ordered*, shipped, sold, or as items in stock. Harmless code words, d'ye see."

"Whatever you wish, Mister Pollock," Lewrie happily agreed, in thrall to crunchy bread and succulent meat zested with mustard. "You do a lot of business in codes?"

"Commerce is a, ah . . . cut-throat business, Mister Willoughby," Pollock said with a cryptic smile. "*Ahem!*"

⚓

They rolled down the sloppy streets along the waterfront levee, once they'd returned their hired mounts to the stablery, savouring the sunset and the cool, river-sweet air. A trifle stiff-legged, it must be admitted, from spending nigh the whole day in the saddle, and their fundaments, chafed thighs, and challenged leg muscles complaining.

Watching their passing image in one of the rare, large, glass storefront windows, Lewrie was put in mind of a brace of virgin girls toddling homeward after their first experience at "All-Night-In"!

"And, there's your men, Mister Willoughby!" Pollock pointed out as Rue Toulouse dead-ended at Levee Road.

"Drunk as lords, I'll warrant," Lewrie growled to see them all asprawl at their ease in cane-bottom chairs round a rickety table by the entrance to a lowly sailors' café. "Damn 'em, I *warned* 'em to stay sober! Much good that does, with sailormen," he despaired.

"They look fairly sober to me, Willoughby," Pollock countered, back in his fully civilian and "innocent" role once they had returned to civilisation.

"Hoy, Cap'm Willoughby!" Quartermaster's Mate Toby Jugg lazily called, lifting a wooden piggin by way of salute, without rising or doffing his hat; playing his own role to the hilt, and loving every second of it, Lewrie was mortal-certain.

"Aye, Cap'm L—" Landsman Furfy, that dim but capable Irish side of beef began to say, just before his mate Liam Desmond kicked him beneath the table. "Ow, Liam, whad'ye do 'at . . . oh."

Neck burning at Jugg's impertinence, but knowing that he would have to play up game, Lewrie only sauntered to their table, his hands jabbed deep into his trouser pockets most *unlike* naval officer fashion to join them. Clenched into fists, but jabbed deep.

"Havin' a free day, are we, lads?" Lewrie casually enquired of them, rocking on his heels with his wide-brimmed "wide-awake" hat far back on his head, and with a faint grin on his face. "Not gotten all 'three sheets to the wind' yet today?"

"Oh, nossor," Jugg idly replied with a smile. "For I e'spect th' last few days o' sportin' done 'em in for a bit. 'Make an' Mend' it 'tis, t'day, sor. 'Caulk or Yarn' an' all."

"Short o' th' 'blunt' today, sor," Desmond added.

Damned if they weren't drunk at all; tiddly, perhaps; "groggy" for certain, but no "groggier" than they'd be by the Second Dog Watch and the second rum issue aboard *Proteus!*

"Toby . . . Mister Jugg's been keeping a weather eye on us, sor," Clancey, the youngest lad in his party, good-naturedly griped, lifting his own pig-gin in Jugg's direction in mock salute. "Too damn' good, beggin' yer par-don, sor."

" 'Sides, our money goes fur'der with th' doxies, we don't drink it all up, sor," Furfy dared to contribute with a childish enthusiasm.

"An' would ya be carin' for a 'wet' o' yer own, sor?" the irrepressible Jugg solicitously enquired. "For 'tis good Dublin stout, as sure as yer born, so 'tis."

Lewrie goggled at him for a moment, nigh apoplectic at Jugg's effrontery, fighting the urge to A. jerk hands from pockets, B. curl into vises, C. leap, D. strangle.

"French beer?" Lewrie scornfully managed to croak at last.

"Faith, but that's filthy muck, sor!" Jugg hooted in mirth as he finally got to his feet and came within arm's reach, showing Lewrie the yeasty contents of his piggin. "No, 'tis real Irish stout, brung upriver on good Mister Pollock's little brig, sor, an' not so *horrid* dear, e'en then, agin wot th' Frogs an' Dons charge fer their piss. Want a sip from mine, sor?"

"Christ, no I . . . "

"Need a private word, sor," Jugg muttered from the corner of his mouth, darting his eyes at Pollock to include him. "Been aboard our prize, sor, and I knows for sure about her, beg pardon."

"Aha!" Lewrie barked, stepping to the table to pour himself a glass of *vin ordinaire* from an earthenware jug. "Aye, Jugg, we should take a short stroll with Mister Pollock."

All three took a few paces apart from the rest of the crewmen, facing south across the river to the prize ship and the emporium hulks, where belfry and taff-rail lanthorns—oil lights or candles—were now cheerfully aglow for late shoppers, casting long, dancing glades across the Mississippi, which itself had put on its gay blue-grey nighttime masquerade, instead of its day-time muddy-brown.

"She's our prize, sure 'nough, Cap'm . . . Mister Pollock," Jugg im-parted, rocking on his heels and wearing a grin as he lifted his mug to take a leisurely sip, using that gesture to point at the hulk. "We went aboard her this mornin', so we did . . . Cap'm Coffin and th' First Mate, Mister Caldecott. Actin' like we might buy her, like."

"Absolutely certain," Lewrie stated.

"Oh aye, sor," Jugg said with a snicker, turning to look at him. "For I'd left me mark on her, by way o' speakin'. When we woz anchored at Do-minica an' sleepin' aft in th' mates' cabins for a spell, I carved me name in her

fancy overhead woodwork, right above 'er master's bed-cot . . . me name an'
Erin Go Bragh, sorta. 'At woz still there, plain as anythin', sor. Down below,
when soundin' her well, I found Mister Towpenny's cribbage board, too, wot
he woz so proud of and missin' so sore after they marooned us. One he
shaped hisself, sure, sor. Foot o' th' orlop ladder, t'woz."

"Any clue as to who claims her ownership, then, Mister Jugg?" Pollock
asked in a side-mouthed mutter, looking outward, and to an idle observer
merely engaged in casual banter.

"Slow-coach ol' feller in charge o' her Harbour Watch, Mister Pollock,
sor. He said t'ask for a merchant name o' Basternoh, or some such, who
bought her, recent. I 'spect yer Cap'm Coffin kin tell ya more about that,
since 'twas 'im did th' bulk o' th' talkin', but . . . seems I do recall a banker
feller name o' Merrypaws was tied up innit, too, mebbe bought inta her as a
'ship's husband' . . . even help with th' financin', did anyone buy her, sure."

"Bistineau, and Maurepas, was it?" Pollock pressed, perked up as sharp-
eyed as an owl.

"Aye, 'em names sound more like it, certain, sor!" Jugg agreed.

"Aha!" Pollock chortled half aloud, rubbing dry palms together. "Now
we're talking. Now we're in business at last, gentlemen! For I am familiar
with both those worthies. *Monsieur* Bistineau is as crooked as a dog's hind
leg, a right 'Captain Sharp.' He'd steal the coins off his dead mother's eyes,
and Maurepas! Monsoor Henri Maurepas, he's rumoured to have been involved in some shady dealings in the past. The plantations he's scooped up
for a song off people who fell behind with their loans . . . I imagine either,
or both, can provide us valuable information, do I put the thumbscrews
to 'em."

"Ye would, sor?" Jugg asked, surprised. "Fer real, an' all?"

"Manner of speaking," Pollock off-handedly quibbled.

"Aww," Jugg rejoined, sounding hellish disappointed.

"She's floating high above her waterline," Lewrie said. "So I s'pose her
cargo's long gone?"

"Ev'ry stick gone, sorry I am t'say, sor," Jugg told him with a mournful
look. "Her holds're as empty as an orphan's pantry. Not just her holds, neither, Cap'm, sor. 'Er second bower an' least kedge ain't there no longer, an'
all her spare spars an' sails've been sold away. Cable-tiers are empty, too.
Though, I 'spect 'at had more t'do with a need t'lash her bow, stern, breast
an' spring-lines t' th' shore t'keep her moored agin th' river currents."

"Then who do they expect to buy her, I wonder?" Lewrie said with a snort, recalling again his one reading of the prize's manifest, imagining middling-sized bags of prize money winging away.

"Most-like, that bastard Bistineau would be more than happy to play ship chandler and sell you her own fittings back as spanking new . . . at a hellish-dear cost," Mr. Pollock sneered with a matching snort. "Yes . . . Captain Coffin and Mister Caldecott *could* tell me more, well . . . a *bit* more, and for your sharp eyes and, *ahem* . . . sagacity, I thank you, Mister Jugg. I do b'lieve I should look them up at once. After your trip aboard her, Jugg, I do believe we have a lead at last!"

"Thankee kindly, sor," Jugg replied, doffing his hat from long practice; though peering quizzically at Lewrie for the meaning of the word "sagacity."

"Good, clever work, Jugg," Lewrie congratulated.

"Er, ah . . . thankee, Cap'm, sor," Jugg said to him, plumbing to the approximate meaning of his praise. "Hoy, ain't she a handsome wee thing there, sors? 'At cutter comin' upriver."

They all turned to gaze upon a smallish single-masted craft not so far downriver, coming up slowly against the relentless current with all her fat jibs and huge gaff mains'l winged out into a starkly white cloud of canvas against the blue of the river, and twilight. She flew a Spanish flag, and Mr. Pollock cupped his eyes with his hands to peer hard at her, even without the aid of a telescope.

"Spanish Navy cutter," Pollock announced at last. "An *aviso* . . . a despatch boat. From Havana or Veracruz, most-like, making the round with the latest mails. Though they do have a few like her at Mobile and Pensacola for *guarda costas*."

"A problem for us, is she?" Lewrie fretted half aloud.

"Oh, I rather doubt it . . . Mister Willoughby," Pollock amusedly dismissed. "Had the Dons tumbled to your presence, you'd have been in cells in the *calabozo* days ago, hah hah . . . *ahem*. Had the Spaniards a single clue about our business, they'd have sent a frigate!"

"Well, that's reassuring," Lewrie said, scowling at the man.

"Being Spaniards, they won't land the mails 'til next morning"—Pollock chuckled—"after a good supper and a run ashore. As well known as I am, no one'll think twice of me wandering over to the Cabildo and asking the latest news in the Place d'Armes. It's what everyone else does, God knows. Tonight, though . . . *ahem*. It might be a good idea if you and your hands, being strange new faces, didn't do their drinking and carousing near yon cutter's crewmen, hmm? Make it an early night?"

"Aye, I'll see to it," Lewrie vowed. Though, after his carouse with Char-ité Bonsecours, even an orgy in the Pigeon Coop cabaret would prove anti-climactic, and making it an early night held no charms whatsoever. Twiddle his thumbs in his rooms alone? Polish his boots and bed down by ten? It sounded like a hellish-dull evening.

BOOK FOUR

Prospero: Lie at my mercy all mine enemies.
Shortly shall all my labours end, and thou
Shalt have the air at freedom. For a little,
Follow, and do me service.

-*THE TEMPEST,* ACT IV, SCENE 1
WILLIAM SHAKESPEARE

CHAPTER TWENTY-ONE

*W*ell before noon the following morning, more than a few events came to pass in the parlours, offices, taverns, lodging houses, and streets of the town of New Orleans.

At the corner of Rue Royale and Rue Toulouse, Jim Hawk Ellison was breaking his fast and taking in the latest informations from his men. Piping-hot cornbread, white hominy, and a rasher of bacon, with a pork cutlet aswim in gravy, and strong rum-spiked and sweetened chicory *café au lait* kept hands and mouth busy, while his watchers' reports occupied his mind.

"Don't see how we'd manage, comin' upriver," one of his men, Silas Bowman, said in a hunch-shouldered low mutter over his plate of eggs and bacon. "Fort Saint Charles and the Rampart batteries're too strong. Got eighteen heavy pieces, twelve- and eighteen-pounder guns, an' set for a wicked crossfire, Jim Hawk."

"Crossin' Pontchartrain don't look too good, either," another man, a disguised U.S. Army sergeant named Davey Lumpkin told him. "Fort Saint John can slaughter anybody tryin' to cross the produce fields. Even with all the swamp-drainin' they've done, it still's too marshy for anything but men afoot, too."

"Guess it'll have t'be done from the inside, then, boys," Jim Hawk Ellison decided as he slathered molasses on a buttered slice of pone. "Come prime trading season, we'll have to float men downriver in flatboats, rafts, and keel-boats, dressed 'country.' The Spaniards won't think a thing of 'em, and everybody comes armed with rifles or muskets, and they're used t'seein' that too. Peyton, what're those Englishmen been up to? Been keepin' a sharp eye on 'em?"

"Hell, Jim Hawk," Peyton Siler, another disguised soldier, said, "yest'a'dy they rode way out east all th' way t'Lake Borgne and ate a meal outten a basket. Never could get all that close, but I could see 'em with my glass. Spent a long time pawin' an' head-cockin' over some map they brought with 'em. Pointed north and east a lot, they did. Up that way, there's Fort Coquilles . . . hmmm? *Knew* they warn't straight."

"Well, I do declare!" Ellison chuckled over his laced coffee.

"Tore some kinda paper inta itty-bitty bits 'fore they left," Siler said on, winking. "Oncet they got outta sight, I picked up what I could of it. Whole lotta numbers, was all. Couldn't make no sense of it."

"That's all right, Peyton," Ellison told him. "They were up to some kind o' devilment. And now we know they got something t'hide."

"They stopped 'bout halfway back t'town," Siler continued. "I saw 'em get down an' paw th' ground. It's high an' firm. They looked right pleased with whatever it was they saw there."

Ellison already had a map of the environs engraved in memory. He smiled at that news. "Firm ground? Sounds t'me like they spotted a good place t'place defences an' guns . . . so maybe the rumours aren't true. Won't come down from Canada, like we thought. They mean t'land somewhere out th' end o' the Chef Menteur road an' strike fast, twelve or fifteen miles away from the town! You see anything out there could stop 'em, Peyton?"

"That'd be th' onliest place that might hold 'em up, Jim Hawk," Siler decided after a long, contemplative rub of his unshaven chin. "If they come so far south o' Fort Coquilles, that is. But it'd be a chore, 'less they had a *whole* lotta small boats."

Ellison snickered, keeping his own counsel as he sipped coffee. The American Army, even if that bastard General Wilkinson did lead it, could muster 20,000 militia *plus* regulars and infiltrate around 2,000 into New Orleans. Half the rest would march on Natchez and overwhelm its pitifully small garrison, the other half would sail down from Kentucky or the Wolf River bluffs to pick up the Natchez detachment once they'd won. With Natchez silenced, the Spanish would have no warning until the makeshift "armada" swung round the last bend above the city, which would be the signal for the infiltrators to cause general havoc and pave the way for the main force to land!

"Anyone have any luck talkin' up that crew o' theirs?" Ellison enquired as he set his cup aside.

No one had; the new-come strangers usually made taciturn, early nights of things, and what desultory conversations that Ellison's men had drawn them into, all that could be learned from them was that they came from Ireland or England once and were loyal to their court-martialed former naval officer, who was a fairly good-natured sort, and a terror with the ladies.

"Wide open out there," Ellison muttered, once those reports were done. "East o' town. Wonder why the Spanish haven't fortified it or even planned against a Lake Borgne landing?"

"Too marshy, really, Jim Hawk," Siler said with a shrug. "That road's the only way, and h'it's not much t'speak of."

"Wish *we* had a navy, big as the British do," Ellison said with a scowl. "Oh well, maybe someday. But there's twenty thousand fightin' men in Kentucky an' Tennessee, just rarin' t'go. Does President Adams and Congress ever get done wranglin' and jabberin', give us the signal t'go ahead, well . . . "

"Hey, what 'bout 'at 'ere girly feller, Jim Hawk?" Silas Bowman asked with an eye-rolling leer. "Er wuz he'un really a she'un after all?"

"Oh, I was pretty sure she was a she, soon as she came outta th' lodgin' house, Silas," Ellison whispered back. "Took off her hat and shook her hair out 'fore she got to her door. Right before those two bastards come boilin' out an' tried t'slit my gizzards. I still don't know who she is, and for damn' sure can't stick my nose anywhere round her street, after that. Silas, maybe you could sniff around there . . . ask a slave who owns that house, or who-all lives there, so I can narrow it down. Gotta admit, I'm damn curious 'bout that little gal and what her connexion might be t'that mysterious Willoughby fellah."

"Ah'll do 'er, Jim Hawk," Bowman assured him with a deep nod.

"Well . . . maybe ya shouldn't get *that* close to her, Silas," Jim Hawk teased with a leer, creating a bit more mirth at his crowded table. "Rest o' you boys . . . today it might not hurt t'sneakify round all the forts an' such. Get a count o' th' garrison an' whether they live in barracks or sleep out. Then . . . "

Meanwhile, back at the *pension* at Bourbon St. and Rue Ste. Anne, Capt. Alan Lewrie (or Willoughby, take your pick) heard the rumbles of a dray waggon in the brick and cobbled streets, and all but levitated off the mattress as he flung himself from his left side to his right. He crammed a fluffy, cool goose-down pillow over his head to shut out the creaky-screechy-rumbly din, then fell back asleep.

Aboard the Panton, Leslie & Company emporium hulk, Hippolyte and He-lio de Guilleri, along with their weedier cousin from Saint Domingue, Jean-Marie Rancour, and the elegant Don Rubio Monaster, bought some few things with their illegal gains that they thought might come in handy on their impending new piratical foray. Fresh, and reliable, British gunpowder—pistol and musket priming powder most especially—was paramount in their purchases. Jean-Marie bought himself a new long-barrelled pistol, one with rich and glossy walnut stocks and grips, and a glossy blued finish intricately chased with hair-thin silver inlays, with a bright brass powder flask, replace-ment lock spring, and a bullet mould and sprew-snip, all in a velvet-lined walnut case. Jean-Marie already owned four pistols, but a man could never have too many. Besides, he'd been awed by a woodcut print of the infamous buccaneer Blackbeard, of the last century. Blackbeard was depicted bearing an awesome number of pistols on his person: in his waistband, the pockets of his coat, in his hands, and even more holstered in a long and wide canvas rig that hung down on either side of his chest, like a priest's scapular. Black-beard had also been shown with burning slow-match fuses in his wild hair and beard. That *might* be a touch *outré*, Jean thought, but the firepower he would have at his fingertips!

His new weapon matched the calibre of three others in his collection and had a narrow steel shank on one side so it *could* hang from his waistband, just like the real, old-time pirates! He would gladly have bought its twin, so he'd have six, but he'd lost at *Bouré* and the Pharoah tables two nights running, so his funds were very tight.

"So dear, though, Jean, *mon cher ami,*" Rubio Monaster said with a sniff after they left the below-decks stuffiness for the fresh air on the covered for-mer quarterdeck, and shared a round of ginger beer.

"But long-barrelled and *rifled*, Rubio," Jean-Marie enthusiastically an-swered. "With my grandfather's duellers I inherited, now I own three rifled pistols. I would trade my two smoothbores if I could for this English pistol's mate. In a boarding, firepower is ev—"

"Shhh, Jean," Helio cautioned with a growl. "With the Spanish Navy cut-ter here, the less talk of such things, the better. Everyone in the Place d'Armes was talking about the missing Havana *guarda costa*. For now they think a British warship or privateer took her, but . . ."

"Indeed, Jean," Don Rubio said with a languid smile, "we must be as bland as a *blanc-manger* 'til they are gone. And slip away down south as quiet as mice. Though it would be pleasing for our fellow Creoles to know that *someone* struck a blow against our oppressors. Think of the wonder that would cause!"

"Perhaps it *might* light a fire under the many who sleep through Spanish occupation," Helio gruffly commented. "Perhaps all the bluster and bold talk of freedom would not be so damnably *idle*."

"Well, we could start a rumor that bold local Creoles did the deed," Jean-Marie suggested in a much softer, conspiratorial voice.

"An anonymous letter dropped at the doorway of the newspaper?" Hippolyte posed.

"But would they dare print it?" Helio countered. "The Spanish would shut them down in a heartbeat."

"Bastards!" Don Rubio fulminated under his breath.

"No time, anyway, *chers*," Helio said, scowling. "We're off to sea in a day or two. Dim and slothful as the Spaniards are, a letter like that, and us suddenly absent, even the fools in the Cabildo could put two and two together. We've other business first. One of the Americans trailed our sister home from Le Pigeonnier yesterday . . . lurked outside as if he meant her harm. When we rushed downstairs to confront him, he escaped us in the mists, but we know him."

"*Salaud!* Son of a whore, who is he?" Don Rubio said with a malevolent hiss, bristling up in an instant. "I will kill him myself!"

"He calls himself El-isson," Helio informed him, stepping even closer and lowering his voice to a faint mutter. "The leader of those new-come buckskin barbarians we suspect are here to scout the city for an American invasion, Rubio. Our body slaves have made careful note of all the skulking they do. We know the low-class tavern where El-isson and his band lodge . . . a filthy, gloomy place."

"He would violate her? He would lurk and hope to seize her and ravish her? *Nom d'un chien*, I will call him out at once!" Don Rubio hotly vowed.

"No time for the niceties, Rubio . . . *comprendre*?" Helio hinted, tipping him a grave wink and nod. "He is no true gentleman, so challenging him to a duel would mean no more to him than gold to a hog. He seems more the sort to cheat, anyway. Besides, duels take such a long time to arrange. And, what sort of insult would it be to *your* honour, to waste high-born niceties on a jumped-up peasant, who would sic his minions on you in the dark of night, and back-shoot you, *hein?*"

Helio de Guilleri had known Don Rubio Monaster and his family, the Bergrands, since he donned his first pair of boys' breeches, knew him, and his touchy sense of honour, to a tee . . . and his sheeplike lust for his sister. All it would take would be one word to launch him at their foe, and Rubio would wade in with all guns blazing, if given the chance to do something impressive to redeem Charité's honour or guard her "delicacy" from the advances of a beastly scoundrel. Even knowing his sister and her little "games," Helio himself would have sprung to her defence—it was what brothers were *supposed* to do to guard the family's precious honour. But Rubio was such a wonderful weapon!

"A murder, do you mean, not a duel," Don Rubio replied, nodding in grim, but pleased, understanding.

"Exactly," Helio said with an equally grim nod. "Without their leader, the other American wolves will melt away. Run scared back to Kentucky with their tails between their legs."

"The knife in the heart!" Jean-Marie Rancour breathed, eyes alight with evil mischief and expectation.

"No, no, too messy," Hippolyte de Guilleri drolly quipped. "You would stain a good suit of clothes, up that close with all that blood. Remember on that trading brig, when I stabbed that—"

"A pistol is better," Helio suggested, shushing his brother one more time. "In the dark, as he staggers back to his lodgings."

"Oh, better yet, Helio!" Jean-Marie excitedly piped up. "With a rifled musket! One of those Girandoni air-rifles they showed us not five minutes ago. They're so quiet, the clerk said . . . one little *snap* or *crack*, no louder than a twig, and if you miss your first shot, your . . . *game!* . . . can't take alarm and bolt before you get off a second or third. Though Rubio is such a fine marksman, I doubt he would require more than one, isn't that so, Rubio? Twelve shots in half a minute, the fellow assured me! Think of the advantage a man could have in a melee, *hein?* A decent shot . . . half a dozen men of passable skill firing ten or twelve shots in half a minute would *massacre* a ship's crew!"

"Six men could equal the volleys of a whole regiment, *oui!* Oh, I wish we had enough money to buy more than one for Rubio to use when he pots that American," Hippolyte exclaimed, catching his cousin's enthusiasm and picturing in his mind the crew of a proud royal Spanish frigate being slaughtered like a cloud of passenger pigeons in a boarding action. "If we asked Monsieur Maurepas for an advance, took some of the seed money account . . . as a material investment, hmm?"

"Four at least, for us," Jean-Marie added. "They aren't *that* expensive. We could put down payment for four now, then get the rest from old Henri for the balance!" Jean-Marie was almost tail-wriggling and prancing in place, like a tot at first sight of his birthday pony.

"We would be invincible!" Hippolyte gushed.

His elder brother, Helio, thought that over for a second. He was seized by visions of a stalwart battalion of rebel Creole gentlemen marching under bright French Tricolours, with a band playing "La Marseillaise" as they strode bravely near musket range of an entire Spanish brigade, taking aim and strewing them flat as easily as reaping sugarcane stalks.

"We should get six," Helio announced. "For now. With them, we gain more profits from our cruise and can buy more later."

"With six, we could ambush the American upstart *and* that damned *Anglais,* too!" Hippolyte softly crowed. "All at once, the same night. Pay him back for what he did with Charité, even if . . . "

"And *what* did *that* dog do to her?" Don Rubio Monaster demanded before Helio could even think to slap his brother's arm to shut him up. Rubio, though, knew the answer to his jealousy even before they could confirm it. Their tight faces, stiff postures, and queasy shrugs said it all.

"She came out with us to Le Pigeonnier," Hippolyte had to admit, red-faced with embarrassment. "In her usual 'costume' . . . *n'est-ce pas?* The *Anglais,* Willoughby, came in, too, and she dared us to engage him . . . to see if he might be dangerous to us, and, you know how bold she can be, when we wouldn't go . . . one thing led to another, *Bouré,* then drinks, then they, ah . . . left together, round . . . "

"He spent the night with her?" Rubio gasped with a cold twinge under his heart, even as he darkened with rage. "The *salaud,* that . . . English *bastard*! The *cochon,* pig . . . ravisher!" he spluttered.

So dearly did he crave her, it could never be *her* failing that made her go off with the Englishman . . . could it? Women—girls!—with heads so easily turned were frail, weak, and biddable, even ones bold and *outré,* which boldness and unconventionalism in Charité made her even more maddeningly desirable.

No, Charité was so young still, so in love with Life, galloping through it with her head thrown back in a laugh. Once her "enthusiasm" palled, surely she would settle down at last, would consider becoming the wife of a stalwart, bold, and assuringly steady fellow from a lineage as distinguished as hers, would take as a lifelong lover one who had gladly shared all her adventures, had been dashing and brave . . .

"They are both dead men," Don Rubio Monaster stiffly promised, manfully fighting the tears of disappointment that stung the corners of his eyes for being denied her wholehearted love, though his for her was boundless. He would *not* un-man himself with tears before his future in-laws; he would disguise his upset with righteous anger. "They are dead men, *mes amis*. At my hands, both of them, in the same night!" he heatedly vowed.

Mr. Gideon Pollock sat down to a light first breakfast with his "wife," a mere piffle of *café au lait,* half a canteloupe, and only one *croissant.* He'd take a second, more substantial breakfast with business associates, but Colette would feel neglected if he didn't humour her desires for close, intimate, and talkative domesticity, a semblance of a righteous man and wife's routines.

Colette was little darker than Pollock's heavily creamed coffee, as lightbeige as expensive letter paper, with long, straight and lustrous raven-dark hair, now demurely pinned up behind her ears, with deep bangs over her brows and crimped, springy coils depended on either side of her face. Her eyes were hazel, nearly as green as dark emeralds, and almost Asian-almond shaped. The palest yellow morning gown she had on perfectly complemented her hair, eyes, and complexion.

Colette smiled, tweaking up the corners of her generous lips as she poured them both refills of coffee; which smile forced an appraising wry grin on Pollock's face, too, recalling the night before, when her hair had been free of pins and combs and had fallen loose to the top of her sweet, round buttocks, had fanned out across the pillows as she had lain invitingly, her body dusky against the paleness of the bed linens.

Mr. Pollock congratulated himself again for having her, despite his lack of height, imposing physique, or handsome features. *Wealth,* Mr. Pollock had found, atoned for almost anything, and he was nothing if not *very* well off after his years of neck-or-nothing adventures and toils. If it hadn't been for a legitimate wife and three children back in Bristol, where he ventured only once every three years, he would have been sorely tempted to avow Colette his *only* woman, for she was the most pleasing, most passionate and *abandoned,* yet fine-mannered lover ever he had had.

Five hundred English pounds she had cost to buy from her former owner and keeper, two thousand silver Spanish dollars; even more to set her in this grand *pension* and furnish her *appartement* in a style worthy of her sham status . . . even more to provide her with a slave cook, handmaiden, housemaid, and an *elderly* yet *wakeful* footman. And fees and bribes to the slothful Spanish authorities to start, then expedite, her manumission papers. And the price paid in embarrassment as those authorities leered and nudged each other to see the proud little *Inglese* twist-face prig turn red to free his paramour, whom he could have kept in bondage as his harem toy at half the cost and trouble . . . the way they maintained their own.

Loco, utterly besotted . . . behaving like an old colt's-tooth, a witless cully of a boy over his first milkmaid, he certainly was . . . and *delighted* in his folly. Did Panton, Leslie & Company allow him, Mr. Pollock would gladly chuck return voyages to England, gladly shed Kingston, and settle for a lesser post as company factotum permanently assigned to New Orleans, for the entrancing town, its burgeoning trade, its future promise, and *Colette* were equal opportunities to his mind.

He could keep an eye on her faithfulness and escape the damnable, hellish pangs of jealousy and dread he felt whenever he had to sail off and stay apart from her for months and months on end. He *knew* they could never *really* marry, even in a city so casual about its licentiousness, so hypocritically, sinfully . . . Catholic!

Mr. Pollock himself was a rock-ribbed Scot Presbyterian.

"You wish me to ask in the markets about your mysterious young girl, *cher?*" Colette quite innocently posed. *Seemingly* innocent.

"Hmm . . . what?" Pollock flummoxed, with a twitch of his head at the picture of her sauntering and sashaying past hordes of leering and lustful idle Creole "gentlemen," returning the sly grins of a muscular Free Black dandy, even of an impressive slave horseholder! "No, no . . . "

"Can it be you tire of me, *cher* Gideon?" Colette gently teased. "And your *m'sieur* Willoughby's White Creole girl in male clothes fires your imagination, hmm?"

"Oh, rot!" Pollock replied with a shuddery laugh to realise he was being lovingly twitted, as all older lovers would be by their much younger and more desirable paramours.

"My dearest love," Colette said, turning serious as she put down her coffee cup and folded her hands together on the table. "You allow me to be . . . decorative, but you never let me be the wife partner that I am to you, *cher.* Hermione and I," she said, naming her stout and darker older maidservant, "have many sources. She knows the slaves to all the *grands blancs* families, and they see *everything, n'est-ce pas?* I . . . am on casual speaking terms with many of the town's young ladies. The *jeunes filles de couleur* who are . . . kept. Their masters and beaus share their gossip when they come home from the cabarets, the pillow talk, the amusing tales? I *know* you wish to protect me from . . . "

"No, dearest, I must insist that . . . " Pollock began to splutter.

As dearly as Colette actually loved her wry little Englishman, there were times that his not-so-hidden jealousy, his fear of losing her, was maddening!

"Allow me to aid you, please, Gideon? Just this once?" she almost begged, reaching across the table to take his hands in hers and squeeze reassuringly, batting her long lashes like a fearful kitten. "I already know . . . Hermione and I have already learned . . . that this girl is not a Bonsecour. They have no young, unmarried daughter. And the Darbone brothers you mentioned have not been in New Orleans for at least a month. Their manservant boys were disgusted that they had to leave the city and go up towards Pointe Coupee to the Darbone lands . . . They despise the crude field slaves and are terrified that *anything* could happen to them so far away, if old man Darbone or *madame* takes a dislike to them. Three sass-mouth Darbone house slaves already died of whipping, after the Pointe Coupee rebellion, Gideon. *Comprendre?*"

"Well . . . "

"Let me call Hermione in, please, *cher* Gideon? Let her tell of what she has already heard?" Colette cajoled.

"Hmm, I s'pose . . . *ahem,*" Pollock grudgingly assented, unable to deny his entrancing mistress anything. Almost anything. He did desire an answer to Lewrie's mystery—just so long as he could keep Colette from laying eyes on the impressive lout!

"Hermione?" Colette said, tinkling a porcelain bell by her place setting. *"Ici, s'il te plaît."*

"M'amselle wish?" the husky older woman asked, coming in from a mostly unused kitchen, wiping her square hands on a dish-clout, swiping at her garish satin headcloth. "Oh la! Dat girl who go about at night like ze *gentilhomme? Mon Dieu.*"

The gist of her gossip (gleaned from a kitchen maid who was friendly with one of the oyster shuckers owned by the proprietors from the Pigeon Coop cabaret) was that the girl, who was uncommonly pretty, was no Bonsecour at all, but lived in a grand *pension* on Rue Dauphine and could be seen sneaking home arm in arm with two young men, always the same two. Both a groom and a girl body servant belonging to one of the houses on Rue

Dauphine—"No bettah'n dey should be, and *mon Dieu,* don' get me started on dem, *m'sieur* Gideon!"—said that they had both seen her, sometimes with the two young men, when all three of them would go into a house together. Sometimes the girl alone, dressed in suitings but with her hair free, would come traipsing in at cock-crow. For sure if Hermione asked a slave who worked a produce plot on Bayou St. John and came into town at dawn with his owner's cart of greens to sell, he'd tell her the same and could show her the right house, even tell Hermione which floor where the candles got lit, after she went up to her *appartement!*

"Oh, dey say she a *high-born* Creole gal, *m'sieur* Gideon . . . but not de finest sort, *hein?*" Hermione concluded.

"But we could ask about her for you, *cher,*" Colette perkily assured him, "and I'd lay you any wager you wish that the secret is not a secret at all . . . That sort of delicious gossip surely is already the common coin in *this* town! Let us try for you, *mon cher!*"

"Well . . . just so long as you don't stray into a neighbourhood where Hermione could not protect you, dearest. Perhaps you had best take Scipio along to chaperone both of you. He may be getting on in years, but he still can appear forbidding, does he put a scowl on . . . *ahem,*" Pollock at last conceded.

"You are the *dearest man,* Gideon," Colette murmured, her eyes locked on his with the promise of a most magnificent night of reward.

"The mails, *m'sieur,*" Henri Maurepas's personal assistant and clerk announced with his usual unctuous air as the banker entered his inner sanctum. A fashionable thimble-shaped hat, gloves, and cane were taken from him and placed securely in a tall oak armoire that had come all the way from Paris as Maurepas strode to his imposing desk and sat down with a sweep of his coat-tails. Without a word spoken, a slave in formal livery tiptoed in with a tray bearing a coffee service and a candle-warmed silver-plate pot.

"Merci," M. Maurepas said in a distracted and bored grunt, as he almost always did to indicate that he had taken note of the service done him . . . but they should both now get out and let him get to work.

He sorted through the many letters. There was one pile that was local business; those he shoved aside to concentrate on the few others that had come aboard the naval cutter. To his disappointment, none of his latest correspondence was from France, not even from distant kin. Certainly, there had yet to

come a reply from the Directory in Paris to his many letters urging support
for a rebellion in Louisiana . . . though there were some outdated newspapers.

Ah! Two letters directed to the bank, one from Havana, with a date scribbled on it that was much earlier than the second, which came all the way
from Ciudad de México.

Both were in Spanish, a language he detested. No matter how flowery and
elegantly written, Spanish could not hold a candle to the grace of a cultured
man's French.

> . . . *to inform you, Most Esteemed* Señor *Maurepas, that, given your*
> *previous requests directed to His Excellency the Captain-General, com-*
> *bined with the humble pleas of your fellow bankers in the Colony of*
> *Louisiana and the city of New Orleans, His Most Catholic Majesty*
> *has graciously given assent to the shipment to the Colony of a consider-*
> *able sum of silver specie, with which to ease the regrettable shortage of*
> *coinage which has, of late, caused such a hardship upon his Most*
> *Catholic Majesty's subjects residing in Louisiana, due to the regrettable*
> *outflow of specie which the import of diverse American trade goods has*
> *caused. The Captain-General of His Majesty's American possessions*
> *having received His Majesty's gracious permission, the Captain-*
> *General at Havana has ordered the Captain-General of New Spain at*
> *Ciudad de México to order the mines at Potosi to refine, mint, and pre-*
> *pare for shipment pieces-of-eight and dollars to the amount of—*

"*Sacré nom de Dieu!*" Henri Maurepas almost screeched in amazement,
choking on the smoke from his morning's first *cigaro*, doubling over and
hacking for a good two minutes before he could trust himself to reread the
sum, and breathing *very* carefully 'til he had managed to pour himself a
restorative, throat-clearing tot of brandy. It was followed by a second, larger
one that he sipped in a celebratory but very thoughtful fashion.

Coined money *gushed* northward into the coffers of the barbaric Yankees
to pay for their flour, wheat, corn, lumber, and such, their whiskies and furs,
hides, tobacco, and cotton. With the war, most of the merchant ships that
came to trade in New Orleans were American, too. Yankees ending buying
Yankee goods passing through the city and very little of the profits *stuck* to
French or Spanish fingers. Hence Louisiana, New Orleans, and Maurepas's
bank were forever short of coin; which shortage drove up the price of everything needed or wished, even local goods.

Spain had ignored the problem for years, halfheartedly closing the Mississippi to American traders for several years, which had been a disastrous policy that had fomented mass smuggling and even *greater* corruption and graft, was such a thing possible.

Now, with the river open again, but Spain locked in a war, even wealthy bankers had to scrimp and scrounge to maintain comfortable cash reserves to loan out, and as to what their borrowers offered as payment, *pah!* M. Henri Maurepas had to lease several warehouses to hold consignments of molasses, sugar, rice, and cotton 'til it could be sold to someone, someday, before the mice, insects, or the ever-present damp ruined it, and he thought himself fortunate did he make a *2 percent* profit!

Shelling out so much silver to Lanxade and Balfa to reward their sailors, paying shares to those foolish youngsters who would foment a rebellion, after the *hellish* cost of buying artillery, weapons, and the pirate schooner for them to play with, had put him in a worse spot, and if they ever tired of their little "adventure" or failed to take more prizes to sell on the sly, failed to bring in more "free" goods for the scalpers like Bistineau to front, he and his firm could go under!

Now, though . . .

Six million dollars in hard silver coin could be his salvation. His bank's share was to be a fifth of the total, charged against his "holdings"—lands, future crops, outstanding planters' loans, or warehoused goods—and with that money he would be solvent again . . . for a *few* more years at least. His loans could be repaid in coin for a change, he could loan more . . .

Or! Maurepas quietly mused, taking another sip of brandy and picking up the letters to reread them. He leaned far back in his chair, with his brandy glass resting atop his substantial paunch. All would come aboard a single, undistinguished, fast ship from Veracruz, one not too obvious as a treasure ship, nor one so grand as to draw the attention of any prowling British man of war or privateer; nor the free-roving so-called privateers of other nations. Soldiers would be aboard, of course, a full company drawn from a trustworthy regiment based in New Spain, a Navy crew to be provided, skilled gunners . . .

Both letters cautioned that the shipment was a matter of strict confidence, that upon receipt and perusal of the letters, they were to be handed back to the Governor-General, and that any idle mention outside his firm could result in harsh punishment, etc.

Hmmm, Maurepas further mused, a sly grin creasing the corners of his eyes and lips. "Hmmm," again, aloud this time.

A fast ship, was it, and undistinguished? A shallow-draughted one, he thought most likely, so it could ascend the river quickly and cross the bars near Fort Balise without the risk of unloading all, or a part, of the cargo, thus exposing it to greedy prying eyes.

Guarded by a "trustworthy" company of soldiers; well, that was a wry jape! The local garrison was made of weary, jaded place-servers and half-illiterate peasant clods; half the original Spaniards had run off or died, replaced with ne'er-do-wells too lazy to work an honest trade. So what would a regiment in New Spain consist of? A few hidalgo fops as officers, a few grizzled, over-aged sergeants, and the rank-and-file mostly local-born Mestizos, even Indios straight from the bean fields, still jabbering away in Nahuatl or some other savage language. Ill-trained, ill-clothed, poorly led, and indifferently armed, crowded elbow to elbow and at sea for the first time in their lives, perhaps? She'd not be a royal galleon, perhaps not even a fast frigate! What did the letter say, how did it phrase it? Ah!

"... *manned by a crew drawn from the Marina Real.*"

The Spanish didn't dare send one of their few valuable warships to sea, afraid of drawing too much attention, fearful of *losing* it, and neither Tampico nor Veracruz were good harbours for ships of worth. New Spain—Mexico—lay far to the west, down at the bottom of the Caribbean's and the Gulf's prevailing winds, Henri Maurepas knew. Though he had never been a sailor, he knew that much. A square-rigged ship could spend *weeks* beating windward to the mouths of the Mississippi. A brigantine, barkentine, or schooner would be more weatherly. Hmmm . . .

Maurepas pondered whether he should tell the de Guilleris about this. This punishing war could last for years and years, and Spanish colonies would continue to suffer as Spain grew even weaker, less able to defend her American possessions. What guarantee was there that *all* the local trade would *not* be American in five years?

The United States and the British had designs on Louisiana already. Could his bank survive an invasion by either? Even if by some miracle a French fleet and French army fought its way through the British blockade, sailed upriver, and reclaimed them, what surety could he have that the radical Directory in Paris and all their Jacobin rabble-rousing sentiments would be amenable to money, to rich men like him?

Now, if he had all six million secretly cached at his plantation, and only tapped now and again for working capital, he could easily explain its partial presence as better-than-average fortune, due to his conservative and sagacious business sense. And he already knew all there was to know how to make things look legitimate on paper!

Well, not *all* of it. If he told the de Guilleris and those oafs Lanxade and Balfa, and they actually succeeded in *taking* it, he'd have to go shares, would not realise more than the fifth that the Spaniards originally intended his bank to have. But that would be 1,200,000 dollars more than any of his competitors, and all of it free and clear of pledged assets and sureties! Such a windfall was certainly nothing to sneer at.

And finally, *could* such a sudden shower of money actually create a real rebellion, result in a real reunion with beloved France, Henri Maurepas shudderingly, hopefully wondered?

"*Laclos, venez ici, s'il vous plaît,*" he called out.

"*Oui, m'sieur?*" his reliable longtime aide asked from the door.

"These letters from the Captain-Generals, how did they come?"

"The usual post clerk brought them, *m'sieur,* with all the rest."

"The same as *any* letter, Laclos?" Maurepas pretended to gasp.

"Well . . . *oui, m'sieur?* Why?"

"We'll see about *that!*" Maurepas answered with a deep scowl. He shot to his feet, shouting for his liveried slave. "Those hapless idiots! I shall be at the Cabildo, Laclos . . . giving them a piece of my mind at how slipshod they are!"

What a wonderful pretence that would be, Maurepas thought as his liveried slave handed him his hat, gloves, and cane. He would hand the letters over as instructed but would fume that they'd lain on someone's desk overnight, able to be read by just about *anyone.* If not his, then what of the letters sent to his competitors, *hah?* If anything happened to their precious consignment of silver, it would be all *their* fault!

Meanwhile, back at the *pension* . . .

Capt. Alan Lewrie, RN, sensed a slight buzzing noise round his head and idly swept one free hand to shoo the pesky flying . . . thingy. Which herculean effort woke him just long enough to take note that it was a good hour past dawn, and a slit of honest sunshine blazed in the gap in the nearest window draperies; that he could, for once, sleep in like the idlest civilian ever born; and that his lips were dry yet his bottom pillow was damp with drool and stuffily warm.

He rolled over, cramming the cooler top pillow under his head, with his face towards a dark corner, not that demanding daylight, and, for good measure, both smacked his lips and essayed breaking a bit of wind. Mildly eased, and with grit-heavy eyelids, the bold adventurer drifted off once more to what he deemed a *damned* well-earned rest.

At the grander, much more spacious de Guilleri city residence, Charité finished packing her rakish seagoing piratical men's clothes in a single heavy sailcloth bag and drew the rope strings taut, knotting it to keep it shut. A second change of clothing, to be worn on the trip down Bayou Barataria, was already laid out on the bed; this one consisting of a rough, *écru* shirt and a nondescript skirt of dark blue *cotonnade,* a short, decorated carmagnole vest, and a *garde-soleil* . . . a sun bonnet. Cotton knee stockings and her well-polished boots stood by the foot of her bed. Though she might go in disguise as a backcountry woman riding in a *pirogue,* Charité would be damned if she would squish and slop through bayou and swamp muck barefooted. At Capt. Balfa's *vacherie,* she could change into her pirate's rig, *damn* what the backward local women thought of it!

Her smallsword, sash dagger, and pistols were cleaned and oiled, the pair of smaller pocket pistols already loaded but not primed, with tompions in the muzzles to keep out the damp. Her slim poignard that she'd strap to her left forearm she had honed to razor sharpness.

For the rest of her last day in New Orleans, though, more feminine things awaited her; a high-waisted gown of the brightest cornflower blue that almost matched her eyes, one that fell straight without the aid of confining corsets, one with an only slightly daring scooped neckline, puffy shoulder flounces, and tight sleeves. With it was a wide straw bonnet adorned with gay ribbons and flowers, and the tiny matching silk parasol with which to flirt. White silk stockings and cunning little slippers dyed dark blue; even if heeled, common shoes were better suited to the perpetual slime of New Orleans streets.

She had finished her *toilette* seated in front of her dressing table, had lotioned, powdered, and pampered her face, neck, and shoulders before carefully daubing on the minimum of makeup allowed the genteel daughters. She crimped and brushed her lashes, though, to *nigh* the bold look of the *demimonde,* for she was not yet a matron and, frankly, did not think that she could ever submit to such a stolid and boring child-ridden propriety, not 'til their grand design had borne fruit.

Charité stood before her *cheval* mirror and unlaced the ties of her sheer dressing gown, then tossed it towards her bed. She slid her palms down her sides to her waist, over a tight-laced *bustier* atop a thinly woven *chemise,* turning slightly to either side to appreciate her slim and youthful body, lifting her hands under her breasts, as if to press them together for a deeper cleavage.

She smiled and blew herself a teasing kiss as she shifted both feet a bit more apart, lowering her rapt gaze to her slim and shapely thighs, revelling in recalling how she'd wrapped those fine legs about that *coquin*—that rascal—Alan Willoughby. Looking up into her own eyes again, she tried out a sultry, smouldering pout.

"Non non," she whispered, giggling, discarding that passionate look for a wide-eyed, innocent come-hither, all but biting her lip in trepidatious desire. "Better, oh là." She chuckled before making a cross-eyed face and sticking her tongue out at herself.

"Hunh!" was her Black *"maman's"* sour comment.

"You hush," Charité told her, rewarding her maidservant's sauce with another cross-eyed tongue-shot, "and don't tell me they'll *stay* crossed if I keep that up. Push me into my gown."

She stood patiently to be gowned, shod, tucked, laced, and adjusted, to be adorned with earrings and matching necklace, swaying from one foot to another and crooning to herself, sleepy-eyed but her head cocked in wonder at her own beauty as she was rigged out for the day, became an adorable, desirable perfection before her very own eyes one more time. A little shopping, a delicious dinner, and a few glasses of wine . . . some coy flirtations with her lashes, parasol, and laced fan with the town swains of her acquaintance, perhaps a former lover or two; punctuated with the pouty tale of being summoned upcountry for a family gathering on one of their plantations, to explain her, and her brothers', absence. It would be more a necessary chore than her usual pleasurable stroll and sampling of her beloved city's treasures. They would depart after full dark, taking a closed coach to the nearest boat landing on Bayou Barataria, and then it might be *weeks* of enforced solitude aft in a well-guarded cabin aboard *Le Revenant*—the celibacy of an Ursuline nun or Capuchin monk!—surrounded by swaggeringly masculine sailors. Hmmm . . .

"Fetch me pen, paper, and ink, *maman*," Charité ordered suddenly, impishly inspired. "I must write someone a note."

She consulted her tiny, cunningly wrought timepiece. It was not yet nine in the morning; would Alan Willoughby still be slug-a-bed, or was he the sort to be out and doing at the crack of dawn? she wondered. A note to his *pension*, or would it better serve to be sent to Panton, Leslie's shore establishment? Hah! Both, just to make sure!

CHAPTER TWENTY-TWO

An' th' top o' th' mornin' to ye, Cap'm, sor," Toby Jugg said with a jovial tone to his voice and a sham tug of his forelock, as if making *salaam* to an Asian potentate . . . or a poor Irish crofter to his landlord. "An' wot a foin mornin' h'it be, at 'all an' at 'all."

"Oh, pack it in, Mister Jugg!" Lewrie replied with a groan and a weary scowl. "'Tis too *'foin'* a morning for your 'Jack Sauce.' Have you seen Mister Pollock yet?"

"Come an' gone, sor, in a bit of a dither," Jugg informed him as Lewrie hefted the teapot off the candle-warmer in the Panton, Leslie shore warehouse offices. There seemed enough to make a cup, so Lewrie poured himself a mug-full, hoping for the best.

"Did he say what'd . . . dithered him, then?" Lewrie asked, making a face at the bitterness of the tea, despite a liberal admixture of two spoonfuls of sugar and a hefty dollop of cream.

"Borryed Dempsey an' Mannix, said he needed eyes t'do some watchin', an' loped off, sor," Jugg said, taking a sniff of the teapot and slinging what was left out onto the cobbled street to start a new one. "Desmond, Furfy an' t'others are keepin' their eyes on th' Americans. An' th' Yankee Doodles're keepin' an eye on us, too, sor. 'At lout 'cross th' street, sor? Been strollin' back an' forth th' better part of an hour, an' about wore 'is eyes out lookin' in th' same shop windows, each lap he makes."

Lewrie flung his mug of tea into the street, taking the time to peer at the buckskinned, raccoon-capped watcher, who spun suddenly on his heels and took an intense interest in the creaking overhead sign-boards that jutted out from the storefronts.

"Clumsy buggers they is, sor," Jugg said with a faint snicker. "Liam said some o' their lads skulkin' round th' town forts was so obvious, they might as well been carryin' surveyor's rods."

"Well, pray God our lads are better skulkers," Lewrie breathed, "though I rather doubt it."

"Th' local Cuffies're best, sor," Jugg said, spooning tea from the un-locked caddy into the pot, then turning to stoke the fire so he could get a fresh batch of water to a boil. "I 'spect ye niver took a bit o' notice that a slave followed ye all th' way here, Cap'm. Nor did th' Yankee feller who trailed ye take note o' him, neither," Jugg pointed out with a droll wink.

"They what?" Lewrie responded, with an urge to go "Eep!" or run out into the street and search for his pursuers. "Where?"

"So many of 'em, they blend in damn' well, they do, sor," Jugg almost chortled. "Who'd spot one Cuffy in a crowd, when New Orleans is et up with thousands of 'em, and most as alike as peas in a pod, sor? To th' likes o' us, anyways."

Lewrie had sauntered down to the streets after shaving, a sponge bath, and a change of clothing, completely oblivious to anyone lurking or follow-ing him. He couldn't *recall* being stalked on his way to a hearty breakfast. All the way to the warehouse and store, he had idly ambled, savouring the sights, tastes, and smells, and hadn't suspected a blessed thing! Even if Jugg took him by the hand and led him to his trailers, he doubted if he could re-member seeing them mere minutes before, and that shameful lack of aware-ness gave him cause to shiver with dread. Lewrie could understand the competing Americans tailing him, but . . . had the Spanish authorities sicced watchers on him and his men? Had they tumbled to his true identity?

"At least we're not at war with the Yankees," Lewrie thought out loud. "They're up to no good for certain, but it ain't all directed at us, thank God." And for Toby Jugg, of all people, to enlighten him . . . that nettled him, too. "The Cuffy, though. He might be a Spanish spy, and that *is* a danger!"

"Amen t'that, Cap'm, sor," Jugg gloomily agreed. "Though I . . . beggin' yer pardon an' all, Cap'm Lewrie, but it don't seem t'me a Don would trust a Cuffy t'do his spyin', not a blue-skin slave Cuffy, even a fancy 'Bright' in liv'ry. Such work's fer freeborn Spaniards, most-like. Clerks an' soldiers an' such, sor? 'Ese Creole Frenchies, they ain't *quite* as cruel an' haughty with th' Blacks as th' Dons are, even do they own most o' th' slaves here'bouts, so . . ."

"You think the Black watchers've been sicced on us by the local Frog Creoles for some reason, then, Jugg?" Lewrie speculated with one eye screwed nigh shut in a quizzical expression. "Perhaps our pirates, who got wind of our presence, somehow?"

"'At'd make th' most sense, aye, sor," Jugg cagily answered, in faint amusement. "Could be one o' Mister Pollock's competin' traders done it, but there's no way o' tellin', not without we grab one of 'em an' make him talk, like."

"That sounds like a good idea," Lewrie said, perking up at the idea of doing something to forward their endeavour and to atone for his blissful blindness in the streets. "Let's take a stroll, get one of them to follow us somewhere quiet, then grab the mis'rable bastard and wring it out of him."

"Aye, we could, couldn't we, sor?" Jugg mused aloud, scratching his chin whiskers in sly delight. "Might be we'd have need o' Furfy, one'r two t'other lads t'keep watch fer us, block 'im in from a'hind."

The kettle came to a boil and began to rattle its lid, claiming their immediate attention; they were British, well . . . English on the one hand, Irish on the other, and a fresh pot of tea could bring even bloody donnybrooks to a temporary halt. Lewrie saw to the teapot as Jugg took up the kettle with a filthy towel to guard his hands, so he could pour boiling water over the fresh leaves.

The second thing to claim their interest was the arrival of one of those aforementioned Black slaves, this one in a muted livery, with a short, white side-curled wig on his head, and a letter in his hand.

"I 'ave ze letter fo' a *Capitaine* Weel, uh . . . Weelo . . . "

"That'd be me . . . Willoughby," Lewrie announced, and the neatly garbed house servant left off trying to puzzle out the odd name on the outside of the folded letter and handed it over. His hand remained out in silent demand.

"Oh," Lewrie said, clawing into a trouser pocket for local coin. Whatever denomination of *peseta* or *peso* he produced wasn't the liveried servant's going rate, it seemed, for the fellow heaved a weary sigh, all but made an audible sniff of disdain, but closed his palm over it and stalked away. "Can you follow him, Mister Jugg?"

"I could give it a go, sor, aye . . . cautious-like."

"Good, 'cause I don't know him or his livery from Adam, and as for who'd send me a letter, if it ain't Pollock . . . " Lewrie muttered as he broke the still-warm wax seal (one without any identifying impression stamped into it of either aristocratic crest or the initial of the sender's surname) and read it quickly. "Well, damme!"

"Ain't Mister Pollock, sor?" Jugg asked, mystified by Lewrie's sudden elation.

"Er . . . no, Jugg," Lewrie gruffly told him. "From a lady, but a lady whose servant you *must* follow, all the way home if you're able."

"That'd be th' one wot dresses like a man, then, sor?" Jugg enquired, slyly bland-faced and innocently hiding his droll simper well.

"The one who claims she knows rich men who want their own ships, Jugg," Lewrie sternly retorted, "and most-like aren't that choosy over how they get 'em! Her name's Charité Bonsecours, but I don't know if that's quite true, after talking to Mister Pollock. I need to know as much about her as I can, if she does lead us to the people who back our pirates. Pollock's trying, too, but we can't trust to him alone."

"We leave this place abandoned, then, sor?"

"I'll leave Pollock a note," Lewrie impatiently stated, nettled again by Jugg's impertinent quibblings. "We're to dine at a place name of . . . de Russy's," he said, referring to her note, "round one. Plenty of time for Pollock to get here and get caught up. Speaking of . . . you dawdle much longer, that slave'll be out of sight, Jugg."

"Arrah then, sor, aye aye," Jugg reluctantly responded, as if he wished to dispute being sent on a fool's errand but did put knuckles to his brow in salute before sloping off.

Damn the man! Lewrie fumed to himself; *His eye-rollin' impertinence, too, like I don't know what I'm about, and he knows best!*

If the Spanish *were* alerted to their mission, were keeping eyes on him and his people . . . today he *must* take a chance and rush things with Charité, press her on her mystifying offer of a ship and get her to introduce him to those rich men she'd boasted of knowing.

Pollock'll have a fit, Lewrie decided as he quickly wrote a note to the man on a torn-out ledger page. *Press Charité for her address so I can write her whilst I'm gone? Hah! Call on her and her lordly Creole family? Bet* that'd *make 'em dance a pretty jig!*

He warned Pollock that he *suspected* that he'd been followed . . . by whom, well, that *was* the question, was it not? Despite the risks, he felt it necessary to keep his outwardly "innocent" appointment with the girl, with no one to watch his back.

Despite the risk of arrest as a British spy, Lewrie found that he was *vibrating* with excitement, like to jump out of his skin. There was a tiny *frisson* of dread, of course, but . . . the girl was the real lure. Maddeningly outlandish and entrancing, so desirable! Would they have another long afternoon bout of "the needful"?

Lewrie pegged his note where Pollock was sure to find it, then impatiently drew out his pocket watch to check the time. His dinner appointment was two hours off, and the tea leaves *had* steeped, so he poured himself a fresh, bracing cup and forced himself to sit down and sip it, fretting over just how he would frame his questions, how subtle he'd have to be. If Charité knew the people who *financed* the piracy, did she know more than she let on about their business, too?

"Damme!" Lewrie muttered of a sudden. "My cundums!"

He'd have to rush back to his set of rooms and fetch them, now they were fresh-washed and lightly oiled, before . . . with luck . . .

*All do*z*en?* he fretted; *I bloody* hope *so!*

CHAPTER TWENTY-THREE

*H*e had been forced to pace and stew in front of the *restaurant* she had named, de Russy's, for Charité had been coquettishly and coyly late, but more than worth the wait once she had turned a corner and had sashayed up to him, her tiny parasol spinning flirtatiously and her blue eyes aglow with both impishness and delight. As intriguing as she was when garbed as a young gentleman, when properly gowned as a young lady, she was a vision of femininity.

Dinner had taken the better part of two hours, with light and mostly innocent and inconsequential conversation, though Lewrie did get a chance to suggest that he wasn't long for New Orleans, if Pollock had his way. She had expressed regrets over that news, but her *innuendos* promised both a grand send-off on his trading expedition and a hearty welcome upon his swift return. Hidden meanings crossed her features, along with half-lidded girlish innocence, mixed with part sultry seductress, and delayed wanton abandon, making him squirm on his chair.

He trusted to her taste, let her have her head when it came to the menu that Charité almost knew by heart. A thin and tepid celery broth had resulted, just right for a warmish tropical day; then a zesty crabmeat *rémoulade*, followed by a palate-cleansing mixed green salad, fresh from the Lake Pontchartrain garden plots. That had gotten them ready for grilled shrimps as big as his thumbs, and lemony seafood crêpes that contained a meaty fish mélange and sauce that was heavenly from the first hot bite to the last cooled forkful.

Lastly had come a syrupy sweet trifle sort of pudding, lush with local oranges. So many wild oranges grew thereabouts (so he was amusingly told) that the local farmers fed most of them to their hogs . . . which made for a succulent Sunday ham!

"My last fine meal, *aussi, cher* Alain," she sadly imparted, "for I must leave the city and go visit my papa and maman upcountry. I hope I do not have to stay as long as Easter, but certainly I should be back about the time you come back from the wild Indians . . . if they do not scalp you, *n'est-ce pas?*" She giggled, then quickly went serious, reaching her fingertips to touch the back of Lewrie's hand. "I will pray earnestly that they do not . . . for you have such a fine head of hair, *mon cher*. And the savages have such horrid habits when it comes to shearing White people . . . of their hair and their . . . other things, *hein?*" she teased with a fetching blush and grin. "I do believe I would miss them all . . . equally. Oh là, *l'addition*. Will you take care of it, *cher?* Then, we shall go for a stroll. It will be good for your liver."

"Nothing wrong with my liver, Charité," Lewrie had said, claiming intimacy with the use of her Christian name in public; to which she made no prim objections.

"Oh, you English . . . you do not understand how important one's health depends on *la digestion* and proper care for one's liver!" she teased. "Look at your John Bull . . . so choleric and pasty-fat . . . so full of nothing but roast beef and *beer*! No wonder he is always so red in the face, *hein?*"

"A long walk, did you intend, then?" Lewrie had wondered aloud.

"Oh, lazy-bones!" Charité fondly teased him. "If not a long stroll, you have another healthful exercise in mind, *peut-être?*"

"Hmmm," he leered.

"Oh, oui!" Charité squealed. *"Plus vite, plus fort, mon étalon!"* And Lewrie gladly obliged, picking up his pace and slamming his groin against her firm and springy young buttocks. The taut bed-ropes supporting the mattress groaned and skreaked, the wooden bedstead parrot-squawked at its joins, and Lewrie himself groaned, panted, and uttered triumphal steer-like grunts as he thrust as she commanded: harder and faster . . . certainly not deeper, for he was already sheathed up to the hilt in her upraised, kneeling body. Charité clawed the pillows, the sheets, face pressed into a pillow now and then when her pleasure made her squawl out loud, shudder, then writhe and thrust back against him like a maddened serpent, grunting and lowing like a

heifer being taken by a rutting bull, her grunting a counterpoint to his that increased in fury and urgency 'til . . .

"*Ah-ahh!*" she screamed. "I go, I go so . . . *mon Dieu!*"

A moment later, it was Lewrie who threw back his head, roaring incoherently as he burst in her like a flaming carcass-shell, jerkily thrusting through the last melting moments 'til he *had* to rock back on his heels and gasp for air, dragging her back with him, his grasp firm on her soft, sweaty-cool hips. Charité, still sobbing with ecstacy but as if in need of yet even more, shuffled back to him quickly on palms and knees, to half squat, splayed wide across his lap, rocking up and down to either side, petulant-sounding to milk the last *frissons* of sensation from him, to keep him pressed hard against her innermost flesh. He slid his hands up to cup her breasts from behind, wrap his arms about her, and hold her close to his heaving chest. Her arms took hold of his to keep him there, her head weakly lolling on his chest.

"*Formidable* . . . so *formidable, mon amour,*" she barely croaked.

"You are indeed, sweet'un," he responded, muttering huskily in her damp mane of hair, some of which stuck to his mouth. "*Vraiment!*"

"You have lied to me," she accused, suddenly.

"Hah?" Lewrie gawped, stiffening in shock.

"You *can* speak French . . . when you care to." Charité chuckled.

"Only enough to get in trouble, dear," he laughed, greatly relieved that her plaint was harmless. To further distract her, he slid a hand down her sleek stomach and belly to her thatch, playfully twining his forefinger in her love-matted hair, flirting even lower round her clitoris, where his member was still sheathed inside her, making her roll her head, moan, and giggle.

"I am split . . . I am ruined, forever," Charité vowed in a weak whisper. "*Zut!*" she cursed a second later, as Lewrie limply slithered from her at last. Matter-of-factly, without shame, she flung herself forward to the headboard and piled pillows, rolled over face upwards, and swiped her damp hair from her forehead, with her fine, slim legs still wide apart, knees slightly raised as if welcoming another romp before sunset or suppertime.

Lewrie shuffled forward to recline alongside her, admitting to himself that he might *not* be the "All-Night-In" Corinthian he had been in his wilder twenties . . . After four blissful bouts he was just about utterly spent, and a longish nap wouldn't exactly go amiss. He snaked an arm under her neck and about her shoulders, getting no closer for a bit, as they lay there and genteelly "glowed" . . . perspired . . . on the nearly soaking sheets.

"You will miss me among the savages, *mon* Alain?" she pressed at last, rolling to her side to face him, propped up with a hand under her head.

"Desperately, *ma chérie*," he earnestly, nigh honestly vowed, rolling his head to look at her and seeing her impish expression. "And you? *Et vous?*"

"*Et tu*, Alain," Charité amusedly insisted. "Not the impersonal *vous*, but the intimate *tu, mon étalon*." She stroked a hand over his hot chest, a fingertip circling his near-side nipple.

"Your stallion, hey?" He chuckled, feeling risible after all as she teased.

"Ah, *oui*. The stallion *le plus puissant*. You spoil me for . . . After you, the most powerful, what man could ever compare, *mon amour?*" Charité said, frowning for a second and lowering her eyes as if she had said the wrong thing, had come close to reminding him that other lovers had existed, would exist in the future.

"Then I'd best hurry back to New Orleans before you run across a better," Lewrie suggested, tongue-in-cheek. "So we can have days and *days* like this. Days and nights . . . early mornings, the crack of dawn?"

"Oh la, I tempt you so much, you would surrender all your other lovers for me, Alain?" she asked, trying to be light, but with a slight edginess in her voice, as if his reply actually mattered.

"Hah! What *other* lovers?" he barked with laughter. "Damme, if you haven't spoiled *me*, d'ye know. If I *had* one, or a round dozen, a 'wife' in ev'ry port, I'd toss 'em *all* off a cliff, aye. Charité, you are *sans pareil*. Lovely, passionate . . . abandoned. Maddening! There, ye see? Another French phrase. We keep this up, I'll *parler* . . . "

She rolled half atop him, embraced him, twined with him and bestowed a dozen fond kisses to reward such gallantry.

"Oh, pooh!" she said after suddenly breaking away, pouting *very* prettily and desirably. "It would all end in tears. I could not have an *Anglais* lover! You are not even *Catholique!* A heretic, Protestant . . . 'Bloody,' born and bred to kill the French, and Catholics? Never, not in a thousand years, could you be acceptable. What Papa and Maman would say . . . my brothers!"

"Well, don't they say that 'love conquers all'?" Lewrie jested.

"Oh, we marry, and I am disinherited?" Charité huffed, though still pressed against him, up on her elbows. "I must go to a *British* seaport as your kept woman, your wife . . . when you admit that you cannot even keep yourself? *Zut, putain!*"

"Well, nobody said . . . " Lewrie began, daunted by her intensity.

"And then you give me babies," Charité further fantasised, one hand flying in objection as if swatting flies, "and after a few, I am the fat, dull *matrone* and you take your pleasures elsewhere, *hein?* I become hideous to you? *Non!* I wish *never* to be a *matrone*! No matter how grand the man, there is so much *more* to life, *certain*! I wish to do more with *my* life than marry, breed, and die anonymously, Alain."

"Well, *I* think you're famous," he essayed, much confused.

"Even so . . . " Charité said, her heat evaporating as she turned pensive and lay down atop him again, her head on his shoulder and her voice muffled against his neck. "I would have *your* babies, Alain. I would be your *belle amie*. Just so long as I am the *only* one!" she concluded, with a mock-fierce nip at his earlobe. "And when you are among the Indians, you do not take a lover there!"

"Well, I might be more among the Yankee Doodles than Indians," Lewrie said, yelping as if really nipped and playfully wrestling with her 'til he had her under his weight, her wrists pinned by his hands.

"Oh, they are even worse!" she snarled, wriggling and thrashing.

"How fair could they be, in their homespun junk, and all muddy barefeet?" Lewrie snickered, feeling even *more* risible as she squirmed most fetchingly under him, belly to belly, even pinioned as she was. "You wouldn't trust me out of your sight, would you? Would you? I thought so. You'd have me *clerking* for Pollock, here in New Orelans. All ink blots and smudges on my nose, in a countinghouse, instead of adventuring."

"No, you can have your adventures, Alain," she insisted. "Just so you come back to me . . . often. Always," she softly, fondly, added.

"But what could I do to earn a living, if I don't go venturing for Panton, Leslie?" Lewrie innocently asked, thinking it about time to try to dredge some information from her.

"I *told* you, *cher*, Learn the river trade from your adventures, prove yourself, then . . . meet with those wealthy men I mentioned, who wish to own their own ships before the Americans control *all* the shipping trade," Charité reiterated, turning still between his thighs. "If you wish to begin at once, I could introduce you to *Monsieur* Maurepas, the banker, He is in touch with . . . oh, *zut alors! Putain!* I cannot. You must go upriver, I must go to my parents' plantations. It will be weeks and *weeks* before I could introduce you properly."

There's a name t'conjure with! Lewrie silently exulted, to hear one of Pollock's suspicions almost confirmed.

"Though, he is . . . many of his associates," Charité hemmed and hawed, writhing beneath him as if spurred more by dread than pleasure. "They are proud Creoles, Alain, *tu comprends? French* Creoles, who hate the Spanish subjugation and wish to be a part of *la belle France* once more. France is strong, and Spain is weak, and they believe that *someone* must save them, before the

Americans . . . or you 'Bloodies' eat us up!" she spelled out for him, though turning the traditional epithet for Englishmen to a joke, instead of a taunt. "You must be careful in your dealings with them, *mon coeur,* before one of them spins out some fanciful dream about revolution against Spain. Oh, how do you English say, to . . . " she asked, frustrated.

" 'Take it with a grain of salt,' d'ye mean, love?" He chuckled. "D'ye mean that, one . . . or a lot of 'em . . . might want me to smuggle arms? Start a Louisiana *Navy?* Turn privateer, or some such, and take *Spanish* prizes? Bein' a former naval officer might *tempt* 'em?"

Damme, that *was knacky of me!* he quietly chortled; *Perhaps I* can *do 'subtle'!*

"*Oui,* with the grain of salt, *vraiment,*" Charité quickly agreed.

"But *you're* happy enough under the Spanish?" he further asked.

"*Mon amour,* I am most happy this moment, under *you!*" she teased with a coquettish stirring under him. "*Mais non,* the Spanish . . . such a *horrible* set of tyrants. And so bad for trade as well! Everyone I talk to says so. Papa, *Monsieur* Maurepas, our factors . . . If I were a man, *I* would be tempted to do something rash. To rid Louisiana of any *taint* of Spain . . . even their idioms!"

"When I met you, you came *close* to being a man," Lewrie pointed out. "Though . . . thank God you aren't. Most *surely* aren't!" he said, sliding down her so he could kiss her nipples and circle her areolae on the tip of his tongue.

She knows more than she wants t'tell me, Lewrie furiously schemed; *Her papa's in on it, I'll wager, maybe even her brothers. Damme . . . have I already met 'em, two nights ago? They were all so alike, and . . .*

"Oh la, Alain," Charité said, sounding as if she was mournfully wailing in exasperation at men's folly, "I fear, if someone gave you a chance to fight, do what you were trained for, you would *leap* for joy, and turn . . . *pirate,* if you thought it would be grand adventure. And, paid enough! Men . . . *mon Dieu!*" she spat in a flouncing huff.

"Something in what ye say, Charité darlin'," he frankly seemed to confess, breaking off his teasing ministrations to look her in the eyes. "I never *did* get many opportunities to . . . swashbuckle. Boring blockade work in all weathers . . . paper wars and ink smuts? Boresome. Hellish-boresome, most of my undistinguished naval career was. But I doubt I'd *really* do anything that damn fool."

"*Bon!*" she approved with some heat. "Good!"

"Not 'til they promised I'd be an Admiral," Lewrie cagily japed. "Not 'til it looked like it'd *succeed*. Look at John Paul Jones, that Yankee Doodle. Catherine the Great of Russia made *him* an Admiral over her whole fleet! Why, there's been dozens of ambitious Royal Navy men, taken service under foreign colours, some with the Admiralty's connivance and blessings, too, who didn't look like they'd *ever* make senior Post-Captain in their own service.

"The Swedes even made *me* an offer . . . not much of one, but," he added with a deprecatory shrug, suddenly inspired to feel her out even farther. "Not a *command,* actually—not a ship of my own. *Arsenal* clerking, counting cannon barrels or some such. I turned 'em down and tried for merchant service . . . where I'd at least be at *sea,*" he lied.

"You *would* be tempted," Charité stated, peering closely at him, not in the expected disapproval at such insanity that she had evinced just moments before, but in a speculative, calculating . . . *weighing* of his sentiment, with the faintest hint of a smile touching the corners of her mouth and eyes . . . as if he'd said or done something clever.

"Well, if they threw *you* in," he japed, shrugging again and forcing an inane grin onto his phyz to quash her slightest suspicions.

"Oh, la! Oh, *zut alors, mon chou!*" Charité suddenly snapped as she turned forceful in her attempts to slide out from underneath him. "The hour! It is growing dark, and I must go!"

"Oh, damme, no!" Lewrie said with a crushed groan. "Surely you could stay for a *little* longer, darlin'. Just a quarter hour more?" he entreated, gone all pleading puppy-eyed. He sat up, though, rocked on his heels once more as she lithely sprang down from the high bedstead *au naturel,* as boldly bare as she'd been born, fetching her discarded chemise off the back of a nearby chair and wriggling it down over her head. *Damme, we were almost there, too!* he thought; *This close to . . .*

"Lace me up, *cher?*" she asked, clapping her undone *bustier* to her chest, perkily, impishly smiling. "I must be home, quickly."

"What if I won't?" Lewrie pretended to pout.

"Then I must walk home as undone as a whore, and I will blame you for it, *mon chou,*" she threatened. "And there will be two *dozen* challenges to duels slipped under your door," she added, cocking her head at the doorway to his set of rooms.

"Well, as we said in the Navy . . . 'Growl you may, but go you must.' Damme!" he cried, springing naked off the bed. He seized her, burying his face in the hollow of her neck. "I simply *cannot* get enough of you, me girl!"

"Nor I you, *cher* Alain," she conceded, "but . . . I leave in the morning, you go upriver in a few more days, so we *must* part sometime. Only for a *little* while, *mon amour,* I promise! How do you say, that a parting is . . . something-something?" she crooned, embracing him with her fingers caressing his head and his hair against her as if to give comfort. "A short absence . . ."

" 'Absence makes the heart grow fonder,' " Lewrie recited, lifting his head to swing her length against his nudity. "I'll make you a new'un t'go along with that, too. 'Brief partings make *rencontres* all the sweeter . . . and urgent yearnings, the passion even fiercer.' Hmm?"

"You just made that up?"

"Aye."

"You are a *rare* Englishman . . . with the romantic soul of a true Frenchman," Charité admiringly declared. "Are you *certain* you weren't born French?"

"Quickened in Holland, but born in London. Son of a penniless rogue and a disinherited heiress, dammit all." Lewrie snickered.

"No matter, *mon Anglais,*" Charité said, wide-eyed and serious, all but biting her trembling lips as she bestowed the sweetest little kiss on his mouth, "for . . . *je t'aime,* Alain *mon chou. Je t'aime!*"

"Darlin'!" Lewrie gasped, stunned right down to his curling toes by her sudden declaration of love; not intimate fondness, but her true love. Wondering what the Devil to *do* with it, but . . . !

When in doubt, lie like Blazes, Lewrie told himself; *It surely won't cost me much, and she might even halfway believe it!*

"*Je t'aime, aussi, ma chérie . . . ma petite biche,*" he growled in reply, his forehead pressed to hers. "You darlin' little doe-deer, I adore you, too. Ev'ry lovely inch of you."

Well, that *seemed t'make her happy,* he thought as they embraced even tighter. And, despite her protestations, it *did* lead to a frantic tumble back onto his bed, and one more glorious, feverishly passionate romp, spare cundums, her expensive chemise, the lateness of the hour, her family, or society's expectations bedamned.

Oh, make him happy, Charité told herself at the same time; *Men! So easy to entrance . . . and enlist! He will aid us. For me. And it* will *be pleasurable for both of us. And he is so adorable, I think I truly* am *falling in love!* Well, perhaps *I could.*

It was well past seven in the evening when he handed her down to the street and walked her the short block from Bourbon Street, up Rue Ste. Anne to

Rue Dauphine, where she insisted that they must part at last. Now, on public view, their behaviour had to be most circumspect and formally courteous. Lewrie gallantly doffed his hat and swept it across his chest, was just about to make a "leg" in *congé*, she about to drop him a brief curtsy and elegant incline of her head in parting as well, when it suddenly struck him that he *still* hadn't plumbed the matter of her address. He'd had other things on his mind.

"When I return and wish to see you again, how do I reach you?" he asked suddenly. "Where do I send my best regards?"

"To . . . Mademoiselle Charité," she seemed to stumble for a moment before resuming her gay, coquettish airs. "Write me at La Maison Gayoso. Twenty-Six, Rue Dauphine."

"Not Mademoiselle Bonsecours?" Lewrie pressed, hat in hand and shamming amiable, fond confusion.

"Our *concierge* will see that I get it," Charité attempted to explain, for one brief instant almost snippish with him, before relaxing into her customary air of flirtatiousness. "My parents and family . . . for now, *mon chou*, for only a while longer, just my given name, please? Until you are well settled in New Orleans, *n'est-ce pas?*"

"Well," he quibbled, shuffling from one foot to another.

"And you will keep your lodgings while you are upriver, Alain?" she asked with a disarming smile. "When I return, I may write to you there?"

"No, I'll . . ," Lewrie flummoxed, considering that he would most-like never see her again, that his secret doings would be finished by the time she got back to the city; then hit upon a sudden inspiration. "When I come back, I expect t'be *much* richer, and I'll take a grander *appartement*, not a low, single room. Where I may 'entertain' you in proper splendour, and . . . discreet privacy, hmm? Oh! You could pick it for me! Choose it and help me furnish it to our, ah . . . our mutual satisfaction?" he said with the suitable anticipatory leer. "Try the Panton, Leslie offices first, though, and I'll come running."

Aye, feather a nest, he smugly thought; *women just adore that!*

"*Je t'adore!*" Charité cooed under her breath, her eyes glowing under the brim of her fashionable bonnet, and the parasol carried over her shoulder spinning in delight. "But of course, I shall be *more* than happy to help. And I shall be distraught every day that we are apart, Alain, *mon coeur*. 'Til then, though, alas," she said with a tremble of her lip and a forlorn hitch of her shoulders and a heartfelt gulp in her voice. "*Au revoir, mon cher* Alain! Trust that I do love you . . . madly!"

"And I you, Charité . . . as mad as a Hatter, as a March Hare!" he declared. "English sayings . . . I'll explain them all to you, soon."

"You will have to!" She chuckled. "Soon. *Le plus tôt possible, mon amour* . . . as soon as possible, my love. Again, *au revoir!*"

A slim hand gloved in lace net almost reached out for him, but she remembered her distinguished place in Creole society—in public at least!—and dropped him a slow and graceful curtsy, that elegant incline of her head, then she was gone in a trice, rising and spinning away down Dauphine without a backward glance, as if all their fervent day had never transpired.

Lewrie shrugged to himself and turned away as well, clapping his hat back on his head and fiddling with his sword-cane. He walked a few paces back down Rue Ste. Anne as if to return to his rooms or to head for the part of town where the most eateries were located . . . but then paused, theatrically felt his waist-coat pockets as if he had forgotten something, and turned back to lean his head round the corner, once he'd almost assured himself that no one was watching him. A few lamplighters were sluggishly making the rounds with their ladders and port fires, igniting the entire hundred (some scoffed and said only eighty) publicly funded streetlights of which New Orleans could boast. In the entryways, above the high stoops of shops and houses, private lanterns were already lit and feebly glowing, throwing little pools of light and even deeper skeins of darkness. But he could pick her out by the pale colour of her gown, the flounces on her hat, the now-furled parasol in her hands, as she flitted from one illuminated pool to the next . . .

A moment later, and she'd melted away into an iron-gated entryway of a blank-walled building. *Close enough,* Lewrie decided, thinking that his sauntering past the place would blow the gaffe. He would recognise the building again, counted it off as the twelfth from his corner, on the north side of Rue Dauphine, and from the look of the place at his acute viewing angle, it would most likely turn out to be one of the many walled-courtyard *appartement* houses. No more than three storeys above the street, but with spacious sets of rooms on all four sides to face the central courtyard. *Eight appartements or twelve?* he speculated, seeing no sign of commercial establishments on the ground floor. *With their own stabling out back, it'd be even fewer,* he deduced.

Ste. Anne began on the east side of the Place d'Armes, the main city square by the riverbank; Rue St. Pierre ran down its west side, so . . . how did they number their houses? Outward from the centre, the lowest numbers starting on those two streets, or from Rue de l'Arsenal on the east straight to the west? *No matter,* he thought with a sniff; *She'd said number 26. Unless she's been lying like a dog right from the start!*

He shrugged again and drew out his pocket watch. It was nearly eight! Long past time for him to hare back to the Panton, Leslie & Company warehouse offices and catch up with Mr. Pollock, to see what he'd learned today, and proudly impart to him what he had garnered. A growl from his innards warned Lewrie that it was long past suppertime, too. Frankly, he suddenly felt ravenously famished, now that the most important items of his activities list were done, and he had only the idle Spanish to fret about.

Play-acting and fucking! Lewrie happily pondered as he strolled along, clacking his cane on the pavement; *Both* damn' *good for buildin' an appetite, ha ha! Lewrie, you sly dog!*

Down Ste. Anne to cross Bourbon Street, then down to Rue Royale, headed for Rue Charles, where he thought he might take a little amble in the Place d'Armes before diving into the commercial jumble round Levee Road, where it was darker, poorer-lit, and the streets narrower, filthier, and nigh abandoned at this hour.

The first two thin and muffled shots, the twiggish *crack! crack!* made him slam to a stop, head swivelling to track the confusing echoes that swirled from God knew where—closer to the river, or westward down Royale? A third *crack!* and by God that *was* a shot, quickly followed by a chorus of harsh shouts and the discharge of a weapon and a keen whine of a ricochet off brick! Definitely westward down Rue Royale, near St. Pierre or Toulouse!

Lewrie took a hesitant step in that direction, recognising the shouts as being made by English speakers. His men from *Proteus* or some of Pollock's men? Instinct made him reach under his coat and pull out one of his double-barrelled Manton pistols, then spurred him to turn in the direction of the commotion.

The fourth thin *crack!* was much closer; so was the musket ball that droned past his ear and spanged off a wrought-iron balcony pillar with a departing harpy's howl inches from where he'd stood dithering but an eyeblink before!

The fifth shot forced him to throw his body flat in one of the 'tween-lamp pools of gloom!

CHAPTER TWENTY-FOUR

*L*ewrie feverishly searched for a betraying cloud of spent gunpowder to mark the shooter's position, but saw nothing. He perked his ears for the telltale sounds of a nearby marksman reloading, the rattle of powder horn on a muzzle, the tinkle of a ramrod—nothing! He got his feet under him, spotted a deep doorway further west down Royale . . . popped up and turned as if to dash for it . . .

Crack! A second after he had flung himself down again, a ball went zinghumming over his head, and Lewrie was up and running for the shadowed doorway, reaching its shelter and flattening himself against the east side of the vestibule, out of sight for a moment as he cocked both firelocks of his Manton pistol, tore off his "wide-awake" hat and put it on his fisted left hand . . . stuck it out as if fearfully taking a peek, and . . . *Crack!* came another shot that spun the hat like a top on his fist after the ball had taken a round bite from its brim!

He swung out—head, shoulders, and gun hand in plain view—to see the faint gleam of a bright-metal movement. Laying his gun hand over his left forearm, he fired one round, absorbing the recoil upwards for a second, then levelling again and firing the second barrel towards the slightest vertical glint of lamplight off what he took for a musket's barrel. The Manton belched two large clouds of blackpowder smoke, in which he slithered away, low to the pavement in a duck-walk to another deep entryway farther off.

With his second double-barrelled Manton, he fired off a round in the general direction of his last vague target, then ducked under the resulting pall and sprinted the short distance to another entryway on the south side of the street, this time.

He heard no more *Crack!* aimed against him; after a long minute he took note that there were no more shots down Rue Royale, either. A loud chorus of shouts and curses, aye, but no more gunfire. He traded the spent Manton for one of those single-shot pocket pistols, then set off down that way. Halfway there, skulking from one shadow to another, it suddenly struck him . . .

Twig-crack . . . no powder smoke or ramming! Four shots, got off in less than a minute, at me! he furiously thought; *Bright-metal, not treated blue or brown. Hell's Bells, someone's got a Girandoni rifle!*

"Mine arse on a band-box!" he seethed aloud. "I find out who it was, I'll have his *nutmegs* off! Pollock's hen-head *clerks* sold . . . *pah!*"

He could not go back the way he had been walking, that was for certain, to attain the relative safety of the evening crowds strolling in the Place d'Armes where, one *might* assume, the Creoles didn't take pot-shots at each other all *that* often. Even if the shooter was long gone, the commotion would surely draw the Spanish foot patrol and the idle curious, and he'd much rather not have to answer their questions or be recognised and recalled later.

A slight distance more and he'd be at the intersection of Rue Royale and Rue d'Orleans, but d'Orleans dead-ended behind the impressive cathedral, and Lewrie could not recall but one narrow alleyway leading to the square, where the odds were good that he might re-encounter the bastard who had shot at him . . . or meet up with Spanish soldiers, who'd block both ends and delight in questioning or arresting the first foreigner they came across.

There was nothing for it but to keep on westerly down Rue Royale at least as far as St. Pierre to get to the Place d'Armes, then Levee Road—right into the crowd he could see gathering at the scene of the *first* shooting he'd heard! At the least, Lewrie thought, he could blend into a much larger crowd and sidle through it with eyes curious and wide, play-acting an idle gawker . . . hoping that the reek of gunpowder on his person wouldn't be noticed.

One last desperate and intense study of the intersection he had fled, and Lewrie shoved his pistol back into hiding under the tails of his coat, and he launched himself from the deep doorway, sword-cane in his right hand once more to peck out a languid pace down towards that hubbub and growing knot of people near Rue Toulouse, hoping that once near there, he could turn down St. Pierre to the square, on a well-lit and peopled street . . .

"Empty yore hands, yew English sumbitch!" came a harsh whisper from an unlit doorway he had just passed, almost in his left ear, and chilling him to his bones. He felt the prick of something sharp right through his layers of clothes in the small of his back!

"I was shot at, too," Lewrie managed to say, though just about as frightened as he had ever been. "Back there, at Sainte Anne street!"

"Huh!" came the faceless response, with the slightest shove of the sharp object against his skin. "Gimme 'at sword-cane."

"You're American . . . one of Mister Ellison's men?" Lewrie asked as he let his cane clatter to the cobblestones. He winced to think that he hadn't spotted his assailant lurking in the shadows, had not got a *whiff* of his stench as he passed him, for up close now, the reek of a crudely tanned deerskin hunting shirt or fringed trousers was overpowering. "Damn you!"

A rough hand groped under his coat, discovering one of his twin-barrelled pistols. Lewrie could hear the man sniff the muzzles.

"It's just a cane, and I shot back at whoever shot at me, that's why the—" Lewrie tried to explain, insulted to be man-handled.

"Yeah . . . *shore* it is," the man sneered.

"There's another Manton, both barrels fired. A pair of pocket pistols, too, *not* fired, and couldn't hit anything over ten paces if my life depended on it." Lewrie announced. "I heard shots, *rifle* shots, fired down your way, before they shot at *me*. Like twig-cracks? Quick together? Was that how it was down yonder? If you're with Mister Ellison, you came aboard the emporium ship with him . . . you saw the Austrian sharpshooter rifles, the Girandoni *air*-rifles? That's all of a sound they make, a twig crack. *Think*, man!"

A hand hammered onto his left shoulder to spin him around to face his accostor and his wide-bladed ten-inch skinning knife, as big to Lewrie's eyes as a Scot's claymore. And he *was* an American, clad in a mix of homespun and leather, glaring face and eyes beneath a massive coonskin cap with the mask on, with glittering brass beads in its eye sockets winking from the street lamps' lights.

"How d'I know ye didn't have a hand in shootin' Jim Hawk? 'At ye didn't sic some o' yore men t'do it?" the man accused.

"Why the Devil would I?" Lewrie shot back. "He doesn't even owe me money!"

" 'Caws yore an English spy, come here t'scout New Orleans 'fore ye take it fer yore own, an we got in yore way, an iff 'n Jim Hawk dies I'll draw out yore innards an' roast 'em on a stick right b'fore yore eyes. An' 'at'd be just fer starters," he vowed with a feral grin.

When among the Muskogee towards the end of the Revolutionary War, Lewrie had *heard* of savage tortures, so he could not help gulping in dread, but . . .

"And you and Mister Ellison are here to scout the place so *you* can take it before we do," Lewrie retorted, "but *we* came to hunt down pirates who stole a rich prize ship from us. That ship moored highest upriver of the emporium hulks. Looking for a large, black-hulled, and red-striped schooner. Some of the men with me survived being marooned on the Dry Tortugas, and they could recognise both the schooner *and* the faces of the pirates. *That's* why we're here, the only reason. I am a Post-Captain in his Majesty's Navy. Unless you and your party had anything to do with the piracy, we'd have no *cause* to shoot your leader! And how is Mister Ellison, by the way?"

All that truth, carefully mixed with lies, discomfited the man, Lewrie could see. His fierce glare subdued, replaced by a thoughtful but puzzled expression.

"We stand here with your knife drawn much longer, man, and we'll draw the Spanish watchmen, sure as Fate," Lewrie suggested. "Neither side needs that, for God's sake. *Keep* my damned Mantons if you wish, but shouldn't we try to blend into that crowd yonder? Find out how it stands with your Mister Ellison, hmm?" Lewrie gently urged.

"Put yore hands down," the man growled, shoving both of Lewrie's pistols back at him. "Anybody gets caught with fired guns, it'll be you, not me. Pick up 'at cane o' yor'n, and we'll go. Mind now, I'll be right at yore back. Play me false, and I'll cut yore kidneys out."

The first frontiersman turned Lewrie over to another member of Ellison's gang while he went inside the mean tavern to pass on what he had learned. Lewrie and his guard stood near the door, where he could see inside. Ellison was propped up on a threadbare settee, biting his lips, grimacing as a Creole surgeon worked on him. Now and then, he'd let pass a faint groan, then take a sip of whisky from a tall tumbler as the surgeon probed and plucked inside a plum-purpled wound high on his right chest. They rolled Ellison on his side so the surgeon could feel about, then use a slim scalpel to excise a rifle ball from under his shoulder blade. That forced a cry from him, but Ellison's torment came out in a battle-roar, or the snarl of a cornered bear. From that incision, a shiny .51 calibre ball appeared, one that Ellison demanded be laid in his palm. Which plucky, courageous *geste* raised great cheer among his anxious men and even made Lewrie feel relief.

To the Creole doctor's chagrin, whisky was poured right in the raw wound, more poured over his needle and thread before they'd let him stitch the lips of the wounds together. As he finished his work, with generous batts of absorbent cotton and linen wrappings, Ellison sat up on the settee, half reclined on one padded arm. He had a long whispered conversation with Lewrie's captor, then crooked a finger to summon Lewrie to him.

"You got shot at, too, didjya, Willoughby?" Ellison muttered.

"With a Girandoni air-rifle, the same as you, it appears, sir," Lewrie said, pointing to the ball in the man's hand. "By the Spanish, most-like. Why they didn't just arrest us, I've no idea, but they've apparently tumbled to our . . . doings."

"And you're a Captain in the British Navy, are ye?" Mr. Ellison snidely smirked, though wincing against his pain.

"Right enough," Lewrie breezily admitted. "And you are a serving officer under American colours, or . . . in a civilian capacity?"

"The Army of the United States of America, sir," Ellison admitted. "Temporarily, ah . . . detached. And were ye happy with yer beach, out t'Lake Borgne, Captain Willoughby?"

"It'll serve main-well, Mister Ellison," Lewrie confessed, once he got over his surprise. "And your improvised river fleet?" he asked, taking a stab in the dark. "Much shorter distance to go, I'm bound."

Hah! Got it in one! Lewrie hooted to himself to see Ellison's chagrined expression. *In his shoes, that's how* I'd *pull it off!*

"I don't *think* ye had a hand in my shootin', sir," Ellison told him. "But the Spanish sink their teeth inta things, they'll not care fer either o' us bein' here. My man says ye told *him* ye come to hunt pirates that stole yer prize ship, well . . . that won't wash any better than spyin' out how t'invade. Ever hear folks say, 'once bitten, twice shy'? Uh-huh, good. Me an' th' boys'd take a dim view of ye, if you an' your people were still in New Orleans, come mornin'. Ye are, then it's 'Katy, bar the door.' "

"That translates much like your hairy fellow's 'ki' ye,' does it, Mister Ellison?" Lewrie japed, playing up game even if exposed.

"Why, I do b'lieve it do, Captain Willoughby," Ellison managed to snicker. "*Somebody* drew my blood . . . an' no man tries t'kill *me* an' lives. If ye get my meanin'."

"Neither I nor my men were responsible, sir, 'pon my word of honour. And my name is Alan Lewrie, not Willoughby, so you'll know who to damn, do I prove false," Lewrie declared. "I sincerely regret your wounding, sir, and wish you a speedy recovery," he added, offering his hand, which Ellison took and shook gingerly. "Though I must caution you, sir, that you and your men might find it expedient to, ah—what *is* that picturesque American word?—ske-daddle? . . . before the Spanish find they've failed."

"That's my lookout," Ellison said, retrieving his hand. "Yours is th' Spanish, *and* us. Luck to ye, Captain Lewrie, fer you're quite a plucky bastard, but . . . don't let yer string o' luck run out. Good-*bye*, sir. Skedaddle, yer own self, and *adieu!*"

Lewrie took that for as good an exit line as any and turned to shoulder his way through the anxious throng of hostile Americans for the door, thence to the far side of Rue Toulouse, was just about to leave the vicinity by heading for Rue Chartres when a Spanish patrol finally made its appearance. He casually turned on his heel, leaned on his cane, and got on tiptoe to see over the crowd of onlookers as if he was just another curious ogler.

"Kentuckians," Lewrie sneered to no one as the hastily dressed soldiers shoved their way through the back of the crowd. "Tennessee trash! Ought to run 'em all back to their kennels!"

Deal with that hint, do! Lewrie fervently thought at the back of the Spanish officer as he got to the door of the tavern. *And take* that, *Mister Jim Hawk Ellison, of the United States Army! Now, if I can only get back to the docks before the Dons try t'kill* me *again, I'll be a* damned *happy man!*

CHAPTER TWENTY-FIVE

*L*ew . . . Willoughby!" Mr. Pollock barked as soon as he'd entered the dockside warehouse offices. "Where the Devil have you been? We've been beating the bounds for you, the last two—"

"I've been out getting shot at, act'lly," Lewrie drawled, as if such happened daily, "me and that Yankee Ellison both, and nigh the same instant. Two ambushes . . . though Ellison got the worst of his. Anything to drink?" he asked, tossing his hat on a table, drawing his spent pistols from underneath his coat, and peering about for fresh powder, ball, wadding, and wine. Liam Desmond fetched him a glass of *vin ordinaire*, which Lewrie tossed down in three gulps.

"*Shot* at?" Pollock gawped. "How? When? By whom?"

"Why, with an *air*-rifle, Mister Pollock," Lewrie scathingly replied, "halfway to here from my lodgings, not a quarter hour past. With an air-rifle your clerks sold *someone*. So was that American, Ellison. Saw the ball they cut from him . . . fifty-one calibre. I told him that *we* didn't do it, that it must've been the Dons . . . unless *you* ordered it, and I lied to him unwittingly. Either way, they've tumbled to us and said were we still here come dawn, 'h'it wuz, Katy bar th' do-er' or some such," Lewrie said in sarcastic imitation. "You *didn't* set up an ambush of Ellison and his men, did you, Mister Pollock? Didn't sell the Americans any Girandonis they might've used to pot-shot me? Didn't sell a few to the Dons, did you?" he cynically demanded.

"No to all of it, sir!" Pollock retorted, as if such nefarious doings were beneath him. "You're *certain* it was Girandonis used?"

"*Damned* certain, Mister Pollock," Lewrie vowed, crossing to the sideboard for a refill from the wine carafe. As he poured, the hinges of the door squeaked, and Toby Jugg and Seaman Furfy came tumbling in.

"Oh, there ye be, sor," Jugg said, sounding relieved for a rare moment before turning laconic once more. " 'Twas a spate o' shootin' a little while ago. Big commotion round th' tavern where them Yankees lodge . . . "

"Captain Lewrie tells us someone shot their leader, Mister Jugg," Pollock gloomily informed him. "Took shots at the captain, too."

"Who'd want both of us dead, sir?" Lewrie asked. "The Spanish?"

"Some'un shot at th' Cap'm?" Furfy barked, round-eyed in alarm.

"Hesh yourself an' listen, lad," his mate Desmond chid him.

"I can't see the Spanish . . . " Pollock fretted, nervously chewing on a thumbnail. " 'Tis not their way. They've more to gain by arresting us and holding public trials. The old firm and I live or die on their stance towards us, and I haven't heard the least rumour, felt the faintest stiffness in how they deal with us . . . not even the slightest sidelong glance! Especially on this trip, given the, ah . . . *ahem*."

"Well, if the Dons didn't do it and the Yankees swear it wasn't them," Lewrie posed with a grim frown, "then who? Our *pirates*, maybe?"

"More likely than the Spanish, yes!" Pollock agreed. "Something we did or said, our presence revealed somehow to them, put the wind up them!"

"Perhaps they recognised Mister Jugg and put two and two together?" Lewrie wondered, looking at the survivor of the marooning, almost accusingly. "Then why the Devil didn't they shoot *him*, 'stead o' me, I ask you? *He's* the man, could point 'em out! And why shoot Ellison at the same time? Far as we know, *he's* not here t'hunt 'em down."

"We don't know that," Pollock countered. "They *seem* to prefer Spanish victims, but the bulk of the merchantmen that dock are Yankee ships. They carry desirable imports and fat chests of coin that buy New Orleans's export goods. If the pirates had taken one of theirs . . . "

"Ellison's a temporarily seconded American Army officer," Lewrie told him. "We both, ah . . . admitted our bonafides. Said he hoped that we liked our dinner t'other day out by Lake Borgne, sir. They've kept us under their eyes almost from the first, I'd expect. And he asked did we find the lake shore suitable for our purposes?"

"Ah-ha!" Pollock responded, like to strangling on that revelation. "*Ahem!* (*large* twitch-whinny!) Did he! Though . . . two may engage in the same game, sir. And accomplish two tasks in one, as we've been charged. Perhaps the Americans even intend to use the loss of several of their merchantmen as a legitimate *casus belli* . . . the elimination of a pirate's nest as an excuse to the wider world for *their* invasion."

This revelation was news to Lewrie's hands, who had thought they were merely nabbing pirates who'd harmed their mates. They nudged and poked each other, sharing confused but sly grins. After all, no one had yet laid out whether they were Scotching Yankee invasion plans . . . or sketching out their own. Either one would suit, so long as it made for a unique adventure.

"Could your firm have unwittingly sold the Girandoni air-rifles to *whoever* it was used them tonight, sir?" Lewrie asked. "Might your ledgers contain *names* or your clerks recall faces?"

"By God, yes!" Pollock chirped excitedly. "We haven't sold that many. One had hopes they'd find a market, but the novelty may've . . . "

"Then perhaps we might enquire of your clerks tonight, sir?" Lewrie impatiently said, nigh snarling.

"I'll send for my head clerk," Pollock declared, animated now. "Um . . . Mister Jugg, might I impose upon you to row over to the hulk and fetch the fellow here?"

"Aye, sor," Jugg replied, heaving himself off a table's edge in a trice. "Quicker'n two shakes of a wee lamb's tail, an' th' first be a'ready shook," he took the time to jape, taking Dempsey and Mannix to do the heavy work.

"That slave who brought my note," Lewrie had to ask before they could get out the door. "Did you . . . "

"Lost 'im soon's he turned west on Dauphine Street, sor, sorry t'say," Jugg informed him with a hapless shrug, then dashed off.

"The, ah . . . Bonsecours slave, sir?" Pollock asked. "The note you mentioned in your message to me . . . from the suited, booted, *ahem* . . . young woman?"

"The very same, Mister Pollock," Lewrie replied, pouring himself another glass of wine by the sideboard. Now that he was safe and alive, surrounded by well-armed men, the usual shaky let-down that came nearly to overwhelming him had appeared, and he needed some "liquid" fortification. "Jugg placed her man in Dauphine Street, but I managed to tail her right to her door, Mister Pollock," Lewrie explained, feeling rather "sly-boots" and clever. "I'm to write her at the Maison Gayoso, number twenty-six Rue Dauphine . . . no last name for now. Now, whether she really lodges there or merely uses it as a convenience, I still don't know, but I saw her *enter,* and it didn't look as if there's a handy back exist. No stable gate. So, Charité . . . "

He waited for Mr. Pollock, the part-time, "job-lot" British spy to offer him at least *grudging* congratulations for skulking and observing so skillfully, but . . .

"A young lady by name of Charité may very *well* reside, there," Pollock somberly told him, holding up an objecting hand, "but I must inform you that, according to my own queries, not a single Bonsecours dwells on Rue Dauphine."

"So . . . it's an assumed name," Lewrie said with a crestfallen shrug, as if it didn't really signify.

"Indeed, sir, enquiries made by my, ah . . . domestics," Pollock flustered, all but tugging at his neck-stock, which Lewrie intuited as nervousness on his part to even come close to admitting that he had a "shore wife," not a "domestic."

Domestics! Lewrie silently scoffed; *Mine arse on a band-box! Is that what they're calling kept "mutton" these days? Hah!*

" . . . in point of fact, the Bonsecours family *have* no daughter, certainly not one named Charité," prim Mr. Pollock continued, looking a tad red-faced to broach the topic of Lewrie's mysterious young chit. "Further, Captain Lewrie . . . they also learned that those young gentlemen who accompanied her your first night at the Pigeon Coop cabaret—I recall you mentioning them as the Darbone brothers? That wouldn't be possible, since the Darbone family's sons have been upcountry for at least the last month, entire. My, ah . . . people, after nosing about the help at the Pigeon Coop, have determined that your girl's, ah . . . unconventional masquerade, her true identity beneath it, rather, is an open secret among that cabaret's habitués. As is the identity of her companions, sir."

Pollock, like all good spies, full-time or amateur, paused then, bestowing upon Lewrie one of those detestable "I know something that you don't, and you must beg for it" looks.

"And?" Lewrie archly demanded, after trying to wait him out and not have to beg; a losing proposition he'd found, after years of dealing with old Zachariah Twigg and his compatriot, Mr. Jemmy Peel.

"They are all three de Guilleris," Pollock almost simpered with a top-lofty smugness. "Helio and Hippolyte, and their sister, Charité."

"So . . . who are they, when they're up and dressed?" Lewrie off-handedly queried, pretending closer interest in his wine, wishing to God that this was a private conversation, with none of his seamen present to hear him proved a gullible cully . . . again.

"Very rich, distinguished, longtime French Creoles who've resided in New

Orleans fifty years or better," Mr. Pollock informed him, looking as if he was manfully trying to stifle a look of sympathy for just how easily beguiled and "bamboozled" Capt. Lewrie could be. "Ah!" Pollock exclaimed, snapping his fingers before turning to his ledgers in a bookcase. He leafed through one, mumbling to himself, then "Hah!" escaped his lips.

"*Thought* the name was familiar! Two years ago, the de Guilleri family placed an order with us for a china service, made in Paris, settings sufficient for twenty guests, ah ha . . . well, who am I to quibble with legitimate goods first sent to Holland for *trans*-shipment, hmmm? Delivered to, *ahem!* number twenty-six Rue Dauphine, ah ha! Devil of a row with Madame de Guilleri, had to unpack it all to assure her none were broken, all were there, um-hmm . . . They live on the second storey. Does that comport with what you observed, sir?"

"Well, I didn't *act'lly* . . . " Lewrie had to fuddle. "Didn't get that close. Peekin' round barrels, corners, and such."

"Final payment referred to the, *aha!* . . . Henri Maurepas bank, damn my eyes!" Pollock chortled, whacking the ledger shut in triumph. "And where have we heard *that* name, hey, Lewrie? Agent for your prize ship, cross the river? Factor for the de Guilleri plantations up by the Saint Gabriel settlements, *and* . . . chief factor for that swindler Bistineau's store as well! Intriguing, how all these names cluster together," Mr. Pollock asked with a parrot-like cock of his head and a lop-sided, ghastly smile. "Ain't it?"

"So she *could* steer me to the people who back the pirates, as she *claimed*," Lewrie further intuited, taking what comfort he could from being "played" like a fiddle. "So I *must* see her again, after she gets back from her Easter visit to her parents . . . "

"Leaving town, are they?" Pollock said, wincing in thought.

"For a few weeks, at least. I told her I was going upcountry on your be-half, and we should get together once we're both returned," Lewrie ex-plained. "Though, given all you've learned for us, we might be able to strike out before . . . "

"A disturbing information, though, Lewrie," Pollock said with a "shush-ing" hand raised once more. "An oyster shucker and a swabber at the Pigeon Coop, spoken to by my . . . domestics, further told them that the younger de Guilleris, and an impoverished cousin of theirs by name of Rancour—Jean Rancour—seem to have come into some money of late and are spending *very* freely. More so than they did when on their absentee parents' allowances at any rate. And that the cousin, who hasn't had two farthings t'rub together since his family escaped Saint-Domingue, has been gambling very *deep* and doesn't seem to mind his losses all that much. Far be it from me to decide for you on this matter, but were I in your position, I might begin to . . . "

Whatever it was that Pollock wished to impart was interrupted by a soft and hesitant tapping on the glass panes of the office door.

"Come!" Pollock cried, whipping out his pocket watch as if his head clerk had been fetched in record time for a row cross the river's fierce currents. "Hah!" he cried, though, once the door had opened.

Damme, what a vixen! Lewrie instantly thought, seeing a woman enter, her beauty and the richness of her ensemble half-concealed by a light, hooded cloak against the misty night airs. For a second, he could espy a stout older Black who remained outside, one who held his lanthorn on a pole in one hand, and a cudgel in the other.

Bright . . . 'Fancy,' an Octoroon or better, Lewrie appraised to himself, nigh to uttering "Woof!" and ruing that he hadn't "sampled" the town's more exotic females after all. *What a stunner!* he further thought as the woman tossed back her hood, put in mind of the half-European, half-Hindoo *bints* he'd seen in the Far East, with her eyes so almond-shaped and a teaspoon away from Chinese, or something . . .

"Gideon!" the young woman happily cried out, stepping close to him, her exotically alluring eyes alight with mischief, or a victory; certainly with affection, which made Lewrie think *Aha!* to discover Mr. Pollock's close-held secret at last. "*Mon cher,* you must hear . . ."

"Colette, ah . . . *ahem!* You shouldn't, ah . . . " Pollock flummoxed, blushing hot as a farrier's forge. "Mean t'say . . . "

"Madame Pollock, I presume?" Lewrie brightly intruded from the other side, stepping forward quickly. "Allow me to name myself to you . . . Alan Willoughby, one of your husband's associates. *Enchanté, madame!*"

The young woman inclined her head, preening-pleased to be named "Madame Pollock" whether it was a thin fiction or not. She offered her hand French-style, which Lewrie dashingly took, sketching a kiss on the back of it. Mr. Pollock actually growled as she dropped him a curtsy.

"Er, um, yess," Pollock hissed. "My dear, this is men's . . . "

"We 'ave found the girl who meets with Monsieur . . . Willoughby!" Colette Pollock gushed, all but bouncing on her toes with excitement. "*Maman* . . . pardon, my maid, *messieurs* . . . finds she is a de Guilleri. I and Scipio, our man, find where she live, *oui?* A Bayou Saint John boy on 'is produce cart show us. And as we watch, you never guess, Gideon!"

"We know, dear, so . . . " Pollock patronisingly tried to say.

"The de Guilleris, they decamp!" Colette protested. "A washerwoman who work for the D'Ablemonts in the downstairs, she say Charité come home after dusk, dress-ed *très* fine. Then, full dark come, both her brothers come home, *très rapidement. That,* Scipio and I are there to see! They have hide *guns* under their cloaks, and we have *heard* the shooting noises somewhere in town while we wait, before—

Christ shit on a biscuit! Lewrie thought, his innards chilling as the implications of *that* struck him; *She? . . . No, it* couldn't *be!*

"Soon, come two more young *gentilshommes,* with guns *aussi,* with a country coach," Colette breathlessly imparted, almost gulping at her own daring. "Dress-ed mos' rough, *comme des Acadiens?* Like Acadians I mean, the huntsmen, *comprenez.* I ask Scipio to go talk with coachman, *après* young men enter, *oui?* And I *see* them in the upstairs windows, Gideon! *Et,* coachman tell Scipio they hire him to take ferry over river to the Bois Gervais road, only pay for *short* trip, *n'est-ce pas?* Tell *him,* they will take boat down bayous there. *Ensuite . . .* pardon, *then,* few minute later, *all* come down, and enter the coach, and *la jeune fille,* Mademoiselle Charité I am thinking, is dress-ed *à la rustique,* Acadian, *aussi! Carmagnole,* bonnet, skirted, *avec* the boots? All 'ave long and heavy canvas bag, same as sailors? The coachman whip away *très rapidement, comme un fou . . .* like the mad!"

"Ho-ly . . . God!" Lewrie slowly breathed, realising the guilty import of all that Pollock's "wife" had seen. "Damme, I've been . . . "

"It would, ah . . . so appear, sir," Mr. Pollock sadly commiserated, sounding so earnestly sympathetic Lewrie could have gut-shot him on the spot if he didn't have a pack of witnesses!

My God, I've been had! Lewrie scathed himself, just about ready to reel off his feet and plunk himself down in a chair; *How big a fool have I been? She was* in *on it all along. She was laughing up her damn sleeve, they* all *were, playing me like a piccolo from the—*

"You are pale, m'sieur Willoughby?" Colette Pollock solicitously enquired of his pallor, his febrile, anxious look; his silent lip-mumbles and scowl, too, it must here be noted.

"Bloody *wonderful!*" Lewrie distractedly grunted.

The tiny bell hung over the office door gave off a gay tinkle, and in breezed Toby Jugg, with Mr. Pollock's weedy head clerk in tow.

"One would s'pose this may be 'gilding the lily,' in a manner of speaking, *ahem,*" Pollock began, "but, about our consignment of air-rifles, Mister Dollarhyde . . . how many have actually been sold, and to whom, might you be able to recall?"

"Locking the barn after the horses have . . . shit!" some present almost heard Capt. Alan Lewrie disgustedly whisper.

"I b'lieve only a dozen, so far, Mister Pollock, sir," the clerk fussily replied, referring to his own ledger book after being told by Jugg, most likely, why he was being summoned cross the river in such a hurry, and at that hour. "One to Mister Willoughby here . . . "

Sold, mine arse, it was s'posed t'be a gift! Lewrie thought.

" . . . four taken on by Mister Whiting for his trading post up at Natchez, one to a *m'sieur* Columbé . . . said the local rodents eat up his garden something sinful, and . . . the other six to a party of city men."

"And, might you have their names available, Mister Dollarhyde?" Pollock impatiently prompted.

"Most odd, that, Mister Pollock," Dollarhyde simpered. "I did a brief demonstration, and they placed down payment on four, yet not an hour later, returned with the money for six, and paid in full."

"Names? *Ahem?*" Pollock harumphed.

"A Monsieur Monaster . . . *Don* Rubio Monaster, actually. He was most insistent on that point, really," Dollarhyde recited, looking up from his book for a second, "one to a Monsieur Rancour, J. . . . and the rest to a Monsieur de . . . Gool . . . de Gweel . . . Damn all Frog names."

"De Guilleri, hah!" Pollock barked, uncharacteristically slamming a palm on the top of his desk.

"Rancour," Colette mused aloud, "Gideon, is he not a cousin to the de Guilleris? *Oui*, I am thinking he is. And Don Rubio, oh la!" She chuckled, looking as if she would fan herself. "His papa was the Spaniard, but his maman was the Bergrand, and they raise him, for his poor papa die when he is little . . . killed by the Indians. He is the *très* handsome *gentilhomme*, mos' dashing? *Aussi*, he is—'ow you say?—the . . . crack shoot? All girls adore him, but he only has eyes . . . "

"Damn!" Pollock spluttered, slamming a fist on the desk this time. "Damnn, damn, damn!"

"Gideon, *cher* . . . What 'as distress-ed?" Colette asked.

"I must ask you to leave things to us, Colette," Pollock gruffly told her. "You've taken enough risks tonight, and there's an end to it. Scipio will see you safely home. I fear we will be discussing our, ah . . . business matters far into the night. They'd only bore you, *ahem*. I'll be along, soon as I'm able, so why don't you . . . "

"You have done us a great service tonight, Madame Pollock, for which we all . . . and I'm sure I speak for Gideon as well . . . " Lewrie found wit to say, "are extremely grateful. As I'm certain he'll tell you, once he joins you at home. *Merci, madame. Merci beaucoup!* You were very brave and clever."

If you *won't at least give her grudging thanks, then I will,* he sourly thought; *And why she stays with a clot like you 'tis a wonder! Thoughtless, churlish . . . and ugly, to boot!*

"Wot'd I miss?" Toby Jugg whispered to his compatriots who had been present the whole time. Once clued in, he could not help musing aloud. "Now I think upon it, sor, 'mongst them a'titterin' sprogs on 'at pirate schooner, one of 'em *coulda* been a girl, i' fact!"

And ye didn't recall 'til bloody now, *ye thick-headed Irish bog trotter?* Lewrie silently accused, his anger building, now that he was over his shock, to a sulky, but well-deserved pet; *Never thought to even bother mentioning it 'til . . .* damn *his blood!*

"Gideon, I do not *comprendre,*" Colette gasped, fingers flying to her lips, and paling most fetchingly. "You speak of *pirates?* But I . . . I thought you merely wish to discover . . . ah! So *that* is why the two *capitaines* call on the de Guilleris the other day?"

"*What* captains?" Pollock cried.

"The washerwoman *chez les D'Ablemonts* we speak to, *cher?* She say two famous heroes, both *Capitaine* Jérôme Lanxade and the Acadian, *Capitaine* Boudreaux Balfa, are visitors to the de Guilleri *appartement* . . . She say she see them the . . . several time. Mos' recent, a few day ago, she say! Oh, Gideon, you are in danger, *mon coeur?*"

"Go *home,* Colette," Pollock insisted, almost shooing her to the door. Relenting, he finally said, "I am in no danger, my dear, have no fear. There's, ah . . . underhanded commercial finagling afoot, and those old rogues are involved with some noted families to pull a sly one over on we despised outsider traders. A *coup de commerce?* But with your quick wits and sharp eyes, my dear, Mister Willoughby and I are in a fair way to Scotching it before it costs us tuppence, ha ha!"

"You swear?" Colette warily asked, still upset and dubious.

"Cross my heart," Pollock *cooed* to her, sketching on his chest. Blushing again, even redder than before, he vowed, *"Je t'adore, chérie."*

And, blushing herself but immensely pleased by his rare public declaration of love, she pecked him on the cheek, smiled, and departed.

CHAPTER TWENTY-SIX

*S*he isn't aware of your, ah . . . " Lewrie somberly asked once the door was firmly shut, chiding himself for being infected with Pollock's characteristic mannerism.

"I sometimes wonder, Lewrie," Pollock replied, shaking his head. "Well, then! *Ahem!* Took the ferry to the south bank, did they? Most odd, indeed." Pollock clapped his hands together as if suddenly convinced of something, then crossed to a tall desk to produce a map, which he spread on the larger, lower desk's surface. "Were they fleeing back to their parents' Saint Gabriel plantings, they would've coached round this way," he pondered, waving a vague hand over the northwestern end of the map. "Could've hired a *shalope* to sail them up the Mississippi to one of their plantation landings, but they didn't. Why?"

Mr. Pollock frowned at the map, drawing a candle stand closer so he could see the better, and traced an idle finger along the southern bank opposite New Orleans.

"Fleeing down the Mississippi?" Lewrie idly speculated.

"For that, a hired *shalope* would've served, Captain Lewrie," Mr. Pollock gravely countered. "Had they taken a boat, going with the current, they could already be ten miles downriver by now. Getting away in perfect comfort and laughing up their sleeves," he growled with growing frustration.

"Then why'd they dress so rough, Mister Pollock?" Liam Desmond, who had been present for most of their musings, had the temerity to interject;

most-like catching Toby Jugg's attitude, Lewrie feared. "Yer missuz said they wore whatcha-call-ems . . . rusticals, wan'it, sor?"

"*Mauvaises*," Pollock supplied off-handedly, "Means tattered, or thread-bare. *A la rustique*, they say of the Acadians, who live . . . To pass without notice 'mongst the Acadian settlers, by God! Balfa! *He* lives down south."

Mr. Pollock's finger traced a hypothetical route down along one pencilled-in, iffy track, from the ferry landing on the south bank to a true, plotted bayou, tracing further to where the bayou intersected a river, and . . .

"They're bound down the Ouatchas River," Pollock exclaimed. "I'd stake my life on it!" Pollock declared, now all fervent brusqueness. "The Ouatchas connects with Bayou Barataria, where that rogue Balfa farms. And I'd not be surprised to learn that one of the plantations along the Bois Ger-vais Road, *on* the bayous, is conveniently owned by one of our suspected conspirators, aha!"

"They could hide their schooner *this* far up the bayous?" Lewrie asked, frowning over Pollock's map. "It looks too . . . "

"God, no!" Pollock snapped. "Even the Ouatchas, or the Bayou Barataria, is too shallow, narrow, and twisting. Backcountry people use *pirogues* on the creeks and bayous," pronouncing the word as "*peer*-ohs," and sounding impatient with Lewrie's wits. "You've seen them, not a foot of freeboard, four inches or less actually in the water? They're poled or pad-dled. Trees overhang so low, they *can't* be masted. Float on a heavy dew, they do! Right through any swamp, good as a highway."

"Damme, don't snap at *me*, sir!" Lewrie retorted. "We must have *pirogues* of our own, go after them . . . "

"You'd blunder about like a blind man in Vauxhall Gardens' hedge maze," Pollock scoffed right back. "*They'd* need a good guide to find their way . . . which I'm sure they already have, which you don't, sir. And I very much doubt you could buy one with a keg of gold coin, with the best bein' Acadian, and them so clannish. Acadians'd never trust an Englishman, not after we expelled them from Canada after the Seven Years War. Secretive, backward—"

"I'll not sit and wring my hands!" Lewrie declared, his chagrin and anger at his gullibility and his attempted murder now bubbling over and directed at the handiest subject. "I'll not allow 'em t'get away, and wail about what a *shame* it is . . . sir! All these bayous and such . . . they lead to the sea, eventually?"

"Ah . . . to Lake Barataria," a much-chastened Pollock said, now cowed into politeness by Lewrie's outburst. "Thence, into Barataria Bay, which has deepwater passes into the Gulf—"

"Here?" Lewrie almost snarled, stabbing a finger at the mouth of the bay. "Grand Terre Island, right?"

"Beg pardon, sor," Toby Jugg hesitantly spoke up. "I hear tell . . . tavern talk from th' auld gammers who *mighta* gone privateerin' in their younger days, d'ye see woz all . . . Some say Grand Terre Island, and Barataria Bay, woz th' grandest place t'wait fer passin' Spanish treasure ships, sor," he revealed, eyes shifting in old guilt, perhaps?

"Do tell, Jugg." Lewrie said with a knowing smirk. "Say on."

"Good anchorage, sandy holdin' ground, back o' th' island, an' sweet-water springs ashore, sor," Jugg continued in a gruff, off-hand tone. "Twelve'r fifteen foot o' depth, bay an' isle brim-over with a seafood bounty. Some say there's booried treasure on Grand Terre, to this very day, sor, sure! East Pass better'n the' western . . . I heard."

"Deep enough for their schooner or prizes," Lewrie exclaimed. "Balfa's place conveniently halfway from New Orleans, so far up no one could pursue them . . . a planter house and barns just over the river to cache stolen goods. Damme! They must be running all the way down to Grand Terre! They're bound to sea! Where my frigate can *smash* 'em!"

Fearing *very* overt action, Pollock gave him one of those cringing, mouse-pawed, appalled expressions of his, as if Lewrie had gone madder than a hatter, was about to run as *amok* as a rogue elephant.

Your safe little world about t'be tipped over? Lewrie silently sneered; *Damn' right, it is, and too bloody bad!*

He'd been led by the nose since boarding Pollock's trade brig, since Captain Nicely's *supper,* off his feed and balance; led round by his "member" almost from the moment he'd stepped ashore in New Orleans, too. Now, their pirates' identity had been discovered, and it was his time to re-don the Royal Navy's brutal harness.

Idling's over, me lad, Lewrie thought, steeling himself to the task at hand; *You've eat your last lotus. I'll run 'em . . . That bitch! That lying little whore! How large a fool must I look to my sailors right now? How much of their respect have I lost by being such a . . .*

And here he'd been, feeling twinging-guilty to "abuse" a sweet young girl's "adoration"! Hah!

"We must be got downriver," Lewrie firmly said. "Soon as dammit . . . sooner! *Proteus* is lurking off the Mississippi passes. I must get her underway for Barataria Bay at once!"

"What, d'ye mean tonight, sir?" Mr. Pollock fretfully asked.

"If not by midnight, then no later than dawn, aye," Lewrie said, impatient to get back to doing what he did best, *where* he did his best . . . at sea. "How long would it take your brig to gain the Gulf, with the downriver current to speed her along?"

"Well, no more than four or five days downriver, but . . . *ahem!*" Pollock whinnied, having himself a twitch-neck crooking fit. "I fear, though, that for my ship, my firm, to be involved so publicly would be quite impossible."

"And why the bloody Hell *not?*" Lewrie barked, hands clasped in the small of his back, four-square on his feet, as he would stand upon a quarterdeck. A chilly hush fell upon the gathered sailors, knowing by their captain's tone and the eerie change of his eyes from a merry blue to a flinty Arctic grey that Mr. Pollock was "gonna catch it"!

"Panton, Leslie & Company is only *marginally* associated with Crown interests, and, ah . . . activities," Pollock tried to exposit in a calm, reasonable tone. "We are not, never have been, directly under Foreign Office orders, not like your fellow James Peel, Captain Lewrie. Nor am I, no matter what you might have told or *assumed*, actively engaged as a Crown agent . . . nor have I *ever* been, d'ye see. I observe, I *listen*, might now and then make harmless and innocent *enquiries* when in town, but . . . I fear that either Mister Peel, Admiral Parker, or your Captain Nicely, ah . . . over-sold how *much* direct aid to your . . . expedition, *ahem!* I might render, so . . . "

"You *did* intend to smuggle us away once we'd cut a throat or two?" Lewrie brutally stated. "Left bodies piled in the streets?"

"So long as I or Panton, Leslie were not, ah . . . exposed to the Spanish, sir, yes," Panton tremulously confessed, "so long as you managed the task *covertly*, without . . . I am merely a businessman, sir!"

"If not your brig, then what about one of your *shalopes*, or a lugger?" Lewrie pressed. "One of your river boats stout enough for the open sea? Give us a few extra hands off the brig or your river boats, and we'll manage things on our own! Could you manage *that?*"

"Well, of course, sir, that wouldn't, ah . . . " Pollock said in evident relief that nothing would stick to his shoes if things went badly. "A plausible excuse for your sudden departure would be necessary, I do think, though, so the firm doesn't—"

"Tell 'em you fired us for buggery," Lewrie quickly suggested, prompting a hearty laugh from his hands. "For all I care, let 'em believe we stole the damn' thing, too! Just so we depart *soon!*"

"Well, I do have have a decent seaboat and send correspondence aboard her to Jamaica," Pollock allowed, perking up a bit as an alibi sprang to mind. "You could claim to carry—"

The door opened and that damnably merry bell tinkled again, freezing everyone in a hostile *tableau* as Mr. Caldecott, the First Mate off the *Azucena del Oeste,* wandered in.

"Ev'nin', all," Mr. Caldecott called, tossing off an idle doff of his hat, and obviously cherry-merry in drink. "Heard the rumours in town? Shootin's and harum-scarums, though the Dons've only found one victim, so far. Some buckskinned turd . . . "

"We heard!" both Pollock and Lewrie snapped at the same time.

". . . even more excitement makin' the rounds," Caldecott breezed on, too tipsy to take umbrage. "The whole town's bellied up to the bar counters t'celebrate the treasure ship they heard was coming."

"Treasure ship?" was the chorus of *everyone* present, making the idling sailors leap to their feet in sudden and intense interest.

"Bless me, sirs. Don't know how much stock t'put in the tale," Caldecott explained, beaming, "what with how excitable Dons and Creoles can get, but . . . word is that the banking houses got told *tons* o' money was t'be sent here, fresh from the Mexico City mint. Place d'Armes is so crowded, you'd think it was a saint's day pageant. Fireworks, band, and all, by—"

"And did they say, ah . . . how much was coming, Mister Caldecott?" Pollock asked, his eyes slit in avaricious calculations.

"Oh, bloody *millions,* sir!" Caldecott happily replied, pouring himself a glass of wine from the sideboard carafe. "A million pounds in real money. And that was the *low* guess. The more wine, the higher."

"Damme!" Lewrie marvelled at their pirates' daring. "They're not fleeing, Mister Pollock . . . they're off to try to *take* it!"

"Henri Maurepas," Pollock shrewdly mused. "Is he bound up with the conspiracy, he must have been the one that told them about it."

"All the more reason for haste, sir," Lewrie exclaimed. "Catch them in the act, nab 'em red-handed. Your boat, sir . . . instanter!"

"With the bloody treasure ship alongside, *arrah?*" Liam Desmond muttered in awe of the possibilities. "Jaysus, Joseph, an' Mary!"

God A'mighty! Lewrie frenziedly speculated; *A million Spanish dollars'd be a quarter million pounds. Captain's share is two-eighths so . . . sixty-two thousand, five hund . . . JESUS CHRIST!*

"Right, lads, we're off!" Lewrie cried, banging his hands together in urgency. "There's nought we may do to the local villains, this Maurepas or Bistineau, Mister Pollock. No time to scrag 'em, but . . . did someone put a flea in the Spanish authorities' ears once the money is taken, hmmm? Let those idle bastards in the Cabildo do our work?"

"I do imagine something could be, ah . . . arranged," Mr. Pollock decided with one brow slyly, contemplatively cocked.

"And look to the safety of your emporium hulk as we sail, sir," Lewrie further said, gathering up his discarded things. "Bistineau's store . . . is it nearby to anything *you* value?"

"I don't . . ."

"We came t'get our prize ship back, but that ain't in the cards, Mister Pollock," Lewrie quickly explained. "Her cargo's lost to us as well, safely cached in that bastard's store and warehouse. We can't have either, I mean to make sure no one profits from her. Just before we set off, I intend to set 'em all afire and burn 'em to the ground . . . and the waterline!"

BOOK FIVE

Prospero: Now does my project gather to a head.
My charms crack not, my spirits obey, and time
Goes upright with his carriage. How's the day?
                    -*THE TEMPEST*, ACT V, SCENE 1
                    WILLIAM SHAKESPEARE

CHAPTER TWENTY-SEVEN

*B*oudreaux Balfa squatted on the lip of the canvas-covered cargo hatch, horny bare feet and stout, suntanned shins splayed either side of a smallish wooden keg, a prosaic bulge-sided 5-gallon barrico that one could find anywhere liquid goods were sold . . . though this one had neither tap nor bung. The lid, which had been hatcheted open, had the King of Spain's royal crest burned into it, so one might have mistaken the barrico for one containing only the costliest, smoothest, brandy for aristocratic tables, but . . .

Capitaine Boudreaux Balfa, *L'Affamé*, dipped his hands into that 5-gallon barrico and ran his fingers through silver, not spirits. If the Mexico City mint workers hadn't cheated their masters, a 5-gallon wooden barrico *should* contain 1,000 pieces of silver, 1,000 Spanish *dollars*. Less the tare weight of the keg, Balfa knew from his previous lootings, the mint simply shovelled loose coins into a barrico 'til the heavy scales balanced at 55 pounds, about as much as a government dock worker or slave employed at public works could lift by himself. If a mint employee pocketed a few on the sly, well . . . it was almost expected. Balfa rather doubted that the count would come out exact, but then . . . who the Devil cared?

"Ahh-*yeee!*" Balfa cried in a high, thin two-note howl of victory. "By Gar!" he shouted, drumming his heels on the deck and tossing a double handful of coins high aloft, without a care where they landed.

A pistol shot drew his attention. That whippet-lean boy, Jean-Marie Rancour, was flinging silver dollars over the side so his friend Don Rubio could shoot them like ducks on the wing. Most shots went wide of the mark, but again . . . who the Devil cared when there was so *much* money for the taking?

A quick pair of shots below-decks sounded, muffled but distinct, followed by the scream of a mortally wounded man and the keening howl of a survivor of the ship's crew whose hiding place had been found, as he was dragged from the side of his slain comrade and hauled up from below for the further amusement of the triumphant pirates.

Balfa squinted with concern when he saw that one of the sailors who fetched the survivor up was his own son, Fusilier; he was a bit relieved, though, to note how his son hung back from actually manhandling the poor, doomed bastard. No, it was those two brothers, Pierre and Jean, who held the man by his upper arms and lugged him onto the deck, laughing and taunting the fellow, crying out to their fellow buccaneers that a fresh victim had been discovered.

Fusilier trailed behind their victim's scrabbling bare feet, an ashen cast to his features, eyes flicking right and left as if in some fever, his cheeks red, and gulping in trepidation.

Boudreaux Balfa did not want his son to follow in his bloodied footsteps; he'd adamantly decreed, for his poor, dead wife's sake, that *L'Affamé* would be the last pirate of their clan, that he would make an honest living on the land that piracy had bought them, that Boudreaux would make sure that Fusilier and Evangeline would grow up respectable and in the fear of the Lord, if he had to kill them to do it. He would leave them property six *arpents* wide and fifty *arpents* deep, from their good dock on Bayou Barataria to far back into the cypress swamps, with channels and sloughs for rice fields, enough solid land for cotton and sugarcane, enough cleared land where thirty or fourty head of cattle could graze, on his *vacherie*, twice the herd any neighbour could boast.

Three hundred *arpents*, over 250 British acres, enough to support generations of Balfas in comfort and self-sufficiency—if it wasn't in debt now and then in bad years with bankers and crop factors in the city. His old "trade" could provide a hedge against its loss.

So when the de Guilleri brats and their cohorts had come ghosting up to his landing the night that Boudreaux had invited friends and neighbours over for his monthly *rustique*, to sing the old French homeland tunes and those of long-lost Acadia, to dance barefooted on hard-packed dirt or softer grass, to drink and feast and court and carry on, well . . . Even if they'd come "dressed down" like the old feudal landlords or *aristos* of the Court at Versailles did when playing peasant among their lessers, once they'd gotten him aside and had imparted their fabulous news, the temptation had simply been too great. His son, Fusilier, had begged and pleaded for just *one* adventure by his side, and Fusilier had been too hot-blooded and eager to be denied, despite his promises to his dead wife.

"Madre de Dios, por favor, señores, no!" the fresh victim cried in a squeaky child's despairing voice, crawling on his knees with tears streaking his face, searching for just one with mercy in his heart.

Instead, he was hauled to his feet, held pinioned from either side as a burly but sweet-faced crewman strode up to him, laid a hand on his shoulder as if to reassure him, then jabbed a wide dagger into his belly . . . once, twice, and a third time, roaring with laughter as he did so. With a feral shout, half a dozen buccaneers hoisted him up and flung him overboard, cheered their own boldness, then broke up to hunt down any other lurking survivors.

Boudreaux nodded with sad pleasure to see Fusilier blanch and dash to the opposite bulwarks to puke up his meagre breakfast. At his side was the teenaged boy who'd fetched up the latest victim. *He* was heaving because he had no stomach for seafaring, and even a moderate chop turned him grass-green, quite unlike his older brother, Pierre.

Fusilier had no stomach for *this, bon!* Balfa thought. And this would be the last voyage for both of them. There was so much silver stowed below, their shares could support their lands for the next hundred years if they were frugal. No buccaneering scum as friends . . .

Pierre and the seasick younger Jean, those itinerant La Fitte brothers, had come up the bayou between cruises, looking for land and opportunities, they'd *claimed*. They had idled on his hospitality, did the least possible to repay it, and spent most of their time spooning his lovely but naive daughter, Evangeline, and turning Fusilier's head with tales of loot and plunder. Balfa had trusted neither one out of his sight, sure they were sniffing round for his hidden wealth! He'd been ready to run them off when the de Guilleris turned up, and once this adventure was done, he'd be glad to see the backs of the La Fittes.

"We did it, Boudreaux, *mon vieux!* We did it after all!" Jérôme Lanxade cheered, capering and performing a creaky horn-pipe, coming up to embrace him, buss him French fashion on both cheeks, then pound him on the back. "So easy, it was nothing! Spaniards . . . pah! What a pack of toothless monkeys!"

Yes, it had been easy, so incredibly easy. The intelligence in the letter to banker Maurepas had been like all vaunting Spanish self-delusions, but an empty sham. That so-called company of stalwart soldiers had been thirty-odd idle, seasick Mestizos in shabby uniforms with poorly kept weapons, half-Aztec riffraff led by a fat sergeant, a brace of equally low-down corporals, and a pair of down-at-the-heels officers, one of whom, the senior *capitano*, had offered to surrender if he could join their merry marauding band for a share of the money!

The cannon were good, but their powder was poorly milled, damp with age and indifferent storage, and the "well-drilled" naval gunners—one per piece as gun-captains—outnumbered by spiritless, cowardly, and clumsy gutter-sweepings. Only the schooner's *capitano* and his naval officers had put up much of a fight once their vessel had stalked up to cannon-range, and those hellish, quick-firing air-rifles had put him and his quarterdeck party and helmsmen down in the first minutes, leaving the rest of the crew leaderless and adrift. *Le Revenant* had more swivel-guns—in the old days, they'd not been termed "murderers" for nothing!—and they'd had those air-rifles in the capable and deadly accurate hands of the de Guilleris, so the gun-captains, loaders, and rammers, along with the frightened, swaying infantrymen, were blasted off their feet faster than any troops could bear, with half the soldiers shot in a single, brutal minute! After that, no one could resist their howling, shrieking, sword-waving boarders, and the thing was done.

"Too bad we can't keep this schooner of theirs," Jérôme Lanxade went on. "Might salvage her guns if we had the time, but . . . "

"No disguising her," Balfa spat. "She gotta go down, wit' all de evidence, by Gar."

"Give her a good cleaning, Boudreaux, a clean sweep down fore and aft, she could serve as our second raider," Lanxade posed, sweeping at his thin and rakish mustachios, "like scrubbin' up a whore over in Havana before you board her, hah? We'll get you a suitable ship, never fear."

"Won't need one, Jérôme," Balfa said in a covert growl, telling truth if only to his longtime compatriot, perhaps the only man aboard whom he could trust. "So much silver, come to hand so easy . . . like I gets de shivers dat another prize push our luck. My luck, *hein?* By damn, I see all dat silver, I feels de rabbits runnin'. We get all o' dis ashore and split up, I callin' it quits."

"*Damn* the bastards!" Helio de Guilleri was raging as he came stamping heavy boot-heels up the companionway ladder from below. "Bedammed to all lying Spanish bastards! *Cochons, salauds!*"

"What is the matter, *m'sieur?*" Lanxade broke away to ask him.

"I've counted kegs, *Capitaine* Lanxade, counted them twice, and there aren't enough to make six million dollars!" de Guilleri seethed, lowering his voice at Lanxade's urgent hand gestures so their sailors wouldn't hear that they'd been denied a single *sou*. "There is not one ten-gallon barrico aboard, just five-gallon kegs. A thousand dollars each, none of the ones that hold two thousand!"

"*Putain, mon Dieu!*" Lanxade spat, blanching beneath his swarthy life-time sea tan. "*Mon cul!*" he gravelled, teeth grinding.

"My ass!" Balfa groaned, too. "Dey didn' hide some down among d'eir water butts an' salt-meat kegs? How many barricos you find?"

"Only two thousand, *Capitaine*," Helio de Guilleri told him in a grim mutter, nigh snarling as if it was he who'd been robbed. "That only makes fifty-five tons of silver, no gold. Here!" he spat, making them look at a small ledger book. "Hippolyte found this aft, in their *capitaine's* cabins, in the mint official's bags. It says they carried only a *third* of the total shipment!"

"By *damn*, d'ose Spaniards get clever after all!" Balfa hooted with inex-plicable laughter after a moment of thought. "Sent one ship close inshore to Texas Province, like lubbers feelin' d'eir way scared o' open water. But, dey done put de rest in two *more* fast schooners! Figure dey lose one, but de rest sail far out at sea . . . Might now be off Fort Balise, safe as lambs! But, *mes amis*," he slyly pointed out, "we still got two millions of it!"

"Lads won't be happy, though, *cher*," Lanxade griped, plucking at his fin-ery most fretfully. "They think we're fools, they've been cheated some-how . . . bad thing to do, to fail in our trade."

"*Ah, mais oui,*" Balfa uneasily agreed, grimacing over the tales of what had happened to even the greatest pirates who'd lost the trust of their crews . . . who'd seemed to lose their magic "touch."

"For now, there is rum, wine, food, and loot," Lanxade supposed, peering about the schooner's decks to see his crew busy with newly captured muskets and pistols, new cutlasses and infantry hangers hung by new baldrics over their shoulders. Dead men's hats were being quarreled over and gambled for, as were coats, waist-coats, shoes, and the few pairs of salvaged boots. "Rest of her cargo, the butts of Mexicano wine, and that peasant-brewed *pulque* and ar-rack . . . that can keep them satisfied for a while. Quiet, fuddled, and too drunk for a proper counting. Proper thinking."

"Enough silver for each hand t'get two, three keg apiece, right away," Balfa cannily speculated. "Delay de reckonin', *n'est-ce pas?* Set aside dead men's shares, in plain sight?"

Poor and poltroonish as the Spanish resistance had been, they still had managed to slay or mortally wound at least seven of their buccaneers before going under. Wives, children, and lovers were due a lost man's "lay." Or what Balfa and Lanxade could later *swear* was a proper share, after . . . deductions.

Those wounded, but not mortally, were owed bonuses, too, depending on whether they'd lost something off their bodies; an eye, hand, digit, or foot, a leg . . . a "pension" paid in one lump sum if their seagoing life was curtailed by disabilities.

"You fear your own men?" Helio de Guilleri asked with a gasp of surprise. But then, he was used to absolute obedience and deference from house slaves and street *nègres,* those below his social class. It never occurred to him, would never occur to any of his cohorts, that the piratical trade was the freest sort of democracy.

"They discover the sum we took is off, yes," Lanxade whispered, wondering if old Boudreaux might not be quitting the trade at the best time, after all . . . and might it not be in *his* interest to do so, too.

"Well, this schooner is worth a lot, too, so couldn't they wait until it, and that British prize, were sold, and we—" Helio asked.

"Non, mon cher!" Lanxade hastily objected. "This schooner must disappear, and quickly, before the Spanish begin a search for her. If they lose a *guarda costa* lugger, a few local merchant ships, that they could abide. Blame the *Anglais.* But a royal vessel, with two million dollars aboard? Even *they* would be stirred to action."

"Well, take her back to Grand Terre, unload her, and strip her of anything useful," Helio pressed, sounding almost *whiny* to them.

"Tow her back outta Barataria Bay, den sink her in deep water," Balfa cagily suggested, "so nobody ever see her again, by damn."

"Sink her?" Helio gawped, louder than he'd meant to. "Why can't she be *sold* . . . to some stupid Yankees, perhaps?" he plaintively posed as if ruing the loss of a single *écu* of her worth.

"*Sink* her?" his sister Charité demanded, stalking up from astern to join them, her dainty left hand fisted about the hilt of her smallsword in sudden dismay, and her knee-high boots drumming on the decks. "*Sink* her, will you, *messieurs?* She's the equal of *Le Revenant,* with better guns aboard her. We need her to begin building our own fleet! Helio, tell them! Carriages could be built, the artillery could then be used ashore . . . for our Creole army, for our coming revolution!"

"We were just discussing that, Charité, *ma soeur,* uh . . . " he lamely stammered, blushing under his sister's indignant glare.

"*Capitaine* Balfa has been *promised* a ship of his own," Charité continued, her colour high over any less-than-zealous enthusiasm for their cherished cause. "*Et voilà,* here she is. When word gets out, hundreds of men will come forward to crew her. *Capitaine* Balfa then can choose only the best. The others can enlist in your regiment, *mon frère*. They will come like . . . that!" she exulted with a boyish snap of the fingers of her free right hand.

"*Tiens,* there is a difficulty, Charité," Helio muttered, gazing away, unable to meet her eyes. "We will speak of it later, if . . . "

"Let us speak of it now, Helio," she countered. "Or is it too complicated a matter for a mere woman to understand, *hein?*"

"*Quel dommage.* We're out of targets, alas," Don Rubio Monaster pretended to mourn as he and her cousin Jean-Marie casually sauntered up to join the leaders of the expedition, which was to their minds a natural right. They were still smirking over the "hunter's bag" they had shot or skewered while there yet had been survivors from the Spanish vessel's crew or armed guard. "*Eh,* something is amiss? Why all the long faces? We *did* just win a great victory, did we not?"

"They insist that we must sink this ship after looting her," Charité informed him with the slightest plaintive sound, as if looking for a supportive voice to champion her argument.

"Well, I suppose we *should,*" Rubio said with a simper. "When a *blind* Spaniard could recognise her a mile off, ha ha! A pity surely. But, we can salvage her artillery and such."

"Hidden far up Barataria Bay, she'd be safe enough, as safe as *Le Revenant* has been," Charité hotly pointed out. "*Cher Capitaine* Balfa to command her, with *two* ships to prey on the Spanish *cochons.*"

"I quittin', me," Balfa baldly told her.

"What?" Charité spat, aghast at that news. "But, you *cannot!*"

"Losin' dis ship, de Spaniards git too stirred up," Balfa laid out in a calm voice. "My share be more'n enough t'get by a long time. Got a bad feelin', *mademoiselle*. A longtime sailor's 'sight,' " he added with a shiver.

"But!" Charité spluttered for a moment, then turned icy cold. "*Très bien, m'sieur,* "she said, distancing her demeanour. "If you have a . . . foreboding, then . . . we could promote a promising mate for command of this schooner. And honour you for your contributions."

"We cannot *keep* her, *chérie,*" Helio gravely told her. "It is a risk we cannot take."

"But we *do* need a second ship, yes?" Charité snapped, rounding on him as if he'd let her down, too. "If not at once, we could make a third cruise with *Le Revenant* and take a suitable merchant ship, then add to her armament with this ship's guns, yes? With news of this success, recruit more eager volunteers to man her, yes?"

"Well, of course, but . . . " Helio quickly agreed with a shrug of his shoulders, mostly to cool her ardour.

"Then I have a promising man in mind who seems more than eager for adventure," Charité schemed. "That mercenary former *Anglais* Navy man, Willoughby." She blushed as she raised that possibility to them, the mention of his name and nation. "He is nearly penniless, dismissed his service, and will do anything for riches. A very useful man who can be . . . lured." She blushed, too, to describe her lover in such a harsh fashion when the thrilling memory of his hands, his lips, his thrusting body was still fresh in her mind. "He would do *anything* for me, *n'est-ce pas?*" she intimated with a cruel grin forced to her lips.

"Not if he's run off in terror!" cousin Jean-Marie Rancour hooted with dismissive scorn and glee.

"Jean!" Rubio cautioned, but it was too late, and Jean-Marie waded in deeper despite the elbow aimed at his mid-ribs.

"We did for both of those uppity *poseurs,* didn't we, Rubio? The *Anglais* and that nosey *Américain* Ellison who followed you, Charité . . . that night you bearded the *Anglais?*"

"What . . . did . . . you . . . do?" she angrily demanded, breathing slowly but hard enough to flare and collapse her delicate nostrils.

"Shot both of them," Rubio gruffly confessed, nose-high for his motives, his actions, to be questioned. "Just before we gathered at your house to leave. They were *not* gentlemen!" he haughtily declared.

"Oh, you arrogant . . . stupid . . . " Charité raged, surprising all of them by leaping at Rubio to hammer her fists on his chest, driving him towards the starboard bulwarks; surprising them, too, by loosing a sudden flood of tears amid her ire.

"Rubio didn't *kill* him, the *Anglais* I mean, Charité!" Jean-Marie cried, trying to seize one of her arms as Helio went for another. "He put a scare on him, was all. He ducked too quick for a clean shot, he got off three shots at us, and got away! Helio and Hippolyte did for that El-isson. He and his men were dirty *Américain* spies, and I wager your *Anglais* pig is one, too, so . . ."

"Pompous, idiot. Vain and *jealous*!" Charité shrieked just as they peeled her off the startled Don Rubio, squirming and kicking at his shins in vain. Don Rubio Monaster went as pale as a winding-sheet, slack-jawed in astonishment at her reaction. In that instant, he realized he'd *never* possess her, that all that had passed between them had been "kissing cousin" teasing. Another, a *despicable* other, held her heart, and Rubio suddenly despised her, hating that *Anglais* with an equal revulsion—could have shot her as gladly as he'd shot at the Englishman. A new weapon, the man's agility and return shots; to get that close yet *fail* because he didn't use his old Jaeger rifle, hadn't been familiar with the Girandoni! His own righteous action had slain his hopes and dreams . . . and someone would have to pay!

Charité calmed, much too suddenly for any of them to credit, as if the eye of a Gulf storm claimed her rage. Her arms went out at her sides to fend off those who held her, nodding in grim understanding . . . brought her hands prayerfully together under the tip of her nose, to think . . . to *bide*.

"*Très bien,*" she finally muttered. "Very well. You enrage the *Américains* to find who shot their leader. You enrage the British merchant company, and *they* will try to avenge Alain," she bleakly sketched for them, clearing her too-tight throat several times.

"We can deal with any—" her brother Hippolyte disparaged.

"No! *Mon Dieu,* you have even wakened the Spanish!" she retorted. "Better you had . . . but it is much too late for second thoughts or *sense,* is it, *messieurs?*" she accused. And, like the gust-front of an *ouragan,* her icily controlled rage sent a *frisson* of Arctic chill over the bloodied deck. "*Zut, putain!* Goddamn your foolishness! You have put everything we've worked for at risk. You may have just destroyed our most cherished dream!"

It was too much for her. At last Charité Angelette de Guilleri hitched up a wracking sob, unable to master it, and girlishly dashed at her tears. Damned if she'd weep in front of them, but . . . she spun on her heels and ran aft for the looted Spanish captain's quarters for a precious space of privacy.

"Hmmm . . . well then," *Capitaine* Lanxade said, breaking their stricken *tableau.* He twirled one end of his mustachio, frowning as he listened carefully. It was much too quiet, suddenly. Even the rowdy, brawling, drunken buccaneers had been silenced by her unseemly cries, her attack on that arrogant, half-dago fop, Monaster.

Fierce and merciless as they could be, *Le Revenant*'s buccaneers were sailors after all. Simple folk for the most part, they carried their emotions close to the skin, could slay a longtime shipmate over trifles in a drunken rage, then weep for days over the deed once they sobered up. Superstitious— even religious when all else failed—they'd been appalled to have a woman aboard ship at first, for that was as dangerous as whistling on deck, which might summon vengeful wind at such disrespect for the old sea gods.

Yet Mlle Charité had proved so entrancingly lovely to behold, so sunnily dispositioned, that she had endeared herself to them, and their string of successes with her aboard had made her almost a talisman, the scrappy mascot that brings good luck.

And didn't she handle a smallsword or light hanger as well as a man? Wasn't she a passing-fair shot, also? They could eagerly, and had eagerly,

raped and murdered women passengers or slaves aboard some of their
prizes, but this young girl of theirs was different! She was sacrosanct, not to
be groped, touched, taken, or even spoken of by any hand in a scurrilous
manner. What upset *her*, then, upset *them*, and if they got angry enough
over the sight of their "pet *jeune fille*" raging in such a brokenhearted way, so
contrary to her usual demeanour, then those who caused it stood in peril of
being chopped into stew meat!

All Lanxade could hear for several long moments were the creaks and
groans of the two lashed-together hulls, the slats and bangs aloft from un-
tended yards and booms, and the drum-slapping of freed rigging. Then
there came a faint growl and rumble of displeasure from several sailors, and
he and his old mate Boudreaux Balfa shared a queasy look. From their long
experience of dealing with the fractious and unpredictable sort of men who'd
go pirating, they both feared that there would be trouble over this . . . even
before the revelation of the shortage of expected loot.

"Women!" Don Rubio said with a lofty sniff, as if he had never placed
much hope in so frail a vessel. "Were she not so foolish, she might eventually
come to understand . . . "

"Shut *up!*" Lanxade harshly barked at him, taking sides in front of his
men so they wouldn't end up turning *him* to chutney. "You men! There's *tons*
of silver to be shifted, *oceans* of drink to salvage. Get back to work, before a
British or Spanish man-o'-war interrupts us!"

"*Mais oui!*" Balfa quickly seconded. "Let's gather our spoils, *mes amis.
Allez, vite, ah-yee!*"

The de Guilleri brothers, with cousin Jean-Marie, wandered off to commiserate with poor old Rubio, closely grouped about him to give their condolences for the vagaries of brainless girls.

Lanxade and Balfa drifted forward towards the prize schooner's forecastle
and belfry, where they could confide in each other, casually stepping over the
odd stripped and looted body that hadn't been tossed overside, as if they
were no more than ring-bolts or coils of rigging.

"*Un emmerdement*, Jérôme," Balfa said in a raspy voice. "We've really
tromped through de shit dis time, by Gar."

"We need to get this ship off the sea and out of sight, *vite*," Lanxade muttered from the corner of his mouth, a confident grin plastered on his phyz for
the crew's sake.

"Get de lads drunk an' stuffed wit' meat, too, before dey start cuttin' dose
bébés' t'roats, too. Our crew likes *her*."

"Boudreaux," Lanxade said, leaning on the lee bulwark cap-rails and gazing out to the empty southern horizon, where even more trouble might pop up, all guns and officiousness. "Do you remember what it was we said, back at the Dry Tortugas? About showing these amateurs what real piracy looks like?"

"Hmm, ouais," Balfa said with a shrug, trying to recall.

"Two million dollars won't go that far with our lads," Lanxade fretted. "Not with Bistineau, Maurepas, and that goddamned Rebellion Fund of theirs each taking a cut, what is due our *very* young, stupid . . . employers, too, *n'est-ce pas?* How are your shivers, *mon vieux?*"

"Oh, dere be a whole *herd* o' rabbit run up an' down my spine!" Balfa told him with an uneasy chuckle. "Why?"

"All of a sudden, I feel them, too, *cher,*" Lanxade confessed to him, turning to smirk. "Your talk of retiring makes me think that it may be a good time for me to 'swallow the anchor' as well. Havana or Cartagena . . . they are both delightful cities, where a well-respected—dare I even say famous!—former privateer could retire ashore," he said, preening at his mustachios and posing with a hand on the hilt of his smallsword like a grandee. "Well settled, famous, and *rich.* A well-built house overlooking the bay, perhaps? An honourable and respected and *wealthy* gentlemen, *hein?*"

"Oho!" Balfa gleefully grunted. *"Some* aspirin' lad of ours will take *Le Revenant,* sail her away to better pickin's. We can't kill dat girl, though," he speculated, making no real objection to a betrayal as he leaped on the most troublesome matter with his usual blunt acuity. "I stagger back to N'awlins, tell Maurepas an' dem a tale o' mutiny when de lads see all dat moncy, and I got away by de skin o' my balls. Who *know* where dey go after dey cut dem *bébés'* heads off, haw haw!"

"And I was slain after a gallant and heroic bit of swordplay?" Lanxade airily fantasised, drawing in his corseted stomach to make a more dangerous figure to his own mind. "Fierce as I *tried* to defend the poor young gentlemen, ah . . . *quel dommage,*" he said, simpering.

"Oh, *mais oui,* you kill a *dozen* before dyin'." Balfa snickered.

"But then . . . what *will* we do with our little *mademoiselle?*" Lanxade quibbled with a sober sigh. "She lives, she'll talk sooner or later, and her parents, the Spanish authorities will run us down. I wish to fuck my way to my dotage, Boudreaux, not get garotted before I've had a chance to amuse *all* the pretty wenches of Cartagena."

"We come up wit' somethin'," Balfa muttered, though what that would be, he hadn't a clue. He really *didn't* want little Charité fed to the 'gators and crabs, but what other course was there?

CHAPTER TWENTY-EIGHT

*A*hoy, the boat!" Midshipman Grace shouted from the entry-port with
the aid of a brass speaking-trumpet, though his challenge was by rote, since
Proteus's people had known who it was that approached her for the past quarter hour, in mounting expectation and curiosity.

"*Proteus* . . . aye aye!" Quartermaster's Mate Toby Jugg, senior hand
aboard the *shalope* shouted back, thrusting one hand skyward as if in triumph, with four fingers spread to announce the arrival of a Post-Captain
as well.

Gilding the lily, that, Lewrie thought of Jugg's display, for when coming
back aboard, Lewrie *was* HMS *Proteus*. Four fingers and "aye, aye" were for
unknown Post-Captains arriving, to tell how many sailors should turn out as
the side-party. After a long, fretful, civilian, and covert absence, though, the
more Navy ritual, the better, for it meant a return to sanity, security . . . and
his own identity.

Lewrie almost squirmed with anticipation, that itchy-innards, leg-jiggling impatience he recalled from his boyhood when his father, Sir Hugo,
had gruffly announced that they'd coach to town the next day. The dawn
would *never* come, it seemed, before he got that first orange from the
fruiterer's, that first peek at new toys, first sweet-sticky candy after being
good, studious, and *quiet* for *so* long!

His eyes flitted hungrily over his magnificent frigate. *Proteus* in his absence had been maintained in spanking "Bristol Fashion," with First Officer

Mr. Langlie in his stead as acting-captain, aided by Lt. Catterall and Lt. Adair, and that "temporary" Third Officer Lt. Darling, whom Capt. Nicely had fetched him. Lewrie could find nothing to gripe about in her appearance or her readiness.

And there those worthies were by the starboard quarterdeck bulwarks, wide grins plastered on their faces, just about ready to give up Sea Officer "stoic" and whoop like punters at Derby whose horse led the last furlong. His whole crew looked to be gathered on the gangway and glad to *see* him . . . happier than he had a right to expect.

Their *shalope,* a wretched craft only fifty feet on the range of the deck and never meant for extended seafaring, sidled up to *Proteus* like a timid trout shyly nuzzling up to a great sea bass. After they left the Mississippi Delta, even Lewrie's cast-iron constitution had been challenged to seasickness aboard the *shalope,* so it was with avidity that he took the single easy step from the *shalope*'s low entry-port to the main-mast channels, man-ropes and boarding battens of the frigate's starboard entry. A moment later, Lewrie stood on his own decks once more, doffing his much-abused wide-brimmed hat in salute to the side-party, the wail of bosun's calls, the stamp-slap of boots and hands on muskets from the Marines, and the doffings from both officers and crew.

Once his honours had been rendered, Lewrie gleefully smiled and whooped himself to send his civilian headgear sailing as far off as possible. He skinned off his hideous shiny-green coat and tore at the buttons that bound him into that tight, striped waist-coat.

"Lemme help, sir!" his steward, Aspinall, joyfully offered as he came near. "God A'mighty, sir, but . . . these're a tad . . . garish!"

"Burn 'em if you wish, Aspinall," Lewrie sniggered.

Then there were his officers to greet, his middies, Bosun Pendarves, and his Mate, Mr. Towpenny, now returned to robust, full-fleshed health after his ordeal on the Dry Tortugas. And there was his Coxswain, Andrews, eyes alight with relief that he'd returned at last.

Where's that bloody Nicely? Lewrie fretfully wondered, a glance upwards assuring him that Capt. Nicely's broad pendant still flew aloft; *Command of a, hah! . . . squadron o' one gone to his head?*

As if "witched" up by the very thought, the bulkhead door to the main deck opened below him as he still stood on the starboard gangway. The Marine sentry on that door stamped and presented his musket in salute, and Nicely began to emerge . . . beaten to it, though, by two balls of fur that streaked so close to Capt. Nicely's feet that he staggered for a moment like a

Scotsman dancing over crossed blades, as his cats, Toulon and Chalky, came flying up the starboard quarterdeck ladder in a full-out, softly thundering, feline gallop.

"And *there's* my lads!" Lewrie cried, going down on one knee to welcome their arrival, and he didn't care who witnessed it, either, so fondly happy to see them again. And oh! but didn't they twine, mew and trill, stand on their hind legs, and sniff him over, make snorting, open-mouthed sounds as he stroked their heads. They kneaded and gently clawed at his trousers, and made a great ado over him.

"Ah, Captain Lewrie . . . back at last, I see," Capt. Nicely said once he'd gained the quarterdeck, standing a few feet off, cocking one brow in wary fashion. "The deed's done, sir? Our pirates' foul business stopped, I take it?"

"Not quite, sir," Lewrie told him, looking up, half his attention still fixed on his insistent creatures. "The prize was looted and stripped of anything useful, a dead loss to us. A dead loss for them, too, 'cause we set her afire on our way out of town. Set alight a Yankee emporium ship, too, but that was accidental, really. Let me get below, back in uniform, and I'll tell you all, sir. We know where our pirates are bound, d'ye see, sir, and . . . there's a chance, just a *chance*, mind, that when we catch 'em, they *might've* stolen a shipload of silver the Dons were sending from the Mexico City mint, and—"

"Silver?" Nicely goggled. "A whole *shipload* o'—?"

"Coined silver, sir," Lewrie said, rising to his feet, despite the protestations of his cats. Chalky, younger and spryer, took hold of his trousers at the left knee and scaled him like a tree trunk. "We . . . *ow!* . . . heard rumours in New Orleans the sum might be at least one or two millions. Spanish dollars to British pounds'd be . . . "

"Jesus bloody Christ!" Capt. Nicely breathed in awe. "And you think you know where they're bound, sir?" he further asked, his mouth moving afterwards in a silent mumble of numbers-juggling. "Five hundred thousand bloody *pounds?*"

"I do, sir," Lewrie said with a sly smile, with Chalky draped over his unbuttoned waist-coat, and going for his shoulder as agile and intent as a squirrel. "Where they'll *likely* be, if they're not at . . . *ow!*, stop that, Chalky, damn ye . . . if they're not at sea seekin' the booty this instant, sir."

Lewrie looked down as he felt claws on his right leg as Toulon gathered himself for a (clumsy) ascent of his own. Lewrie knelt to let the heavier, older cat have his other shoulder, to spare himself a few more bleeding nicks. Toulon nuzzled, head-butted, and snorted, whilst Chalky went in for more playful love-nips. Needless to say, both were purring as loud and rattly as carriage wheels on street cobbles. "For what I have in mind, sir, we'll need to retain the *shalope*. She's very shallow draught, and can go . . . *ow!*"

"Mister Langlie," Nicely bade, swivelling about. "I'd admire if you order yon . . . *shalope*, taken in tow, then get us back underway."

"Aye aye, sir," Lt. Langlie said, flicking a wary gaze betwixt Capt. Nicely and his own Capt. Lewrie for a moment. Now that Lewrie was back aboard, the request should have gone to Lewrie first, then to him. Lewrie cocked a brow at Langlie, as if to say that he would set things right once he and Nicely were below in his great-cabins.

"The course to steer, Mister Langlie, will be roughly Nor'west, a touch of Northing, for Barataria Bay," Lewrie instructed. "Know that place, Mister Winwood?" he asked of his stolidly prim Sailing Master.

"Not personally, no, Captain," that worthy slowly replied after seeming to give the matter a long, ponderous think. "Though I have in my possession a *fairly* trustworthy chart of the area in question."

"An out o' date, typical slap-dash French or Spanish chart, an hopeful fiction, most-like, but . . ." Lewrie genially scoffed. "Consult it, anyway, Mister Winwood, and give Mister Langlie the proper heading, then fetch it to my chart space, so we may all refer plans to it."

"Aye aye, sir," Mr. Winwood replied.

"Good Christ!" Lewrie said with a grimace once he was below in his private quarters, inhaling the stench of ram-cats. "Aspinall!" he started to accuse, "have you slacked off your scouring whilst I . . . "

"Beg pardon, sir, but . . . " the lad muttered, wringing his hands. "The little fellers *seemed* t'take to Cap'm Nicely well enough so long as you were still aboard, but oncet you set off for Louisiana, it got sorta . . . grim, sir. Spent half their time sulkin' for lack o' ya and t'other half prowlin' th' ship in search o' ya, the poor little beasts did. I 'spect they felt a bit put out with a stranger aft. Gave up their sandbox for 'is clothes, the deck canvas . . . his shoes an' hat, sir? Lurkin' about, peein' on his pillows an' bed sheets . . . hissin' an' spittin' whene'er they saw him, too, sir. I *tried* t'scour things fresh with vinegar, e'en smoked th' cabins with tobacco, but the wee lads're nothin' but sneaky an' clever, the little pranksters. Cap'm Nicely didn't take t'*them*, I tell ya, too, sir."

"And what of *my* clothing, Aspinall?" Lewrie dubiously said, as Aspinall bustled about, prating and fetching him fresh breeches, knee stockings, and shirt. Lewrie held the shirt up, sniffing it warily.

"Oh, no harm t'yours, sir!" Aspinall grinned. "When they were their lowest, they'd curl up t'gether on yer dressing robe. It seemed t'comfort 'em. But nary a whizz did they ever make on it. Though I *did* have t'brush off a couple pounds o' hair, now an' then, d'ye see. Now . . . here's a fresh-pressed neck-stock, sir, and yer waist-coat. I got a pitcher o' cold tea brewed, just th' way ya like it, and . . . "

It was all Lewrie could do to walk from one end of his quarters to the other for his lovelorn cats, who twined round his ankles.

"Right, then," Lewrie said with glad sigh of satisfaction once he was properly and comfortably garbed in complete uniform, less gilt-laced coat and cocked hat. "Do you pass word for Captain Nicely, the ship's officers, and Marine Lieutenant Devereux to attend me."

"Aye, sir," Aspinall responded.

"And uhm . . . Quartermaster's Mate Jugg, as well," Lewrie added.

"Well, that should cover it," Lewrie concluded, looking at his officers gathered round his desk and the pertinent chart spread atop it. HMS *Proteus* bowled along on a goodly slant of wind, her larboard shoulder firmly set to the sea, and heeled over about fifteen degrees. It felt *good* to flex his legs and balance again, good to hear the hissing, swooshing muffled roar of her hull parting the waters. "Two-pronged assault, not so very far apart that either party is dangerously isolated from the other, I trust."

Grand Terre was about five miles long and perhaps a mile wide at best, a low-lying sandy barrier island. It, and its smaller eastern twin, Grand Isle, barred the southern end of Barataria Bay, leaving a poor choice of entrances to the bay. Between the two was the deepest, though *Proteus*, with her seventeen-and-a-half-foot draught, could not probe too deep between the isles. The borrowed *shalope* would lead the assault, armed with swivel-guns and 2-Pdr. boat-guns, whilst *Proteus* would stand in as close as she dared to support with her 12-Pdrs.

It was an uneasy conference, when all depended on Toby Jugg's dim "recollections" of older sailors' talk, with many a "so I heard" qualifier flung about; and Jugg shiftily avoiding how he'd gathered such knowledge . . . or under which flag he'd gained his "experience."

Jugg sketched out three possible sites that the pirates might use. One was on Grand Isle's Nor'west tip, on the right-hand side of the best channel; the other was on Grand Terre Island's Nor'east tip, on the other side of the pass. The last, least likely "So I heard of, oncet, sors" was at the far West end of

Grand Terre by the shallower inlet. A schooner could get in there, but not a deep-draught prize to be unloaded and stripped.

At both of the most likely sites there were freshwater springs and rills ashore, dense stands of timber for firewood or huts . . . off the ground like Indian *chickees* to deter the venomous snakes that the "auld sailormen" had mentioned. Indeed, there were reputed to be easily recognisable Indian mounds there—wide, tall, and slope-sided, erected God knew how long ago, and for unfathomed uses. There were mounds of oyster, clam, and mussel shells, too—garbage middens from centuries of native settlement, of fishing, raking, and cooking.

Proteus and the *shalope* would close the coast once it was full dark, launch a cutter and a spying-out party on the evening of their arrival to determine which spot the pirates might be using. If they were even *there*, of course; *if* Barataria was more convenient than any inlet farther west, like Atchafalaya Bay, or . . .

Were they present, all four of *Proteus*'s boats would be used to land a mixed party of seamen and Marines, who would march a short distance overland to take the shore encampment under fire. At the same time, the *shalope* would go for the pirates' ship and any capture they might have made, curling round behind to block their escape.

If they'd come *down* Bayou Barataria or the Ouatchas River, like Mr. Pollock had supposed, it made sense to imagine that they would run back that way if overpowered, poling and paddling like mad in *pirogues* to escape, to lose their pursuers in the maze of *coulées* or bayous that they alone knew. The *shalope*'s light guns and swivels could slaughter the dugout log canoes and flat-bottomed boats.

"Now, as to who leads which," Lewrie posed, gesturing for them to take seats and accept glasses of claret, now they were finished with the chart. And this was the sticky part.

As commanding officer of HMS *Proteus*, one who had already earned his captaincy, Lewrie customarily should have left the hard chores to his junior officers, for how else could they ever gain notice with Admiralty except by the successful doing of some brave deed, mentioned favourably in their captain's report of the action. Of such things a successful career was made, promotion and advancement earned, command of their own warships someday "bought" with bloody, fatal risks.

Yet Lewrie wished to be in at the kill, to see firsthand, or *cause* firsthand, the deaths of the de Guilleris, Lanxade, and Balfa . . . that cousin of theirs, that Don Rubio Monaster who'd most likely taken the shots at him and was reputedly as tight as ticks with them all . . . do *something* with that lying slut Charité, though he did admittedly feel squeamish qualms should *she* be slain.

"Mister Devereux to take all his Marines for the landing party, it goes without saying," Lewrie declared with a grin, knowing how his elegant and efficient Marine officer relished independent action. They lifted their glasses to each other, Devereux smiling wolfishly.

"Mister Langlie, as First Officer, to oversee our frigate's approach inshore, sir," Capt. Nicely said with a grunt, knowing that Lt. Langlie would be crestfallen. "If I, as temporary commander of this squadron, may deem best, hmm?"

"With Mister Adair to assist," Lewrie said. "Mister Catterall to lead the seamen of the shore landing and take charge of the boats' progress to the beach."

"Thankee, sir!" the burly Catterall hooted with glee, ready to elbow everyone within reach to gloat over his good fortune, even if he could be a bobbing corpse not two days hence.

"We *do* have Mister Darling handy," Nicely posed.

"Your pardon, Captain Nicely," Lewrie gently objected, "but he is not *known* to the ship's people. Neither, for that fact, is Mister Gamble, tarry and efficient a Midshipman as he's served in my absence. If I may, sir, as *Proteus*'s captain, I prefer her own people to participate. After what the pirates did to some of her people, they have a personal stake, if you will, in the—"

"Mister Darling and Mister Adair, with Lieutenant Langlie, will manage *Proteus*," Captain Nicely decided, "whilst *I* shall take overall command of the boat party, and *you*, Captain Lewrie, shall command the *shalope*."

"Well, sir!" Lewrie gawped, trying to finesse his objection politely and squirming uneasily in his chair. "Dear as I'd wish to see things done to a proper turn, d'ye really think that—"

"Damme, I do, sir," Capt. Nicely rejoined, all smiles and verve. "Privilege of my seniority, d'ye see. Oh, we'll not get in the way of the younger lads who need to make their names, but! If those pirates are in there, and *if* they've been successful, I would no more be able t'sit by and fidget than I could abide t'watch another man eat my supper . . . then tell me how tasty it was, hah!

"Are we successful, I intend to write fulsomely of all participants in my report to Admiralty, so no one'll suffer for want of credit. Call me an old war-horse if you must, Captain Lewrie, but I can't turn down the chance for real action . . . and so I shan't."

Gold fever, more like, Lewrie uncharitably thought; *in this case, silver night-sweats!*

"Very well, sir," he said, knowing that further quibbling could be deemed insubordination. "In that case, I'll need Mister Adair and a midshipman with me . . . Mister Larkin's an energetic laddy. And at least eighteen hands. Mister Darling and Midshipman Gamble may stay aboard *Proteus* to second the First Lieutenant."

"We'll have four more hands, at any rate, sir," Lt. Adair glumly told them, still disappointed to not play a larger role. "The men Mister Pollock loaned you off his brig . . . once word got round that we could be in the way of *substantial* prize-money, those four asked to speak with me and ended up taking Ship's Articles. Since they already had their chests and kits, their guinea Joining Bounties are all profit to them too, sir."

"In at the kill, Lewrie!" Capt. Nicely cheered. "They desire to be in at the kill! As to your request for your own Lieutenant and Midshipman to accompany you aboard the *shalope*, I say 'done, and done,' ha ha!" Nicely slapped the desktop with his palm as if to seal the bargain. "And a full bumper with all of you, gentlemen, from my own stock of wines . . . a toast to our complete success!"

Which boisterous slap and cry elicited ominous hissing, moaning, and some spits from Toulon and Chalky, now well hidden 'neath the starboard side settee.

They even despise the sound *of him, by now,* Lewrie sardonically thought as Aspinall produced a brace of claret bottles; *Either that, or we're in for a whole lot o' trouble!*

CHAPTER TWENTY-NINE

*T*hey're there, sir," Lt. Langlie told him once he'd gained the deck. "Two big schooners anchored off the tip of Grand Terre, on the West side of the channel. Mister Jugg recognised the black'un, that set him and our party on the Tortugas, but the other is even bigger, a tops'l schooner that we didn't recognise, sir."

Sop to his ego and career prospects, Lewrie told himself; *The bold, unsupported probe, but not the lion's share of any battle. Damn! They did take a prize. Just one, so it must be a rich'un. Talk about your silver fever! For I think I've caught it!*

"How close did you get, sir?" Lewrie quickly asked, just about shaking himself to clear his mind of avaricious images. "Did you see any preparations dug? Batteries or watchtowers?"

"We grounded on the beach, sir," Lt. Langlie proudly announced, glorying in his small but risky part of the endeavour boldy done. "On those flat-topped Indian mounds, we could see a *few* sentries. We got within about half a cable, I'd reckon it, before we feared their firelight might expose us, sir. They're *celebrating*, sir! Three sheets to the wind, as drunk as lords . . . lots of caterwauling and fiddling, capering and dancing." Lt. Langlie snickered, his teeth shining in the darkness as he broadly grinned. "Long as we observed 'em, the sentries atop the earth mounds came and went, spent half their time jawing with their shipmates down below, and sneaking swigs from crocks or bottles when they thought no one was looking. No batteries, sir, no entrenchments that we could spy, though Mister Jugg *thought* he saw springs set on the black-hulled schooner's bower and kedge cables."

"So, an hour 'fore dawn, and they'll most-like be falling-down drunk and insensible," Lewrie surmised. "Better and better! A grand night's work, Mister Langlie. Damned fine!"

"Thank you, sir!" Langlie gladly replied. "And thank you for the opportunity, to—"

"No one saw you and your party, d'ye think?" Lewrie fretted of a sudden.

"Don't think so, sir, no." Lt. Langlie told him, pensive for a moment. "No hue and cry, that's for certain."

"Well, that's fine, then," Lewrie decided, letting out a much-relieved sigh. "And thank *you*, Mister Langlie, for an arduous task, nobly done."

"Er . . . aye, aye, sir."

"If you will, sir, I'd admire the *shalope* fetched alongside, so I may go aboard her," Lewrie ordered, turning stiffly formal. "I give you charge of *Proteus* 'til my return, or the completion of our little enterprise, sir. Get her as deep into the channel as you think practicable, Mister Langlie, and her guns well within range, even the carronades if that's possible."

"Directly, sir!" Langlie assured him.

"Damme, I like this frigate hellish-fine, Mister Langlie! Just as she is . . . paintwork included, hmm?" Lewrie declared, chuckling as he clapped his First Lieutenant on the shoulder.

"I'll take good care of her, sir. No worries."

"I have none, sir," Lewrie replied. "Especially knowing that any scrapes and such'd be *your* sad task to repair, once back in port!"

Boudreaux Balfa and his son, Fusilier, toiled away on the dark bay side of the captured Spanish schooner, shifting kegs from her entry-port to the sole of a dowdy, paint-peeling, and flat-bottomed lugger, a single-masted boat that could go almost anywhere up the bayous or the *coulées* that a *pirogue* could go . . . if one knew the maze of waterways like the palm of one's hand, as did Balfa, his son and several of his neighbours who'd come along on the raiding cruise. Kegs of silver were shifted from the lugger to their flat-bottomed boats and *pirogues*, their shares for participating . . . as well as "a little something extra" that Balfa and his neighbours would rather not have the others know a thing about.

Chère, mo lem-mé toi, oui, mo lem-mé toi,
avec tou mo coeur, mo lem-mé toi, chère,
comme tit cochon lem-mé la boul!

He sang softly, covertly, perhaps to hide the sly guffaw at the trick he was playing on all of them, else he would be roaring out loud.

Dear, I love you so, yes, I love you so.
With all my heart, I love you, dear,
like the little pig loves mud! Hee hee hee!

"Papa, the others," Fusilier Balfa fretted in a whisper. "If we steal dem blind, dey come after us an' kill us!"

"Naw, Fusilier. Come dawn, ever'body gonna shinny up dere own side, I tell ya," Boudreaux softly snickered. "We just takin' our own shares a little *early,* is all. For safekeepin'. *Comprends, mon fils?*"

"I don' know," Fusilier timidly objected, counting off a new keg as it was manhandled across their lugger to a waiting *pirogue;* that would make twenty kegs so far, he reckoned. And more was coming.

Just in case a Spanish *guarda costa* or one of those perfidious British men-o'-war ran across them before they'd reached the safety of Barataria Bay, over eight hundred kegs had been put aboard *Le Revenant,* so if one ship was taken, the cruise wouldn't be a total loss for the survivors. Fusilier's papa had told him on the sly that the take was nowhere near what their buccaneers expected, but that he was to shut his mouth about that until the whole cargo was broken out and the truth revealed . . . in the morning, when their crew would be groggy and hungover, *perhaps* gullible enough to settle for what was in hand.

There was enough rum and *arrack,* enough barricos of rough Mexican wine, to keep the men pliable and "hot" enough to work the ships back to Grand Terre, but not sober enough to wonder where the rest of the money was. Dread of being taken by a passing warship had sped their labours in shifting *some* of the cargo, then breaking off suddenly and setting sail homeward, with the rest soon to be "discovered."

Balfa and Lanxade would declare that they would take less than their customary shares, so the men would not be cheated. Just as soon as the de Guilleris and their arrogant compatriots were accused of supplying them with false information, a nebulous (but hopefully believable!) plot would emerge with the banker Maurepas, to skim off some of the silver as soon as it landed in New Orleans . . . Jérôme Lanxade would even suggest that Maurepas, Bistineau, and the de Guilleris might have conspired to steal some of the silver from the prize *during the night!*

Which would conveniently explain why Boudreaux Balfa was taking some tonight, and wouldn't Jérôme be surprised! Balfa gleefully thought as he shouldered another heavy keg from one of his cousins aboard the prize and carefully set it by the others in the lugger's amidships. He reckoned that he might be able to make off with about 40,000 silver dollars, which he *might* split with Jérôme . . . or he might not. Maybe even 50,000, if the water in the creeks, *coulées*, sloughs, and bayous was up, and they could float that much away.

Did he take a reduced share of the loot in the morning, not the 200,000 he was due but only 50,000, say, the Balfas would be rich for life, rich beyond imagining, when he combined his *public* share with a little, trifling, miniscule *private* one, even if he had to give half to Lanxade to mollify him once he found that his imaginative fabulation was *true,* hee hee!

And just to be on the safe side, he had a *second* lugger for a quick departure, once the share-out was done, before anyone with quick wits could suspect him. After all, come dawn those witless play-acting *bébés* would be feeding the crabs; the prize schooner would be emptied, stripped, and burned; and *Le Revenant* awarded to the strongest, loudest-voiced, and quickest-witted pirate who wanted to stay in business.

"*Vite, vite, mes chers,*" Balfa stealthily urged. "*Un autre . . . beaucoup d'autres!* Another . . . a lot o' others!"

"It's so pagan!" Charité tittered as she sat cross-legged on a blanket atop one of the ancient Indian earth mounds where she and her brothers and kin had, by right as "leaders," put up a trio of lean-to shelters for the night. "Like something out of an old book."

Firelight flickered high and heathen from several bonfires on the beach, from cooking fires where cauldrons simmered and black-iron pans sizzled up savoury things. The flickering yellow and orange glow from so many fires lent an unreal aura to the shoreline for over fifty yards from end to end, from the beach line to the scrubby bushes above the beach, where the wood had been gathered, and illuminated the tall trees that shrouded their secret lair and the betraying sight of the ships' masts from view from any passing searchers. The light was reflected back onto the rough buccaneer camp by the bleached-bone whiteness of other, lower mounds of oyster, mussel, and clam shells that had been heaped up first by aboriginal Indians, then added to by White fishermen, wanderers, and outlaws. They were not as tall or as deep as the roughly flat-topped earth mounds, but they snaked along like a miniature mountain chain, slumped into each other a bit inshore.

The camp could boast a few rare tents, but most huts were of fresh-cut saplings and thin limbs, over which scrap canvas or blankets had been draped . . . more lean-tos, hastily thrown up by their sailors or built for them by the many wild rovers who made a precarious life along the bay and the inland lake. Wild, eerie, and isolated as these remote isles were, some few people did reside there and even more camped temporarily. And Barataria had been a pirates' lair and "hurricane hole" for ages. And where there were pirates and bold buccaneers, there would be the chance for quick profits off their witless free-spending.

Almost as soon as their mast heads had been spotted, red-sailed luggers had veered down to them, and somehow the word had spread, drawing rowing boats, swamp craft, and *pirogues* full of hopeful entrepreneurs. Cooks had built lean-tos and fires, shrimpers and crabbers had turned up with their catches, farmers had arrived with bushel baskets filled with pod peas and corn for boiling or "roasting ears." Fruit, backcountry wines, pigs, chickens, and goats, carefully hoarded bottles of costly cognac or apple brandy from dearest *la belle France,* turned up for sale. Flounder, mullet, and mullet roe, even humble meat like muskrat, 'possum, rabbit, and raccoon sizzled on little spits and peeled twigs, their aromas blending with that of fresh corn-breads.

There were half-naked Spaniards and Canary Islanders, very poor Acadians, and even a few French Creoles who'd fallen on hard times; some light-skinned Free Blacks, swarthier *nègres* who just *might* be Maroons escaped from their masters' plantations and eking out a meagre existence as honest runaways, or even a few sly-eyed ex-slaves now in a predatory armed marauder gang like that of the devilish Saint John, whose murderous horde *were* known to lurk along the west shore of the bay.

There were cooks, there were gamblers, and there were *putains,* too, of all nations and races. Some of those women danced singly as the drunken sailors danced to the music of the itinerant musicians. Some, nude and glistening, put on a show to music to lure tossed coins, then the "socket-fee" from the pirate who was the most enflamed. They flung themselves down under a lean-to and grunted in time with whoever had found them fetching, then sponged off in the salt water of the bay, standing knee-deep between the many grounded boats before going back to look for a fresh customer.

"*Capitaine* Lanxade said they only *think* they know how to celebrate," Helio ventured to say, now that Charité *seemed* to be her old self again, after her hysterical tirade of a day or two before. "This is nothing to the old days, he said. These modern buccaneers of ours can't hold a candle to the wild men he knew in his youth."

"And we've only seen three fights," Don Rubio added with a disappointed sniff. "And none of them to the death." Warily, Don Rubio still distanced himself from Charité's side. For if she could forgive her brothers and her cousin, even speak civilly to them again, yet she still gathered her brows together and scowled at him whenever it was necessary for them to converse, her voice distant and cold.

"The night is still young," Jean-Marie Rancour commented with a hopeful chuckle and shrug. "One never knows . . ."

"Hmmph!" Charité said, turning to look at Helio and Hippolyte. "Even if this is only a dim shadow of an old-time pirate gathering, it is still a wondrous show. Tortuga and Topsail Island . . . Port Royal, before the earthquake destroyed it. Nassau, on New Providence, before *Capitaine* Woodes Rogers cleaned it out. And him an old pirate, too!"

"No honour among thieves, the saying goes, *chérie*," Helio cited.

"The firelight, the Blacks," she rhapsodised in spite of him, quite romantically taken by the scenes, the smells. "So much nudity on display! Why, one could almost imagine us transported among those savage corsairs of High Barbary . . . in Algiers, where the sultans buy beautiful virgin girls for their *hareems*!"

"Christ!" Hippolyte sneered with a disparaging groan. "Novels! Romances written mostly by eunuchs in a Parisian garret! There's not a single thing worth a *sou* in fiction books!"

"Most written by *Anglais* eunuchs!" Jean-Marie guffawed. "French writers at least *have* the 'necessities' to write romances. From experience, not their imagination."

Charité frowned over that comment, her lips pursed in an argumentative *moue* as she thought of telling them a thing or two about how equipped with the "necessities" *some* Englishmen were, but didn't.

What was done was done, she told herself, and she'd never see her Englishman again. There was tonight, though, this heady and rapturous pagan display to savour. Tonight, she was not a patriotic revolutionary, she was . . . Mary Read or Anne Bonny, notorious girl pirates of ancient fame!

She sat cross-legged on the ground in breeches and boots, with a sheathed dagger in her sash, a blade up her sleeve, pistols at her hips, and her trusty sword standing close at hand. In her lap there was a coin-silver charger for her supper plate, looted from a Spanish captain's quarters, and she used heavy, ornate silver utensils from a dead man's sideboard.

She dined on roast goat and pork, like the bold Caribbean *boucaniers* had, on peeled shrimp and rice, corn on the cob, peas, and cornbread. By her right knee stood a large silver tankard, the piratical rogue's sort with a clear glass bottom, so big it could hold a whole pint of beer, half a bottle of wine, or an entire flask of brandy or rum. This night, it was strong, heady, amber rum.

Dining *al fresco* but hearty, swigging rum in a savage firelight, witnessing a bawdy, raucous carnival to celebrate a victory, a grand coup, a magnificent adventure. Oh, it was simply wondrous!

The bonfire smoke and cook-fire smoke wreathed and melded with a rising mist to encapsulate the scene, as if Nature made for them a ghostly theatre. She would remember this all the rest of her life!

CHAPTER THIRTY

"Fog, dammit t'hell!" Lewrie growled under his breath, clinging to a larboard shroud aboard his borrowed *shalope*. "Should've expected that. Should've *known* better!"

They were standing into the deepwater channel between the isles, both of which were now invisible behind the dank banks of mist; astern of them would be *Proteus*, but she was invisible, too, and just before dawn there would be very little sea breeze and a next-to-nothing land breeze, either. On what dying wind-memory that still stirred the sea, they barely made steerageway, and their *shalope*'s gaff mains'l and jibs limply sagged and rustled like a too-large shirt on a starving man.

Lewrie peered astern, past the vessel's tiny quarterdeck, where the enigmatic Toby Jugg tended to her tiller-bar. *Proteus* spread *acres* of sail and had a much longer waterline; even on this slack wind she'd amass a knot or two more forward progress and, unless her lookouts were keen might loom up blind and trample the *shalope* under her forefoot. Even if she avoided colliding, a drastic hauling-off would steal all her hard-won speed, and it would take a quarter-gale to get her moving, again! Worse, sheering away cross-channel could strand her on one of the invisible shoals, and she'd be out of the fight before it had even begun, leaving Lewrie and his small party vastly outnumbered.

"The bay's shallower, sir," Lt. Adair said, coming aft from the leadsmen in the bows who swung for soundings, passing their discoveries aft by hand signals, not the usual cries.

"Yes, and?" Lewrie snapped, wondering if there was a way to recall the landing party, wait for a better, fogless morning.

"Shallow water heats faster than deep, sir," Adair said on. "As the bay heats, it should make a touch more breeze and thin this fog."

"This humid air, though, Mister Adair," Lewrie countered. "As the bay water warms, it'll make for a *thicker* fog. To clear would take hours . . . far past dawn. Round *noon*, by the looks of it."

"It has thinned a tad, sir," Lt. Adair hesitantly opined. But, as if to bely that hope, a thicker bank of fog loomed up ahead, slowly rolling down to swallow them and cut their visibility to a mere stone's throw ahead of the jib boom and bowsprit. But it had been *driven* down to them by a slightly stronger breath of wind, and the sails rustled and meagrely filled out; tackle blocks and parrel-balls clink-clanked or groaned, and for a few moments Lewrie could hear the burbling sound of the *shalope*'s hull making a knot more way through the water.

And the fog *seemed* to thin a trifle!

"'Bout a full cable's visibility now, sir!" Lt. Adair pointed out. "Aye, sir . . . thinning. With a touch more wind now, too."

"Fine for us," Lewrie muttered, looking aft as if he could sear through the foreboding mist. "We're gaff-rigged, fore-and-aft, but . . . it might be a 'dead muzzler' for *Proteus*, square on her bows. She'll be stalled in-irons, and helpless."

And without his frigate's artillery, there'd be no support for his assault on the buccaneer's camp, no support for the landing party, either. If Lt. Langlie could not even *row* her into range, much less in *sight* in this fog, using her 12-pounders at Range-To-Random-Shot, then Lewrie's small and divided assault force might be massacred, half by half, and there'd be nothing Lewrie could do to prevent it. Worse, it would take much too long to send a boat to shore to re-call Captain Nicely's men, to go about and *try* to find *Proteus* in the fog!

Lewrie crossed his fingers behind his back, knowing that, for better or for worse, they were now committed. But the breeze *did* feel fresher, and the fog *did* look just that much thinner, so . . .

"Damme, that smell . . . " Lewrie said, as a sour odour arrived on that slight wind. He lifted his face and sniffed deep like a hound.

"Cook-fires, sir!" Lt. Adair exclaimed in a guarded whisper as he, too, picked up the reek of wood-ash and smoke, spilled, fried-out fats and cast-off gristle from meats, and the low-tide tang of boiled shellfish. "We must be *very* close to the Nor'east tip of Grand Terre, sir . . . almost onto the camp!"

"Alert the hands, Mister Adair," Lewrie bade, forcing down his frets and donning the steely, determinedly confident air of a leader sure of success. "Muskets and pistols loaded, but not yet *primed*. Do you and Mister Larkin oversee that personally, sir. Mister Jugg, helm over a bit . . . pinch us up to larboard half a point, no more."

In for the penny, in for the pound, Lewrie grimly thought as he tried the draw of his sword in its scabbard; *and pray* God *don't let me get half these men killed in the next hour!*

Lt. Catterall simply bloody *hated* snakes and felt his skin go icy as he shied from another particularly dangerous-looking serpent, his sword-point aimed at its hideous cotton-white mouth and fangs as he gave it *two* sword lengths of berth, eyes darting all round to avoid stumbling into another as he fled the latest one.

Grand Terre Island was working alive with the bastards, and Lt. Catterall was *already* miserable enough. From the moment he'd stepped ashore, he'd been swarmed by midges, gnats, whining mosquitoes, and *wren*-sized moths. His exposed skin itched like mad from their stings or bites, his face felt puffy and "pebbled" with mosquito welps. Grit and mud still filled his shoes from wading sightless through the marshes, puddles, and rivulets. His feet chafed and squished with every step, and he'd splashed mud and foul-smelling wet *something* higher than his knee buckles. Catterall even vaguely envied soldiers; they could wear "spatterdashes" from their shoe soles to the crutch. Boot would have been better, but his single pair were new, and he hadn't imagined he'd need them this badly, so . . .

Their extremely slow, groping march from the beach on the south shore through the forest's tangles, thorny shrubs, and clinging vines had been a horror, too, utterly mystifying and confusing. For hours, it had been black as a boot, and he'd barely been able to see his hand in front of his face. Everyone was forced to shamble, shuffle, and put each foot ahead of the next on sheer faith, led by a few Marines who'd been woodsmen.

The halts were many, the progress treacle-slow, and the forest was an eerie foe to seamen, Marines, and civilised gentlemen used to open fields and *sensible* terrain. Owls hooted, *un-named* things cawed and chirped; insects sawed and squeaked all about them, and armed men shivered and took fright at every unexplained rustle close by in the underbrush. Once off the beach, the air had been dank and close, too warm for woolen uniforms, too dense to breathe comfortably, stinking with raw, oozing dankness and putrefaction, with foul, sappy odours.

Then had come the fog, just as it was *almost* possible to see, making the march even more ominous, and each scampering rodent was an enemy scout dashing off to give the alarm, and . . . !

There were bare-tailed rat-like things that grinned, as big as bloody *spaniels* scurrying away almost at their feet; ring-tailed and masked beasts that chittered and growled; 'possums and raccoons, Lt. Devereux had whispered to calm them, and all quite harmless. Humped, hard-shelled lizardy creatures called armadillos, disturbed squirrels in the trees, whose sudden barks could startle Catterall to crying out!

"Halt here," a Marine hissed ahead of him, "passin' th' word, we halt here fer a bit."

"Hold here," Catterall repeated as loud as he dared, both arms outspread to indicate a ragged skirmish line for his men. It was all taking too long, he thought; in the dark and this pre-dawn fog it was possible they'd gotten hopelessly lost, and when the sun rose they'd find themselves far from where they were needed, unable to hit the pirates' camp in time to coordinate with Captain Lewrie's seaward attack. The pirates would be awake and ready for them, it'd turn into a disaster, and . . . !

"Passin' th' word, there . . . awf'cers, front," the Marine said in a raspy, weary whisper.

Lt. Catterall almost tiptoed forward, trying to go quiet, but the many scrub bushes and palm-like swishing greenery made that a forlorn hope. He finally made out two men who stood before the kneeling sailors and Marines, men in cocked hats peeking round a thick cypress at something: Devereux and Capt. Nicely.

"Smell them, sir?" Devereux asked with a happy grin. "We are there. They are there, just yonder, the other side of this wall."

"A wall, sir?" Catterall said, trying not to sound "windy" to his comrades-in-arms. "Damme, not a fortification, is it?"

"Irregular," Capt. Nicely hesitantly opined, wiping sweat from his brows with a calico handkerchief. "Not *laid* stone, perhaps . . ."

"A dug entrenchment, with a firing step behind it?"

"Damme," Capt. Nicely groused softly. All evening long, all during the ferrying, then the arduous trek through the swampy wastes, Nicely had practically boiled over with energy and enthusiasm. Now he was taken aback by an un-looked-for obstacle. This fog, though it was thinning as a light wind sprang up, combined with the fearsome-looking fortification, was almost the last straw, and his eagerness seemed flown from him; the imperturbable Capt. Nicely was just about ready to chew on a thumbnail in worry. In the fog, the frigate and the *shalope* could not support them, or even *find* them, and now this! And it was impossible to call off the ships, to withdraw. If the fog dissipated and the ships attacked without the shore party, the pirates might just sail farther up the bay, beyond reach, without the landing party ravaging and surprising their encampment!

"No sentries, though," Devereux took note.

"Might've heard us thrashin' about and already mustered behind this wall, just waitin'," Catterall grumbled.

"Don't croak, Mister Catterall," Capt. Nicely chid him.

"Their fields of fire haven't been cleared," Lt. Devereux said in further assessment, pointing at the stumps of downed trees and the many small trees that still stood, the irregular clumps of scrub bush that remained. "Damn' shoddy way to maintain a fortification, really. The low places here and there *could* mask small cannon, but . . . "

"We're too few to attack that." Capt, Nicely sighed. "If it *is* manned, our villains are alerted. Might there be a way around?"

"No time for that, sir," Lt. Devereux said with a hitch to his voice and a fatalistic shrug. He began to strip off his red coat and bright brass gorget, unwind his scarlet officer's sash, and discard his sword baldric with its rectangular brass plate, removing his sword from the frog and holding it scabbarded in his left hand. "You gentlemen will excuse me for a few minutes, sirs?"

Devereux crouched down and warily sneaked from one large tree to the next 'til he'd reached the scrub, his spotless white shirt and breeches melding into the mists, *hoping* that he was mostly invisible, briefly praying that no marksman or sentinel behind the forbidding wall had already taken aim at him.

"Sweet Jesus," Devereux whispered as he steeled himself, then rose to a half crouch and sprinted to the cover of a clump of bushes. Halfway there! Dry-mouthed, panting, fear-sweat popping on his skin, he scanned the wall for danger. It was one thing for him to stand by his men and order volleys. He stood the same odds as a private facing enemy fire then, but this!

There was more sand than grass near the foot of the irregular, rough-surfaced impediment . . . as if a lane *had* been cleared. Nearer-to, it didn't exactly look intentional, its forward slope too gentle to impede a determined infantryman. So what . . . ? Sprint again!

He crunched to the base of the wall, gasping like a hound, fears gibbering at his brain, his nerves twanging like harpsichord strings, chest upon its lumpy, irregular roughness as he tried to quiet the bellow's roar that came from his own frankly scared breathing, wanting to shush noises that his slightest movement made, the hollow tinkling and gravelly—

What the bloody Hell?

His left hand came up from his sword hilt to take up a palm full of loose, broken, sharp-edged but weathered shells! Clam and mussel, larger sun-bleached oyster shells. The smaller shells he rolled in his hand like dice before very quietly putting them back in place. Fighting to contain his giggles, he crept to his left under one of the high heaps 'til he reached a low saddle between mounds, peeked cautiously over it, and felt another giggling fit swell up, which he quickly stifled, then got to the business of reconnaissance, wishing he'd thought to fetch away pencil and paper.

It wasn't a wall at all! Lt. Devereux silently exulted; *just a garbage midden!* The sleeping pirates' camp was just the other side of it, stretching perhaps fifty or sixty yards along the far shore, under the looming bulk of a series of odd flat-topped earth mounds, and them sloped so gently that he could almost mistake them for natural rises. The shoreline wasn't an hundred yards further north, with boats drawn up on the beach. Two schooners could almost be made out in the mists, anchored perhaps two hundred yards from the beach in deeper water, a black-hulled, red-striped schooner and another. Lt. Devereux despaired that he'd left his short pocket telescope in his coat. After a long few minutes of observation, he crept back beneath the cover of a high point in the mounds, steeled himself once more for the unseen sentry's musket, then dashed back to rejoin his fellow officers.

"Well, damn my eyes!" Capt. Nicely gasped when told the nature of that forbidding "fort."

"Allow me to suggest, sir, that we bring our men up to the foot of the shell heaps," Lt. Devereux said as he donned his uniform again. "Load muskets and pistols, my men to fix bayonets as well, then wait for our ships' arrival. Once the camp's well stirred to confront that threat, would be the ideal time to strike right to the beach, cut right through their camp and take possession of the earthen mounds, so our musketry has the only high ground, forcing the pirates to clamber up in the face of our cutlasses, bayonets, and muzzles, sir."

"Damme, I like it, Lieutenant Devereux!" Capt. Nicely chirped, suddenly reinfused with pep and vinegar. "Like it, indeed, hah hah! And *two* schooners, did ye say, sir? A prize they've taken, or . . . "

"One flies what looks to be a French Tricolour, sir. T'other has no flag aloft," Devereux replied as he hung his rank gorget about his neck once more and clapped on his cocked hat, taking time to set it in the regulation manner. "Though the wind is limp, sir."

"Harbour Watch aboard 'em?" Nicely pressed.

"Couldn't tell, sir," Devereux said with a wry grin as he took his telescope from a side pocket of his coat. "I quite forgot to put this in my waistband, so . . ."

"Then let's be up against your heaps, sir, and I'll squint at 'em myself!" Capt. Nicely cheerfully, eagerly declared.

CHAPTER THIRTY-ONE

Capitaine Jérôme Lanxade has slept aboard the pirate schooner, avoiding his soon-to-be-disappointed and angry sailors as long as he could, savouring the safe privacy of her master's quarters. Lanxade had slept alone too. None of the churlish drabs who had flocked to their camp had caught his eye. Besides, with so much loot soon to be his, he could afford to be picky. In New Orleans, where he would soon close out his accounts and pack up his valuables, there were at least a round dozen young *courtesans,* or bored and "sporting" wives of his acquaintance, some "obliging" young unmarried girls who'd be glad to give him a rousing send-off on his "honourable retirement" across the sea to "parts unknown." The sorts who didn't laugh when he took off his finery and revealed his taut-laced corset!

A shambling steward fetched him a silver pot of hot *café noir,* and he sipped from an ornate Meissen china cup and saucer as he shaved himself—never trust unruly pirates with razors to do it!—and combed in fresh hair dye, then pomade, through his thinning locks, daubing new wax on his pointy mustachios and twirling them stiffly horizontal.

He then shucked his silk dressing gown and donned his constricting "appliance." Jérôme Lanxade never let a steward or body slave do it for him; that felt demeaning, making *"Le Féroce"* an object of fun, not fear! He laced it as tight as it could go, going almost purple in the face before he drew on his snug breeches and buttoned them up.

Capt. Lanxade heaved a worrisome sigh, then, fully dressed at last, went out on deck for a welcome breath of fresh but moist, mist-laden air, the dawn's first *cigaro* alit in one hand and a fresh cup of bracingly strong coffee in the other. He scowled at the beach, at the sleeping camp, and was satisfied that most of their henchmen would be *weeping* with hangovers, too fuddled to think straight when he and Boudreaux Balfa broke their sad news. Most of the scows and *pirogues* were gone. The *honest* backcountry folk had packed up and left once they'd sold their last goods. In the wee hours of a pirates' celebration, it was dangerous to linger too long among the red-eyed murderous!

Lanxade looked over at their prize schooner. There stood old Boudreaux himself, just arisen and yawning like a shambling swamp bear, stretching to get the kinks out, scratching his hide and even grating his back against the schooner's main-mast!

Lanxade rehearsed his plan for betraying the youngsters in his mind once more, once the hands were *hot* and outraged, as he would *make* them. Bind them all first, *then* do the reduced share-out, *then* offer the ships to the unlikeliest, most despised mate among them, setting them to fighting among themselves whilst he and Boudreaux made their getaway cross the bay and into the bayous—without getting savaged like sick sharks by the rest of the pack and torn to bloody gobbets! What happened to the de Guilleri men, their whey-faced cousin, or that arrogant peacock half-dago afterward was of no matter to him, though, he doubted the men would kill Charité to ensure her silence. She was too well liked. They *might* turn her loose eventually, Lanxade imagined, send her back to New Orleans after they sailed under their new leader, and there'd be nothing she could do about it—long after *he* had departed for safer climes, that was certain!

Oh, she might get "used," of course, protected, then raped, by the strongest to emerge as *capitaine*. Jérôme even wished he could stay to rape her himself. After all her empty flirtations with him, Charité *deserved* a come-uppance, the "servicing" of a *real* man who knew . . .

"*Eh!*" a sailor up forward by the fuming galley funnel cried. He pointed over the bows, eastward towards the main channel. "A *ship!*"

"What?" Lanxade responded in a shocked screech, blanching with alarm. A drunken sailor roused himself in Lanxade's way as he strode forward, got shoved to the rails, where he began to puke over-side.

"Strange ship!" the sailor up forrud added. "Guns run out!"

"To arms!" Lanxade bellowed, seizing the lanyard on the ship's bell by the forecastle and clanging away with it. "All hands on deck! Dammit, dammit, wake up, you bastards! Up, and man the guns!"

He glowered at Boudreaux aboard the prize, was pleased to see him capering an alarm of his own among his few crewmen who had slept aboard her. The camp, though! Lanxade leaped to a swivel-gun by the starboard bow, jerked the tompion from its muzzle but found that no goose-quill fuse was handy, no slow-match burning, no tinder-box. He swung the light gun's barrel skyward, stepped back, puffed on his *cigaro* to a red-hot tip, then stuck it against the touch-hole, hoping that a pricked cartridge bag had been left loaded.

Bang! A faint howl of musket or pistol balls shot into the air, and that stern, startling noise was enough to rouse the campsite, roust out the last pig-drunk heavy sleepers aboard *Le Revenant*.

"Nom d'un chien," Lanxade angrily hissed as he saw to his own personal weapons. The strange vessel—a good-sized *shalope*—advanced on him, bows-on. "You Spanish dogs have bitten off more than you can swallow this time. We'll show you what a real fight is!"

But, what was this? A stronger whiff of wind abeam the *shalope* flirted out her flag, and it *wasn't* the crowned red-gold-red of Spain but the red, white, and blue crosses of . . . "The *Anglais?* The hellish *Anglais?*" Lanxade yelped in stupefaction, realising that that distant prize they'd taken off Dominica might have spelled their ruin! Vengeance had come upon them, with lit fuses and bared steel!

Small ship, though, Lanxade thought, imagining a small *crew* to put up against his cut-throat *desperados*. He might win after all!

Off the same American smuggling brig that had yielded Toby Jugg as a reluctant "volunteer" a year or so before, HMS *Proteus* had also garnered a dozen or so deadly-accurate Yankee-made Pennsylvania rifles, bound for rebel general Toussaint L'Ouverture and his officers on St. Domingue. Those that hadn't ended up in the hands of Capt. Lewrie or the ship's officers, Marine Lieutenant Blase Devereux had appropriated for his keenest marksmen when posted aloft in the fighting-tops. Picking off enemy officers might be deemed by *some* to be ungentlemanly or dishonourable, but Lt. Devereux was one, as was Captain Lewrie, who ascribed more to "All's Fair in Love and War," that Fair Fighting was for dim-witted fools.

"I believe they're sufficiently stirred up and misdirected," Lt. Devereux muttered, once he'd taken another peek over the top of a low spot in the shell midden, noting how those pirates able to rouse themselves and stand erect after their night's excesses were all peering and gesticulating at the *shalope*'s approach from out of the mists. "Do you think, sir, that we should take advantage of their astonished condition . . . even if the Captain has yet to close with them?"

"I do believe we should, sir!" Captain Nicely was quick to say "Aye," drawing his work-a-day smallsword from its plain black scabbard. "Up and at 'em, Mister Devereux . . . and God uphold the right!"

"Marines . . . *shun!*" Devereux bellowed. "Marksmen to the tops of the mounds! Rest . . . form line! Marines . . . level!"

Muskets came up to shoulders, the fixed bayonets wanly glittering in the misty dawn.

"Cock yer *locks!* Take *careful* aim . . . *fire!*" Devereux howled.

Barely thirty yards away, stunned, hungover pirates stumbled to their feet, not understanding the orders in English but knowing that danger was present. They came slithering out of their lean-tos, fighting bleariness and their encumbering blankets. Some *saw* the invaders, whose red coats, rarely worn aboard ship but for ceremonial duties and Harbour Watch, blossomed atop or behind the bleached shell hillocks as red as poppies . . . or blood. The buccaneers barely had time to blink or rub their disbelieving eyes, to shout a quick warning before those muskets barked and spat great spouts of powder smoke, before some much sharper cracks from rifles stunned their ears.

"Reload!" Devereux yelled. "Marksmen, look for ralliers!"

"Proteuses, *up!*" Lt. Catterall shouted in an irate steer's roar, the leather-lunged sort of cry that could carry from the quarterdeck to the bowsprit in a full gale of wind. "Level! Take aim . . . *fire!*"

Catterall's sailors, who far outnumbered the Marine complement, popped up from behind the shell mounds on either flank of the Marines, dressed in their usual slop-trousers, loose shirts, and tarred hats or head rags. Less used to musketry, or the rigid weapons drill of their compatriots, they were; but there were more of them, their targets were within a long *pistol* shot, and "Brown Bess" would not be denied.

Reeling, scurrying buccaneers were scythed down, at least ten by the Marines' initial volley, perhaps another half dozen claimed by *Proteus*'s less-skillful sailors. A few cooks or vendors were killed or wounded, people who'd stayed to sleep off the night's revels, The gape-mouthed *nearly* innocent who stood still too long, in the wrong place at the wrong time, fell howling beside the panicked bloody-handed guilty, while others spurred into witless flight amid scared buccaneers. A raddled and terrified whore or two, rushing from their borrowed beds, were gunned down as well. Massed volleys of musketry were as uncaring as clouds of grapeshot.

"Recover and reload!" Lt. Catterall roared, over his frights in the eerie forests and never happier than when challenged to mindless combat. He cocked his pistol's lock, took a huntsman's lead on a running pirate with a musket in his hands, fired, and whooped with joy to see him tumble over and sprawl, instantly lifeless.

"*Pick* your targets . . . make 'em count, lads! Take aim, and . . . *fire!*" Lt. Devereux commanded, sweeping his sword blade chopping down.

"*Merde!*" Boudreaux Balfa gawped at the first shots, eyes fixed on the approaching *shalope* with her gunports open. "*Oh, merde!* We be up 'shit's creek.' Fusilier? *Viens ici,* son, come here, quick."

"He's not aboard," Pierre La Fitte told him as he scrambled up from below-decks. "He and Jean went ashore . . . after you went to sleep."

"What? I *told* him . . . !"

"They went to see the girls, get, ah . . ." Pierre confessed.

"Damn you! Damn your little brother, too! Fusilier get poxed, by damn I kill you *both!*" Balfa vowed. "We gonna lose de prize, maybe lose *Le Revenant,* we don't act quick. Get de men together, take dem to Lanxade, so he can man de guns! I cut de cables, an' let dis bitch go on de tide. Move, man! *Vite, vite, allons!*"

"I get my little brother," Pierre objected. "The Spanish have us for certain. All we can do is run for it, And I won't let those *salauds* hang him. I'm taking a boat for shore, then . . . " Pierre backed his decision with a hand about the hilt of a large dagger. "You can do what you like."

"Mutinous dog!" Balfa sneered, spitting at the man's feet. "Go, den! Run wit' your tail 'tween your legs, faithless son of a whore!"

Pierre was overside in a twinkling, paddling like mad in one of the hollow-log *pirogues.* Balfa shouted for his remaining sailors to go to *Le Revenant* and man the guns; he'd take care of their prize and all their silver. He'd be with them in a twinkling. Or . . . not.

That damned Pierre was right, things were all up with them, and it was time to obey the old maxim of *sauve quie peut;* run like hell and save what one could! Balfa ran forward and plucked a heavy boarding axe from the foremast arms chest. He stood, straddling the nine-inch anchor cable a moment later, and began to hack at it. It took only a few powerful strokes to part it, then leap out of the way as the last strands exploded apart, the inner end snapping inboard, and the bitter end slithering into the murky depths of the bay.

The Spanish schooner began to sidle sternward, driven by an incoming tide, began to make a slight leeway, even under bare poles, to the faint land breeze. Balfa ran aft and quickly did the same to the stern kedge-anchor cable, but realised that the prize would drift 'til she took the ground on Grand Terre, perhaps no more than two miles to the west. He'd have to burn her.

Bare feet thundering on the mid-ships companionway, Boudreaux Balfa dashed below and snatched a lit lanthorn from a hook set in one of the overhead deck beams. And, dire as things looked, he started to grin a sly little grin.

He and his Acadian friends and neighbours had gotten a *bit* more than carried away shifting coin kegs during the night, like they would when snacking on the peanuts their slaves insisted on growing. Greedy arms and hands had loaded hundreds of silver-filled barricos aboard a *fleet* of *pirogues*, flatboats, and luggers, leaving only half the 1,200 kegs that had been aboard. Six hundred thousand Spanish dollars!

"Spanish never know where it go," Balfa mused, starting to titter and wheeze over his little *geste*. "Dem *bébés* and Jérôme never know, neither!"

By the light of the lanthorn in his meaty paw, Balfa lumbered all the way forward to the cable-tiers and the Spanish bosun's stores. He ripped out fresh, resiny spare planking, rigging rope, loose oakum bales, and kegs of paint and linseed oil, and liberally sluiced down the cable-tiers and the decks. Another lanthorn hung overhead, but not for long. It was filled with whale oil, already hot and runny from being lit all night, and at once it made a dandy splash of fire.

Amidships, there were looted sea chests, hammocks and bed linen by the bale, too, and a second lanthorn set them alight quickly. Aft, the mates' and captain's quarters were full of papers and trash, with even more lanthorns available. His tortuous straw mattress, torn open and scattered, went up in a twinkling, and serve it right for his itches, by damn!

Balfa went over-side to larboard, what had been the dark, unlit side the night before, where a last little flatboat trailed from its painter at the foot of the main-mast chain platform. With two pistols in his belt, a dagger and cutlass on the boat's sole, Balfa freed the boat and began to row round the schooner to go save his boy.

"Take aim . . . *fire!*"

Atop their earthen mound, the first crackle of musketry snapped the de Guilleris from their rough beds as if a bolt of lightning struck the hillock, all sudden blue-white light, sizzle, and thunder *crack!* Hippolyte and Helio, sharing a lean-to, both sat up quickly, gasping as if throwing off a shared and terrifying nightmare, cracking heads on the bound-together saplings in a flurry of arms and legs and thrashing blankets, their eyes blared owl-wide in alarm. They were bootless and coatless, their weapons laid handily aside, but for long moments, any thought of dressing or arming themselves was lost in shaky fumblings as they tangled with each other . . . even as a second harsh volley rattled out, and shouts and screams assailed their ears. Hippolyte crawled to the open end of the lean-to and began to stand with a boot in hand, hopping as he raised his foot to draw it on, but the humming of musket balls past his head, and his older brother's sweeping arm, threw him flat.

"Keep down!" Helio growled in his ear. Regaining his wits faster than Hippolyte, Helio groped for his boots, writhed on his side to don them, then belly-crawled on his elbows and knees for his weapons.

"Rubio! Jean!" Helio yelled.

"We're with you!" Don Rubio shouted back, from behind the lean-to he shared with Jean-Marie Rancour. Both had slithered out to hide behind its insubstantial shelter, dragging boots, clothes, and rifled muskets with them. "Charité? Stay down, *chérie*. We'll deal with it!"

Don Rubio stomped into his boots and fastened his sword about his waist. He clapped his egret-plumed wide hat on his head, flung up the tarpaulin that had covered the lean-to, and reached between the saplings for his pistols to jam into his waistband, then warily stood up, hands working the complicated mechanism of his Girandoni air-rifle. A fresh air-flask buttstock had to be screwed on, the magazine under the barrel topped off with lead balls.

"*Mon Dieu, merde alors!*" Jean-Marie quavered as he gathered up his clothes and guns, hands visibly shaking and his white face pinched. "Who is it, Rubio, what's *happening?*"

Don Rubio Monaster didn't answer him. The son of a pure-blooded Spanish hidalgo, a genuine Creole, did not *panic,* as that weak-kneed Rancour boy did. He was *born* to command, born to lead lesser people!

His eyes did widen in shock, though, much as Jean-Marie's did, to witness the camp and its doings. Their bold pirates, the hangers-on, and the whores were dashing about like witless chickens, scrabbling in their bedding for their portable loot or their weapons, crying aloud in chaos, and not knowing which way to stumble! They swarmed as unknowing as bees from a hive that someone had shot from long-distance, wheeling and darting ready for vengeance, but unable to discover where the shooter was.

"There! At the shell mounds!" Don Rubio cried, pleased that he could keep his head, feeling that he was as sanguine as a professional soldier to re-act so quickly and so well. "Jean, your rifle, quickly. Helio, Hippolyte! The shell mounds! *Shoot* at them!" Another volley was fired from the shell heaps, the powder smoke almost hiding a ragged double line of men dressed like sailors!

"*Garde vous, mes braves!*" Rubio bellowed down to their sailors. "*There* is the enemy, in the oyster piles! To arms, I tell you, and *fight* them!"

On the next mound east, where some sentries had been posted, he saw from the corner of his eye a buccaneer or two raise their muskets and shoot back, which cheered him greatly. A second later, there was a lone cracking discharge, and one of the sentries screamed as he was struck in the forehead, his skull and brains erupting in a gory spray behind him before he tumbled back on his heels, arms and legs spread as if he was crucified. Don Rubio spotted the shooter atop one of the higher shell heaps, a soldier in a red coat, white cross-belts, white breeches, and knee-high spatterdashes, with a white-laced tall hat upon his head. He wasn't from any *Spanish* regiment Don Rubio had ever seen, but he raised his air-rifle, took careful aim, and fired as the soldier laboured to ram a ball down the muzzle of his weapon.

"Damn!" he swore as his shot merely clipped the man's hat, making him jump back in alarm and slide-tumble down the far slope of the mound. Don Rubio cranked another ball into the firing chamber and recocked his rifle, hearing a faint hiss as he did so, as the demand valve opened. The gun smoke was thinning, as was the mist, and he shot at another red-coated soldier stand-ing behind a waist-high slumped heap of shells. This one he struck, with a feral whoop of joy as he cheered his own skill, though the air-rifle still was shooting high . . . as it had when he'd tried to kill that damned *Anglais*, Willoughby, in New Orleans! His target flung a hand to his breast and dropped like a stone!

Don Rubio heard the cracks of other air-rifles firing near him as Helio and Hippolyte finally got into action. By his right side, he heard another crack as Jean-Marie summoned up his nerves and entered the fray, shrilling thinly as he saw one his shots kill a sailor, too!

"Stay down, Charité!" Helio was yelping. "Go down the back of the mound and get to the beach. Get aboard the schooner!"

There came another murdering volley from the red-coat soldiers, scyth-ing down a few more witless buccaneers in the camp, forcing those with guns or cutlasses in their hands to duck and slink backwards, in the direction of the beach and the grounded boats. Rubio noted that *some* of them were start-ing to form up and return fire.

There was another belated crack, then the mallet thuds of balls striking flesh, and Jean-Marie's left hand was clawing at the sleeve of his shirt as he sank to his knees with a look of utter astonishment on his face, his mouth opening and closing like a boated fish. A moment later, and there was a flood of bright blood spilling from his mouth, down the front of his fine white shirt!

"Jean! Poor Jean. Oh no!" Charité wailed, standing in the open with her hands to her mouth.

Another of those damned red-coat men atop a shell heap! Rubio saw him lowering his weapon to reload it and *knew* that this marksman was Jean's slayer. Aiming at his waist this time, Rubio fired at him and saw the bastard spin around and stumble, dropping his weapon as he pitched forward and slid down the face of the mound in an avalanche of old shells. "Got him, aha! Charité, get down! We men will fight them for you!" he shouted to her, plastering a bold, confident, *dangerous* smile on his face for her benefit.

"Marines will . . . advance!" they all heard a powerful voice cry. "Poise muskets, and *for*-ward . . . march!"

"Oh, hell!" another, deeper voice was bellowing. "Proteuses . . . cutlasses and bayonets, and . . . *charge*!"

"English!" Helio spat. "They're *Anglais*, the 'Bloodies'!"

"The *Anglais?*" Hippolyte gawped. "Run, little sister. Run for your life! Get aboard the schooner, now!"

"Up here, you men!" Don Rubio shouted, waving his arms to catch their buccaneers' attention. "Get on the mounds and we'll shoot *down* at them. Hold the mounds! *Kill* the *cochons!*"

He had heard somewhere that the high ground was preferable in a real battle. Helio came round him to his right-hand side and looked down at his cousin, Jean-Marie Rancour, but that unfortunate youngster had already died, his lungs and mouth filled with blood, and his eyes already glazing over.

"His rifle," Rubio Monaster callously snapped between shots as a dauntingly long line of Britishers tramped over the oyster heaps and slithered down the front faces, whilst the *Anglais* dressed as sailors came swarming more quickly from the flank, cutlasses waving aloft, in full, bloodthirsty cry. "His four pistols, Helio. *Use* them!"

"Damn you, Rubio, Jean was just a . . ." Helio de Guilleri swore as he dashed tears from his eyes with his shirt sleeves, but gathered up the pistols and the air-rifle as directed. Hippolyte, still crouching by the lean-to, was already firing his Girandoni, fast as he could aim, pull the trigger, and crank, and Helio could see that his shots were telling, so he knelt and began to shoot as well.

The *Anglais* quickly took half a dozen casualties, dropped right at their feet. They stumbled as they tried to step over the bodies, and their ragged charge all but skidded to a halt. Pirates were clambering up atop the mounds, walking backwards as they loaded, primed and fired right in the Englishmen's dirty faces.

Charité had not obeyed them but had snatched up Helio's rifle, and was inexpertly, clumsily working its action to fire a few rounds of her own, making Helio and Hippolyte shake their heads at each other at her foolishness . . . sadly proud of her all the same.

"First rank . . . take aim! Clear them off the mounds! Fire!"

"*Those* bastards!" a blue-uniformed naval officer was bellowing down below them, waving his sword in the air and pointing with a pistol in his other hand. "*Shoot* those bastards, lads! Kill 'em dead!"

The volleys stuttered out, loud and deep-toned, and buccaneers on the forward slopes went tumbling in heaps. Their hands on the east mound were completely scythed away, and another young man with a sword in a blue coat shrilly led an impromptu charge to its top. Their few men who had rallied below the centre mound, where the de Guilleris and Don Rubio fought, were shot down, or broke and ran round its edges for the beach.

"Run, Charité, run!" Helio ordered her again, even as musket balls whined about them like deadly bumblebees.

"Second rank . . . the centre mound! Take aim . . . fire!"

Stunned by the suddenness of the deaths below her, Charité at last came to her senses. She went as pale as milk, might have fainted if she'd waited a second longer to flee, but managed to turn round as quick as a spider and scramble on her hands and knees to the back of their mound and slide down the far side on the seat of her breeches, a hand still gripped white-knuckled on the barrel of her air-rifle. Her pinned-up long hair had come undone, and she instinctively reached up to let it spill, praying a silent prayer for poor Jean-Marie; praying, too, that the "Bloodies" wouldn't shoot a woman, a girl so pretty!

She felt her lips begin to tremble, her teeth chatter uncontrollably, and tears stung her eyes. Sobs arose from the wrenching tautness in her chest. She got to her feet at the foot of the mound, her legs feeling juddery and weak, her feet oddly disembodied as she tried to run to find a boat.

"*Mademoiselle!*" Boudreaux Balfa's son, Fusilier, dashed up, in company with another young lad off *Le Revenant*. Both were armed, and Charité was glad for their company.

"Damn you all! Come back here!" the other youngster yelled at the few boats still in sight, Those who could had scrambled into any slight hull that would float and were fleeing northward, dangerously overloaded in most cases. There wasn't a single *pirogue* left, as far as they could see along the shore! "A boat! Where's a boat?"

"We must swim out, *mademoiselle!*" Fusilier said, trying to be calm and brave but almost shivering with fear. "Get aboard our ship and sail out of here."

"No, we won't," Jean, the other lad, dispiritedly growled, and pointed to the large *shalope* not a quarter-mile off from *Le Revenant* and their prize and stalking up slowly but remorselessly, a British Navy ensign atop her main-mast.

"We must swim, or die," Charité determined. "Somewhere we'll find someone to pick us up."

"Papa will come for us," Fusilier added, perked up considerably. "He *must!*"

CHAPTER THIRTY-TWO

*H*alf a point more to windward, Jugg," Lewrie snapped, his eyes fixed upon the black-hulled schooner. As they neared her, she turned from a dark smear in the fog to a substantial and detailed fact. He could hear firing off the larboard bows, coming almost abeam now; distinguishable pops of single muskets, the sharper crack of his Marine's Pennsylvania rifles, now and then the collective *Chuff!* of a volley fired all at once. They were *late*, the wind was perverse and fickle, his landing party might be getting knackered, and his *shalope* was closing too slowly to overwhelm the pirate schooner. He had no need for a telescope to see her crew scurrying to prepare to fight. She had been bows-on when they could first make her out through a thin patch of fog but was now slowly swinging to bare her starboard side, her blood-red gunwale stripe oddly bright and ominous as they let out on her kedge cable and hauled in on the spring-line on her bow cable. Lewrie could see a flamboyantly garbed figure on her quarterdeck, waving his arms and shouting.

"'At 'd be Jérôme Lanxade, sor," Jugg grimly informed him, "'at peacocky one, yonder. Allus *woz* a flash bugger."

Six gun-ports each side, my survivors said, Lewrie speculated; *four-pounders or six-pounders, mixed perhaps. Our battery, God, what a joke!* They had swivels and boat-guns, so short-ranged they couldn't use them 'til they were close-aboard, would have to eat one or two of Lanxade's broadsides before getting that close. He'd *try* to be stoic, in the best Royal Navy traditions, but the odds didn't look good!

Steer for her bows, lock bowsprits, and board her up forrud? he feverishly schemed; *Haul off and cross her stern might work, too, if there's depth enough.* Mr. Pollock's borrowed *shalope* only drew eight feet, slightly less without a cargo. Yet if they ran aground short of the schooner, it would mean the death of them all; if they crossed her stern so slowly that they caromed off her kedge cable, they'd be just as helpless, could end up stranded close to the beach, drifting to ruin, whilst the schooner cut her cables and escaped!

And there was still no sign of *Proteus!*

"Ship burning beyond her, sir!" Midshipman Larkin cried.

"They *did* take a prize!" Lewrie exclaimed, finally reaching for his telescope. "Damme, they've fired her!"

"With all the *silver* aboard her, sir?" Young Mr. Larkin yelped.

"Sonsabitches," Lewrie gravelled, outraged that all this might be for nought, beyond justice, of course . . . and vengeance.

He lowered his telescope, lips gloomily pursed. That schooner beyond the black-hulled one was ablaze from end to end, wren- or mouse-sized flames scuttling along every inch of her standing or running rigging, and great clouds of smoke beginning to belch from open hatches.

"Mister Larkin," Lewrie stolidly ordered. "I'll have all the swivel-guns shifted to starboard, along with the grappling hooks and throwing lines. We'll board her starboard side to starboard side."

"Oye oye, s— Aye aye, sir, mean t'say," Mr. Larkin chirped. Whenever he was excited, which was rather often, the lad easily lapsed into a cottager's brogue.

"Mister Jugg," Lewrie said, rounding on him. "Pinch her up to weather, like we'd grapple to her bows. But at the last moment I want you to slew about and go alongside her near side. We'll give 'em grape and langridge, point-blank, then board her."

"Aye, sor," Jugg said with a firm nod of understanding.

"Ah, sah?" Andrews whispered, plucking his attention back. "I think she's openin' her ports, sah, ready t'fire."

"Nothing t'do but grin and bear it, hey?" Lewrie tried to jape.

"Good God A'mighty," Andrews whispered.

Lewrie turned his attention back to the pirate schooner, just as the first of her guns exploded in a gush of powder smoke, a sharpish slamming noise, with the scream of solid shot coming . . . ! Passing! Warbling off easterly, a clean miss!

"Bear up . . . bear up!" Lewrie snapped, pointing to the north. "Duck out of their aim, Jugg . . . thus!"

The schooner blotted herself out of existence as four more guns fired, making a dense, drifting wall of yellow-grey powder smoke along her engaged starboard side, sulfurous and reeking. Shot howled harpy-like, and a cannon ball nipped at their *shalope*'s larboard stern quarters, another slammed into her midships larboard bulwarks but caromed off after wrenching a large bite of timber from her with the parrot-screech of shattered wood. One screamed low over the deck, its unseen passage trailed by a tunnel of tortured air that shimmered like the uprush from a red-hot forge. The last was another clean miss!

As the spent powder smoke drifted southward, the schooner's bow swam out of the newest mist; jib-boom and bowsprit, figurehead, beak, rails, and nettings . . .

"Helm hard up, now!" Lewrie rasped, coughing on the guns' lees.

Jugg put the tiller as far over to starboard as it would swing, his weight, and Dempsey's weight, pressing on the bar, and the *shalope* began to turn.

"Stand by grapnels, Mister Larkin . . . stand by swivel-guns, at close range," Lewrie called out. "Christ!"

There the schooner was, her upper railings just a foot higher than the *shalope*'s deck, her glossy black hull shining like a fresh-groomed stallion, so close Lewrie could almost call it spitting distance. Their *shalope*'s thrusting jib-boom looked like it would jam right into the schooner's main-mast shrouds and pin her there helplessly, but after a long, pent breath, the jib-boom slid past by a cat's whisker, and they were sidling up to her at an angle.

"Boat-guns, swivels, and muskets . . . fire as you bear!" Lewrie cried, drawing his hanger and a double-barrelled Manton pistol. His men opened fire, the light 2-pounders barking lap-dog sharp, chewing chunks from the schooner's side without doing much real damage. The swivels, though, atop the cap-rail stanchions, spewed loads of musket and pistol balls nearly straight across her decks, reaping things . . . and people!

"Grapnels!" he snapped as their boat's single mast came level with the schooner's midships. The hooks flew, scraped, and found purchase, and muscle power on the heaving lines hauled their lighter vessel alongside, checking her way in a groaning instant. Their bow met the schooner, bumping and rasping, the stern began to swing in snugly, and there were more bumps and thuds.

All the while, Lewrie, with nothing physical to do, stared with dread at those gaping gun-ports, just waiting for them to be filled by reloaded cannon, for them to spew grape and langridge and murder every man in his crew, yet . . .

"Boarders!" he almost screamed at last! "Away, boarders!"

Up atop his own bulwarks, a long stride across to theirs, and he was hopping down to the schooner's deck, flooding with tittery, joyous relief to see that no more than one or two pirates had tended each cannon, that most of her crew had been ashore. He dashed aft, bumped and shouldered by his own hands, to claim her quarterdeck.

"Vous!" the gaudily dressed captain said, a tall and lean man with a wide but slim set of mustachios . . . and a sword in his hand.

"Strike, ye thievin' cut-throat!" Lewrie roared back. A burly pirate with a cutlass leaped between, shoved forward by Lanxade. The cutlass and Lewrie's hanger rang together once, twice, the pirate two-handing his sword. Lewrie binded him, brought up his Manton with his left hand, and gave him both barrels in his lower chest with the muzzles against his skin, and the man shrieked and lurched backwards like a pole-axed steer, his shirt on fire.

"Strike, damn you!" Lewrie roared again, tossing away his spent pistol, cutting the air with his sword.

"Va te faire foutre, vous sanglant cochon!" Lanxade spat, whipping his long, old-style rapier through the air as well.

"Fuck *yourself*!" Lewrie retorted as Lanxade sprang at him with a distracting foot-stamp and an inarticulate screech of battle rage. Their blades met, parted slithering and chiming, met edge to edge with the next slashes, both men iron-wristed, iron-willed.

"Comin', sir!" he heard his Cox'n Andrews vow.

"Hell ye will, he's *mine*!" Lewrie shouted.

"Son!" Boudreaux Balfa shouted in immense relief when he recognised one of the weary swimmers in the water and quickly sculled over to pick him up. *Mademoiselle* Charité was there, too, with Jean, that little La Fitte brute. Fusilier clambered in first, then aided the girl. Balfa considered leaving Jean, not trusting him one inch, but Fusilier reached for him and hauled him in, while the *mademoiselle* knelt on the soleboards, coughing up water, as drenched as any wharf rat. Balfa spun his boat about, got Fusilier and Jean to seize hold of two oars, and started north, up the bay, for escape.

"*Capitaine* Balfa!" Charité finally found strength to say. "You must go back! Those cowards took all the boats. My brothers!"

A mere hundred yards off the beach, Balfa could hear the firing and the clash of blades, the desperation of French-speaking or Spanish pirates . . . and the encouraged battle cries in English.

"Naw, *chérie*," Balfa sadly said, "dere nothin' t'be done. Best we can hope is we get away. De game's done did."

Charité knew it in her heart, too, as she crept aft near Balfa to cling to the boat's gunn'ls and peer at the battle on the mounds.

"Helio!" she yelled, sitting up on her knees and waving as her elder brother appeared at the back of their mound's flat top, pistols in both hands, looking seaward, looking at *her*. He shouted something, waved as if to drag back the only boat still in sight.

Two horrid red splotches suddenly blossomed on his white shirt, the fine linen and lace punctured through-and-through with .75 calibre musket balls! Helio stumbled forward, dropping his guns, and almost knelt as if to recoup his strength . . . then pitched, tumbling and sliding down the back slope of the mound like a bundle of cast-off clothes from a rag-picker's barrow.

"*Nooo!*" Charité screamed, grief, protest, and horror together.

"Gotta go, *chers*," Balfa urged. "*Vite, vite!*"

Topman Willy Toffett scrambled up the slope of an earth mound, gasping, almost clawing with his free hand for purchase, grasping his heavy Brown Bess Sea Pattern musket in his right. He had been scared at first, but seeing so many pirates—some he even recognised from his ordeal in their grasp, their marooning on the Dry Tortugas—on the run, or *dying*, had perked up his courage considerably. A Marine ahead of him, Private Doyle, a fair-decent bastard for a Lobsterback, was kicking muck in his eyes as he scrambled, howling eagerness, his musket held in both hands. "Hah . . . hah!" Doyle cried as he engaged a pirate who rose up atop the lip of the mound, bringing his bayonet-fitted musket level, thrusting at the sword-armed foeman's belly, but the pirate whipped up a pistol and shot him in the chest.

One of 'em! Toffett thought, panicked again as Doyle fell back the slope, head-down and instantly killed. *He was* one *of 'em aboard that schooner, the one who killed Midshipman Burns, all those slaves in the water!* Toffett howled inarticulately as he reached the top and swung his musket like a quarterstaff at the man's legs, knocking him off his feet long enough for Toffett to take proper hold and get into the drill he'd been taught four times a week since "volunteering" into *Proteus*. Thrust!—partially parried by the bastard's sword. Recover. Thrust again, step forward inside guard. Butt-strike, up from below-right to level, the heavy brass-footed stock smashing into the bastard's mouth with a toothy *Crunch!* to send him sprawling on his back! Plant left foot forward! Thrust! Toffett screamed just as loud as the pirate as he sank six inches of triangular steel into the foe's belly, folding him up like a jackknife! Twist, stamp, and Recover! "Yew murd'rin' *son 'fabitch*!" Stamp! Thrust, into the enemy's unguarded throat! *Lean* on the musket like shoving a capstan bar, and twist and *grind,* saw back and forth! "Yew filthy goddamn *whoreson! That* fer Mister Burns! *That,* fer them Cuffies! *That,* fer ol' Doyle!"

"Don't make a meal of 'im, lad!" Marine Sergeant Skipwith said almost in his ear, beaming with delight. "Six inch o' bayonet's good as a yard fer *his* sort!"

And Don Rubio Monaster, whose aristocratic ancestors had been hidalgo since the *Reconquista* of Spain, and charged into battle with El Cid against the Moors, died with the taste of blood and cold metal in his mouth, and his elegant breeches full of shit.

Hippolyte de Guilleri could only hear a whistling noise in his ears as he scampered to the back of the mound, terror making an empty, cold pit in his middle, and his bowels watery. Time and motion slowed to a crawl as he saw Rubio get spitted, as he took hopeless guard with his sword to oppose the sailors and soldiers running at him, him alone as the last defender, all by *himself,* and it was *so* unfair, he didn't *mean* to kill all those people, and he pleaded with God that he was now sorry to have taken such perverse pleasure from killing, but hadn't it been in a righteous cause, for Louisiana, for France, so . . . !

Hippolyte stamped his foot and slashed with his sword, howling at the hard-faced men who swarmed at him from every corner, trembling inside despite his wish to be brave, go game.

Maman, don't let it hurt! he wailed to himself as his blade was easily knocked aside, and he saw the flicker of a heavy cutlass coming at him sideways. It cleaved like an axe into the side of his neck . . . and it *did* hurt, *very* much, a white-hot agony in his head, his throat, and a second was rammed into his groin with so much force that he was lifted up on tiptoes. It redoubled the agony, brought forth a scream through the bubbling blood he was drowning in, his last breath.

And then there was an officer in a blue coat standing over him as he sank to his knees struggling for air; raising a pistol in his face, inches from his eyes, and the bore was as wide as a cannon, and then there was a hot, reeking, scalding wind on his face, bright amber light like the fires of Hades then . . . *rien*. Nothing.

He ain't a hop master! Lewrie wearily thought as he caught his enemy's blade on his, twisted his wrist so it slid off his own, jabbed under to force him back, then swept his hanger up to high-left to stop another slash, counter-sweeping under at his belly, again, missing . . .

Elegant as Lanxade dressed, he wasn't the product of some languid fencing-master's *salle d'armes*. He was skilled, quick, and steel-wristed, and fought with the desperate savagery of a back-alley brawler, the cut-and-thrust he'd learned at sea in close-quarter murder.

They swirled about each other, leaping, stamping, and clashing. All the other pirates were down, the schooner was theirs, and his hands stood watching their captain's fight. If he stumbled or fell, looked about to lose, Lewrie was sure that a dozen muskets or pistols would take Lanxade down the next instant. Surely, Lewrie thought, Lanxade knew he was a dead man even if he won, and, tiring as Lewrie was, the issue was in doubt! Swordplay was the most strenuous and enervating way to fight, and his one-on-one "duel" with Lanxade felt like it had been going on for half an hour, not one or two minutes!

Lanxade clashed, drew him wide left, then whipped under, *thrust* with a mighty shout and stamp, but Lewrie met it, whipped off a flying cut-over, forcing Lanxade's longer rapier low and left, wide-open . . . !

Lanxade, panting and gasping as loud as Lewrie, instinctively cut right, was left high and wide, *vulnerable* for once, backed against the schooner's taff-rails, and Lewrie put all he had into a slash that would *gut* the bastard from his left hip to his right breast!

Lanxade bellowed rage and defiance, even as Lewrie's hanger cut his clothing open like a berserk tailor's razor. Blood sprang from a slash on Lanxade's left thigh, another gout from his right shoulder. Something went *Twang-twang-twang!* and Lanxade fell back with his sword hand on the taff-rail to recover, his stomach and belly swelling like he'd suddenly become pregnant, and Lewrie was stunned motionless for a second or two.

"Bloody *Hell*." Lewrie gawped.

"*Merde alors!*" Lanxade snarled back, using that second granted him to glance down and see his waist-coat and shirt slashed open, and the severed laces of his whale-bone corset standing out like hedgehog quills! "*Sale chien!*" Lanxade screamed, shoving off the railing, and brought his rapier up in a wild slash at Lewrie's head, which he ducked, tried to slash back downwards in the blink of an eye, but that was blocked by Lewrie's right shoulder against his forearm, and Lewrie rammed the point of his hanger deep into Lanxade's stomach, no longer protected by canvas, whale-bone, or lacings, right through the gap he'd made with his slash; deep as he could, the whole length of the honed back-blade savagely twisted to ease its withdrawal. Lanxade tried to bring his own rapier back far enough to stab, but Lewrie took hold of his wrist, feeling the man's oar-stout strength going.

Lewrie looked into his eyes, glaring utter hatred, getting the same hatred back. "Fuck with *my* sailors, will you? *My* prize you took . . . *my men* you almost murdered! *My* Midshipman you gut-shot and left to die, you . . . miserable . . . *bastard!*" Lewrie raged, almost in his ear. "Now die, and roast in the fires of Hell!"

Lewrie stood back, jerked Lanxade back on his feet as he tugged his bloody hanger free, then jammed it up under Lanxade's jaw, through soft tissue and tongue, into his brain!

Lanxade jerked and jiggled like a dancing marionette at a Punch & Judy show, his rapier clanging on the deck as it dropped from nerveless fingers, then he was falling backwards over the taff-rails, arms, legs, and coat jerkily windmilling as Lewrie shoved him over-side, to create a cannonball's splash as he plunged deep under. Lewrie peered down over the schooner's transom to see Lanxade surface once, strangling but incapable of movement, before he went under again, to sink slowly, lifeless eyes almost yearning for air, and the light.

Drowned, a last thought in the final dark: *I died rich, hein?*

Lewrie spun about, sagged against the taff-rails, and peered up at the French Tricolour which still flew aloft. "Get that damned rag down, someone," he croaked, dry-mouthed and desperately weary. Cox'n Andrews came to his side with a leather bottle of brandy, and a suck or two at that helped. He was leery of the round-eyed awe his sailors showed him, but hoped that awe cancelled out his previous lost respect ashore.

"Been below, sor," Toby Jugg reported. "They's kegged silver in th' hold, not too much, though. Pris'ners say th' bulk o' h'it woz on their prize, still."

They looked West. The pirate's prize was now a half-sunk hulk, a bowl of sullen flames beneath a monstrous volcano's pillar of smoke, adrift and almost beached. Even as they watched, the fire reached the unpillaged powder magazines, its kegs and sewn cartridges at last. She exploded with a dull roar, a staggering series of blasts that shot flaming debris and fingery smoke trails up and outwards, each bigger than the rest. And with each explosion came a glittering in the sky like the coloured embers of a fireworks display; tiny, *silvery* bits that glinted as they spiralled out over a half-mile radius, all new-minted and mirror-like in the rising sun.

"Oh!" Lewrie lamented. "Ooh!" went his sailors. "Aw, *shit!*"

"Boy, you get in your brother's boat," Balfa ordered after they met up with the grim-faced Pierre in a small gig by himself. "You an' him row like Hell one way, we go dat way, dey don't cotch us all in de one bite, *hein?*" Balfa still had two loaded pistols in his belt, but Pierre only had one, and all the rest had been soaked useless in their swim. Bad as things looked, hard as it was to see old Jérôme meet a hard end as they rowed past to the west of the fight, his neighbours still had his hillock of silver, and the fewer greedy survivors of this day, the better; especially those quick-witted La Fitte brothers.

"Row where?" Pierre snarled. "We don't know the way through . . . "

"Away from *dis!*" Balfa mirthlessly hooted. "Due north, get in Lake Barataria, skirt de shore, de bayou take you free, you stay wit' de wide channel. Get t'New Orleans, den it up to you, dat."

"We have no money, we've lost it all," Pierre carped.

"Oh, here," Balfa grudgingly said, pulling out his coin-purse and tossing the bulging sack over, pretending generosity. "Dat get ya new kits, passage outta Looziann'. Don' worry 'bout payin' me back, *chers*. De least a *capitaine* can do for good hands, *hein?* Go on, now. Hug de right bank, t'rough dat op'nin' dere, see it? Right bank, all de way, an' don't go wand'rin' off in a *coulée*. Dey be 'Cadiens live 'long dere, dey steer ya right, feed ya an' put ya up 'til ya get back t'New Orleans, an' *bonne chance, chers!* Maybe we go sea-rovin' again, together. Never can tell!"

Pierre weighed the bag in his hand, couldn't see that Boudreaux Balfa had another on him, and decided to make the best of what little was left him. He motioned his younger brother, Jean, to join him in his boat, and they set off. Balfa bade the morose Mademoiselle Charité take the steering oar, and he sat beside his son on a rough thwart, an oar in his hoary hands. "Let's row hard, now, Fusilier. All de way home, and say a *strong* prayer we get away wit' our lives, by Gar!"

"Sir! Sir!" Midshipman Larkin cried, hopping from one foot to another in excitement. "There's a rowing boat out there, sir, off the larboard bows. They're not *our* people, sir!"

The damnable fog had not quite dissipated, but it had thinned considerably, now more a haze that hid the horizons. Lewrie put his telescope to his eye and swept the nearer waters. There were a *lot* of boats, most nigh-lost in the northern haze, some to the west . . . ah! That'un! Two men rowing, a lad and a gammer, one man with his hair bound back in a horse-tail steering with a sweep-oar . . . about two miles off and going strong.

Up to the Nor'east, Lewrie could almost make out a second boat with two men in it. "Mister Jugg?" he called. "Use my glass and tell me if you recognise anyone in these two boats nearest us."

Jugg trotted up from his task of helping secure their prize and took a long gander with Lewrie's telescope. "'At 'un up in th' Nor'east, sor . . . don't think I know them fellers," he said after a long moment. "Left-hand'un, though . . . 'at's Boudreaux Balfa at 'er starboard oar, as big as life, sor! We goin' after 'em, Cap'm?" he eagerly asked.

Lewrie took his telescope back, extended the tubes to full magnification, and eyed the closest of his known foes. "Damme!"

He grunted as if punched in the stomach as he recognised another person in Balfa's boat: Charité! She'd turned to peer astern anxiously and he spotted her long mane of chestnut hair, her soggy shirt plastered to womanly breasts. "The murderin' bitch. Do we have a boat handy?" he loudly demanded, rounding to peer about the schooner's deck. "We're off after 'em, if we have t'paddle logs!"

"Two, sir," Midshipman Larkin responded. "Our *shalope*'s jolly boat, and . . . that," he said, pointing over-side at a scrufulous *pirogue* tied up alongside their captured schooner's larboard chains.

"Cox'n Andrews! You, me, and four hands in the jolly boat, men who can row like Blazes!" Lewrie quickly decided. "All to have muskets and cutlasses." With the shore fight seemingly done, and Capt. Nicely in charge of that, there was nothing to deter him from wrapping things up, nabbing Balfa . . . and getting a personal matter finished. "Mister Adair . . . take charge here 'til I get back. Send word ashore if you're able, and tell Captain Nicely where I've gone."

"Aye, sir," Lieutenant Adair crisply replied.

"Hands for the *pirogue*," Lewrie bade to his crewmen. "Any volunteers to . . ."

"Me, sor," Toby Jugg quickly spoke up. "Sorta personal, like."

Lewrie looked him in the eyes for a moment, then nodded assent.

Just 'cause he once knew *the bastard* . . . ! Lewrie thought with a mental shrug as he headed for entry-port; *no reason* not *to trust him*. Jugg and his two almost inseparable mates, his fellow Irishmen Mannix and Dempsey, followed Jugg into the *pirogue* as Lewrie took charge of the tiller of his own rowboat. "Shove off, out oars . . . and let's be *after* the bastard!" Lewrie urged his hands.

As their boats began to surge in pursuit, he did take a moment, though, to wonder if he could shoot a woman if he caught up with Charité.

"Dey gainin' on us," Balfa muttered, arm muscles bulging as he dug deep with his oar, laying out almost prone at each stroke to sweep their boat faster; almost ruing that he'd rid himself of the La Fittes, now that they needed fresh, strong backs. "Gonna cotch us . . . I think. Dat *pirogue* . . . she be . . . faster, her," he grunted 'tween hard strokes. His tongue was about lolling out, and Fusilier's youthful power was nearly played out, too. The girl could steer adequately, but she'd not last five minutes on an oar. "*Mam'selle* . . . dat rifle o' yours . . . you can use it, *hein?* You good shot?"

Helio had showed her how to use the air-rifle, though she didn't consider herself a crack shot. Charité had opened the magazine tube as they'd rowed past *Le Revenant,* when the La Fittes were still aboard, to count remaining rounds. There were only seven. Helio and Hippolyte had bragged how far it could shoot . . . She angrily swiped the sleeve of her shirt over her eyes to blot the fresh tears that the thought of them evoked. They were prisoners of the hated *Anglais,* now, on their way to a British noose, cruelly wounded, or . . . dead and gone!

Everything was lost! Ships, crew, the silver, and when news got to the Spanish, the surviving de Guilleris would face arrest and trial and the *garotte* in the Place d'Armes. All they owned would be forfeit, even if her parents and sisters had had no knowledge or part in their planned revolution.

Her own fate was the bitterest of all to savour; she would die not as a martyr for France, but as a fool, an utter failure who'd gotten her brothers killed, a lunatic with a demented dream! And Creoles, even those who *might* have taken up arms with them, would be cowed into silence and ineffectiveness! Louisiana and New Orleans would stay part of Spain!

Better to die now, Charité bleakly thought, fantasising a tale told of a *brave* but foolish girl who'd slain her heartless, pursuing Englishmen and died in *battle,* than to be abased in a court like Joan of Arc, then strangled in the public square.

"*Mam'selle?*" Balfa prompted.

"I can use it, *Capitaine*," Charité grimly promised. "When the time comes, I will. I'll not be taken, *non*."

But oh, it would be hard to die, when she'd only had nineteen sunny years. Couldn't there have been many more, in a Louisiana that was free and French again, her holy duty done?

"Hoy, the boat!" an *Anglais* shouted from a boat on their starboard quarter. "Lay on your oars and surrender, in the King's name!"

"Shit on your king!" Boudreaux Balfa hooted back, "an' kiss my rosy 'Cadien ass!" In a mutter, he added, "De time be come, *mam'selle*. Try your eye, an' I'll be ready wit' my pistols for when dey gets real close."

Charité abandoned the sweep-oar, pulled the air-rifle up off the boat's sole, and cranked the stiff loading lever to chamber a ball, then turned on her thwart to take aim, frightened to death but determined to take at least one despicable *Anglais* with her before she fell.

"We know who you are, Boudreaux Balfa!" the *Anglais* bellowed in a quarterdeck voice, shambling half bent over to stand in the bows of his boat. "Charité de Guilleri! Surrender, and no harm will come to you!"

She started with alarm, chilled that the British knew her by name! Over the sights of her rifle, she peered at the officer in the bows, a "Bloody" *cochon* in a gilt-laced coat, face shaded by a large cocked hat, hands cupped to his mouth. *He* would be her target. She cocked the valve mechanism to the air-chamber.

The officer lowered his hands, took off his hat as his boat got within sixty yards, and a long musket shot . . . *Him? Mon Dieu, Alain?*

A spy, a glib liar, an arch foe of all she held dear! *Crack!*

Her first round was short and to the right, but Alain's oarsmen faltered, and she'd forced him to duck, rocking his boat alarmingly. Cold-bloodedly now, Charité reloaded and recocked her air-rifle, then brought the rifle's stock back to her shoulder, her fluttery fear now departed, her hands and body no longer shivering. Charité de Guilleri was filled by a calmly righteous and vengeful anger.

"*Pirogue*'s gettin' close, *aussi, mam'selle*," Balfa cautioned.

As if she was still Papa's little prodigy hunting quail in a cut-over cane field, Charité swivelled to face dead aft and put a well-placed ball square in the *pirogue*'s bows, forcing all three men in it to lay flat and fall back as they abandoned their paddling.

"Give it up, Charité!" Willoughby—whatever the lying bastard called himself—shouted over. "We won't hurt you . . . swear it!"

Vous! she thought, utterly revulsed that she'd let him even put his *hands* on her, that she'd given him her body, her affection, and her foolish trust, her . . . *love*! Her skin crawled at the recollections of how they'd, how he'd . . . ! *"Vous êtes fumier!"* she cried. "You have already hurt me to my very soul, you . . . 'Bloody'!"

Charité dashed her sleeve over her eyes again, blinked her vision clear of tears, took a breath and let it out slowly, found the instant of perfect stillness, and fired.

Phfft-tack!

The ball hit him square in the chest, just under his heart, and the force of it punched the air from his lungs, slugged him backwards to splay over the forward-most thwart with his head on the jolly boat's damp soleboards.

Merciful God! Lewrie frantically thought as agony engulfed him, unable to draw breath, vision darkening; *I'm killed!*

CHAPTER THIRTY-THREE

*A*h-*yee!*" Fusilier Balfa cheered her accuracy, all but clapping his oar-chafed, bleeding hands. *"Vivat, mam'selle!"*

"Hell wit' dat," his father, Boudreaux, snarled, dragging them to sobriety. "Dat only slow 'em down for de little while, den dey *really* be mad wit' us. Gotta get a lead on 'em. Row or die, *chers.*"

And, for a few minutes, it seemed as if Charité's awesome shot *had* bought them a lead. The *Anglais'* rowing boat had come to a stop, the *pirogue,* going alongside it, and both receded into the lingering bay mists. Balfa bade Charité to bear off Nor'westerly to throw them off, and reach the closest maze of marshes, cypress and mangrove swamp, not Lake Barataria, which lay due North.

Both men were spent, though, the act of rowing a muscle-searing agony. Their breath roared like a forge bellows as they panted for air, and both were hang-dog, drooling with exhaustion.

"Oh, *mon Dieu.*" Charité gasped as she fearfully looked over her shoulder and spotted the much faster *pirogue* off their starboard quarter, re-emerging from the haze. "They have found us, *messieurs.*" Sure enough, the paddles flashed more quickly, and the *pirogue* swung about to run parallel with their boat, just out of pistol-shot. The sailor in the middle of the *pirogue* held a musket at the ready.

"Sorry, *chérie,*" Boudreaux Balfa wheezed, letting his oar slide aft. "Can't do no more. We tried." He pulled a pistol from his belt and let it lay in his lap, handing the other to his son.

Charité abandoned her steering oar and test-cocked her weapon; a snap of the trigger only produced a faint hiss. Its unreliable buttstock flask was expended. In spite of that, she levered a ball into the breech and brought it to her shoulder, the pretence of a ready gun more of a final act of defiance. A way to die in battle.

"Hoy!" the paddler and steersman seated in the stern of the *pirogue* shouted as he set aside his paddle and took up a musket as well. "Hoy, Boudreaux Balfa . . . ye auld cut-throat!" he added, sounding nigh cheerful, not threatening. "Ye auld mud-foot!"

"Who dat?" Balfa warily called back, squinting in confusion.

"An auld shipmate o' your'n!" the man hooted. "One ye didn't reco'nise when ye marooned 'im on th' Dry Tortugas . . . come t'take ye in, Boudreaux!"

"An' who be dat?" Balfa quickly asked, laying a cautioning hand on his son's gun-arm to force it down. "Bide, *cher* . . . we ain't taken yet," he whispered with a disconcerting wink. "May *not* be."

"Ye knew me as Patrick Warder, Boudreaux! Though th' Navy knows me as Toby Jugg! Throw yer weapons over-side and put up yer hands."

"*Nom d'un chien!*" Balfa exclaimed. "Ol' Paddy *Warder?* Ah-yee, you little t'ief! Stole a hundred *Anglais* pounds offa me and run off. Damn if I don't forgive you dat, long ago, and now you wanna arrest me and my son here, Fusilier, let de British courts hang us bot' an' end my *patrie*, by Gar? Dat he hard, Paddy . . . damn' hard."

"Shoulda swung *years* ago, Boudreaux," Toby Jugg called back. "I figger this'll be *delayed* justice. Why I jumped ship an' run, 'coz I couldn't hold with wot you let 'at ol' demon Lanxade git away with in th' last war. Waddn't privateerin', but murd'rin' piracy . . . "

"An' you steal my moneys. You a *saint*, Paddy? Swear, I didn't know you, all dat fine beard ya got, *cher*," Balfa cajoled, playing for time. "All dese years, too. By Gar, I know you, den, I'da let you go in a spare boat, wit' no harm. Always liked you, Paddy, you *know* dat!"

"Oh, aye!" Toby Jugg snickered. "Right! Give it up!"

"My boy Fusilier be innocent, Paddy, dis his first trip, swear! *Mort de ma vie!*" Balfa wheedled, open-handed with his pistol below the boat's side. "Fine, you take *me* for hangin', 'cause I prob'ly done sin enough for it, *some* time in de past. Can't *recall*, but . . . let Fusilier and dis sweet *mam'selle* go,

Paddy. You want see a pretty *jeune fille* like her on de gibbet, kickin' an' stranglin' in de noose, an' no one t'pull her legs t'make it quick?"

"She lowers 'at damn' rifle o' hers or she dies right here an' now," Jugg gruffly promised. "She's th' Cap'm's girl from New Orleans. One 'at went a'piratin' as a man. One 'at killed him, too, an' *all's* a reason fer her t'do th' 'Newgate Horn-pipe,' Boudreaux."

"He is surely dead?" Charité interrupted, aiming at the sailor amidships of the *pirogue,* but her gaze darting to Jugg.

"Looked hellish like it 'fore we paddled after ye, miss, aye."

"Bon," Charité cold-bloodedly stated. "Good."

"Guess ya got us, den, Paddy," Balfa said with a weary sigh of surrender. "An' dis was my *last* trip, too. Be damn' hard, though, to get cotched an' die wit'out a chance t'spend dat Spanish silver we got away wit'. Hope *mes amis* an' neighbours have joy of it. *Ah-yee.*"

"What silver?" Dempsey, the armed sailor, demanded.

"You t'ink I plan t'quit de old trade, I don't fiddle my ol' *ami* Jérôme Lanxade?" Balfa chuckled. "How much silver you *find,* 'board dat Spaniard, hah? Eight hundred t'ousand or so, was all, when we'd took two *million!* Oh, dey be a pile left on *Le Revenant,* but . . . you ask Paddy, dere. We promise de crew *six* millions, but de Spanish send it in *three* boats, an' dis mornin' was gonna be *grim* when dey find out we don't have it."

"Ye cheated yer auld mate, Jérôme, did ye, Boudreaux? I allus knew ye were a greedy auld shark, by God!" Toby Jugg mirthfully mused.

"Where is it, then?" Dempsey snapped.

"Mes amis, 'Cadien friends o' mine, take it away las' night," Boudreaux Balfa explained, shrugging. "Don' even tell *me* where it be, 'til I gets back home on de bayou, Paddy. I don' go back, dey'd split it . . . leave my poor 'Vangeline a *bitty* share. I *do* get back, I'd get *all* my share. Won' tell *you* where it be buried, by Gar, 'cause you're outsiders, an' *Anglais* to boot. Same th' same sort who kick us outta Canadian Acadia, *hein?* Go huntin' it, dey most-like kill you an' feed you to de pig an' 'gator, dem," Balfa slyly, "sorrowfully" told them.

"Ah . . . how *much* ye git away with, then?" asked Mannix, the sailor in the bow of the *pirogue,* his mouth agape in greed.

"Couple hundred t'ousand, wasn't it, Fusilier? *You* counted dem kegs," Balfa asked his son.

"More dan dat, Papa," Fusilier chimed in, cleverly catching his father's drift, and marvelling at the old man's craftiness.

"You let us go, we *could* go shares," Balfa hesitantly pretended to hint.

"Ah, but you go back to your Navy, dere's no way you'd trust *moi* t'get de moneys to you, *ah-yee*. So I guess we *all* gotta go broke."

"Fack th' Navy." Dempsey snickered, lowering the muzzle of his musket a trifle. "Wot *kinda* share we talkin' of, mister?"

"Here, now, Dempsey!" Jugg warned him. "He's a sweet-tongued auld imp o' Hell, he is, an' most-like ain't got tuppence left. Cap'm Lewrie trusted—"

"Cap'm's dead as mutton, Toby," Mannix sourly pointed out. "I 'llow ye, Cap'm Lewrie woz a decent sort, but now he's gone, who's to take charge o' *Proteus* . . . one *more* o' them top-lofty, floggin' shites . . . a piss-proud, Irish-hatin' *English* officer-bastard? No thankee!"

"We're way out here," Dempsey seconded. "Outta sight o' anybody. Who's t'say we didn't get kilt by th' pirates we woz chasin'? We don' go back, nobody'll come lookin' after us. Rest o' th' ship's off'cers ain't like Cap'm Lewrie, Toby . . . no skin off *their* arses if they come up a few *Irish* hands short. Not with all th' silver still aboard 'at prize schooner t'caper over."

"An' didn't we allus plan t'take 'leg-bail' o' th' Navy, iff'n a prime chance turned up?" Mannix eagerly seconded. "*Think,* man! We get listed 'Discharged, Dead,' 'stead o' 'Run,' an' no one'll *ever* be seekin' us! Free an' clear, an' in money, t'boot! How much in pounds is yer silver, then, mister?" he greedily asked Balfa.

A keg apiece, Balfa alluringly told them. A thousand dollars in silver was 250 English pounds, a lifetime's earnings to the average tar, and that set them to gabbling again. Balfa hid his smile; all the rest would be "negotiations." They'd already become a pack of *putains* . . . now they were haggling over their bed price!

"*Capitaine!*" Charité desperately interrupted, aghast that *he'd* betray her, too; her heart broken anew over the loss of her last illusion. "If you and your friends keep all our money, you lavish it on *Anglais!* . . . there's nothing left for our revolution! Would you have my brothers die for *nothing?* Don't you want to be *French* again?"

"Moonshine from de start, girl," Balfa snarled, snatching that rifle from her numb hands. "Money's *always* what matter! Dis toy gun outta air, *mes amis,* don' worry 'bout her! Your mates go along, so what *you* say, Paddy, *mon vieux?*" He hated to do it to her, but . . .

"I've a wife an' two babes on Barbados, Boudreaux," Jugg morosely said, sighing. "A *bitty* plot o' cane, bought *clean,* but we've worked damn' hard an' honest t'git it, keep it. I'd lose it all, if . . ."

"Send for 'em," Balfa breezily suggested. "How *big* your place?"

"Five acres."

"By *damn,* Paddy!" Balfa laughed. "Land in de piney-wood, north o' New Orleans . . . back o' Baton Rouge? . . . go for penny an *acre,* not a *arpent!* Keg o' silver buy you a *plantation,* big house, fine coach, an' a regiment o' slaves! Be set for life, you."

Toby Jugg—Patrick Warder or Tobias Hosier, and an host of aliases he'd given ship captains over the years—looked at Mannix and Dempsey's child-like, prompting expressions, knowing that if he didn't agree, they'd most-like shoot him down, so eager they were to desert. Without Capt. Lewrie, what would he be? A new captain would bring a "pet" to supplant him as Quartermaster's Mate, reduce him to being an Able Seaman again. But, if he was "dead," his name cut from ship's books and Admiralty registers . . . and with a pile of money . . . !

"Ye're still a thief, Boudreaux," Toby Jugg allowed at last. "One keg, me arse! *Five* keg a man, an' no debt o' auld I owe ye, for ye *said* ye forgive it long afore."

"*Ah-yee!*" Balfa cried, all but tearing his bushy grey hair out at the roots. "You starve my *famille,* starve my *chickens!* Five kegs, *mon cul!* Two, an' be damn to ya. You live *good* on two kegs, that's five hundred *pounds!* North Loosiann' be fulla heretic Protestants an' I hope dey *burn* ya! Fulla 'Mericains an' skinflint Yankees who take de coin off your dead mother's eyes. You *deserve* t'live dere, Paddy!"

"Four kegs, Boudreaux," Jugg countered. "After all, wot's your life worth, you an' yer son's?"

"Mist be burnin' off," Boudreaux pointed out suddenly. "We'd better get along, *chers.* Your men row dis boat, 'cause we played out, but we can still paddle a *pirogue* . . . "

"Not without a firm price an' yer Bible oath on it, Boudreaux," Jugg insisted. "They spot us, we'll remember we're 'True Blue Hearts O' Oak' an' haveta settle fer our share o' th' prize money. Let's say three kegs an' have done."

"*Mon Dieu, merde alors!*" Balfa surrendered, knowing that his old ship-mate Toby Jugg was right. "T'ree keg each, my word on it," he said, crossing himself.

"Mannix, you get in their boat. Boy, you come into ours, and I'll thankee for yer 'barker,'" Jugg ordained. "We'll tow you on a short painter 'til we strike th' far shore. Fire off a shot ever' now an' then . . . your pistols first, o'course, t'keep 'em guessing back down South. Miss? Ye want t'play a man, well . . . take up 'at oar an' help Mannix row 'til auld Boudreaux's got his wind back. No harm will come to ye, me own oath on't. Jus' sing small an' be thankful ye still got breath in yer body, for ye slew a decent man . . . for an officer . . . an' he did right by me, I tell ye."

Charité slumped down on the sternsheet thwarts, knees drawn up, and her arms hugging her breasts. Everything she'd had in life was lost and gone, even her last, leery trust in "dear old" cheerful *Capitaine* Balfa, who had just sold her out! She would live, the *Anglais* sailor swore; she'd return home . . . but to what?

CHAPTER THIRTY-FOUR

*O*h, God," Capt. Alan Lewrie weakly whimpered, his hands shakily feeling over his chest. His head lay cradled in Cox'n Andrews's lap, and Andrews was gently undoing his waist-coat and shirt buttons. Air! *Pain!* He could barely draw breath, and his heart thudded so strongly and quickly, it felt like a kettledrum at a bloody concert. *Hot* pain thrummed knot-like 'twixt his stomach and sternum.

"Be *easy*, sah!" Andrews commiserated.

"Easy! I'm bloody dyin' and . . . *ow!* Damme, but that hurts!"

Hold, a tick! Lewrie puzzled; *Heart's bangin' like a racehorse! Hurts, but . . . what the bloody Hell?*

"Ya ain't killed, sah!" Cox'n Andrews wondrously exclaimed. "Ya ain't even bad *shot*, praise de Lord!"

Lewrie fumbled at his bared chest, coughing and still gasping for breath, each one searing pain through him. His fingers came away smeared with blood! "What d'ye call this, then, damn my eyes!" he querously quibbled.

"Faith, sor," Liam Desmond, one of his oarsmen, cried, holding a silvery .51 calibre rifle ball 'twixt thumb and forefinger. "Found it on th' soleboards, sor! Must o' bounced right off ya, sure. Shot went *pish!* 'stead o' *crack!* Like that duck ya shot comin' upriver, sor . . . when th' air-flask was spent? Mother Mary, but you're th' lucky'un an' there's a tale for th' tellin', Cap'm, sor!"

"Mebbe we starts callin' ya 'Iron-Bound' 'stead o' th' Ram-Cat, sah." Andrews tittered, immensely relieved and slightly teasing.

"We will *not!*" Lewrie snapped, struggling to sit upright despite his sailors' protests. He gaped downwards, thinking it *must* have been a weakly propelled shot, for all of Charité's remorseless accuracy. It had further been blunted by his white leather sword baldric that angled cross his chest, by a doubled-over gilt-laced coat lapel atop it, and lastly, by the insubstantial obstacle of his waist-coat and shirt that had absorbed most of the ball's force. Even so, his flesh had been split by its impact, and when he gingerly massaged his chest near the seeping, slight wound, which was already swelling and turning the most garish shade of purply green in a bruise as wide as his hand-span, he thought he could feel something broken inside—a rib or two perhaps, his breastbone chipped, maybe? *Dented?* Thank the Lord, indeed, though, there wasn't a gaping, spurting, grape-red *hole* in his hide!

"Damn my eyes, but she shot me," Lewrie wheezed. "She actually *shot* me! Tried t'kill me!"

Not that I really blame her . . . much, Lewrie told himself with chagrin; *'Tis a bloody wonder some woman didn't try ages ago!* And by the queasy expression on Andrews's phyz, his longtime Cox'n must've been wondering the same thing.

"Where is she?" Lewrie demanded, head aswivel in search for her.

"*Way* off yonder, sah," Andrews had to say, waving northward at a fog-hazed horizon. Lewrie couldn't spot another boat anywhere.

"Damme, we've lost 'em. But if Jugg is still after 'em . . . we might get lucky yet," Lewrie sadly decided. "*Might* have 'em in irons by nightfall."

"We head back to de ship, Cap'm?" Andrews solicitously asked. "Ya need t'let Mistah Hodson an' Mistah Durant, de Surgeons, tend to ya, sah. Bind up yer ribs an' such?"

"Aye, Andrews, that'd be capital," Lewrie was forced to agree. "It strikes me that I might've done enough and *more* today for King and Country. I've *earned* myself a lie-down!"

"Amen t'dat, sah," Andrews said with a chuckle. "Make y'self comf'table as ya can, an' Desmond an' me'll fetch ya back to *Proteus*, quick as a wink. Mebbe Jugg *will* cotch dat girl for ya, an' . . . "

"Ah-*hemm!*" Lewrie growled at that unfortunate slip, tossing in a grumbly "Arr!" for good measure as he pressed his handkerchief over his wound and eased down to sit on the gig's floorboards, seepage and the state of his uniform bedamned, to lay against the forward thwart. Half prone, he found it easier on his ribs to breathe.

Andrews and Desmond got the gig turned about and set themselves a slow but deep-biting stroke that would get him to safety and still not completely exhaust them, and the metronomic rumbling creak of oars in ungreased tholes, the thrust and glide of the boat between strokes, and the gurgle-chuckling of passing water began to lull him.

Do I really want her captured? he asked himself, puzzling over why he didn't utterly despise her and wish her heart's blood, since she'd come damned close to spilling *his*. All in all, Lewrie reckoned, it had been a shitten business they'd done . . . but it was done. And even if Charité escaped, once the report on this affair was published in London papers the tale would make its way to New Orleans sooner or later and it would be up to the incensed Spanish to do the *real* dirty work. In spite of all the depravities she'd been in-volved with, he could almost pity her, when the Dons got their hands on her.

Luck to you, girl, he thought, lolling his head back to admire the clearing, bright blue sky; *but,* damme *if I ain't pleased t'be shot of you!*

He *would* have laughed at his play on words, . . . but he suspected it would hurt.

EPILOGUE

Miranda: O, wonder!
How many goodly creatures are there here!
How beauteous mankind is! O brave new world
That has such people in it!

—THE TEMPEST, ACT V, SCENE 1
WILLIAM SHAKESPEARE

CHAPTER THIRTY-FIVE

Crack! went the Girandoni air-rifle, little louder than the dry snap of a twig on the forest floor, and the wily old tom turkey leaped as its tiny skull was shattered, wings flapping, breaking into a staggering run for a second or two before it realised it was dead and fell in a feathery heap.

"*Waaw!*" Peyton Siler marvelled. "An' at a hun'erd paces, too!"

"Damn if 'at don't beat all, Jim Hawk!" Georgie Prater cheered, as loud as he dared on the lawless Natchez Trace without drawing undue attention from a roving Chickasaw or Choctaw band, a pack of frontier outlaws, or down-on-their-luck and desperate travellers. "Wisht I'd o' bought me one, too."

Jim Hawk Ellison painfully rose to his feet from where he knelt, still stiff from his healing wound, one hand dug into the bark of the tulip poplar tree he'd used for cover at the end of his stalk. "Damn' if it *ain't* a God-Hell wonder, at that, boys. There's gonna be a lot o' surprised squirrels in Campbell County once I get settled. Eat on squirrel an' dumplin's ev'ry goldarned night."

"Dependin' on whether ya find a wife t'cook 'em for ya," Siler said with a sly chuckle.

"Figger, with what I won off those two sailor boys in Natchez, I just might manage, Peyton." Ellison gently laughed along. "Georgie, I'd much admire did ya go fetch Mister Tom. Still got a hitch in my get-along." And Georgia Prater dashed to do his bidding, though not without an Indian's caution to go silently and skirt the clearing roundabout near the trees, his Pennsylvania rifle at the ready.

"Leastways, somethin' good come outta Looziana," Siler grunted. "B'sides gettin' outta New Orleans with our skins still on, and a wind down our gullets."

" 'Tis a filthy, damp country, Peyton," Jim Hawk commented as he slung his air-rifle over his shoulder, a wary eye kept on the dark and thick woods even so, for an unwary man on the lonely Natchez Trace was as good as dead, and even a party as large as his could still be taken in ambush, did they ever let their guard down. None of them would lay in easy sleep 'til they reached tiny Nashville. "At least we can say that we came all this way, saw it, and had us a little adventure. But I'd not give you five dollars for th' whole damn' place. Why Congress is hagglin' over sendin' an army down there t'take it, well . . . more power to 'em, but they've not had t'live in it like we did. They decide to try 'er on, I'll hoot an' holler loud as anybody else, an' pat 'em on the back as they march by, but . . . no thankee."

New Orleans, Spanish Florida, and Louisiana would, Jim Hawk was certain, be American someday . . . but not anytime soon, as he reckoned it. President John Adams already had himself *half* a war, a quasi war with France, and he doubted if he'd be able to bring Congress round to his point of view before the coming elections. If Jefferson got in, *he* might manage it, but . . . soon as Jim Hawk was back in Nashville, he'd put his reports in the mails to Washington City, along with his letter of resignation, and head back to the Powell's Valley to make a new beginning; a secure, settled civilian life, after years of war and filibustering for richer men. He had 250 Spanish dollars in his saddlebags, and that was enough for a man to found a mountain empire! So something good had, in truth, come from Louisiana!

"You foolish, foolish girl!" Papa Hilaire de Guilleri fumed yet again. Since he and Maman Marie had rushed back to New Orleans, he'd whiplashed between bawling, drunken grief over the loss of his sons and his *patrie*, to jibbering dread of exposure, trial, and garotting, to anger directed to her, the only living target for his icy wrath. "What were you *thinking*, you . . . "

"To free Louisiana," Charité numbly tried to explain once more, her voice meek and her hands primly folded in the lap of her soberly black mourning gown. "For France, Papa, for—"

"Empty-headed, patriotic *nonsense!*" her elegantly tall and lean, distinguished father cruelly shot back. "Fervent twaddle for things an ocean away, and nothing to do with us, I tell you! And if the Spanish ever learn of what you did, we're all ruined. You're . . . *débile*! You led your brothers into your—"

"Your sweet and gentle *cousin*, poor Jean-Marie, *aussi*," Maman coldly fumed from the other side of her father's study, plying a fan as if to drive off summer heat. Charité didn't know which of them was crueller to her, her dashing *beau idéal* father or her elegantly gay and flighty mother, for Marie de Guilleri had been, still was, one of the most beauteous belles of her generation, the toast of the city and of the grandest Creole society. "Rubio Monaster, who might have married one of your sisters had he lived, made the *finest* match between us and the Bergrands," she accused, daintily daubing at her dry nose with a laced silk handkerchief.

Their banker, Monsieur Maurepas, had summoned them and had spread a plausible lie to explain Charité's stumbling return to New Orleans in a nameless Acadian's *pirogue* and care. Maurepas's sorrowful tale had hardly been necessary, for a week or more at least, since New Orleans had been rocked by the fire that had levelled poor Monsieur Bistineau's old store and warehouse, *and* the simultaneous fire that had erupted aboard a newly arrived ship for sale, on the south bank of the river, *and* the way the used ship had lost *all* her mooring cables and had drifted onto the American emporium ship, burning her to the waterline as well! It had required the garrison turn out, the forts to be manned against any attempt to seize the port city. On top of that, only two of the three treasure schooners had come up the Mississippi, the third feared lost, and that caused even *greater* consternation.

Given the circumstances, the tragic murder of four of the town's most promising young gentlemen at the hands of the cut-throat runaway rebel slave St. John's evil band, while hunting and fishing on Lake Barataria, had almost gone un-noticed! Rumours had flown. Charité had escaped; been raped by the *nègres*; had stopped off with an Acadian family due to slight unhealth and hadn't been with them . . . yet had almost lost her complete wits in grief. *Quel dommage, n'est-ce pas?* It was well known that Charité had been the toobold, outdoorsy, and *de-sexed* sort of girl, too *outré*, too modern, so . . .

"To think I nursed you at my breast, viper!" Maman Marie snapped. Her fan beat like a hummingbird's wings. "Drinking, gambling, running the streets in men's clothing, associating with whores and rogues . . . and reeling home as drunk as a *nègre!*"

"Maman . . . " Charité weakly beseeched, eyes grimaced in misery.

"Carrying weapons, playing at pirate like a . . . " Maman accused. "Whoring, most likely, too! Shameless, thoughtless, little . . . slut!"

"But, Maman!"

"You as good as murdered my fine sons yourself, whore! How I wish *you* had been the one taken from us instead!" Maman swore.

"I wish I was, I *wanted* to die, I . . . "

"Scheming as bold as a dragoon in public, where anyone might've heard you," her father chimed in from the other side of the study, his worries of a different stripe. "God knows how many other grand, distinguished young people you will end up dragging to the garotte if the Spanish ever learn the truth. How many parents will be blamed as well, though they knew nothing!"

"We will end up penniless at the least, idiot-child! Hounded from New Orleans and Louisiana," her mother bewailed, rocking with impending ruin on her gilded chair. "All our wealth and security, lost. Forced to flee among the filthy *Américains, mon Dieu!* Penniless, you hear me, girl? Penniless and damned by every good Creole family whose happiness you have destroyed, bah!"

"She is mad, *chérie*," her father sternly declared. "Her mind is gone. I have spoken to *Docteur* Robicheaux, who thinks she is utterly *débile* . . . perhaps has been for some time."

"That will not excuse what she did, Hilaire!" Maman wailed, then sniffed into her handkerchief. "The Spanish won't care *when* she . . . "

"Only if they ever learn the truth, Marie," Papa cautioned, one hand raised to make his point in peaceful deliberateness. "If we play our parts properly, they never will. The bishop knows nothing, and he will preach a fervent sermon against the rebel slaves, as if our sons truly died at their hands." Hilaire de Guilleri hitched a deep sigh and daubed his own eyes as he said that. "We must be too stricken to speak, so we will not be forced to say anything to the contrary. After, we will quickly return upcountry, along with Iphegenie and Marguerite, and may stay for months and months. *She*, well . . . will be too grief-stricken to attend, *n'est-ce pas?* Though the thought of placing deer bones and rocks in our dear sons' coffins, to rest forever in our mausoleum is . . . Ah, well. According to what she admitted to us, and what *Capitaine* Balfa wrote us, there can be no trustworthy witnesses to her perfidy. Maurepas too frightened of exposure? Bistineau, too? That *Capitaine* Lanxade and most of his crew dead or captured by the *Anglais*, who will quickly hang the rest on Jamaica? The three *Anglais* sailors, the deserters, are scattered to Baton Rouge or Natchez and have just reason to fear that the Spanish learn where they got their money . . ."

Charité stared unseeing at her hands, clenched white-knuckled in her lap, her eyes averted and her chin down, as she had contritely been ever since she had reached New Orleans and saw her parents. She was just as heartbroken as they, perhaps even more so, just as deeply wounded by her brothers' deaths, the utter end of her dreams, hopes . . .

Yet Papa and Maman had scathed her for days, sputtering in spiteful, hateful rages or accusing tears. Speaking of her as if she was dead, too, over the top of her head as if she was not *there,* and frankly, she was getting irked by their waverings from dangerous hostility to bitter but *arch* grief. As if sorrow was the proper "thing" to do, the sham to portray, whether their hearts were touched or not! And being spoken *of*, not *to*, worse than a dog, given less regard than a piece of furniture . . . !

" . . . only living witness would be *her*, in fact," Papa Hilaire declaimed, sitting on the edge of his ornate desk, swinging a booted foot, a brandy glass in his hand, and a so-clever smile on his face. Charité snapped up her head to goggle at him, chilling with dread. Her parents had always been testy about anything that might taint their family's repute; beyond their semi-secret *amours,* of course, and everyone in Creole Louisiana would forgive *those,* Charité thought. But how far *would* they go to protect themselves, she had to wonder?

Her father gazed dispassionately at her for a long and somber moment, then shook his head in disappointment. "*Docteur* Robicheaux is already convinced of her derangement," Papa said as he turned his attention to his wife again. "He has written us a letter to that effect. Such a condition will require years of . . . care."

Charité winced, ready to burst into tears in fear of lifelong exile on their most remote and meanest plantation, a feebleminded exile confined to the garret to spare them embarrassment; there to turn old and cronish and desperately lonely, with only slaves for keepers. The rest of her life? She could not *bear* it! Dare they risk her with the Ursuline nuns, under a vow of silence? A convent *might* be better, but only just. New Orleans didn't have a proper mad-house, but . . . what sort of "care" did he mean?

"She must leave New Orleans," Papa gloomily intoned. "She must leave Louisiana, sorry to say, Marie. We lose yet another child."

"Leave Louisiana?" Charité dared wail in consternation. "Where must I then go? Papa, please!"

"Hush, you ungrateful girl!" Maman spat, stamping a dainty foot. "No matter how evil you turned out to be, still, we *are* your parents, and we love you despite . . . Trust us to do what little we can in the best interests of our family name, your sisters' futures. And in your own good, though you don't—"

Papa shushed her mother and crossed the room to flair his coattails, take a seat beside her, and pat Maman's hand. Charité knew she was completely doomed, seeing where his sympathy lay.

"*Docteur* Robicheaux suggests that there are several colleagues from his university days," Papa said, squirming a little and unable to look his daughter in the eyes, not completely. "Progressive and clever gentlemen who are achieving marvellous results with the, ah . . . deranged, Charité. In France."

"In *France?*" Charité gasped. Her fear of lonely exile fled her soul in a twinkling, and her mouth fell open in utter surprise.

A second later came a blossoming, blissful joy! She would go to *France?* The very centre of the entire civilised world? The birthplace of the glorious revolution that she'd wished to emulate? A smile of wonder took her features, one she strove hard to disguise but could not quell completely; one she fervently hoped her parents interpreted as one of thanks for saving her life, out of their so-called love for her. Secretly, though, Charite was marvellously pleased, ready to leap to her feet and dance with glee, snap her fingers in their faces in elation!

"A Swedish ship is in port and will soon depart," Papa intoned. "We have booked you a cabin aboard her, and *Docteur* Robicheaux wrote a letter explaining your condition, and how you must be kept in isolation and at rest. A neutral ship, which the British will not dare to board. You will not be disturbed on-passage, *n'est-ce pas?* You will be safe, all the way to L'Orient. Then . . . "

"But . . . where will I *go* in France, Papa?" Charité cried aloud. France *did* have mad-houses, and even if the Revolution had conquered the Catholic Church, there still *were* convents! "I mean . . . who will *care* for me, Papa? Maman?" she fearfully asked, play-acting as if she feared being separated from them forever more. "Will you *really* have me . . . committed to . . . "

She bit her lower lip and sham-trembled like a chastised puppy.

But, France! *Yes!* she thought.

"We have distant relations," Papa told her, squirming a little more as he crossed his legs and put an arm about the back of Maman's chair. "Your mother's kin, the Lemerciers. They live in a very nice little village, a peaceful and bucolic place called Rambouillet."

Ghastly! Charité thought, shivering for real.

" . . . not too far from Paris, really, to the west, I think."

Paris? Yes, Paris, too! She would finally see Paris!

" . . . people of the strictest morals and rectitude . . . "

Boring! Charité almost giggled aloud. She'd find a way to free herself!

" . . . a sober example that might, in time, restore you to proper behaviour, near to one of *Docteur* Robicheaux's colleagues who will . . . "

Doubt it! Charité almost whooped in wicked glee; *not with the fabulous city of Paris but a hop, skip, and a jump away.*

" . . . do not mend your ways, Robicheaux's colleague will indeed commit you, Charité . . . " Papa sternly warned her.

"If you upset the Lemerciers in *any* way, you willful girl!" her mother threatened, and Charité's galloping imaginings came to a hoof-skidding halt, making her cringe for real, and gulp. If she did anything to displease her dull-sounding relations, they'd have leave to sling her into the mad-house? *Eu, merde!*

"We will, of course, provide you with a small remittance," her calmer Papa explained. "A letter goes to them, explaining how you've been, ah . . . bereft and driven witless. That we wish them to spend no more on you, and kerb your former extravagance, too. Once assured that your mind is clearer, they might go so far as to introduce you to some local lads of modest but upright nature or, that failing, settle you in some genteel circumstances, as a housekeeper, or . . . "

"We only wish the *best* for you, *chérie*," Maman insincerely and oversweetly assured her, ready to tear up over her youngest girl's departure, her potentially lifelong absence.

Marry a village dullard? A cobbler? Charité bleakly thought, cringing with revulsion; *Be a housemaid, a matron's . . . servant? Burp her infants and empty night-jars? Ugh!*

"I beg you, Maman," Charité pleaded. "Must I *really* end . . . "

"It is settled," Papa snapped. "It is the only solution," he concluded, once again badly mistaking her dread of dullity for dread of parting, her grimace of disgust at paid servitude or worse for the loss of her family's love!

Who are *these people?* Charité had to ask herself; *Did I really* ever *know them? Paris, though!*

Once in France, did she dissemble well and play up humble, she could make her way to Paris, get her well-meaning relatives to show her the famous sights where the Revolution had taken place! Once there, she could ditch them long enough to seek out men in the Assembly or the Senate, even an august member of the powerful Directory! Press for Louisiana's liberation, tell them what she'd done, had suffered, in the cause of Revolution and its worldwide spread. *Some* powerful man would sponsor her, surely, free her from the threat of commitment and the certain dullness of her rustic relatives! Who knew better than a Creole girl how to cajole, flirt, and beguile, after all? Choose well, and she might end up touted as a heroine of France herself, her story a *cause célèbre*, invited to the best *salons!*

She would obey her parents . . . for a time. She would mind her behaviour aboard ship, and convince her *docteur*-minder that she was as sane as he, cruelly and unjustly exiled. She would convince her relations of it, too, force herself to be helpful, meekly obedient to their strictures, and sunnily sweet; once her grief had waned of course. Or would a lingering wan-ness suit better? No matter!

She would win her freedom and get to Paris, where anything was possible; win support for her cause, for her upkeep. Even *marry*, if a powerful and clever man wished it. She would still give anything for Louisiana . . . and for France!

Mrs. Tobias Hosier, Mrs. Toby Jugg, toiled her stony sugarcane field in the hot Barbadan sun, despairing that their poor plot seemed to produce more stones and weeds than cane stalks this season.

Her hips and lower back ached from her hoeing and chopping, and perspiration soaked her entire body, her shabby work-gown. So it was with weary relief, as well as curiosity, that she observed the arrival of a rider at her tumbledown gate. He called her name and waved a letter in the air.

She shambled back to the house and the yard-gate, fetching Tess from watching the baby on the shabby quilt, swabbing her face and arms on her apron as she accepted the rare letter with a surge of hope that Toby might have included a quarterly draught on his Navy pay, for they might not be able to settle their rent and store bills by Quarter Day, and the next Assizes.

She dipped the post-rider a grateful curtsy, then went back to the porch gallery, out of the unmerciful sun, to sit down and read it.

"Lord above, wot've ye done this time, lad?" she whispered as she saw that it was addressed from "Patrick Warder," from someplace in Spanish Louisiana!

> *Deerest Bess*
> *I hev run from the Navy pet & not intire my idee I sware. I run with much Monie tho & hev got us 1,200 akers in Lueeziana up the Missippi river neer Batton Rooj with plentie left for fine house slaves stock & seed & itt is rich fine land will gro anything ha ha.*

Itt is wild cuntry beginning but ful of Promiss We will hev vary few Spanyerds butt manie Americans for neybors English-spekers tho few good Catholics. We all start with nuthing but will be grand as lords & landed gentry sumday, sware it.

Bess sell all & keep little wot you traysure & take Yankee *ship too New Orlins & I will mete you & dres you fine as a title ladie. Ask of me & call self Mrst. Patrick Warder. Kiss the babes for me & say we will see eech other soon & be happy evermore in Americay. A kiss from me to you & git here soon. P.S. Be shur to fetch along my gud luck Toby Jug. Your luving husbund, ritten at Warderlands Plantayshun.*

CHAPTER THIRTY-SIX

*O*w!" Capt. Alan Lewrie carped as Surgeon's Mate Maurice Durant cinched his bindings tighter. "So snug I can't draw a decent breath!"

"So they will be, Captain," his French-born former physician told him with a sad chuckle as Aspinall helped Lewrie don a new shirt. "Ze bruised ribs and breast-bone knit slowly, so you must expect pain, and think yourself fragile for at least anozzer month before I may say wiz confidence zat you are completely healed, *n'est-ce pas,* sir?"

"Mean t'say I'm to dodder like a Greenwich Pensioner, on light duties like one of our herniated brace-tenders?"

"I fear zat is the apt comparison, sir," Durant said with a sly twinkle in his eyes as he closed up his portable kit-box.

"Not serious enough to put a replacement captain aboard, is it?" Lewrie fretted as he gazed at Admiralty House on the Palisades of Kingston Harbour. After being battered about by higher authorities in the last few months, he was "oft-bitten, *damned* shy!" of meddlers, or those who'd reward their favourites with a posting into a frigate, the finest sort of command the Royal Navy could offer an aspiring young officer.

"Oh no, Captain, no fear of zat," Durant assured him. "You mus' be *lazy* for a time, but zat is not cause for displacing you."

"Oh, good," Lewrie chearly said, perked up considerably. "Lazy I b'lieve I can manage main-well, thankee!"

"Much's you done for 'em, sir," Aspinall commented as he shoved

Lewrie into his waist-coat, "I'd expect 'em t'keep you an' *Proteus* as one for-ever. Much's you earned 'em, sir."

They'd sailed back to Jamaica with their pirate schooner flying British colours atop its French Tricolour trailing astern of them and had created quite the stir of excitement once their reports, Lewrie's and Nicely's, had been read, and the amount of coined silver aboard her had been tallied. The Admiralty Court had *leapt* to condemn the prize, Admiral Parker had bought her in as a fast armed tender for £4,000, to be seconded to a larger, slower cruising ship so he could garner even more loot at sea. And, for his signal service in their recent expedition, Lt. Darling, Capt. Nicely's protégé, had been appointed into her as commanding officer.

Capt. Nicely had finally struck his broad-pendant and departed for a new command of his own, since Admiral Parker realised that he would be much more useful at sea, leading a real squadron, than ever he was as Staff Captain.

"Damme, Lewrie, but you've saved me!" Nicely had grandly stated at his departure ceremony, pumping Lewrie's hand so happily. "Got me a *proper* broad-pendant at last, and made me rich into the bargain!"

They had only salvaged eight hundred kegs of coined dollars off the prize, the rest of the rumoured six million in silver was scattered over a mile of bay-bottom mud or swampy forest when the Spanish prize exploded. Or, as their few surviving prisoners suggested, there never had been that much, and the rest might have made it to New Orleans on another ship. Pollock could bear them the facts when he returned.

Still, eight hundred thousand Spanish dollars was £200,000, and that was nothing to sneeze at. Admiral Parker got an eighth, and Captain Nicely got an eighth, as senior admiral and "squadron commander," respectively. But that still left Lewrie his traditional two-eighths as captain of the successful warship, and that resulting £37,500 was his ticket to a life of imcomparable wealth!

He could buy his farm from Uncle Phineas Chiswick, who resisted the odds with his typical stubborn meanness and absolutely refused to die—if he couldn't take all his own wealth with him, Lewrie suspected. There could be a decent townhouse in London, too, and still leave them £30,000 to place in the safe and solid Bank of England's Three Percents and that would yield £1,000 *per annum*, before the bloody taxes due, of course. A family his size could live as grand as an earl on a sum like that. Why, he could even spare an hundred . . . well, fifty would suit, he idly supposed . . . to dower his penni-less ward, Sophie de Maubeuge, buy things to improve her paraphernalia to help attract a suitable man with decent breeding and fair prospects of his own. Sewallis and Hugh, his daughter Charlotte (those offspring it was *safe* to claim!) would be assured the very best educations, and a leg up for their entry into adulthood. His wife, Caroline, well . . . hmm.

Sudden wealth *might* mollify her, he could hope, might soften her heart enough to forgive his overseas *amours* at last. It wasn't as if any of them had been anything more than temporary foreign "diversions," conveniences, really. And weren't a couple of them mounted under the orders of superiors, "topped" in the name of grim Duty? That Claudia Mastandrea with the bountiful "poonts" in the Italies, and Charité his most recent?

It felt callous to think that Caroline could be swayed by a pot of guineas, that she could possibly be that flinty-eyed and mercenary. Yet . . . Riches, as good as absence, *might* make the heart grow fonder! Too busy to remember despising him whilst spending, getting, feathering her nest, hmm?

Dressed proper at last, Lewrie took his hat in hand and walked to the forrud door, or tried to. Toulon and Chalky had developed a new game with which to plague him. Whether genuinely glad to have him back aboard as their main delight, their security, or their chiefest playmate in "their" great-cabins, or whether this was a holdover from the time that Capt. Nicely had usurped that space, a devious mischief they dreamt up to harass him (when they weren't spraying and marking everything in sight, and thank God they'd stopped doing that!), their sole waking delight, whenever he rose from his bed, desk, or settee, was to dash ahead of him, looking back impishly, fling themselves down in his path with their paws aloft and bellies exposed, and God help him if he *didn't* stoop or kneel to pet them and make fusses over them, else his ankles and stockings were in for "heavy weather."

"Aye, damn yer eyes," Lewrie relented with a put-upon sigh, all but stumbling over their writhing, tail-whicking eagerness. With much "oofing" and groaning, he knelt to placate them, but it hurt some, and was a slow process, too. "God's sake, don't try this after dark, will ye, Toulon? I can *almost* see Chalky, but you, ye menace, you're black as a boot! Yes, big baby. Wubby feel good? Oh, you too, Chalky lad."

"Mister Gamble . . . Sah!" the Marine sentry outside his doorway bawled, slamming his musket butt on the deck and stamping his boots to announce the presence of their newest "gift" Midshipman, Darcy Gamble, who came well recommended by both Admiral Sir Hyde Parker *and* Nicely.

"Oh, hell," Lewrie groaned, caught kneeling, and a cat's belly under each hand. "Come, dammit! Christ!" he added under his breath.

"The First Officer, Mister Langlie's duty, sir, and—" Mister Gamble began to say, stepping briskly into the great-cabins, hat under his right arm, chin high in the proud execution of his duties. He widened his eyes, though, and could not help laughing at the sight of his captain on his knees.

"Yess, Mister Gamble?" Lewrie drawled, embarrassed, but determined not to let it faze him. He sat back on his haunches and continued petting the cats, careful for his fingers should they get *too* happy.

"My pardons, sir, but the, ah . . . mongoose problem the ship had a few months ago, sir?" Gamble stated, eyes on the stern windows, and all but biting the lining of his mouth to stay sober.

"Oh, the Marines' rat-killin' Trinidad mongoose?" Lewrie asked, as if it was trifling. "Our pagan *Hindoo* mongoose? Aye?" Lewrie secretly savoured the look of perplexity on young Gamble's phyz, wondering if the lad feared he'd landed a berth in Bedlam, not a crack frigate.

"The First Officer, Mister Langlie, is of the opinion that it, ah . . . was a *she*, Captain, sir," Gamble reported, lips quivering as the lunacy of what he was saying struck him. "A *pregnant* she, in point of fact. There are simultaneous sightings of . . . mon-*geese*, one must assume . . . everywhere, now, sir!"

Lewrie shut his eyes and let a bemused smile spread on his face. "Mine arse on a band-box. Yet the rats *are* kept in check, hey? Next match, Mister Gamble . . . put me down for a shilling. On the mongoose."

I'm rich enough now, Lewrie supposed to himself as he slowly got to his feet; *I can afford a flutter!*

AFTERWORD

Ah, N'awlins, the "Big Easy" . . . the city where I once had *four* Hurricanes and closed Pat O'Brien's at dawn, then thought that *I* was Jean La Fitte, after an LSU-Ole Miss football game at Baton Rouge! I'd driven down with a couple of "Good Ol'Girls" from Ole Miss whom I had met in Memphis. Ole Miss lost 66-6, Archie Manning was quarterback and playing in a cast on his arm, so they took the defeat, and their cry of "Hoddy-Toddy, Christ A'mighty," much like Dionysius's Greek followers took *"Evoe!"*, a reason for *serious* boozing.

Thanks to Louisiana State University Press for *The Founding of New Acadia* by Carl Brasseaux and *Africans in Colonial Louisiana* by Gwendolyn Midlo Hall; and to Pelican Publishing of Gretna, Louisiana, for reprinting George W. Cable's 1884 book, *The Creoles of Louisiana* for the description of the city and its citizens' character, or lack of it. He did know them best!

Creole and Cajun character names were chosen blind from the indexes in these books, and others, so if anyone whose family name is mentioned may wish to take umbrage, consider this . . .

I am well armed, and know how to use them.

Boudreaux Balfa's name was inspired by one of my Bluegrass-Americana CDs, where I found several Cajun-Zydeco cuts done by *Dewey* Balfa (are we kinfolk?) and his family band, though I recall that his family reside on Bayou La Fourche, not Barataria, so as Dewey Balfa said in the liner notes, *Toujours Balfa!* and more power to 'em, 'cause they're great! I'm trolling for a free CD, Dewey!

For my rendition of Cajun diction, blame that famous Cajun comic, Justin Wilson, with whom I spent a day doing a couple of TV commercials in Memphis in the '80's, when I was a producer-director at WMC-TV.

For the Tennesseans, I borrowed a few of my own kin from my old stomping grounds round Campbell, Claiborne, and Knox Counties, Tennessee. My maternal grandmother, Mary Susan Bowman Ellison, spoke of a cousin of her youth, Jim Hawk *McLean,* in the Powell Valley, which is halfway between La Follette, Tennessee, and the Cumberland Gap. Every spring, or when a wild hair hit him, Jim Hawk and his cronies would build a flatboat and head downriver to the Mississippi, then raft down to Vicksburg or Natchez, sell their produce and the boat, then buy horses and good breeding stock and come home up the Natchez Trace to Nashville, the Cumberland Trail to Knoxville, all for a lark. They'd sell all but the best mounts in Knoxville, then return to the Powell Valley (originally Powell's!) with half their cash money for the year, so I couldn't resist working a Jim Hawk *Ellison* into the tale!

Yes, there was a Panton, Leslie & Company, a British firm that traded with Indians, Spanish, and frontier settlements. It's mentioned in both *The South In The Revolution, Volume Three of A History of the South* by John Richard Alden (LSU Press) and *The Southern Frontier, 1670 to 1732* by Vernor W. Crane (W. W. Norton & Co.). Both provide "dirt" on the many plots and schemers who wished to expand westward along the entire length of the Mississippi, the United States plans, the British scenarios, and the individual states' activities. And, yes, by 1799, President Adams and Congress *did* wrangle over the costs of a military expedition to boot the weak Spanish out of the Old Southwest! It was up to President Thomas Jefferson to buy it in 1803.

General James Wilkinson *was* a paid Spanish agent, since 1787. No one could figure out how he was paid, 'til someone noticed, in the wake of the Aaron Burr filibustering conspiracy of 1803–04, that it was odd for barrels of flour and meal to go *upriver* from New Orleans. The barrels were too heavy and when finally opened were found to hold sacks or small barricos of silver coins! Wilkinson planned to seize Kentucky, Tennessee, or both, as his personal kingdom, at the same time he commanded all U.S. Army troops in both states or territories.

Thanks again to Bob Enrione at CBS in New York for research on Spanish money, its contemporary value, and how it was shipped. All of the New

World was short of solid specie, and Spanish dollars were good just about everywhere. There *was* a shipload of six million, Bob said, so I got "inspired." Not only is Bob a great source for fun facts, but he also once owned enough brass muzzle-loading naval guns to fit out a brig o' war, and he and his wife are multiple cat "adoptees," hence in the good folks' column.

There really was a Girandoni air-rifle. Austria bought 1,800 to 2,000 of them and "got shot of 'em" right-quick, too. In 1805 Lewis and Clark took air-rifles on the Corps of Discovery trek, and theirs, made in America, worked a lot better. Almost anything else *would*.

Pierre and Jean La Fitte, hmmm. I couldn't *resist* slinging them into a novel set round New Orleans and their future infamous haunt on Grand Terre, in Barataria Bay. Even if they were enigmas! None of my research sources on them—including a Young Adult nonfiction book I bought that tried really, *really hard* to make slave dealing, slave stealing, piracy, and murder sound like just grand, Politically Correct *fun*—can agree on where Jean La Fitte was born: Bordeaux, Port-au-Prince (Haiti), or Cartagena? He was nineteen in 1799, he was *ten!* He went to a military school on Guadeloupe, Martinique, or in France. He was part-Jewish and his family had run afoul of the Spanish Inquisition and had fled to the Americas, Jean being born in 1782. Now, there's a good reason to prey on Spanish ships; they'd tried to turn your grandparents into tiki lanterns! The only point of agreement is that Jean La Fitte was a sharp businessman but a horrid sailor who'd heave up his innards on anything but a dead-calm sea.

Anyway, whether Jean La Fitte was seventeen, fourteen, or *twelve* in early 1799, he *could* have been part of Jérôme Lanxade's crew, serving an "internship" in murder and mayhem, so why the hell not?

Stodgy academics may take umbrage, but let me put it this way: "It's *my* bloody book, so sod you, write yer own! Pee-Aitch-Dees . . . Pee-Aitch-Dees! *Wwee* don' need no stinkin' Pee-Aitch-Dees!" And let me refer any thin-blooded revisionists to my earlier statement about Louisianans' family names . . .

"I am well armed and know how to use them."

⚓

Lewrie's and Pollock's "appreciation" about the best way to get at New Orleans: it was shorter, quicker, and cheaper than trying to float an army down the Mississippi and, at the time, would've *worked!* Could it be that Lewrie's plan mouldered in a soggy Admiralty basement 'til 1814, the mouse-nibbled thing was pulled out and given to General Sir Edward Packenham when he went up against Andrew Jackson? Robert V. Remini's *The Battle of New Orleans* (Penguin Books) lays the whole thing out, though Packenham "screwed the pooch" just as Lewrie suspected any British Army might, since "daring" and "quick" *weren't* in their vocabulary. And will a Commodore or Rear-Admiral Lewrie play a role in it, hmmm?

So, the bad guys have had their "stuff" scattered to the wind, and Lewrie has come out smelling like rose-water again; not only successful, but fairly damn rich for a change, when a "chicken-nabob," fresh-returned from India with £50,000, was thought immensely wealthy.

Will money soften Caroline's heart? Whoever that spiteful and *incognito* scribbler is that writes anonymous letters to her detailing his *amours* has run out of fresh material and knows nothing of Lewrie's Caribbean doings. Might she ascribe to the views of Clinton backers, "That's old news. Let's just . . . move on"? Or will it still be "Hell hath no fury"?

I *planned* on killing off Charité de Guilleri, but she's one of those characters who grows on you. Will she escape her dull relations and find a powerful sponsor, and . . . who *might* it be? We left ol' Guillaume Choundas an American Navy prisoner on his parole, but never count him out 'til you drive a stake through his heart; he's harder to kill than cockroaches. Could it *be?*

Will the cats stop marking territory, now Nicely's gone? Will Midshipman Gamble fit in aboard that floating mad-house, HMS *Proteus?* Will Lt. Langlie's marital prospects towards Lewrie's ward, Sophie, be improved, now that he's in for a goodly share of "chink," too? And those mongeese . . . how *did* the Marines find them so far from India and the island of Trinidad, and how'd they smuggle it (them) aboard in the first place?

Will Alan Lewrie stay tagged as "The Ram-Cat," or will "Iron-Bound" become his new sobriquet in the Royal Navy?

All I can say, for now, is . . . stay tuned, buckaroos, and . . .

Prospero: I'll deliver all.
And promise you calm seas, auspicious gales,
And sail so expeditious that shall catch
Your royal fleet far off~
My Ariel, chick,
That is thy charge. Then to the elements
Be free, and fare thou well~please you draw
Near.

Exeunt Omnes.

~*THE TEMPEST*, ACT V, SCENE 1
WILLIAM SHAKESPEARE